The Prince of the Veil

Book Three of the Exile Trilogy

Hal Emerson

This book is dedicated to

those of you who have read this far.

Raven, Leah, and Tomaz are lucky to have

such faithful companions,

And I am too.

Also by Hal Emerson:

The Exile Trilogy:

- The Prince of Ravens

- The Prince of Exiles

- The Prince of the Veil

In The Land of Aeon:

- The Ring of Eman Vath

- The Lost Kingdom

Oberon's Children

To Die a Thousand Deaths

Bones

Table of Contents

Prologue: The Heir of Theron Isdiel 1

Chapter One: The Guardian of Banelyn 23

Chapter Two: As Luck Would Have It 48

Chapter Three: The Raven Prince 57

Chapter Four: Blue Lines 79

Chapter Five: Loyalty 106

Chapter Six: Commander of the Gate 115

Chapter Seven: Waking 133

Chapter Eight: Council Matters 147

Chapter Nine: The Clock Ticks 165

Chapter Ten: Good Use of a Tent 185

Chapter Eleven: Traveling North 195

Chapter Twelve: Something to Lerne 210

Chapter Thirteen: Innocence 259

Chapter Fourteen: The Final Road 269

Chapter Fifteen: Tyne 285

Chapter Sixteen: The Plains of al'Manthian 310

Chapter Seventeen: The Battle of the Plains 323

Chapter Eighteen: Why? 340

Chapter Nineteen: Elders 359

Chapter Twenty: A New Light 372

Chapter Twenty-one: Crowned 385

Chapter Twenty-two: The Final Charge 396

Chapter Twenty-three: Lucien 403

Chapter Twenty-four: Lucky Scoundrel 409

Chapter Twenty-five: Innocence Lost 418

Chapter Twenty-six: Exiled Guardian 429

Chapter Twenty-seven: Raven Ascending 436

Chapter Twenty-eight: The Wolf of Eldoras 441

Chapter Twenty-nine: Seeing 456

Chapter Thirty: Immovable 461

Chapter Thirty-one: Prince of the Veil 471

Chapter Thirty-two: After 502

Epilogue 514

Glossary

About the Author

Prologue:

The Heir of Theron Isdiel

In the first year of the discovery of the new continent of Lucia, the seven Heirs of Theron Isdiel lost their memories.

It was gradual at first, and went mostly unnoticed among both the Heirs and those that they had led across the Sea. In fact, to many it seemed indistinguishable from the simple kind of fading that occurs with distance and time. A goodly number of those who had embarked across the Sea had perished when first flung upon the rocks and shoals of the shoreline, and while the survivors had managed to salvage many of their provisions and arms, their documents had been beyond saving. What was left of the expedition had come to shore and been unsurprised when the shock and horror of that night had drowned out their memories, and during the next weeks and months, they had little occasion to think of home as anything other than a vague, unreachable haven.

But during that time, while they learned to survive in this older land, this untamed world, the process accelerated. By the end of their first winter, several months after their ill-favored landing, the truth of the loss was undeniable, and no way could be found to stop or reverse it. The Heirs tried desperately to record what they could, but nothing of import seemed to remain, and what little parchment they managed to craft out of animal skin was quickly filled, leaving thousands of memories to die on the vine. By the end of the first year everything that had happened before they had crossed the Sea was lost to them, as if a surgeon had come with a razor in the night and removed the memories while they slept.

It was the First Daughter, the First Heir and leader of the expedition, who felt the loss most keenly. The voyage was her first command, and Theron Isdiel, the Diamond Empress, had entrusted her with it. But as the memories faded – memories of receiving her commission, of standing tall and proud on her ship's prow as thousands cheered for her, memories even of the Empress's face – she fell into a black despair that would not lift. She could not see beauty, could not hear laughter, could not even live without thinking all things had been sweeter in that other land.

Calling it homesickness would be an error. It was not so simple a thing, nor was she so simple a person. She was defined by her ambition, more than anything else, and when she lost her goal, when she lost where she came from, she lost the guiding star that prevented her from running aground on the hidden shoals of greed and jealousy. And with that anchor lost, she crashed against those rocks, and her good intentions broke into a thousand pieces of madness. The dark and hidden part of her ambition came to fill the waiting void, creeping in slowly and silently, like fog that forms in the night and hangs heavy throughout the dawn.

She fought it, though; she did not succumb willingly, that must be said. She knew the perils of this path, and she knew that if she strayed from virtue into vice she would never find her way back. Others could, but not her. The Seventh Heir, the one they all looked up to, he could do it. He had wisdom in him. But not her. And because she knew it, and knew the others knew it, she feared their silent words, the things they must be saying to each other about her leadership, and the fear inside her began to twist and morph into anger and resentment. It was their fault, after all. It always had been. They must have done something on the voyage to precipitate their misfortune – she was not to blame. She was pure and always had been.

Such thoughts fed on each other in a twisted circle, and a terrible idea took shape at the center of the swirling miasma, one that she tried to deny even as she gave birth to it. One that she sought to disown even as she sustained it.

She fought within herself for days on end. The Seventh Heir, who she had charged with exploring this new land, saw their misfortune as an opportunity. He had begun to preach to the others the virtues of what they had been given – the chance to create new lives of which each of them could be proud. They had been given a gift, he said, the likes of which others could only dream about. And with each new word he spoke, she hated him more and more. He saw the world through eyes clouded with dewy drops of hope and wonder; he saw the world as one deluded, as a madman. They had left their true home, and there was no going back now, back to the... to the....

But she could not remember. How could she not remember? It had been exciting, she knew that, or at least thought she did. The Seven Heirs of Theron Isdiel, seeking knowledge, seeking experience, seeking new lands and strange adventures.

But they had always planned to go back. Always. She was sure of it. She was. And now... now they never could.

Why am I the only one of us who still cares?

Water fell on Alana's head as she passed beneath the trees of the lush forest that crowded the upper banks of the sea and harbor they had found, the thoughts still running through her mind, over and over in an unbreakable loop. As night fell, heavy black clouds had shouldered each other across the sky, jostling for position so that only the heaviest made their way inland to let loose their burden. Alana was glad of the water; it helped wash away the taste of tears.

This is the last time I cry. It is the last time I care.

She wanted to return to a home she did not remember, a home *none* of them remembered. They all knew simple things – they could read and write still, though the name of the language evaded them, and the teachers who had given them the knowledge would have passed before them unnoticed. They knew each other from the interactions they'd had in this new land, and the few scraps of parchment they had managed to recover or recreate bore what they believed to be their names. They could use the weapons they had found in their possession, even Praxas with his enormous maul, but they remembered nothing of training.

And nothing of home. All that was left of that land, the only fleeting glimpse of it, was a deep-seated hope in Alana's heart that she would return. There was something there for her, something that beckoned.

She left the edge of the forest and walked into the encampment, smoothly acknowledging the guards who bowed their heads to her in their red-and-brown armor. She moved between the lean-tos that had been built as more permanent winter shelters, passed beyond the long wooden storage sheds and cooking halls, until she reached the center of camp where large canvas tents were still used as shelter. She moved toward one such tent, a large one made of thick, heavy canvas with a water-resistant coating of wax and sap, and brushed aside the entrance flap.

She steeled her nerves, and told herself that this was the only way.

Warmth hit her first, and then light, both coming from the brazier that stood in the center of the tent, allowing heat to build throughout the enclosure even as the icy wind and rain lashed it from the outside. The tent was a dull eggshell color, and shadows played fitfully across the canvas walls as the brazier's light met the hard outlines of roughly crafted wooden desks, tables, and chairs.

Oliand, the short, spry man who she remembered as Fifth Heir — *what does that mean? Heir to what?* — and the one who wore the Aspect of Luck about his neck on a thick leather cord, looked up at her as she entered. He was the only one there. Good, it was as she hoped.

I have to do it. I have to get home.

"Alana," said Oliand with his easy, mocking smile. He had tried to bed her ever since their memories had begun to fade. She had never let him near her, knowing it was somehow wrong even before they had rediscovered that they were related.

"And how are you this fine evening?" His eyes glowed gold in the light of the brazier and the oil lamps. Alana glanced down at the table he was bent over – a hastily constructed wooden affair made from the planks of the ship that had born them here and broken them on the rocky shore, later fortified with boards cut from oak and pine trees. There were maps there, no doubt the ones he had been commissioned to make with their precious supply of parchment. They showed the harbor, the surrounding area, and an area some miles south of them that was deeply wooded and led to a distant range of mountains. Someone had scribbled the words "Hell mist" there, no doubt in reference to the recent expedition that had been lost for days in a fog that had seemingly sprung from nowhere.

The Hellmist Mountains… a fitting name.

"I find myself strangely cold," she purred in answer to his question, favoring him with a smile that showed something akin to a veiled promise. At least, as much of one as she could come up with. She had never seduced someone before.

At least not that I remember.

His eyes caught that promise and glowed a deeper gold.

"Well, then you have come to the right place, my dear," he said, leaving the table and approaching her. "Stand here, by the brazier." He grabbed her by the elbow and pulled her forward, gently but firmly. "It is much warmer here."

Her clenched fist twitched beneath the fabric of her long, concealing sleeve, but the rest of her remained sweet and supple, allowing his hand to skim down the curve of her back and rest at the top of her hip.

"You are soaked through," he said, surprised. "How long have you been out there?"

He pulled back and took the top of her cloak in his hands. She shrugged out of it and let him whisk it away in a flash of movement, leaving her standing in just her form-fitting white garments. They too were soaked through, a fact that was not lost on the roving eyes of Oliand.

"Here, my love," he cooed, coming up behind her and pressing himself against her back as he maneuvered her in front of the fire. "Stand like this; the fire will warm you from one side, and I from the other."

Her skin crawled as he said it, and her hand grasped the hidden handle up her wide sleeve.

You cannot do this. You cannot do it – there must be another way.

I have no choice.

It was so easy, what she did next. It was all like walking through a dream. She turned and embraced him, giving herself to him the way he had always wanted. Their lips met, his moving against hers with passion. She took what he gave her and followed his lead, knowing this was about him, not her.

They moved to the bed in the corner, and she pushed him down onto it. She needed her arms free, could not let him trap her. She embraced him again, then unlaced his shirt and looked down at his chest – at the topaz gem in the rock fixture.

"Take it off," she whispered in his ear.

He pulled back slightly to look at her, suddenly wary.

"Why would you want that?"

She pulled closer and whispered once more in his ear, as she moved her hips against his, stoking his excitement.

"Because I do not want you to think this is happening through luck."

He chuckled, low and throaty. The smell of his breath was like honey and cloves, with a trace of the harsher jab of alcohol. He'd been drinking mead. Her skin began to crawl so badly it was as if insects had begun to writhe just below the surface, and she suddenly felt dirty in a way that a hundred baths could never clean. But she kept herself from showing her repulsion. She had begun – she could not stop now.

"I will take it off," he said with twinkling eyes, "if you take yours off first. I do not want you giving me Commands; I am in charge now."

She smiled outwardly.

It will come to violence after all.

She slowly undid the soft cord that held the top of her tunic closed, and unlaced it. His eyes left hers to follow her motion, as she had known they would. Men were so easily led when they thought they were doing the leading. She pulled her own Aspect out from between her breasts, trailing the heavy stone surrounding the sharp edges of the glittering diamond seductively across her skin. She felt something leave her as she hung it from the bed nearby, and she almost whimpered in pain. The world's colors were suddenly dull and empty in this lesser state, and the raging sounds of wind and rain were frightening in their intensity. How could people live in a world where they were not sure their word would be obeyed?

Oliand followed suit and removed his own Aspect, hanging it next to hers on the post. A change occurred in him – his movements became less fluid, his motions less confident, and his eyes turned from a pure, radiant gold, to a soft, dull brown.

The color of excrement.

Revulsion rose up in her again as she contemplated this man below her – this man who thought he could dare to possess her, she of all people, the First Heir of Isdiel! – but she forced the nausea down.

He will not take me. It will end before that.

He bent his neck and thrust his nose into her cleavage, rooting around like a pig in a sty, and as he did, he shifted his weight in just the wrong way. He had trapped her hand, and his own was slowly running up her side. His arms encircled her, and she realized that he had not been joking when he had said he was in command now. He was not as big and strong as Praxas, not even close, but he was still bigger and stronger than she, and right now that was the only difference that mattered.

It has to be now.

She kneed him in the groin, though from the way their bodies were entwined, the angle was such that the blow was only hard enough to cause mild discomfort. He let out a chuckle and loosened his grip on her arms, recoiling just enough to show her a smiling face that took the action to be a joke. Before he could say a word she pulled the concealed dagger from the hidden sheath in her sleeve and buried it in his stomach.

He jerked in shock, and recoiled from her, going immediately for the discarded Aspects, and she followed him, digging the knife in deeper, cutting through his entrails with a swift, diagonal motion that spilled the contents of his stomach out onto the floor as he tried to twist away.

His face was a pale mask of shock. He grabbed for the Aspects, but she was too fast. Just as his hand hooked around the leather cord, she spun and threw him across the room. He stumbled, blood pouring out from beneath his hands, and fell on the brazier. But before he could make a sound, she spun, threw her own Aspect, the Aspect of Command, around her neck, and spoke to him in the ringing tone of ultimate authority:

"Make no sound."

No sooner were the words out of her mouth than the smell of burning flesh filled the room. Her brother screamed in silent pain and flailed uncontrollably. Tendons stood out hard and sharp along his neck, and his whole body was wracked with pain as he tried to roll away from the burning coals and found himself unable. The Aspect he had hooked with his finger fell in the flames beside him, and began to burn as well.

She raced forward and grabbed it, snatching it out of the fire as Oliand grabbed at her dress; he managed to seize a fistful and tore off half her bodice as he fell to the ground.

He did not rise.

Smoke curled up from his body, twisting and writhing in the air like the lovers Oliand had hoped they would become. Strange. She had always thought the smell of charred flesh would be horrific. It was indeed nauseating, but...

What have I become that I can think such thoughts?

She was not done yet – she needed him to live a little longer at least. She knelt beside him and did something she had not done since they had first landed, since that first death that she had tried to stop, that death on the beach. Her mind flowed back, remembering how Aemon had succeeded where she could not, something he had repeated over and over since their landing.

He could bring them back. She could make them something more.

"*Do not die,*" she whispered into Oliand's ear.

She heard her own heart thumping in her chest like a caged bird as she waited. Seconds passed, and, when nothing happened, she feared suddenly that she had been too late. She had only ever done it once before – how much did timing matter? Panic took her; she needed them all alive, at least nominally so.

And then the burned body moved, and the chest pulled air into lungs that no longer needed it.

A reflex only – whatever is left of him trying to cling to the life he had.

She bent down low and whispered in his ear.

"*From now on, you are my Watchman,*" she Commanded. "*You will show your wounds to no one. You will stuff those entrails back inside you and clean this blood. No one is to know what has happened here. Once you have finished, you will stand here and wait for my return. Do not leave this tent, do not contact any of the others.*"

She pulled back and watched him. The empty brown eyes slowly focused on her, and as she watched they began to burn a sickly green, just as they had the last time she had Commanded someone to remain alive. He bent over and began scooping up his innards in silent obedience.

She moved for the tent's entrance, slipping the Luck Aspect over her head. The added power was like a shot of spirits, sending warmth to all her extremities before it came back to her head. The heat began to gather on the left side of her body, like she was being held too close to a fire, and she looked down to see that one whole side of the Aspect had been burned. She muttered a Command, and the heat, while intense, did not become painful. It would burn whoever wore it next, but not her.

Praxas was next. He was easier.

When she approached his tent, now wearing both Aspects, she saw a pair of guards stationed outside. Golden lines moved in front of her vision, likely from Oliand's Aspect, and she suddenly knew how to pass the guards without attracting attention. She kicked a pebble as she walked, and it flew off at a peculiar angle where it dropped from sight, eliciting a solid *ding!* as it hit some discarded piece of armor.

Both guards' heads snapped around on their meaty necks to look toward the sound, only a few yards to their right. They went to investigate, and as they turned she walked into the tent without even slowing.

She heard Praxas before she saw him; his snoring filled the tent like a swarm of bees. The huge bear of a man had never desired her – something she could not fathom, and neither could most of the other men in the camp. She was the embodiment of physical perfection, as were all the Heirs. Praxas was supposed to be the most perfect, bearing the Aspect of Strength, and while he was indeed fawned over by the camp women for his enormous strength, Alana had never understood it. She hated the way he looked – the heavily muscled brute.

When she approached him in his bed, the snoring increased, and she felt disgust well up inside her once more. The man had fallen asleep in bed while drinking a pot of ale – and when he had fallen into unconsciousness, the container had slipped from his hands and spilled across the floor. With each step, she felt her boots sticking to the ground, and the smell of spirits assailed her nose.

She examined the man and saw the Aspect dangled by a leather thong around his neck on his bare, hairy chest. She strode forward, drew her knife again, and cut the ties that held the Aspect. Praxas spasmed uncontrollably, reaching out with his meaty arms for her, but she now held the Aspect of Strength, and when he grabbed her, she struck his wrists and broke them even as she Commanded him to silence.

The big man bellowed soundlessly, grabbing his hands and trying to rise until she pressed a pillow to his face and held him down. He struggled mightily against her, but it was no use. She had all the strength stored in his own Aspect, and he had saved hundreds of lives in his time here. All of that energy now flowed through her, and soon he stopped struggling. Once he did, she left him, Commanding the two guardsmen to clap him in chains for treason before he regained consciousness.

She went through the soldiers' tents then, a white shadow among the black ones, to the men she had spoken to who wanted what she did. They spread the word, and went with her as she followed the path through camp to each of her other siblings.

One by one she collected them all. Lilia she took even as she walked the path to her sleeping quarters. Timon she struck from afar, hurling a dagger through the canvas wall of his tent to take him in the leg as he paced; Silva she took sleeping, forcing a gag between her teeth and a sack over her head. Each she brought with her to the edge of the camp, to the space she had been out preparing that night, away form prying eyes. She sent men back for Oliand and Praxas as well, and told them to silence any who might see them.

She had them all now, all except the last, the only one she feared:

Aemon.

She sought him out where he slept, one of the newer wooden cabins he had built himself, but he was not there. She looked elsewhere around the camp in the areas he frequented: the sparring ring, the library tent, the armory. He was at none of them. Her stomach began to writhe and clench within her. He knew. Somehow, he knew. He always knew. She circled back through the tents of the other sleeping members of the expedition, all oblivious to what was happening, heading toward where her men waited on the edge of camp with torches, ready to depart with the captured Heirs.

And when she arrived, it was he who found her.

"I was sleeping soundly, not half an hour ago," said a low, soft voice.

She spun as the guardsmen drew their weapons, but there was nothing to be seen. The voice itself was vague and directionless, like an echo in a cave, and on the edge of the camp as they were, between the first row of trees and the last row of lean-tos, there was barely enough light to see their own hands, much less a concealed man. She reached through her Aspects, drawing on them all together, but one by one they shook and failed, then connected with her again, then shifted, then failed, then caught, then failed. The effect occurred between all Aspects, but it was worst with his, always worst with his, because his was the Seventh, the one that capped them all and held sway over life and death. Compared to that, the others were mere trifles.

Except for mine. I can Command him, I can bind him, as long as I can get the Aspect away. The others will be useless. No, no, they are enough to trap him. They are enough to overcome him, and once I have the final piece, I can do what is needed.

"Take the others to the mountains," she said to the captain of her guard, his armor bordered in white to signify his place as her bondsman. "Go now – do not look back, do not stop. Cut down any in your way. I will be there shortly."

They left, fading into the night with their baggage.

That's all the other Heirs are now. That's all the good they are to anyone.

"Where are you taking them?" asked the soft voice.

She cringed, her back teeth grinding. She hated that voice. She did – she *hated* it. Always so calm, so reasonable; always in control of itself, never raised in anger. Always questioning, probing. It spoke too much in too few words, echoing its owner, who saw too much in everyone he met.

"You will soon find out," she replied. The words crackled like fire or lightning as they rolled out of her mouth, invested as they were with the weight of Command. She would not let go of her Aspect now; it was the only one that she was skilled enough to hold in the disrupting presence of the Seventh. She could feel it, warm against the skin of her chest. She had to keep control of it, had to make sure that when he slipped – he *had* to slip – she had the chance to pull him to her.

"No," he said, "I will not."

She found him, finally, in the light of her own torch. He was standing in a patch of shadow that cloaked him perfectly, his black cloak wrapped around him so that only his face was truly visible. She circled away, keeping distance between them, and forced her hands to stop shaking.

"I told you not to go down this path," he said, still unmoving but now silhouetted against the guardsman's bivouac behind him.

"You should never have abandoned Mother," she said, thinking furiously. How was she going to do this? She knew she needed a plan, but she did not have one. She did not make plans – she acted on instinct, always. And now, her instinct was telling her to run.

That is the one thing I cannot do. I need all seven Aspects; without them, I will never be able to go back. I need them all – that is the answer – it must be!

"Why do you think I abandoned anyone?" he asked softly.

"SPEAK UP!"

The outburst surprised her more than it did him. In fact, it surprised only her. He barely even blinked, and did not deign to repeat himself. He knew she had heard him.

"*Give it to me,*" she said, holding out her hand, her voice shaking with both anxiety and power. Neither affected the man across from her, though – he remained where he was, arms folded across his chest, unmoving.

"Give what to you, sister? Be specific."

"YOU ARE NOT MY BROTHER!"

Again, the outburst startled her. Of all the things they had learned about themselves from the recovered manifests, that had been the most startling.

"You are agitated," he said, perfectly calm, "and I understand why. If I had attacked and kidnapped five of my own brothers and sisters I would feel the same way."

"Soon it will be six."

"I thought you said I was not your brother?"

"You are not!"

"Our blood may be different, but our mother is the same."

"She picked you up off the street! You are nothing – you should be a bondsman, working in some field under the lash!"

"None of that is known," he said simply, not showing the least bit of pain at the harsh words. "None of that is in what we recovered. I could very well be highborn as well, but the son of dead parents."

"*No*," she hissed, throwing her rage at him, rage that had been born of love. "Someone highborn would be different. Someone highborn would be like me, like the rest of us – not like *you!*"

"I am sorry that you feel that way."

She spat on the ground. "That is what I think about your sorry. You are always sorry – you always have your own opinion and you never give in to anyone, never even try to see something from another's perspective – "

"I love you as a sister," he said, cutting through the flow of her words with his own, wielding them like the sharp edge of a perfectly honed knife. "I am sorry that I cannot give you more. I would if I could. Or at least I would have, before tonight."

"You fool!" she cried. "I never *actually* wanted more! I have been playing you. I have always played you, and I am playing you now!"

She was laughing hysterically, and she knew that she had crossed some kind of line in her own mind. Maybe she had crossed some time ago, when she had decided to move forward with her plan. Maybe she had only just crossed it now when he had spoken aloud the words she had never wanted to hear, confirmed what she had not wanted confirmed. In those words lay the ruins of all the dreams she'd had.

"We could have ruled this land together," she said, her voice croaking out through a throat constricted by emotion. "I may have wanted you by my side in the beginning, but now – no. I gave up on you long before you gave up on me."

And finally, he moved. She fell back into a fighting stance, raising her dagger and pulling strength from the Aspects, trying to see the future around him, trying to gather luck around her, but knowing both were unlikely to help her now. If he came close enough, his Aspect would cancel hers, and that was all that mattered.

But when he came forward into the light, moving with the fluid grace of water or wind, memories of their time together came back to her. It was not a parade of images, nor a series of events, but a patchwork quilt of feelings, sights, and smells. And touches... the first time his hand had touched hers when they had landed here and the quickening had started in her chest.

He came forward just enough that the high planes of his cheekbones and the strong curve of his jaw caught the light. His skin was alabaster pale, his lips full and red, his nose a thin, sharp line that seemed to cut the air. He was beautiful, and the sight of him hurt her.

"Send your men away," he said. It was a command, not a request, but delivered in his soft voice, it sounded like a promise.

Close your heart. Do not let him back in.

"You can still make this right," he said, coming another step closer, head tilted slightly and shoulders hunched, hands upright and warding, as if he were approaching an animal that would easily startle. His eyes were a deep violet color, like nothing she had ever seen. They were captivating – they always had been. They changed and shifted in the flickering of the torchlight, going from a scarlet tinged with blue to a deep purple so dark they were almost black.

"*Do not take another step,*" she Commanded. The power of her Aspect could not touch him while he was prepared and buttressed against it, but he stopped anyway, sensing her deadly intent. His eyes took in all of her, encompassing her and knowing her in the space of a second. She realized her hands were shaking, even though one was clenched into a fist and the other clutched the wire hilt of her dagger.

"Alana," he whispered softly, "we can still make this right."

"Do not tell me about right – right is going back home. Right is returning, like we were meant to."

"You do not know that."

"I do! I *do* know that! It is the only answer!"

"Very well," he whispered, his voice quiet as falling snow, more of an impression and a feeling than anything else. "And do you think that when you return, with the blood of your kindred on your hands, that you will be welcomed back?"

She gripped the dagger tighter, but found herself unable to answer.

"Do you think that when you return, having done nothing but land on these shores and kill the ones sent with you, you will be accepted? And most importantly... do you think such a thing will ever give you peace?"

He took another careful step forward; his hands remained up, empty and warding, and she knew that her knife, while powerful, would only do so much against him. He rarely, if ever, fought with weapons. She had seen him disarm Praxas himself in the sparring ring, and use the man's own weight against him.

"I know you; you are not this monster that you think you can become. You are not a cold-blooded killer. I can feel your life, and there is good in it if you choose to let it grow. You have a chance at redemption, the same chance we all have – "

"*Be silent!*" she Commanded. The crack of thunder silenced everything in the nearby vicinity, all wildlife and even the distant fire ceased to make sound, as if an explosion had gone off that deafened them all. She was drawing on as much of the Aspect as she could now, almost as deeply as she ever had. The stone with the diamond gem inside was burning her chest, trapped as it was against her skin.

"You cannot order me," he said, and just that easily the Command was broken and the noise resumed, and indeed seemed even to double in order to make up for lost time. "You cannot win this way. Stop this madness."

"I will never stop," she promised with fervent zeal. "I will never stop hunting you. The Aspects will be mine, and I will make them better than they have ever been. They will give me the power I need, they will help me take what is needed from this land, and I will use it to go home."

She slashed at his knee, and scored a hit. Aemon cried out in surprise and pain, and she pushed her advantage, continuing to speak, endowing her words with power from the Aspect, making them Commands, forcing the world to bend to her will.

"I will return, and I will be welcomed! And they will see that I am a true child, I am the true Heir; they will see that you all, you failed the test of faith. You did not know how to look into the abyss and come back sane – but me, I did!"

The air around them felt tight, and there was a strange swelling inside her. She had never been able to give this much strength to her Aspect before – combined as it was with the Aspect of Strength and the Aspect of Will, she could endow Commands with more power then she had ever thought possible. She felt as though she could command the very air around her. Words came to her lips unbidden, and she spoke in a rolling tone that shook with might.

"Thou shalt BURN!"

Fire appeared from nowhere in a flash of light, engulfing him in a huge gout of flame. It burned with the brilliance of the sun, and as it did she laughed, a baying cry that shattered the last bit of sanity left in her. She grinned, panting like a beast, and spat at her immolated brother.

"I have power such as you could *never imagine!* When I return home, they will not be welcoming a long lost daughter, nor a wayward child. I will be the greatest leader, man or woman, this world has ever seen! They will *bow* to me, and even Mother will –!"

Aemon stepped out of the flame, grabbed her knife, and plunged it into her side.

Shock was all she felt as she fell. There was no way for this to be true – he had been burning. He was dying, she knew he was; she commanded the air itself, commanded all things –

"Your Aspect cannot touch me," he whispered in her ear, "no matter how powerful you become. No matter what you do, no matter what lengths you travel, you will never have my allegiance, nor the allegiance of my soul, which is bound to this stone. I am the Seventh Heir, and if all else fails, it is my duty to stand between you and the innocents that you will try to conquer."

As he spoke, the Aspect of Sight activated itself without her bidding, and images began to play through her mind. She saw herself living for years on years – though she never aged. She searched for him, but all she found was an empty space. His Aspect protected him, at least in part – she could not find him. And as time went on, she saw that what he said was true. He would never bow to her, he would never kneel. Only blood and fire would bind him to her, only war.

"I will find you wherever you run," she hissed. "I will follow you to the ends of this land, and I will kill all that you hold dear. I will spurn you and your adopted people as you spurn me. Go. Go to your savages. Seek refuge in the mountains among them. But I will find you – and I will bring you down."

His violet eyes met her clear ones, clear as glass and just as transparent. He saw the truth in her eyes, and she saw the sorrow in his.

And then he fled. She fell to her knees, clutching her side as blood flowed through her fingers. She grimaced, gasped, as a cold numbness began to spread to the tips of her fingers. Fog rolled through her mind, blanketing her thoughts, hazing everything over. She heard herself calling to the guards, shouting as loudly as she could, drawing them from the edges of the camp. Others came too, those who had been sleeping, those who owed allegiance to the other Heirs, all of whom were secreted away.

With the last of her presence of mind, she stowed the Aspects that did not belong to her inside a hidden pocket of her bodice. When the soldiers arrived, she told them of Aemon's treachery, told them that he had betrayed them all. She did not even have to use her Aspect to ensure their obedience; they simply believed her. It was easy to believe – she was the one left here, wounded, and Aemon the one who had fled. She dispatched them to find him and to bring him back.

As they left, she drew those loyal to her near, and told them what to do. The entire camp was mobilized, and the men were sent out to capture the fleeing Seventh Heir. She had to act quickly – they would soon move to alert the other Heirs and find them missing, and everything needed to be in place beforehand.

An hour later, the guard captain returned to meet her in her tent. They had tried to give her stitches, but she had refused; the Aspect of Will and the Aspect of Strength had already healed the wound. No doubt Aemon had known it would happen – it must have been why he had not tried to finish her. He had known she was all-powerful now, known she could not be killed. Yes, that had to be it. Didn't it?

"My... my lady," the man said, kneeling before her. He was pale as a sheet beneath his black hair, and he was having trouble forming words. "I am – I have been sent here to report to you that... that Aemon was not the only one to betray you."

"What?" she asked, feigning surprise. "He had accomplices?"

"My lady, orders were found in the tents of the other Heirs. The Heirs themselves were not present, and so we searched for them. What we found, in their belongings, on map tables... my lady, I cannot tell you; you must see it for yourself."

He held out his hand and presented her with various scraps of paper, each different, but all in Aemon's hand and bearing the damning words:

Be ready; we move tonight. Take nothing with you; if we fail, we must flee.

"This... cannot be," she said, once more feigning surprise. "Wake Praxas to gather the men. Surely he can not be one of this confederacy."

"My lady," the captain said, shaking his head, "he is disappeared."

She looked between him and the rest of the scouting group that had come to report, giving a masterful performance of innocence.

"Leave me," she said, her voice hoarse. "Give me... give me a moment."

The man nodded, looking both ashamed and proud, as if he had lost his faith in his own lord and gained faith in her. He wore the colors of Oliand – likely, the man had followed him his whole life.

When they had left, she turned to her own messenger, dropping the charade and speaking quickly.

"Bring the Mages. I will need all three – Vynap, Sylva, and Marthinack."

Word went out that evening that Aemon and the other Heirs had rebelled against the rightful Heir, the First Daughter, all of whom had turned cloak to join the savages who called themselves the Veiled Men. The camp mourned, but soon that grief turned to fury that they had been so betrayed, and by their own leaders. Alana rallied them, and soon the hunt was on. They chased Aemon across the country, through the mountain passes, and south, all the way to the Hell Mists and the mountain range they cloaked, miles south of the shores they had landed on. And soon, in that confusion, they came upon the other Heirs.

The details were never fully understood, but the story was clear: the Heirs were taken in the middle of a clearing among a band of natives, those that called themselves the Men of the Veil, all of whom were slaughtered. Aemon alone escaped; the other five Heirs were bound and gagged, their Aspects taken from them by Alana herself.

The men who followed her gathered 'round – as many of them as could fit in the clearing. There were hundreds of them, and they all at one point had sworn fealty to one of the men and women now held prisoner at Alana's feet. These five had betrayed them all, turned their backs on their collective purpose, and tried to kill one of their own, the only one who had remained true to their calling.

When Alana came forward with her Mages, and spoke to the gathered men about proper punishment for these crimes, they shouted for death, and she gave it to them. One by one, the Mages drew Bloodmagic circles around the Heirs, many of whom were weeping and shouting beneath their gags, and one by one Alana stepped forward and slit their throats, spilling the blood of her own brothers and sisters on the thirsty ground. She took each of the Aspects and bound them to her, using the Mages to help her, and from all six she formed a Crown, with her Aspect, the diamond, set front and center. The men cheered, and even the women of the camp, who had been brought along to see their new leader rise, gave throaty calls of jubilation. And when she swore to hunt down Aemon and bring back the final Aspect, to turn it from its master and make it a Talisman of Light that would lead them home from these cursed shores, they all screamed in ecstasy, and swore their undying love to her.

And as Alana watched them, and felt the blood of her brothers and sisters pounding in her veins, felt the heat of the Diamond Crown upon her brow, she knew that this had always been her destiny. This had always been who she was meant to be – she was a figure of legend, a goddess who had only just ascended to her rightful place. She was more than an Heir, more than royal blood, more than a prince or king.

She was an Empress.

Chapter One:

The Guardian of Banelyn

Tomaz watched as a huge block of ceiling fell toward the huddled figures of Leah and Raven. He ran forward as smaller rubble rained down on his head and shoulders, but he brushed it all aside; his limbs were on fire, the Aspect of Strength feeding him power for every life he had saved that day.

With a running leap he dove for them, only barely able to see through the haze of smoke and powdered rubble that choked the air. He turned his body just before he landed, sweeping them both into his arms and rolling with them. Their weight was negligible – he could have picked up ten full-grown men; two slight teenagers barely counted as a hindrance.

The block of ceiling crashed into the spot behind him just as he rolled away. He came up on his feet and turned his momentum into a stumbling run through and out of the immediate circle of rubble, only to find himself on the wrong end of the Cathedral. He spun and looked across the broken dais, where once had stood a ceremonial replica of the Empress's Diamond Throne, now strewn about in pieces and covering the body of Geofred, Prince of Eagles. The nave was still clear, however, though it was now crowded with burning wooden pews, and Tomaz knew that the huge double door beyond that was the only way in or out. The ceiling shook again, and more debris rained down.

"Geofred really wanted to go out with a bang!" he roared to Raven.

But the princeling did not respond. Tomaz stopped and looked down: the young man's eyes had gone glassy and were far away; they looked darker and blacker than Tomaz had ever seen them before. He transferred his gaze to Leah, his young Eshendai partner, and he realized she was not moving – her eyes were closed and all of the blood had drained from her face. He realized he had not seen her move since Geofred had transferred the Eagle Talisman to her.

Or at least had tried to transfer it.

He said it might kill her – he said....

"RAVEN!" he roared, grabbing the young Prince of the Veil by the arm and shaking him, hard. The boy snapped out of his trance – *not a boy anymore, no, not after what he's been through* – just long enough to see Tomaz. He craned his neck up and back to look him full in the face, and again Tomaz saw those eyes, those terrible black eyes.

He's reliving his brother's life. He just killed Geofred – if things are working like they should, that means his Raven Talisman absorbed four centuries worth of memories the moment his brother's heart stopped beating.

A door opened to their right, and then another to their left, and out rushed men dressed in various robes, some deep black, many plain brown homespun, and one or two in gold and white. All of the figures were coughing and shouting.

Seekers – Imperial spies.

Their lair is beneath the cathedral – the tunnels down there must be collapsing, forcing them all above ground.

They were all running and stumbling, fleeing the massive stone structure as it crumbled around them, groping through the blinding haze of smoke for the entrance door. There were dozens of them, though Tomaz knew that there were many more in those vast tunnels that spread out under the entirety of the Inner City of Banelyn. *There must be other entrances and exits – they will be popping up like mushrooms after rain.* He reached a hand to his back, where lay sheathed his greatsword Malachi, the same sword he had forged twenty years before in the Fortress itself.

But before he could do more than make the initial move toward unsheathing the six-foot swath of steel, a huge rumbling *crack* broke through the room, vibrating his bones. He looked up to see what remained of the ceiling's roof split in two and crumble inward, cracks splintering through what was left of the upper walls as well. The beautiful windows, made of stained glass, broke into huge shards of spear-like glass, impaling half a dozen Seekers as they passed below them, killing most and wounding several others.

Tomaz did a quick tally in his head, using the Blade Master training he had been given in the Fortress of Lucien a lifetime ago, back before he had joined the Exiled Kindred to fight the Empire he had once served.

Two men wounded in the arm, one in the leg, five through the gut but only two mortally – none bearing weapons, none over six feet, none with markings of high office or status. None are credible threats or worth risking your life to save.

He released Malachi's hilt, scooped up Leah in the crook of his left arm, and grabbed Raven by the scruff of his neck like a newborn kitten.

Time to go.

His tree trunk legs sprang into action and powered him to the top of the mounting pile of rubble. Beams and stones the size of his head continued to rain down around him as flame licked at the thick tapestries and wooden pews from racks of overturned candles. Dodging left and right around piles of debris, he rushed toward the doors, passing between two huge pillars that still, somehow, remained standing. In a flash of confused images he saw General Gates running ahead before him, already out the door. The princeling was mewling something at him from where he hung immobilized in the crook of Tomaz's right elbow, but nothing could be heard over the rumbling and cracking of the ceiling, and as the terrible ground-shattering impact of the broken pieces of the Imperial Cathedral continued to fall all around him, Tomaz had to rein in the impulse to cuff the boy upside the head.

He is not his right mind; just get him to safety.

He had just passed the final row of flaming pews, buried under fallen crystal chandeliers, when he saw ahead of him, through a haze of smoke that brought tears to his eyes, the huge wooden doors swing closed. Fear shot through his stomach like a jagged splinter, but even as he watched, the building heat began to crack the stone doorframe. The wood splintered and sagged, turning the whole structure into a warped, tangled mess of misshapen planks. There was no other escape but through; it was escape or die. Gritting his teeth, he lowered his shoulder and let out a wordless roar, clutching Leah and Raven to his chest.

Red light flared around him as the Ox Talisman activated itself, lending him strength, and the huge oak doors burst outward in a thousand flying splinters. He opened an eye a bare fraction of an inch, allowing him to judge the fall he was about to make down the long, marble stairs that led from the cathedral doors to the paved city ground. He threw Raven to the side, knowing he could not roll with two people, and clutched Leah tight to his chest. The Prince, at least, was conscious and had a chance of saving himself; Leah would be left to die if he dropped her now.

He managed to push off with one solid foot from the top stair, and for a suspended moment he was weightless and time seemed to slow. The ground came up to meet him, and he wrenched his body around, curling into a ball, and rolled over his shoulder before sprawling both himself and Leah over the hard, tiled ground of the courtyard.

He was up again in the next instant, though, spinning around even as his muscles screamed in protest at such ill use. He quickly scanned the area for the Prince, careful to breathe deep here in the smoke-free air, saturating himself with as much oxygen as he could in order to keep his heart rate steady before he rushed back in to the mounting inferno. He moved forward, his eyes closed to slits, his large body crouched and low to the ground to avoid the smoke now roiling out of the open doorway. Seconds passed, and he began to fear that he had misjudged the throw, that he had sent Raven flying back into the cathedral to his death.

Wait – there.

His eyes lit on the fallen form of his friend, but something was wrong – Raven was not moving. He forced himself toward the young man, working against every finely tuned training tactic that told him to cut his losses, even as the enormous gothic cathedral began to sway and shake ominously. Finally he reached the princeling and grabbed him up, only to find himself confronted by two Seekers who had followed through the enormous hole he had just made in the double doors.

They saw him, screamed, and ran in opposite directions, left and right.

He dropped Raven, picked up two large stones nearly the size of a normal man's head, and threw them, one after the other, pivoting on his back foot as he did. They arched through the air in a strangely graceful way, and struck both men directly between the shoulder-blades, knocking them to the ground and smashing their heads against the hard stone street. Neither of them moved.

Tomaz grabbed up Raven once more and bounded back to the comatose form of Leah. He picked her up as well, just as a gout of flame shot out of the cathedral's entranceway behind him, singeing his hair and armor. He stumbled forward, off balance, but alive and whole. He stopped at a safe distance, many yards away, and used the Path of Polinal technique to calm his mind and check his body.

Bruised right bicep, torn skin over left knee, strained back on lower left side and upper right, likely latissimus dorsi, beginnings of a headache, likely from elevated stress and dehydration. No ligament damage, no breaks, fractures, sprains or tears.

He examined Leah and Raven, who, apart from being unconscious with a dozen superficial cuts and scrapes, did not show outward signs of debilitating injury. On the inside, though? He could understand and help mend the body, but the workings of the mind were foreign to him. He looked up and took in the scene around him.

By the light of the burning Cathedral of the Empress he could see the whole of the Inner City swarming with wave after wave of Kindred men and women in the green, black, gold, and silver that denoted their ranks and specialties. The Seekers of Truth who had fled before Tomaz, those feared shadows that spied on Empire and Kindred alike from the depths of their hidden lairs, had been taken captive. There were two large areas of carnage where Bloodmages had put up a last stand, only to fall to the skilled archery of the Scouts, who had managed to surround them at a distance and feather them with arrows. Several dozen of the sprawling Imperial houses of the Most High, the Imperial aristocracy, were being ransacked by the Kindred and cannibalized for use as hospitals and command posts. Figures in green and black were passing out of doorways with ornamental weapons that were still functional, tapestries that could be cut up for binding cloth, and any stray piece of metal that could be melted down by blacksmiths. Among these could be seen a series of people all in white – Healers, those members of the Kindred that specialized in medical care. They were directing members of the Kindred to bring men and women to various houses as the previous inhabitants were pulled out, bound and gagged. Those would be the Most High, the recent rulers of the city. Many of them screamed about the purity of their blood and their family's history even as they were trussed like pigs for market.

"Tomaz!"

He turned and saw the small, matronly figure of Elder Keri, the Elder of Healing herself, in her white robes at the entrance to one of the mansions. She was beckoning to him with a quick repetitive wave, and even in the midst of the chaos that surrounded her she managed to exude a collected calm. He went to her, moving quickly through the crowd. Others bounced off of him as he rushed past, but he paid them no mind; he was thinking only of Raven and Leah.

Who knows what all those memories did to them? One mind isn't meant to hold all that, especially on top of all Raven has done in the last twenty-four hours. Leading the assault on Formaux with Davydd and Autmaran, killing Tiffenal, running here to Banelyn through the night to warn us of the attack by Dysuna, Prince of Wolves, then fighting through Henri Perci's treachery and finally confronting Geofred... by the angels that guard the Veil, it's a miracle he's unconscious and not outright dead.

His thoughts turned to Leah, his young Eshendai partner, paired with him when she had come to the Kindred several years ago. She was a Spellblade, bound to the daggers she carried, which gave her a certain amount of protection.

But even that might not help her now. Raven, at least, was prepared – he's had the Raven Talisman all his life, long enough to become accustomed to having other people's memories in his head. Leah has never had to endure something like that, and now she's living four hundred years worth of another person's life.

"In here," Keri said quickly when he reached her. She glanced down at the two figures he carried in his arms and her face fell into lines of frustration and anger before reforming into an expression of renewed determination. "Tell me what happened."

They ducked through the entrance of the manor and hurried down a long hallway lined with torn tapestries and overturned tables. Goblets, plates, and various finery lay strewn about, and there were people everywhere. As quickly as he could, Tomaz told her of their confrontation with Geofred, Prince of Eagles.

"He planned this," he concluded, his voice vibrating in his chest even though he tried to keep the words soft and barely audible. Luckily, everyone around them seemed focused on their own tasks and paid little heed to his words. "The Prince of Eagles wanted us to find him, and he planned to have us kill him. He forced

Raven to kill him with Leah's Anchor, and because the Anchor has her blood in it, when Raven killed him, the Raven Talisman pulled the memories out of Geofred's mind and shared them with Leah. She passed out under the strain – he passed out when we escaped the cathedral."

"It transferred the memories," she said quickly, breathlessly, as they turned a corner. "Did it transfer anything else?"

He knew what she was asking, and he looked at Leah, looked more closely.

There were light blue markings at the very edge of her hairline, barely visible even under close scrutiny. He shifted her weight and rolled up her sleeve. His heart skipped a beat and then sank into his stomach with a sense of terrible foreboding. The backs of her hands had marks as well, and they were growing. It was as if an invisible hand were etching a blue tattoo into her skin; even as he watched, the lines thickened, growing bolder and stronger as the Talisman worked its way into and through her.

Talisman? Or Aspect? Did the transfer work the way it was intended?

Tomaz looked up and caught Elder Keri's gaze. She had seen it too.

They reached their destination: the manor's grand hall. It had been a place for dancing and feasting, with a huge fireplace and beautifully painted walls, but was now stripped bare, save only for the molding itself. There were large, blank, off-white spaces on the walls where tapestries and paintings had been pulled down, the thicker weavings then cut up to serve as everything from makeshift bandages to full-length partitions for the Healers who had to do the grisly work of field surgeons. The screams from behind those curtains struck Tomaz in the pit of his stomach; even after all his years in battle, he could not stop the sounds of the dying from affecting him. Men and women rushed past him going both ways, carrying in more wounded, some of them in the colors of the Kindred, but most in the simple homespun worn by the Commons of Banelyn.

Dysuna would not have cared how many she killed in the initial attack. She must have struck immediately, hoping to kill as many Kindred as she could before we closed the gates; the Commons just were caught in-between.

Had they closed the gates? He could not hear the distant sounds of battle here, but judging by the number and type of wounded all around him, he knew the fighting was too intense for a simple siege. The attacking army must have a grip, however tenuous, on one the gates – likely only one, or else the city would have been overrun already.

If the city is not secure, it does not matter what happens to Leah or Raven – Dysuna will kill them without a second thought for what happened to her brother.

He followed Keri as she crossed the room, carefully but quickly breaking through the encroaching crowd of wounded before stopping near the right-hand wall. "Lay them here," she said quickly, motioning to an empty space near the front of the long hall, already covered with layers of blankets. Tomaz complied, and then stepped back.

"Take care of them," he rumbled down at Elder Keri, catching her eye.

"You have my word, Tomaz."

He nodded, forced himself to turn away, and re-crossed the hall. He found himself running a hand through his dense, well-trimmed beard and then his thick mane of hair. His agitation at leaving the two of them unprotected, even here in this makeshift hospital, could not be helped. He had been in too many battles to have illusions about the safety of any place within a hundred miles of drawn swords. But he knew the only chance he had of helping them survive was to man the Black Wall – to find the gate that had been taken, and bloody take it back.

He burst from the house and headed immediately toward the gates that led from the Inner City to Banelyn City proper, where the fighting would be. Breathing deeply, he focused his mind, using the Path again, the technique he had learned so many years ago as a Blade Master in the service of the Empire he now fought.

It is strange to see just how far the world turns.

He relaxed his body into a simple, efficient stride, and allowed breath to come in through his nose and out through his mouth. He focused energy deep inside his broad chest, then flexed his hands, cracked his knuckles, rolled his neck, and re-set what was left of his armor. He had lost too much of it during the initial attack on the city, and then still more escaping the cathedral; holes had been ripped in his chain mail by falling debris, and the leather jerkin beneath was held together by nothing more than sweat, blood, and prayer. His breastplate had been sliced off entirely when a crafty Defender had cut the straps holding it on. But he still had his greatsword, Malachi, and... and maybe something else as well.

If what Geofred said about the Aspect of Strength is correct... then for every person I save, I will grow stronger.

He hurried through the rushing crowds of Commons, refugees from the destitute Outer City of Banelyn that Dysuna had knifed through in her initial attack. He watched them all carefully, or as many of them as he could. A knife in the back here could kill him just as easily as a sword on the Wall. But it looked as though they were all too concerned about keeping their families together and hauling what possessions they had out of harm's way. Many of them held or led small children, who were weeping openly or staring in shock and horror as wounded men and women, some missing limbs, others cursing, and still more crying out in pain and terror, were carted past.

He breached the last ring of Banelyn City proper, the second circle of the three-tier city, sandwiched between the poor Outer City and the affluent Inner City and bordered by the infamous Black Wall. The Wall itself reared up before him, made by the Empress's first two sons, Geofred and Rikard, hundreds of years ago. It towered over him at an almost impossible height; it was unsurprising that it had never been taken until now. The black stone that made it up was nearly unbreakable, which meant that the only entry points for an invading army were the three gates that led north to Lerne, east to Formaux, and south to Roarke. Tomaz concentrated on what he was hearing and realized the sounds of battle were coming from the direction of the Formaux Gate.

Making his way around the perimeter of the city, the crowds of fleeing Commons grew thicker, and the sound of clashing swords grew louder. Soon he found the place where the fighting was – it was indeed the Formaux Gate, which had not been closed. The full sight was hidden from him, even though he towered over the surrounding soldiers. What he did manage to see was that a huge crowd of Exiled Kindred had formed up in front of the opening, where they were engaged in battle. But the fighting toward the front made further details murky. He scanned the area and saw a long set of steps carved into the side of the Wall very close by, providing easy access to the high battlements. He went for them, moving through the gathered people, now mostly Kindred soldiers, with barely a comment.

He took the stairs four at a time and reached the level of the battlements in a rush that startled a number of soldiers. He strode past them without comment, making his way closer to the section of wall above the fighting, passing between ranks of archers who were firing into the gathered Imperial army.

The commanding Kindred officer – a captain with a green cloak – was shouting orders and directing the arrows. A sixth sense must have told the man something was happening – he turned to look at who had broken his ranks, about to rebuke him, but then realized who Tomaz was and shut his mouth with a nearly audible snap. Tomaz ignored him, came to the edge, and looked down from his place on the Wall. What he saw before him was an army of thousands upon thousands marching through the teetering wooden structures of the Outer City in row upon row of tan and gray.

Shadows and fire, it's nearly the size of the Imperial Army itself. How did Dysuna manage to field so many men?

And worse still were towering figures farther back, figures that could only be Daemons, malicious elementals trapped by the power of the Imperial Bloodmages. The mages themselves rode on the Daemons' backs, their billowing black robes cloaking them in shadow as their Soul Catchers, the source of their power, flashed brightly even in the mounting light of day.

A cheer went up among the Kindred, including the archers around him, and he shifted his view to the battle at the gate. The Imperial force was retreating, moving back as if they had lost heart.

Those lines are too straight – they are turning, not retreating.

He shot a look back up at the force crouched amongst the buildings of the Outer City, and realized an alleyway ran down right of the gate, the mouth of which was large enough for a Daemon to just squeeze through.

"STOP!" he roared to those around him as they began to shift, spreading out along the battlements in anticipation of the closing gate. He strode to the captain. "It's a tactical maneuver," he said quickly, staring the man down. It was easy to be intimidating when you stood eight feet tall. "Keep shooting – and train all bows on that alley there, the next attack will come from that direction."

"But – "

"Just do it!" he roared, and the man paled before he nodded and began to give out the orders. Tomaz turned and moved quickly to the tower that formed an edge with the gate below. There was a door there, and it would lead him to the other side, where he could pass the message.

The cheering continued from below, and he grimaced. This was going to be tight – he could only hope the Kindred were not fool enough to pursue.

By the gods, I wish Autmaran were in control down there.

He burst through the door with such force he almost knocked it off its hinges, and continued on through the dimly lit interior of the gatehouse battlements. Men and women were stationed next to murder holes that could be used to stall the enemy as they attacked the gate below.

"Stay sharp," he told them as he passed. "This is not over yet – not by a long shot. Keep your eyes on them, and be ready!"

They all saluted as he strode past. Just as his hand grabbed hold of the metal handle of the door that would lead him to ground level, the cheering died, and a series of bestial roars resounded through the air.

Damn.

He forced his way through the door and began shouting for everyone to shoot the Daemons, to do everything they could to hit the Bloodmages who rode them, but as he peered into the alley, he saw he was too late. The Imperial ruse had worked – whoever had command of the gate had ordered the Kindred to pursue the Imperial force. As he watched, huge forms made of animated stone and wood burst from the alleyway and began killing men and women in droves.

He needed to get down there. He ran toward the back edge of the Wall and unsheathed his sword. The metal rang out with a sweet sound as it left the scabbard, and the weight made him feel complete. As much as he hated killing, he was born and bred for battle, and he could not deny his place at the heart of it.

The Kindred below were being forced back through the gate in a roiling wave of panic. The stairs on this side were a hundred yards down the Wall, through a crowd of soldiers. He looked up and saw the rooftop of a supply depot, twenty feet away and fifteen feet below him.

Shadows and fire, I am going to have to jump that, aren't I?

The bestial sounds of the Daemons intruded on this thought, and all time for deliberation was over. He cradled Malachi against his side, took several steps back, and then ran forward, launching himself into the air.

He landed with a crash that shook his whole body and sent burning cracks of pain up his legs, even as he rolled to lessen the impact. Coming to his feet as quickly as possible on the slippery roofing tiles, he spun and saw the gate before him.

Just as his eyes landed on the sight, a huge rush of sound and air exploded through the gate, and the first of the Daemons was through. Reacting on instinct, he ran for the edge of the roof, and as he did he caught his first sight of the creature. It was an Earth Daemon, one of those most commonly used in sieges. The thing was huge, towering over fifteen feet tall, with legs made of tree trunks and a body and shoulders made of fused boulders. Vines swung about its head in imitation of hair, and its huge lumpy mouth gaped to reveal rows of gnashing stone teeth. In its hands swung a long, wicked scythe, one that looked as if it had been stolen from Death itself, and with each swing it sent half a dozen soldiers to their graves. It turned to swipe at the Kindred clustered by the Wall, and Tomaz saw his opening.

He held Malachi up and out of the way, dashed the last several feet, and launched himself once more into the air, this time straight at the creature's back.

It's invulnerable as long as it's connected to the earth, but if I can get the Bloodmage –

But the mage riding the creature saw him, even though the Daemon was turned away. On some silent command, the creature spun with uncanny speed, and the terrible scythe came up to bat him down. The only thing that saved him was the back-hand nature of the blow – the creature was not fast enough to bring the blade to bear, and so caught him with the butt of the haft, crashing the hardened wood so hard into his chest that the air left his lungs in a *whoosh* of breath that left him weak and gasping as he slammed into the paved stone road.

There was a ringing in his ears, and above that he heard cries of dismay. His hands were empty – Malachi was gone. His vision cleared just enough for him to see what was happening in front of him, and what he saw was the huge foot of the Daemon descending toward him. He rolled out of reach just as a dense leg of enchanted wood drove into the ground, creating a crater where he had been seconds before. He kept rolling, used the momentum to come to his feet, and then ran for his life.

"TOMAZ!"

Along the periphery of his vision he caught movement – a figure too small to be a solider pulling an immense piece of metal through the crowd of shouting spearmen.

Mother of – !

He changed course and ran for the boy; the Daemon roared out a confused challenge as it searched for him.

"TYM, MOVE!"

The young blonde-haired boy that had come along as Davydd's camp aide tossed the greatsword into the air and dove out of the way just as Tomaz was about to bowl him over. Reaching out as he passed, Tomaz caught Malachi by the hilt and kept running, circling to his right.

Earth Daemons draw power from the ground. I have to get it off the ground, have to do something to break its power –

He rounded the other side of the building and came out behind the Daemon, still sprinting as fast as his legs could carry him, heart pounding in his chest like a hammer. The Daemon had raised its scythe to take another swipe at the gathered Exiles, but spears had been brought forward now, and it was having a hard time reaching them. With a roar, Tomaz ran forward and swung Malachi into the leg of the Daemon.

Only one type of metal could break Daemon skin, and Malachi was not made of it. The blow, instead of slicing the skin, knocked the Daemon's leg out from under it and sent the creature crashing to the ground.

Tomaz turned and ran, not having any other idea at the moment besides getting the creature back outside the Wall. "Make sure it follows me!" he shouted wildly to other Exiles as he ran past. A score even ran out of the gate ahead of him, shouting and brandishing swords and spears as they cut down the Imperial soldiers who had begun to form back up on the other side of the Wall. Taken by surprise, the force retreated again, even as the other Daemons made their way forward with trumpeting bellows.

Tomaz shot a glance over his back and saw the Daemon turning, the Bloodmage fuming and shouting curses at the beast to get it back under control, but for the moment the creature had the reins. It pursued Tomaz, a sight that sent a tremor through the big man's heart.

Time it right. Breathe in – one – two – NOW!

He threw himself off to the side, and the Daemon went crashing past him in a huge sliding heap of broken paving stones and scattered Imperial soldiers. Tomaz turned and came back, hefting Malachi. He jumped to the fallen Daemon's back and swung the sword at the Bloodmage. The man threw up an arm to block the blow, knowing that as long as he was connected to the beast his skin was hard as rock and impervious to such blows.

Bad move.

Tomaz pulled back the feint, slipped a hand beneath his armor, and pulled out his Anchor, the small piece of valerium metal that made him a citizen of Vale and a member of the Exiled Kindred.

Valerium – the metal that cut through enchanted flesh.

The Bloodmage's eyes went wide, and before he could even scream, the Anchor, formed into the shape of a small dagger that stayed unnaturally sharp, cut through the cowl of his robe and –

The ground shifted beneath them, and the sudden movement shifted the dagger's direction and momentum. The small white dagger sunk into the Bloodmage's shoulder, causing pain but leaving the man alive. The Daemon reared up beneath them, regaining its footing on huge tree trunk legs, and began to swing about, trying to dislodge Tomaz. Both he and the Bloodmage were forced to grab hold of the nearest piece of Daemon they could find; Tomaz clutched at a moss-covered boulder that sprouted granite tips, while the Bloodmage made do with the strand wood-and-moss saddle.

The movement stopped abruptly, and Tomaz craned his neck from his precarious perch to look over his shoulder. The creature's gaze had fallen on the twenty-odd Kindred troops who had come with Tomaz through the gate.

It went for them with a deep, earthy roar.

With a grunt of effort, Tomaz, holding onto the Daemon's back by a huge spur of granite that protruded from the beast like a shoulder blade, reached up and pulled the valerium dagger out of the Bloodmage. The man clawed at his face, but Tomaz knocked the arm aside, losing Malachi in the process.

With a snarl of anger he pulled himself up the rest of the way, finding footing even on the swaying form, and grabbed the mage's black robes. In response, the man grabbed his arm, twisting and shouting words that seemed to crackle and burn, but Tomaz paid them no heed. With a firm grip on his miniature dagger, he slammed the sharp blade into the jugular vein of the Bloodmage, and then, with a sharp tug, pulled the Soul Catcher crystal from around his throat, crushing it in his hand.

The light in the man's eyes faded, and the Daemon exploded out from under them in a thousand pieces of blasted rock. The scythe, which had just swung up once more to reap the souls of a dozen Exiles, clattered to the ground, and as the pieces of the Daemon blew past them, the men and women looked up in wonder.

Tomaz was thrown through air and into the side of the Black Wall itself, and as he hit he felt as though every bone in his body was about to break. But just as the pain spiked, red light exploded all around him, coming from the Aspect of Strength that was etched into his skin. Sudden strength pounded through his veins and the pain disappeared. He staggered up again, trying to find his footing even as the world spun around him. He pushed off the wall, stumbling through the rubble of the Daemon, and realized he had not been wounded in the slightest. His skin had turned as hard as stone, and he felt strong enough to lift a house.

His eyes fell on the Kindred soldiers who would have died from the Daemon's blow, and he realized that what the Prince of Eagles had told him really had been true – he would gain strength with every life he saved.

Heavy treading footsteps sounded in his ears and two more Earth Daemons, one with shoulders made of moss-covered mountain scrag and the other with oak tree arms, pushed forward from the mouth of the alleyway, heading for the gate. A third Daemon came on strong behind them, and behind it, a gathering swell of men, pouring out in a huge tidal wave from both the boulevard and the alleyway. Tomaz jerked his head around and saw more Kindred coming out of the gate, many of them with the long spears and pikes used for fighting Daemons. Their faces were all grim, and Tomaz knew they were preparing themselves to fight to the death – for death it would be. Their force was no match for this kind of constant pressure; they would have a chance if the Daemons were gone, but those spears would never pierce the rock flesh of the creatures.

The Daemons broke into a shambling run, two of them swinging enormous mauls longer than Tomaz was tall, both with a stone head the size of a horse. They saw him and bellowed, opening their huge maws and showing stumpy wooden teeth and throats coated in moss.

Tomaz saw nothing else to do – he had to stop them here. It would be the Kindred's only chance. He reached over his back and stopped, suddenly remembering he had dropped Malachi. He spun frantically, searching the area –

"Tomaz!"

He turned to the gate and saw, again, the little figure of Tym trying desperately to heft the massive greatsword, his fine blonde hair swinging wildly about his head.

"TYM! I swear by the seven hells I will tan your hide if you don not get inside *RIGHT NOW!*"

Tym took the hint and fled, leaving Malachi behind on the ground.

Tomaz picked up the sword and turned back to the approaching army, standing in the midst of the gathered Kindred. The Daemons roared at them, and the Kindred took an unconscious, fearful step back. Tomaz, however, took a step forward, threw back his head, and roared out an echoing challenge as the red light of the Aspect of Strength burned through the holes in his armor. The Kindred on the wall took up the call, and then the Kindred at the gate, until they were all shouting as one. A palpable energy seemed to infuse them all, and as one, with Tomaz leading the charge, they ran forward to meet the Imperials. Something akin to shock or confusion crossed the dumb faces of the huge elementals, and the first one paused, just long enough to allow Tomaz an opening. He dove forward as the Kindred shoved at it with their long poles; he tapped into the power coursing through him, boiling his blood, and he reached out and grabbed hold of the first Daemon's tree trunk leg, wrapping his own huge arms around it, pulling with all his strength. His back spasmed, and his booted feet were actually forced down into the ground, cracking the paving stones beneath his feet; but after an agonizing second of lost equilibrium, his strength won out and he uprooted the Daemon, throwing it off balance and sending it stumbling into the second Daemon, which was sent sprawling to the ground, dislodging its Bloodmage.

Without pause, Tomaz launched himself over the splayed limbs of the fallen Daemon at the unseated mage; he grabbed the man by the scruff of the neck, spun, and threw him straight through the wall of the nearest building.

That gave Tomaz an idea.

He reached down and grabbed the leg of the fallen Daemon, now without its Bloodmage, and heaved with all his might as more strength infused him, granted by the lives he had saved from the Daemons' charge. The hard oak leg *crunched* beneath his grip; his back and shoulders cracked and screamed in protest; he refused to give in. Red light filled his vision and blinded him; power coursed through his body with such fevered brilliance that all thoughts of caution were shoved aside. He took a step, threw his weight forward, and sent the creature flying into the third Daemon with enough force to send them both tumbling backward through the air, end over end, into the approaching Imperial lines.

The creatures landed and exploded, decimating the first dozen ranks of the approaching Imperials, and sending the ones behind running for cover as debris rained down upon them.

Tomaz turned back to the first Daemon as it regained its feet, and ran for it. When he was a dozen yards away he pulled power from his Aspect and pushed off the ground, throwing himself in a high arc through the air. He crashed into the Bloodmage sitting astride the Daemon, and carried him off his perch. Tomaz rolled over the man as they crashed to the ground, then turned back, picked him up by the scruff of the neck, and snapped his neck.

The Daemon, pushing itself back up once again, slumped suddenly to its knees, stunned as the controlling mind that had directed it disappeared. Tomaz took the Soul Catcher from the dead Bloodmage and closed his hand around it, ready to break it; but then a memory of Davydd Goldwyn riding a Daemon at Aemon's Stand came back to him, and he stopped.

He did not stop to question the idea; he slipped the leather cord over his head.

His mind felt as if it had suddenly doubled. He had two sets of arms, two sets of legs. He turned his head, and the Daemon responded in kind; he looked toward the Imperial army, regrouping and advancing once more, and the Daemon's own eyes narrowed. They smiled as one, and then Tomaz imagined launching himself forward into the fray. The elemental fulfilled the thought, swinging its enormous club and trampling the first line of Imperial men as it attacked those behind with a terrifying backhand swing. With an enormous effort of will, Tomaz pulled himself back from the Daemon, and turned to run for the gate.

"Get back inside!" he roared at the Kindred outside the gate; they retreated without needing to be told again. He gestured frantically to the Kindred and Banelyners on the Wall, the former cheering him on and the later watching with something akin to religious awe.

"Shut the gate!" he cried.

No one seemed to hear him or understand.

"SHUT THE THRICE-DAMNED GATE, YOU FOOLS!"

The second yell awakened them from their stupor, and they turned as one and began to shout at the gatehouse inside the Wall, taking up his call. But whoever was inside either was not able to hear or could not comply: neither the metal grating of the portcullis nor the thick wooden double doors moved.

Tomaz crossed the barrier of the black stone and spun to look back. The Daemon was still making its way through the Imperial army, killing and maiming as it went, but as he watched a shape flew in from the sky, something blinding white that crackled with energy; it crashed into the Earth Daemon, knocking it to the ground.

Tomaz felt the shock of the impact both through the quaking earth and through the glowing green-and-red crystal slung around his neck. The new Daemon, blinding white and crowned with a ring of lightning, stepped forward and punched the Earth Daemon, breaking off part of its stony face in a flash of energy that cracked and rumbled across the city. Tomaz, giving the mental command to the elemental to fight back, watched the Earth Daemon give a mighty heave that threw off the new Lightning Daemon; they both came back to their feet, and the two squared off against each other.

We are running out of time, Tomaz thought frantically. He turned to look at the gatehouse and saw nearly a dozen men – Kindred, common Banelyners, and even men in the red-and-black of Roarke – all throwing themselves at the winch that held the portcullis; it would not budge. His eyes flicked up to the chain that held the solid metal grating in place, and he realized that the upper wheel was completely jammed with rust. Likely it had not been oiled in ages – no one had needed to close this gate against an attack in hundreds of years.

Shadows and bloody fire!

Tomaz felt pain across the left side of his face and realized the Lightning Daemon had struck the Earth Daemon once again. If the Kindred were lucky, the elementals would kill each other and explode in the –

That was it. That was the answer.

In a sudden rush of inspiration, he pulled off the crystal from around his neck and ran for the rusted wheel. The metal part of the gate, the portcullis, was made of thick iron bars bound one over the other, and meant to come down in front of the two thick wooden doors that could be barred from the inside. The doors would not stand up to Daemons – but if the Kindred could bring down the portcullis, they would have a measure of security, at least for a time.

He reached through the Aspect of Strength and pulled power from that strange red reservoir inside him, and as the Lighting Daemon fought the Earth Daemon, the two of them grappling and roaring at each other and blocking the Imperial forces, he closed his fist and cracked the Soul Catcher.

Immediately, the Earth Daemon shuddered as if its spine had been broken, and the Lightning Daemon pounced; the Bloodmage riding it, clothed all in white to blend with the creature, urged it on.

"This is a terrible idea," he rumbled to himself.

He pulled back and threw the crystal at the tangled, rusted mess of chain.

The Soul Catcher arched through the air and hit the chain dead-on. The crack in the crystal widened the rest of the way and split the medallion in two, releasing whatever fell power was contained inside. A wave of energy lanced out, blinding

Tomaz, throwing him to the ground, and knocking the wind out of him. The Earth Daemon exploded as well, the spells and enchantments holding it in place violently ripped away; the Lightning Daemon was thrown off and into an already teetering house, that promptly lost the last of its supports and fell, spilling dust and splintered wood over the Imperial soldiers.

A rattling, metallic sound came from above Tomaz, and through the red haze left from the explosion that had knocked him flat, he watched the portcullis descend, making straight for his head.

He rolled, using what was left of his strength, and watched as the metal spikes sunk into the paved stone road inches from his face with a huge, resounding *crash*. There was more motion, and he saw none other than Stannit, the captain of the guard from the razed city of Roarke, bellowing for him to pull back, as he and his men in the black-and-red pushed at the enormous doors. Tomaz threw himself back once more, just as the oaken doors slammed shut in front of him. The last image he had was of the Imperial troops marching uselessly forward, the sound of marching feet not enough to drown out the horrible bellows of the maimed Lightning Daemon behind them.

A cheer went up among the gathered Kindred, and many of the Banelyn Commons who had gathered about the wall with whatever swords or armor they had scrounged up joined them. From Tomaz's right, Stannit roared orders up into the air; more men were on the Wall, in the red-and-black of Roarke, but also the green, gold, and silver of the Kindred. They stood side by side in rows that stretched out all along the battlements, and as Tomaz watched they raised their bows and loosed a wave of arrows. He ran for the nearest set of steps that led upward, and arrived just in time to see another volley of arrows leap through the air, striking the fleeing army below and felling Imperial soldiers by the hundreds.

Imperial horns sounded the retreat, and even the Lightning Daemon, now missing half of its torso and right arm, pulled back as the arrows continued to fly.

Jubilant shouts and cries filled the air from the lips of the Kindred, Commons, and former Imperials, but Tomaz did not join them. He was looking at the gate – and at the far side of the metal portcullis that had been blown off. Somehow a boulder from one of the exploding Daemons had struck a weak point there, detaching part of the metal before wedging itself into the gears, breaking them when Tomaz had blown the chain, and leaving the whole thing skewed to one side. The gate was vulnerable now: this was where they would attack again.

The smell of smoke came to him on the wind, and he held up a hand to block out the light of the rising sun, straining his eyes to see as far as he could into the Outer City. A haze had already begun to build as the Imperial Army retreated, and with a sinking feeling he realized what was happening.

Smoke began to billow even more profusely into the air over the Outer City of Banelyn as the labyrinth of rickety, towering structures began to burn, and the cries of joy on the Wall turned to shouts of dismay. A number of hulking forms were massing beyond the last row of houses around what could only be the beginnings of hastily constructed siege ladders and towers. Tomaz quickly guessed the rate at which the Outer City was likely to burn, then looked up at the distant sun, already its own height above the eastern horizon and partially cloaked by the rising haze of smoke.

By sunset the city would be burned to the ground. The flames would not cross the Black Wall, but as soon as the fires died, Dysuna would attack again. Another commander might wait until the following morning, but with a compromised gate and the cover of darkness… no, she would not. Not the Wolf. They had killed her brother, and nothing would stop her from taking this city and killing them all in return. They would put up a brave fight, and Tomaz knew he would lay down his life fighting to the last breath, maybe even taking her down himself in a fight of Aspect and Talisman, but his conclusion was grim. The army before them was enormous, and the Kindred were ragged from weeks of a forced march. And if it came down to a fight between Dysuna and himself... he had only borne the Aspect of Strength for a few months, while she had been given the Wolf centuries ago.

If Raven could fight, we would have a chance, but even then it would be a close thing, and without him.... I will take as many of them with me as I can, and I will leave blood on this Black Wall the stories and legends will never forget.

Luck was a foreign idea to him. He was a hard man, a practical man. And so he sheathed Malachi and went to work helping the Kindred fortify the Wall as best he could. And in the back of his mind, he relished the way his limbs moved and his lungs breathed, even though the sun beat down and made him sweat and the air was hot and full of smoke. If he was to die, then die he would. But he would enjoy every last breath, every last sensation, until the very, very end.

He would take as much of life as he could get.

Chapter Two:

As Luck Would Have It

Davydd felt as if he were living in two simultaneous realities. In one, he was riding at the head of a column of Kindred Rangers and Scouts toward the distant city of Banelyn, hoping against hope that they would arrive in time. In another, he was being burnt alive.

Autmaran, Commander of the Kindred Scouts and Light Infantry, rode beside him on the left and slightly ahead, while Lorna, Davydd's Ashandel partner, rode on his right. He was lashed to his saddle with thick binding rope to keep him in place, and each shock of his horse's hooves against the hard-packed dirt road sent jolts of pain through his left side. The sun overhead burned down, dissipating the mists that had cloaked the land for weeks and sending sweat dripping down his face. The salt of the sweat stung his open wounds, and he did not think he had unclenched his jaw since dawn. Added to it all, his throat was dry, his lips chapped, and his tongue swollen. Lack of water and the drying, rushing wind were turning out to be fiercer foes than the soldiers of Formaux. If they arrived at Banelyn in this state, they would not be able to put up much of a fight, no matter what the situation.

A Scout appeared from around a bend in the road ahead. "Sir!" the man called out as he caught sight of Commander Autmaran.

"Jansen!" Autmaran called back without reining in his horse. They were going at a slow trot now, trying to keep the horses as fresh as possible while still eking out as much speed as they could. Jansen fell in beside them.

"Sir," he said, "there's a fork up ahead, one that isn't on our maps. I don't know where it came from – it must be recent, within the past year."

"The maps should still be clear on which one to take."

"That's the thing sir – they aren't. The rest of the Scouts say the markers have been cleared; there's no trace of anything, and the roads seem to run roughly parallel. They must diverge farther in, but we will need to scout down them both a goodly way."

Autmaran was silent for a time and then nodded, looking grim.

"Very well. Scout as quickly down each path as you can and report back; try to find which way takes us most directly to Banelyn."

Jansen left, and Autmaran turned to Davydd and Lorna. "I told you we should not have taken this shortcut," he said, his dark eyes narrowed in something bordering on fury. That was not a good sign – Autmaran did not lose his temper. But they were all going on no sleep and little food, and marching with the knowledge that even now their fellow Kindred could be caught in a massacre that they were too far away to stop. It was enough to make even the most stalwart general ready to chew through rocks.

"It was the right choice," Davydd said. "I know it was."

"How can you say that?" Autmaran asked, his eyes flashing. "I must have been insane – now we need to spend extra time scouting both paths, and – "

"Calm down, Auty," Davydd said with a touch of his old ebullience, flashing his teeth at the man in what he knew most people saw as a slightly feral smile. The effect must be even worse now with his half-burned face. He would have gone for a more winning one, but even smiling at all was a feat worthy of epic poetry; the pain from his left side was so intense he was continually fighting off unconsciousness. "I have the Fox Talisman now. Means I'm lucky. My gut told me to take this road – it will get us to Banelyn. It will. You just have to trust me."

"How do you know it's working?" Autmaran asked, his tone softening a small degree as Davydd cringed in pain at a particularly bad flare of heat from the creeping Talisman. Davydd cursed under his breath – he hated people seeing him weak.

"Because it bloody *is*. Just take my word for it – I can't explain."

As he said the words the *thing* happened again, the strange twist that occurred in his vision, making the world turn somehow. It was a small, infinitesimal shift, but every time it happened, glowing lines of beautiful gold shot across his vision, overlaying reality, and he somehow knew things he could not explain.

He gasped as pain blazed through him again, and he bit down so hard on his back teeth that they felt ready to crack. His left side was so raw that the slightest movement seemed to blur his vision with a red haze that obscured the golden lines and broke whatever tenuous connection he had to the Fox Talisman burning its way through his body. He hid the tension as best he could, but he knew Lorna and Autmaran saw it.

"Just keep going," he grated out. " Trust me."

Autmaran looked ready to continue arguing, but then changed his mind, reserving his comments for another time. Another gleam came into his eyes, though, and Davydd's annoyance mounted; the general had wanted him to stay in Formaux, and Davydd would not put it past the man to send him back now.

He won't – he knows everyone is needed.

The tipping point had come when Davydd had shared the memories he had gleaned from the dead Prince of Foxes, among them the intended trap at Banelyn. The debate had ended immediately, and the Kindred had set out within the hour, accompanied by a strange force of fervent Formaux Commons.

Commander bloody Autmaran thinks they'll stay true to us in the heat of battle.

The Formaux citizenry, those of the lowest and most populous class called the Commons, had enabled the Kindred's swift, nearly casualty-free take-over of the most eastern city of the Empire. Commander Autmaran had taken the walls just as Davydd and Lorna had helped Raven killed the Prince of Foxes with Davydd's sword – a chain of events that had led to the famed Fox Talisman, the Talisman of Luck, transferring to Davydd instead of Raven. However, the memories of Tiffenal, Prince of Foxes, had been shared evenly between the two of them, courtesy of another odd quirk of the Raven Talisman.

Another searing flash of pain rushed through him, and it was all he could do to hold on to his stallion, Aron, as the Fox Talisman continued to burn its way down his left arm and leg. It had already taken the left side of his face and torso as well as most of his hip, burning the skin there and leaving it cracked and blackened. He could feel it reaching further, though, and deeper, those golden lines of power tracing their way along his veins all the way through his body.

The pain subsided to a dull ache, and he looked over his shoulder, catching sight of the mounted column of Formauxans on their liberated horses keeping pace with the Kindred more out of determination than skill. In truth, it was because of the Commoners that they had taken the city so easily. When the Baseborn had heard the alarm bells and word had spread that Tiffenal was dead, slain by the hand of Raven, the Exiled Prince, the lower classes had risen up and deposed the vast majority of the High Blood, breaking open the dungeons and torture chambers below Tiffenal's palace and freeing generations of captives.

We invaded the one major city already ripe for rebellion.

Another painful hour passed as they continued on. They were pushing as hard as they dared; a dozen horses had already fallen with broken legs from ruts and holes in the road, and twice that many were down from sheer exhaustion.

And still we must go faster.

They turned a final bend and found themselves at the fork Jansen the Scout had described. It was almost like something from a fairy story: two perfectly good roads in a heavily wooded forest, neither any different from the other. Jansen was there waiting, talking to a dozen or so others in the red-and-silver of the Scouts; both the horses and the riders looked winded.

"What did you find?" Autmaran demanded, signaling for the others to draw rein behind him as he spurred his own mount forward. Davydd and Lorna came with him.

"Sir," the Scout began. He swallowed nervously and shifted his leather-clad hands on his horse's pommel.

"Shadows and fire!" shouted Davydd. "Just bloody *say* it!"

Jansen's head jerked around in surprise and Davydd cursed himself for the explosion, but felt vindicated. Everyone always took so much time trying to find the right words – just *say what's on your mind!*

"Do not stall," Autmaran said, not acknowledging Davydd, but also not apologizing for the outburst. "Tell us what you've found."

"We've found nothing, sir," Jansen said quickly, tearing his eyes away from Davydd's burns and trying to wipe away the queasy look that had crossed his face. "We scouted up both roads, as far and as quickly as we could, but they go separate ways, north and south, with neither turning back toward Banelyn."

"That makes sense," said Lorna, peering out from under her blonde bowl-cut with a bright, insistent gaze, steady as a blacksmith's hammer. "We're still too far out to need to head directly west."

"I hope Raven figured out which one to take," Autmaran said.

"He grew up memorizing maps in the Imperial Fortress of Lucien," Davydd said dryly. "He could probably draw the whole Empire blindfolded and upside down. If he came this way at all, he likely didn't even stop to think about it."

"Jansen," Autmaran said, "keep scouting down both roads until we find some kind indication of which way to go."

"Wait," Davydd said to the Scout. He heeled Aron forward, and then reined him around so that he was alongside Autmaran's dun and the two of them were side by side.

"What else would you have me do, Davydd?" Autmaran asked quietly, though his voice was still strong and commanding; the man was born to make hard decisions. "We need to know which way to go forward."

"It will waste too much time!" Davydd hissed vehemently.

Autmaran looked at him sharply, but did not respond immediately. The Commander was taller than Davydd, who, though tall, was still one of the Kindred Eshendai and therefore built more for stealth than open warfare. The dark-skinned officer stared down hard, his deep brown eyes fierce, and Davydd took a deep breath, trying to calm the fire in his side or at least forget about it for the next few seconds.

"What else would you have me do?" Autmaran repeated.

"Give me a chance," Davydd said quietly, barely moving his lips.

The Commander's eyes grew even more intense, if such a thing were possible – *no wonder Raven gets along with him so well, they were both born with iron rods shoved up their backsides* – and Davydd saw the man's gaze flick to the burnt side of his face, the one glowing with golden veins, before focusing back on his eyes.

"It took the Prince months to teach Tomaz how to touch the Ox Talisman," Autmaran said. "What makes you different?"

"*It* is different," Davydd said. "I can't control it. This one doesn't seem to be about control. It's deeper, it just happens. If I put myself in the situation – "

"Davydd," Autmaran said, his voice carrying a harsher tone now, "you are the reason we are in this predicament to begin with. You are the one who told us to take the shortcut off the main road. The siege is already underway – "

"*Just let me try!*"

The Commander broke off, barely holding back further rebuke. Davydd grimaced as pain shot through him, brought on by the outburst, and the Talisman advanced again, this time creeping into his forearm, amplifying the smell of singed hair and charred flesh that floated around him like a cloud now. And then it happened again – golden lines splintered across his vision, springing from seemingly random points in the air and ground and arcing through space.

"I got us into this," Davydd said, "and I'll bloody get us out. You weren't there when we were in the throne room fighting him; Tiffenal could not be touched. He dodged things thrown from *behind* him. Everything he did came out his way – *everything.*"

He drew in a hissing breath as his calf cramped inside his boot, the Talisman burning so badly that he couldn't stop from shaking.

"And if it doesn't *kill* me, then it will show us the way to Banelyn," he continued through gritted teeth. "You have seen the things Raven can do; you saw what Ramael did when he had the Ox Talisman. I've got luck – *let me use it.*"

He held Autmaran's gaze with all his might, and after a long, tense moment made nearly unbearable by the pain in his side, the Commander nodded.

"Jansen!" he called out.

Immediately, Davydd reached down and grabbed hold of his cramping calf and kneaded it, unable to keep from whimpering in pain. Lorna rode up and grabbed it for him, quickly punching his pressures points with her iron fingers and getting the blood flowing freely once more, though it made him moan out in a mixture of relief and pain.

"Gather all your men in," Autmaran told the Scout, "we're following Captain Davydd's lead until further notice."

Lorna released his leg and he breathed a quick word of thanks, before spinning around and plastering his accustomed grin on his face. He heeled Aron up to the fork and looked both ways. They were almost mirror images. He waited for the golden lines to splinter his vision again, but nothing happened. He could almost feel hundred of eyes staring at his back, Autmaran's chief among them.

Shadows and fire, work already!

He frantically started looking for differences between the roads, thinking that maybe he could at least choose one that looked better, but before he could focus on the task, the burning pain intensified tenfold. It was as if molten gold were being pushed through his veins. The fire rushed to his toes and fingertips, making him feel as though he were about to be burnt alive; he threw back his head to scream in agony –

And then it vanished.

A cool breeze touch the burnt half of his face, and it felt no different than if it had touched unmarred skin. He flexed his foot, his fingers, his jaw: no pain. Elation shot from the pit of his stomach up through his chest, and something in his vision *shifted*. The whole world seemed to tip to the right for no explicable reason. The wind suddenly felt cooler coming that way, and after a moment he thought it even smelled of heated metal. The sounds of breaking stone and splintering wood followed next, amidst shouts of battle, and golden lines flashed across his vision, pulling him.

"This way," he said, pointing right. "It's this way! It is!"

They all looked the way he had pointed, but none of them seemed convinced. The sounds and smells and wind had all faded, but the sense of which way to go, the sudden intuitive knowledge that came with the golden lines, was still there, at least to Davydd.

"It's this way," he insisted. "It is!"

Autmaran and Jansen were clearly looking at him as if he had gone insane, and even Lorna seemed to be on the fence about the matter. Davydd growled impatiently and kicked his horse into a startled gallop.

"Just follow me!"

For a moment, all he heard was Aron's iron shoes pounding against the hard-packed dirt road, and he thought they might actually refuse. But even as the idea crossed his mind, he heard Autmaran shout the order to follow, and the thundering sound of the army breaking into motion swallowed up the silence. Soon, Autmaran and Lorna had both caught up to him, and they were all rushing down the road as it wound its way through the forest. Neither of them looked at him, and he did not look at them either. Likely they were all thinking the same thing.

Shadows and fire, I hope I'm not crazy.

He looked up at the sun overhead. It had just passed the zenith of midday and was descending toward the western horizon – toward Banelyn. If everything the Prince of Eagles had planned went accordingly, then Banelyn was either under attack or would be shortly. The Kindred under Davydd, Lorna, and Autmaran numbered only several thousand, and they were hardly certain that such numbers could make any kind of difference.

But a sharp shock at just the right moment... that's the kind of tide-turning thing that songs are sung about.

He felt the wind pushing against his face once more, rushing past burned skin that felt perfectly healthy. Reaching down inside himself, he touched what felt like a bundle of golden light that clustered somewhere in his gut, and lines of bright gold shot across his vision, all leading him forward along the chosen path. With each stride of the horse beneath him he felt more certain, more confident. Whatever the Talisman – or Aspect – had needed to do, it had done. He was its new master.

He grinned manically, and there was nothing forced about it this time.

Chapter Three:

The Raven Prince

Raven woke to the agonizing sounds of battle, the air thick with the screams and smells of the dying. As his consciousness gathered, he contemplated never moving again, but even as he had the thought, his body rebelled against it. His eyelids snapped open, and he was staring at a ceiling carved with artful crenulations. Memories came to him, of Geofred and Leah and Tomaz, and then the sounds of battlefield surgery punctured his skull like needles and he raised himself up onto his elbows.

He was at the back of a grand hall that had been turned into a field hospital, nestled against the base of one of the painted walls. Healers were moving men and women past a partition opening in front of him. Bare stretches of off-colored wall caught his eye, and he realized tapestries and paintings had hung there until recently. Standing up, he could see over the hastily erected cloth partitions to where an enormous fireplace along the room's far right side held the remnants of a dying fire. He looked up higher and saw a broad, cross-beamed window. The sky was light outside, but not very. He did not know which way that window faced – was it close to sunrise, or sunset?

What happened to me?

The events of the previous night came back to him in bits and pieces, and he found himself reliving in brief the hour of torment he had undergone as his brother's memories had rushed through him. There were flashes of other things too – of Tomaz running toward him, of Leah lying unconscious in his arms. Fire, smoke, and haze that burned the eyes… cowled figures running to escape falling stones and shattered glass…

But what came to him between those images drew him more. The memories that came to him, the ones he had gleaned from Geofred's mind when it had been absorbed into his, those were the thoughts that had him gripping his hands into fists.

The prophecies he knew... most of them are confused, but not that one; not the one that he specifically burned into his memory for me to find.

Fire. Death. Blood.

The images were more specific, but all were variations on that same simple theme. The Empress stood above him, and as she glowed with the siphoned power of hundreds of thousands of souls, smiling and choking the life from him.

The Return begins.

"You're awake!"

Elder Keri came rushing toward him. Her white robes were splattered with blood and gore, the accumulation of the last minutes of countless lives. *Some of that blood is fresh.* That thought triggered another memory – of the Exile girl howling in pain as hundreds of years worth of memories that were not hers rushed through her mind, memories to which she should have never been exposed, memories for which she'd had no way to prepare.

Leah.

"Where is she?" he asked Keri. Along the periphery of his vision he saw her hands stiffen and he knew she understood what he was asking. She grabbed for his hand, but he pulled it away; she grabbed for it again, and this time she was too fast. Her eyes held his gaze, telling him he would get nothing out of her until he was examined.

"Tell me," he breathed.

She took his pulse, counting under her breath. Satisfied, she released his hand and grabbed his chin, covered one of his eyes and then revealed it. The light hurt, little though there was. She grabbed him and dug her fingers into his head, pushing at pressure points that made him wince; she pulled back and nodded.

"Bend over, then back up," she commanded. Raven did as asked; his stomach did backflips as the world spun. He straightened back up.

"Dizziness? Nausea?"

"No," he lied.

"You can see fine? Hear?"

"Yes. *Where is she?*"

She looked him up and down. "Then there's no reason for me to keep you here. Except that you just lied to me. Twice." She pushed against his chest at just the right angle, and he fell back onto the pile of blankets he'd woken on. "You're not going anywhere – no, shut your mouth, I won't answer that question."

Raven's anger must have shown on his face, because she came closer and stood over him, trying to keep him where he was by force of will alone. "You are not just some soldier who switched sides like you were at Aemon's Stand," she said. "You are the Prince of the Veil now, the leader of the Exiled Kindred in this war. You cannot put yourself at risk the way you did then. They way you just tried to do now."

His hard, stony expression never changed, and so she knelt in front of him, her eyes wide and bright, her look emphatic. Something shifted as she looked at him, and softness crept into that look, a softness that drove fear right through his heart. Her eyes changed, and Raven realized she had made a decision.

"I know you want to help her," she said quietly. "But you cannot. Not yet."

"Why not?" he asked immediately, challenging her with his eyes and tone.

"She is beyond help," she said softly. "Her heart stopped an hour ago."

Raven felt a stone drop down into the pit of his stomach, and his hearing faded away until only a sourceless ringing surrounded him. Before he knew what was happening, he was up again, shouldering his way past her –

An iron bar of an arm stopped him, grabbing his tunic and the skin beneath. He tried to push away, tried to get past her, but in the haze of his mind he could not make his arms and body work the way they were supposed to.

"Stop it!" she hissed at him, throwing him back away from the opening of the partitioned area that enclosed him. "I told you because you needed to know, not because you could do anything. She's gone – even you cannot bring her back. You do not have her memories, you do not have her life – you cannot save her."

His vision blurred as his eyes relaxed, focus slipping away, and he staggered sideways. The memories from Geofred came back to him once more, the images of blood and death choking him, drowning him; and the admission Geofred had made that even he, the far-seeing Prince of Eagles, did not know if the transfer would work.

She might not even survive the transfer... that's what he said.

Elder Keri was speaking again, and with a huge effort of will he managed to focus on what she was saying.

"... you are not healthy enough to leave. I need you to lie back down. Something has happened to you, I can see it in your eyes. And I am not talking about the obvious concussion. The same thing that killed her must have injured you in some way. You *must* stay here, Raven. You need time."

His upper lip curled in disgust. Time? What did one more second matter when the people you loved could die? Time only brought on more chance for pain, more chance for others to be taken.

With a supreme effort of will, he relaxed his jaw and managed to force out words. "I am leaving this place," he said, speaking in a stark, level tone. "People are dying out there because of *my* plan. If I am their Prince, then it is my duty to be with them. It is my duty to die beside them."

"Your death will not help them or anyone else," she said. She looked as though she realized she had made a grave miscalculation by telling him about Leah.

"I am your Prince, and you cannot hold me."

"I am an Elder of the Exiled Kindred, one of those who gave you your power, and I am the Healing Elder besides. There is something wrong inside you, and if you take one second to examine yourself, you will see it too."

"Move, or you will be moved."

"Raven," she said quickly, "I understand your pain. But killing others will not bring her back; even dying yourself cannot change what has already – "

As if in a dream, Raven saw himself reach out and strike the beautiful, matronly woman in the throat, cutting off her words. Her eyes went round with shock, and her mouth worked soundlessly. She tried to turn and get past the partitions for help, but Raven struck a nerve cluster in her back, spun her around, and dropped her on the pile of blankets where he had lain recovering. She did not move – she could not. She still breathed, but her limbs would remain paralyzed for an hour, maybe more.

He turned to leave and realized he felt no remorse. He felt nothing at all. News of Leah's death had drained everything from him, leaving behind a ringing, hollow note that spoke of apathy. And even this thought, even this recognition, left no mark in him.

He stopped at the entrance to the small, secluded space he had been given to recover and saw that his armor had been placed at the entrance, carelessly thrown there by whomever had removed it. He bent and grabbed it, slowly slipping it on over his tunic and pants. The motions were all mechanical, and when he settled the black cloak in place over it all, he left without looking back.

Strange, he thought in a vague, distracted way. *My sword is missing.*

He walked through the grand hall, between sheets and piles of blankets. Screams were everywhere, like mortal things, and they clawed and scratched at him, pulled and tugged at his mind, but he was impenetrable. The thought of Leah touched the corner of his mind, the Exile girl with the green eyes and midnight hair, and he wondered vaguely if she had died in pain.

Geofred said she might not survive the transfer. He said it. I just did not believe it.

He left the room, passing by Healers talking frantically to reserve officers, runners delivering messages, more wounded being carried in on stretchers. The more grievously wounded were rushed immediately upstairs to the second and third levels of the house, and the marble staircase was buried in a mad rush of frantic humanity. He left by the front door.

The sky had deepened to the early stages of twilight. The Cathedral of the Empress lay in ruins off to his right, not a single pillar left standing. Destroying it was a huge symbolic blow and cause for Kindred celebration, but Raven's eyes slid past it without emotion. It was a heaping pile of wreckage; he had caused many such ruins, and doubtless would again. He lowered his eyes to street level, and saw men and women rushing about the large square between various manors and minor palaces. Their frantic movement and anxiety seemed pointless.

A command post had been set up in the center of the courtyard, equidistant from the major Kindred-occupied houses, and maybe a hundred yards from the open gates that led to the rest of the city. Figures moved there. Raven walked down the mansion's steps as men and women in the plain cotton homespun of the Commons, brown and gray and off-white yellow, were being herded past him. Children cried in the arms of mothers and fathers or sometimes what could only be brothers and sisters barely a handful of years older. Many of them were carrying what they had managed to salvage from their homes: clothes, shoes, maybe a pouch of copper coins. They looked terrified, but at least they were inside the gates. He had saved them, at least, from Dysuna.

My sister, the Prince of Wolves.

Emotion finally came to him, and it was a bleak hopelessness that settled into his very bones. He continued moving, though. Some part of him was still driving forward, out of habit or routine. But that first emotion led to others, ones he did not care to interpret, and at the center of it all was something that seemed to stir inside him, awakening as if from sleep, like a formerly sedated beast.

"My Prince!"

The voice drew him from his musings, and he looked up as he approached the command post. There were five hunched forms huddled around a large wooden table that spilled yellow scraps of parchment and wide unrolled maps. Various runners in silver and green came and went, leaving reports and taking orders. One of the five hunched forms was waving frantically to him; it was one of the Generals, in their stately green-and-silver uniforms. There were two of them left, Gates and Dunhold, after Henri Perci had killed Wyck, and Oleander had been revealed as a Visigony-made construct.

Geofred said Perci betrayed us it to save the Kindred. Is that possible?

Dunhold was waving; it must have been he who had shouted. Gates looked to have been recently patched up, his arm in a sling and his cheek bearing a bloody bandage held in place with a thick strip of linen twisted around his head. Raven remembered vaguely that Gates had rushed into the Cathedral just before it had collapsed to tell them that Dysuna was invading. The three other figures became clearer as the oil lamps that lined the streets were lit, their flickering fire pushing back night's swift descent. But as the light brightened, it caught something else: smoke. The sky was full of it – that was strange. The whole of the night was painted with a billowing haze that seemed to roll across the city from the south like an evil miasma. He could smell it now too – it was so thick in the center of the courtyard that Kindred were choking on it as they ran.

He crossed the threshold of the command post – really nothing more than the command tent they had used for months now modified so that the sides were open to allow runners in and out. The other huddled figures were revealed: Elder Ishmael, the head of the Kindred Rangers and Rogues; Elder Spader, the Elder of Law; and a tall, square-jawed captain he knew from sight alone, wearing a black cape with silver threading. Likely Autmaran's replacement until he returned.

Autmaran and the others will never make it here in time to help. They'll be a day away at least by the main road, even if they ride their horses into the ground.

"It is good to see you awake, my Prince," Gates said, with a strained effort at courtesy; the man's thick mustache always seemed to bristle with impatience.

"It is good to be awake," Raven said. He looked down and saw that they were pouring over a map of Banelyn. The others each said something to him as well, none of which he cared enough to hear; he let the chorus of voices wash over him as he examined the map. One of the gates had been compromised – the Formaux gate. The entire Imperial army, indicated by stones colored the tan and gray of Dysuna's forces, was located on the other side. He looked up again.

"Are they through the gate?"

"No," Dunhold said immediately, running his hand through his thick black-gray hair as if calming an anxious pet. "We are holding them, but I do not know how long we can go on with a compromised gate."

Raven nodded. He wasn't surprised Dunhold and Gates were in charge here. Both were experts at defense, and between the two of them, the Kindred could hold the Black Wall for months with proper supplies. But neither general worked well under pressure, and as they were – undersupplied, undermanned, and facing Dysuna – Raven was much less confident.

She will be at the forefront of the next attack. As soon as something opens up, she will be there.

A runner arrived; the others turned to listen to the report. Raven ignored her and focused on the maps. There weren't enough men at that gate to hold it.

" ... Henry Perci – "

Raven spun to face the runner. "What about Henri Perci?"

"He – he's led an excursion force over the Wall through a hidden stairwell, the same one we used to surprise the Banelyners when we attacked, my Prince."

"Why wasn't it guarded?" His voice came out flat and cold, without emotion.

"My – my Prince, it *was* guarded, but when Henri Perci came he brought soldiers with him, and there are men in the rest of the army that have flocked to him, his own men from when he was a commander – "

Raven turned to the others. "Did you not spread word of his betrayal?"

They stared at him with open mouths, a sudden wariness in their eyes. He was floating in a blank emptiness brought on by Leah's death –*green eyes that would never see again, a hard, angular face that would never again break into an unexpected smile* – and the only thought that seemed able to draw him out was the prospect of facing Henri Perci in battle and making the man pay for what he had done.

He deserves to die, Raven thought without remorse. He had always viewed death as terrible; he knew too much of it to think otherwise. But not this time. This time he found himself relishing the idea of killing the man, even taking Henri Perci's memories so that he could live the deed a second time.

"We need to lead a counter-attack," he said. He dropped a hand to his side and realized again he was weaponless. His sword, Aemon's Blade, was gone.

"I will lead it," he said, striding forward. "General Dunhold – I require your sword."

The general complied immediately, unbuckling the simple broadsword on an ornate, silvery belt and silently handing it over. As he did, Raven caught movement out of the corner of his eye; Spader had glanced at Ishmael, and the two Elders had shared an unreadable look.

Why should I care about their secrets? Let them have them.

"Captain," he said to the man in the black and silver cloak, "gather what men you have in reserve and come with me."

The man saluted sharply and turned to call for his troops. Elders Spader and Ishmael exchanged a second glance; this time it was sharper, and it spurred the former man to action. Spader approached Raven, his amber robes and short, brown-gray hair both more ruffled than usual.

"My Prince," Spader said, speaking much more formally than he usually did, and standing farther away than Raven would have expected. The man usually treated him like a favored nephew, one that showed promise and was often good for a laugh. But when he caught the Elder's tawny eyes with his black ones now, holding them, it was clear to both of them that the relationship had changed. "My Prince, what has happened? Are you certain you are well enough to lead a charge yourself?"

"I took a walk in my brother's mind," he said. "And I did not like what I found."

"Have you seen Elder Keri?" Spader asked slowly, his eyes flicking back and forth across Raven's face, looking for something that wasn't there. "She said she wouldn't let you out here until you were well enough to endure the stress of your position. I assumed you had spoken to her and passed any kind of examination she might have administered – "

"She knows I left," he said simply.

"I am sorry to insist," the Elder said, his usual dry, amused tone completely absent. "But that is not the answer to my question."

"No, you are right. But it is the answer I gave you."

He pierced the Elder with his stare, doing nothing more than gazing at him, and Spader swallowed hard. The Prince tried to smile reassuringly, but the motion seemed to have the opposite effect.

"Raven," Spader said, stepping forward another pace and pitching his voice low enough that no one else could hear. "What has happened? You are not yourself. What has gone out of you? Something is wrong; what have you lost?"

Memories of Leah flooded him in a rush; his jaw clenched and his eyes stung. "What I lost there is no way to find," he said levelly, looking away as he finished buckling on his borrowed sword, trying to hide the pain until he could safely stow it away once more in a corner of his heart. His hands were shaking; he forced them to stop.

Elder Spader opened his mouth to ask another question, but before he could do so Raven brushed past him in a brusque, informal manner. The black-cloaked captain stood at attention just beyond the edge of the tent, ready to depart. There were at least a hundred men and women with him, many newly stitched or patched up, and many others old and grizzled. A reserve unit. That was much less than Raven had hoped for, but it made sense. The bulk of the troops would be at the Wall; he was left with whatever could be scraped together.

"Let's go," he told the captain.

The man snapped a fist to his black-plumed half-helm in salute and barked orders. They moved off at a fast jog, slowed down only slightly by the heavy armor they wore. They may be threadbare, but they were heavy infantry, and each wore full plate armor, gauntlets, greaves, and a half-helm. For weapons they carried spears in their hands, and wore broadswords at their hips. Raven was not accustomed to Kindred being so well armed – most of them were ambushers, and as such dressed and fought with daggers, short swords, or bows.

Like Leah.

He stumbled, but by the next step he had regained his footing. The captain did not look at him but continued on, staring straight ahead. Raven felt like weeping, but no tears came.

Feeling was his weakness; it always had been.

They passed through the Inner City gate – gray stone guarded by only a token number of Kindred in the green and silver of infantry – and made their way quickly through the streets beyond. The city looked as though a heavy wind had come and tossed it sideways: scattered clothing and furniture littered the paved roads, and the highest buildings, soaring even higher than the Inner City guard towers, had been gutted and turned into look-out posts by the Kindred, dislodging more detritus that swirled around the city streets. As they passed through, careful to step over broken furniture and the flapping ghosts of unmanned clothing, Raven's mind turned to the path they were headed for, the secret, hidden Seeker's stairway. It was the same stair he had used to infiltrate Banelyn when he had sought the Path of Light that would lead him to the Seekers. Back when he had still been convinced that everything was a test.

The same path Leah and Tomaz followed to save my life.

He grimaced and tightened his hands into such tight fists that his nails dug into his palms. The pain and tension forced the memories away, draining them from his mind like blood and pus from an infected wound.

They passed by a small park set up with three wooden stages amidst curving pathways bordered by short hedges and various flowers. Raven realized it was the same park he had seen months ago in passing, the same place where the Imperial aristocracy, the High Blood and Most High Blood, held their slave auctions. Part of one stage had been torn down, and the other two tilted drunkenly. There was blood there, soaking into the wood like an uneven coat of paint.

I hope the slaves... no. No, I won't hope anymore.

The sounds of battle met them as they crossed into the outer ring of Banelyn City proper, the middle third of the city between the Inner City gate and the Outer City beyond the Black Wall. The Wall itself loomed above them now, covering the lower half of the sky and blotting out whole swaths of stars like an ink stain on a beautiful tapestry.

They turned a corner into a thin brick alleyway, then turned again onto a street parallel to the first, and saw in the distance Kindred fighting Kindred. Raven reached out and grabbed hold of the Raven Talisman; the black markings etched into his skin by his Mother grew hot; his mind expanded outward, and suddenly he was taking in thousands of details he had not noticed before. The smell of smoke was stronger, and so too was the stench of fear, blood, and sweat. The shadows seemed lighter, easier to see through, and his hearing had sharpened – enough that he could hear gasps of surprise and disbelief from the men and women behind him as they saw the two groups of Kindred fighting.

Continuing forward, now with an enraged group of Kindred at his back, he searched the crowd methodically, going from soldier to soldier, trying to pick out his target. A thrill ran through him when he found the man: there, in the midst of the attacking group, a tall figure riding a beautiful white horse. As the horse reared back, the beautiful stallion outlined in perfect tableau by the light of burning oil lamps that lined the streets, the rider's long golden hair fell back from a helm-less head, revealing a perfect face and masculine jaw. It was like looking at a moving picture of a fairy story – here was the hero, perfect and true.

Henri Perci.

Beside Raven, the captain in black and silver signaled an attack, and the group of soldiers rushed forward with even more speed, rushing to save their betrayed companions. But before they had crossed half the distance, Henri Perci by chance caught sight of them, and he shouted for his force to split and turn. The black-cloaked captain shouted the order for an all-out rush, and Raven felt a sense of peace come over him. Time slowed, and all worries and care melted away. His beating heart pounded in his ears, but it was distant. The first two lines met and crashed together, repulsing each other before coming back and drawing each other in, like two fierce lovers in a long-awaited embrace. In the bare seconds before battle was upon him, Raven realized he did not feel a part of the men and women standing around him, pushing forward with primal yells on their lips. No, standing here among those who may be breathing their last breath, he felt completely alone. Despite all the lives he had lived, despite what his Talisman had shown him, he did not feel part of humanity.

He was still only seventeen years old, had only been a part of this world for the blink of a cosmic eye, and had only been away from the Fortress for a year. How could that be possible? How could so much have happened in so little time?

He drew his sword.

The forces came together in a crashing roar. The front line of Raven's group gained ground as their momentum carried them forward, but they were just as quickly pushed back; even the heavy infantry were no match for the violence of men fighting to their deaths, fighting with a general who inspired them. Raven pushed forward, moving through the Exiles, and with each step tried to muster up a sense of self, some sense of longing for life, but found he simply couldn't. It was as if that particular human urge had gone out of him. He did not want life anymore, not really.

Death and silence; a release... the perfect summation of my life.

Hundreds of details assailed him at once. The smell of death, sweat, and terror crushed him from all sides. He saw mud caked on the traitorous soldiers' boots, broken blood vessels in their rolling eyes. The air was thick and heavy, saturated with heat and rage. Golden lights winked in his head, the lives of every man and woman around him, each one a bundle of memories and strength he could harvest and consume.

He struck with General Dunhold's sword and killed the first man to cross his path. The golden light of the man's life went out. The world sped up as the Raven Talisman reaped the man's soul and used it to give the Prince new, stolen strength. He moved on to the next man, and cut him down as well, his eyes all the while on the distant form of Henri Perci on his white stallion.

But the tide of battle shifted, and as the Kindred behind him took heart in their Prince's bravery, he was pushed forward at the head of a swelling wave. The movement broke his stride, and he was forced to kill the next man to confront him, and the next one after that. He tried to hold back, some deep part of him realizing that this was too much too fast, but he had no other choice. His head had begun to swim as if he'd downed an entire bottle of wine, the memories of those other men coming to him hot and fast. His limbs jerked and flailed as his reactions sped up too fast for him to anticipate. A sword lanced out at him from nowhere and struck him a glancing blow across the temple, and he realized only then that he had never put his helmet on.

Memories raced through him, memories that were not his. Sensations of pleasure, anger, hatred, guilt, love, all wracked his body as he experienced them anew in the form of other men's lives. The smoke from the burning houses of the Outer City filled his lungs and choked him, even as the gaping mouths of others sucked what clean air there was away. He was drowning in a sea of chaos, and he was clutching for anything that might pull him out, anything at all that might save him.

Motion came to him through clouded eyes and resolved into a man. The solider raised his sword high, and Raven fell to one knee before him. The blade passed over his head and continued on; Raven thrust his own sword through the man's belly, his added strength giving him the power to force it even through the man's leather hauberk.

More life was added onto him, and suddenly the haze in front of his eyes had nothing to do with smoke. Bloodlust and rage seethed and boiled inside him, the last emotions of the men he had killed. It rose up and filled him to the gullet, and he began to choke on it. He felt it overcoming him, submerging him, and he began to lose track of his own thoughts, his own mind.

Another man fell beneath his borrowed sword, and the rage grew. His senses sharpened yet again; he could see individual pores on men twenty feet away; he could distinguish between a million different variations of sound, knew which wailing voice belonged to which dying soldier. And through it all he heard, as though the distant, drawing whisper of a lover's sigh, the cursing voice of Henri Perci.

He turned and went for the former Kindred general, cutting down two more men on his way, fueling his rage, destroying any last inhibitions. This death, this kill, this revenge, it was all he knew and all that time contained. He had never wanted to kill like this in his entire life. It made him feel good. It made him feel *right*.

Henri Perci spun about on his stallion, using the warhorse to stave in the head of a fallen opponent with its wicked hooves. He laid about him with an enormous two-handed bastard sword, with a blade nearly as long as a man was tall. It was slim though, and he whipped it through the air with a devilish speed.

Unhorse him.

Raven was only halfway through the fray, but he had a clear shot. Using the strength and dexterity of all the men he killed, it was a simple thing for him to take aim and throw his sword, end over end, through the crowd of men. The blade flew so hard and so fast it hit the horse's chest and nearly went completely through, hilt and all. The horse immediately faltered, its front legs falling out from under it as its head arched back to whinny one last time at the indifferent night sky before it collapsed. Henri Perci sensed the drop and threw himself from the saddle at the last possible instant, turning the dive into a roll. He came to his feet and was immediately confronted by three men. They attacked as one, with good form, thrusting at the same time, pushing him in toward each other, but they made the mistake of letting him grab up his sword, and with the bastard blade in his hand, he was a matchless force that cut them down in seconds, before they could even cry out.

Raven, cloaked and armored in black, stepped through the last of the crowd into the space that had opened around the fallen general, and the man saw him as he knelt beside his horse. His lips curled and his teeth gnashed together. His eyes narrowed to slits, and he spat out his words like poison:

"Finally, you face me like a man!" He stood, face splattered with mud and gore. "Come – let me show you how a true Prince of the Kindred should fight! Test your mettle against a true Exile, one who has fought your kind since *birth!*"

The former general struck a defensive position and snarled at him, his face now a mask of hate so deep that it went beyond rage and anger to the depths of lunacy. The man hated him in a righteous way, in a way that made him feel messianic and transcendent, the shunned hero slaying the pretender. Raven saw that light in the man's eyes, and as he stepped forward to meet him he felt the cold emptiness return, countering the blazing heat in Henri Perci; the cold hollowed him out and purged him, and the rage and bloodlust of other men's memories turned sharp and deadly.

It was child's play. The traitor's sword lanced out in a perfect thrust, and Raven moved a fraction of an inch to the left, letting the blade pass him by. Henri Perci slashed, trying to use the double-edged blade to cut; his form was impeccable, and Raven should have at least been wounded, but the Prince saw the motion in Perci's eyes, and simply ducked beneath the blade. When he came up again, he was closer still. The taller man tried to use his height, swinging the bastard blade down in a whistling, diagonal arc, but to no avail. They were within arm's length of each other now, and the realization came upon them both that Henri Perci could do nothing more.

He tried anyway. Hacking and slashing like a madman, dancing among the fallen bodies, never losing balance, never breaking stride, but still Raven came on, always one step ahead, always moving closer. Other soldiers shied away from them, leaving them in a pocket of space no one dared to enter. Sweat poured down Henri Perci's face, and even still he did not flag, did not falter. But Raven was too close now, and the traitor had no room to swing his sword.

So he dropped it. The metal hit the slick, blood-wet paving stones with a *clang* as Perci swung his fist, a surprise blow that should have taken Raven completely unawares. But with the speed of several men filling him up, Raven saw the gauntleted fist coming and caught the wrist behind it. With a sharp upward blow, he broke the general's arm, then came forward and dislocated his shoulder. Henri Perci cried out in pain and fell forward, pulled by the motion of Raven's movements. His other hand reached to the ground, desperately grasping amongst the stones and bloody viscera for the hilt of his discarded blade.

Raven stepped and twisted, breaking the hand.

Perci threw his head back and roared in pain, but even then he would not stop. He came up, and in a powerful rush butted his head into Raven's chin.

The blow was painful, and it rocked Raven back a step, making his head spin. He dropped the arm he held, and Henri Perci, unsupported, fell to the ground. Raven's brain seemed to be rattling around inside his skull, and he vaguely remembered Elder Keri telling him he had a concussion. His vision faded to white mist and then came back into sharp focus, then fuzzed once more. But through it all he could see Henri Perci coming forward, forcing the bones of his broken hand around the hilt of his sword. He raised the sword in front of him – only to have the hand and arm caught by Raven, who wrested the sword away with a savage twist.

Thunder broke the silence of the skies, and the falling night opened to let loose a flood of rain. Raven saw through the falling sheets of water his own reflection in Henri Perci's eyes. He gripped the hilt of the long bastard sword and watched as the light in those eyes saw its own defeat and still refused to die.

The sword came down, and the blade bit into the general's neck, severing his spine but keeping his head attached to his body. The light in the eyes went out, but they continued to stare at Raven, to pierce him as the memories of the man flew into his mind. There were so many, and they all came confused by fear and rage, but the brightest of them all stood out even still. It was at the center of everything that Henri Perci had been, a single moment that flashed before Raven's eyes.

"Promise me, son," said an old man, with a white beard and flowing hair, "promise me that you will always fight the Empire and what they stand for."

"I promise," he said, and meant it, with all his heart.

"No," Raven whispered. "No, get out of me, get out of my head."

Flashes of light – a whisper of movement through the woods around them. Swirling motes of dust kicked up by the horses, the bad horses with the red and black of Roarke on them. The smell of woodlands, and blood on Henri's hands.

Raven clutched at his head and began to tear at his hair, trying to pull the memory out of him. He didn't want it – he didn't want it!

"One day," the old man said with a loving, beautiful smile. "You will be a Prince. This is not over. The Empire, the Tyrant will never stop. You – you must promise me – "

He cut off, choking on his words. Henri held his father's hand, even though the rough, calloused fingers squeezed too hard. Charles Perci coughed and sputtered, and then rose up violently from where he lay before falling back. Blood and mucus dribbled from corners of his mouth as he spat out a mess of bloody phlegm. His body twisted and spasmed in pain, and his side poured out a fresh gush of blood.

"Be strong," his father gasped, his eyes focused on something beyond Henri. "They will return, like they always do. And there will come a time when we call for a Prince of the Veil once more. They will need a Prince like Goldwyn — and you will be that man."

More pain and coughing, and Henri Perci watched it through tearful eyes.

"No crying," the man said, grabbing him harshly. His eyes were still clear and blue, like a summer sky. "From this day on, your eyes are dry. The Kindred are in your hands after me — you are strong, and already the Elders talk of you. You will be the youngest general in a generation. And when the time comes for a Prince... it will be you."

Henri nodded, still sobbing, and watched his father die.

The memory was perfect, with a numinous, transcendent glory, and Raven felt tears running down his own cheeks as he cried over Perci's body as the man had cried over his father's. But through it all he could not help but wonder where the evil was — the darkness that would lead a man down the path of such anger and blind hatred so as to betray his own people in the hope of saving them. How could this terribly beautiful memory be the center of a traitor, the defining moment of his life?

Raven's gaze fell on the sightless eyes of Henri Perci, and he saw, again, his own face reflected in them, and deeper still, a reflection of his own soul.

No — he was not like me. He was evil, just like my Mother and the Children.

But the memories did not lie, and as they continued to roll, he found no evil. He found anger, and he found pain, but even when Henri Perci led his men against the Kindred, even then, he gave instructions to disengage as soon as they drew Raven out.

I was his goal this whole time.

Henri Perci continued to stare at him.

"No. No — no — NO — *YOU'RE EVIL, YOU HAVE TO BE!*"

He struck the dead body, slashing at the neck again, cutting farther through the flesh of the corpse. He hacked again and again, then dropped the sword and struck out with his fist, catching the corner of the man's chin. The violence sent Henri Perci's head flying in an arc through the air, his golden hair and beard still gleaming in what light there was. And though the man was gone, his body a crumpled corpse, his memories lived on in Raven, and as they rolled through him, image after image, Raven's rage died, and despair took its place.

What have I done? I have killed a good man.

"STOP IT!" he roared at himself. Kindred around him looked up sharply and then backed away. The battle had ended. As soon as Henri Perci had been slain, the rebel Kindred had either thrown down their weapons in surrender or broken off in smaller groups to scatter through the city streets. But even as the area around them cleared, more soldiers emerged from the tower on the Black Wall that led to the secret staircase. These men were Imperials, dressed in the tan and gray of Dysuna, Prince of Wolves, and the Kindred rushed to meet them.

Henri Perci fought for what he believed in – he gave his heart and soul, his very life, his family, all of his connections to the Kindred, because he believed in his heart of hearts that what he was doing could save them. How is he different from me, the Exiled Prince? How can I condemn him? How can I feel justified in killing him?

He sank to his knees, and the bloodlust began to curl around him again, breaking through the enforced calm that had frozen him inside. The new heat wrapped around him, enfolding him in its arms like a sweet mother, cooing to him in a voice like a rasping, burning sigh. His guilt and shame pounded in his ears; his disgust, both with himself and the world in which he lived, grabbed him by the throat and choked him until his vision began to spin.

This could have been me. Any of these people – all of them – they could all be me! Everyone I have ever killed!

Something twisted inside him, and suddenly the pieces of the world seemed to fall into place. Something came forward from deep within his heart, from the darkness that he had held so long at bay, some black kernel of hatred and fear that he had walled off and cordoned away from the rest of his mind. It expanded, like rising dough, and began to push against the wall he had made to keep it back, making the brick and mortar crack and give. Thoughts broke through the chinks in the stone, slithering into his conscious mind like serpents.

No... he did deserve to die. And he is no different from me, or anyone. Of course not. It makes sense – he is no different because we all deserve to die. All of us. Everyone.

He looked up at the world around him, black and twisted, and embraced it. The wall inside him that had so long held back that part of him that enjoyed the death and the madness, the part of him that was his Mother, disappeared, crumbling into a thousand motes of dust, all to be blown away in the wind of thought.

He was consumed totally, and when he next raised Henri Perci's sword, it was as something different, something dark. He was the Seventh Child, the Reaper of Men, the Lord of Death. He smiled and shivered as a strange euphoria settled over him, and all his doubts disappeared; all of his anger and hatred melted like mist before the rising rays of a black dawn. This was where he belonged – here, in the center of battle. This was what he had been born for, what his Mother had bred him for. Raven was gone, that identity he had constructed as he had tried to flee who he truly was. He was his Mother's son now, through and through.

He smiled, and set about his work.

Chapter Four:

Blue Lines

Leah broke through to consciousness the way a swimmer breaks through the barrier between sea and sky. She sat up with a shattering breath that rocked her entire body, clutching her head in her hands as she wiped furiously at her ears and face, trying to pull something off, something that had kept her down, kept her hostage. Her heart lurched into motion, feeling somehow rusty and dis-used, and the world spun around her.

Blue lines crossed her vision, and glowing forms and figures resolved themselves out of nothing. They spoke to each other, in words too low to hear, and then dissipated again, gone as fast as they had come. More sounds came to her, echoes of voices that sounded far away, and the sensation of a man's warm fingers caressing her face –

The images disappeared and the world around her resolved into a field hospital. She was on the floor, covered in blankets. She realized she was still clutching her face, and she let go and tried to breathe.

Calm down – try to remember. What is happening; where are you?

She thought back as recently as she could and remembered walking into the Imperial Cathedral with Raven and Tomaz… but the rest was gone. The details of the situation evaded her, and a sense of foreboding began to spread through her limbs, making her jumpy.

If you can't remember, then you can't remember. Focus elsewhere.

She examined herself quickly and found nothing broken. There were various scrapes about her and several painful but non-threatening burns. She clapped a hand to her chest, over an ache that seemed to radiate from her heart, but was greeted by a rhythmic thumping that seemed perfectly in order. She tried to stand and found that easy. The small, partitioned room around her did not spin, her stomach did not jump. Good. She took a step, and that was fine, though the old scar down the back of her leg pulled as it always did when she had been in one position for too long.

I've been lying here for over ten hours, she knew immediately. That was the only time that wound began to ache again. And it was only then that she looked down at the ground, and realized she was surrounded by the dead.

Shadows and fire.

There were at least a dozen in the partitioned-off area, crowding the square space set up by hastily-constructed barriers of torn tapestry. Each of the bodies bore a different wound, but all were to the chest or head, and all had obviously been fatal. They were all freshly dead, as well, that much was clear; blood still ran from some of them, and some of them still held their color.

I... was I dead?

She stumbled out of the cordoned-off area, unable to think clearly. Just past the partition, she found herself among a number of other partitioned areas all situated in a large hall. There was a fire burning in a grand fireplace, inside which were huge cauldrons of boiling water that a number of Healers were tending. The fire itself fairly roared, but it looked as though it had only been recently stoked – someone must have given the order to light it again. She looked up and caught sight of a distant window that showed only a dark, black haze.

Haze?

Images flashed through her head of fire, and pieces of memories fell into place. The Cathedral of the Empress... she had been there with Raven and Tomaz and... the Prince of Eagles.

The thought of him hurt so that she physically recoiled, and memories flashed through her head that were not her own as her heart thumped painfully in her chest. The images were grainy and faded now, like detailed paintings corrupted by age, but they came to her. Memories of years spent with the Empress, hate and love for Her in equal measure. Desire for power, desire for control, and then weariness, like a thick, downy blanket, that fell on her and covered everything. Her own memories took over and she remembered the Cathedral falling down around her. But after that was all a blank – how she had gotten out, what had happened to Raven and Tomaz –

Raven.

More memories flooded into her from Geofred's mind, fading and disappearing even as she grasped at them like a drowning swimmer eager for any bit of buoyancy. Images of him growing up, feelings of mingled pride and disgust... and more.

She staggered and caught at the pole of one of the partitions, steadying herself as a pair of Kindred in the white of Healers rushed past her with a gibbering, wounded man slung between them.

Prophecies.

"Shadows and fire," she cursed under her breath as one of them loomed large in her mind, the words of it rolling through her head as if newly spoken. "Oh, flaming shadows and bloody, *bloody* fire."

She lurched forward, moving through the partitions toward the fire, and then went nearly sprinting through the crowded hall beyond, ignoring the protests of Healers who were looking at her like they had seen a ghost.

She had to find him. *Now.*

Her heart gave another painful lurch in her chest, but she ignored it. She reached the end of the hall, rushed through the doorway, and found herself at the top of a wide marble staircase that descended three levels to the ground floor. Healers rushed past her with more wounded, all gravely injured, and Leah realized she had been in the intensive care ward, or whatever passed for such a place in a field hospital.

Geofred said I might not survive the transfer... was he right?

She rushed down the stairs, moving easily through the rushing tide of people, and realized that if she had been knocked out, Raven might well have been too. She reached the first floor landing and seized the first Healer in white robes that passed her.

"Where's Elder Keri?

"C-checking on the Prince of the Veil," the man said, his demeanor that of someone watching a house burn around him as he tried to save the children, all the while hoping that someone else would take care of the fire like they had promised.

"Where?"

"That way – two rooms, then to your right."

She released him and went the way he'd pointed. She passed a series of wounded and barely noticed, rushing through opulent rooms now stained with blood and the stench of death and dying, looking for a woman clad in white with brown hair going gray at the temples. She was getting desperate: she needed to find Raven, and very soon.

He knows why his Mother tried to kill him. It will drive him mad.

If the memories had not done so already, that was. Geofred, for all his strength, had been a wounded man, held up only by a spiteful need to rig the game his Mother tried to play before it killed him. His final act had been one of vengeance, and with that over, he had no more reason to live.

And now, beating behind her temples, was a simple thought, one that ran deep through her. She knew it came from Geofred, and she knew, somehow without question, that it was right. It just made sense.

He needs the Blade. Without it, he's a danger to us all.

She turned right into the hall that must be directly below the one she had woken in; it was full of hundreds of wounded and scores of Healers. Too many people. Her time was running out – if she couldn't find Elder Keri, she would have to make do. She reached out and grabbed a passing Healer – a young man, tall with dark hair.

"Where is the Prince of the Veil?"

"I think back there," the man said, brushing her off even as he motioned to the back of the hall. "I was just reassigned here, though, so I don't – "

She left before hearing the end of the sentence and hurried down the central corridor created by the recently hung sheet-partitions in the direction the young man had indicated, dodging Healers and wounded Kindred alike. Turning a corner at the end of the row, she found herself in a large space covered in blankets and makeshift beds. There were at least a dozen Kindred here, most of them on their backs with bandages wrapped around their heads, and some deathly pale, one in the process of vomiting, helped by a Healer.

Concussion ward, she thought grimly.

Something stirred in a smaller alcove to her left. She turned, hoping for Raven. The form sat up in a strange, jerky fashion, before falling back partially onto the mound of blankets behind it. Leah came forward, and, as the movement of passing Healers blew a curtain back, light from the hall's distant fire filtered through the shifting pattern of bodies and fell on the patient's face.

"*Elder Keri?*"

The woman barely managed to right herself as a rictus of pain spasmed across her face. Leah dove forward, reaching her just in time to keep her from falling back again.

"Elder, what happened?"

"The Prince," she groaned. "I told him he couldn't leave, and he wouldn't listen. He has a concussion, and more than that – something is wrong with him, something deeper. I need to get to him; he needs to be brought out of whatever is taking him over from the inside. His eyes were terrible. I have never seen anything like that before – "

The woman cut off, and for the first time seemed to realize to whom she was speaking. Her eyes went wide and bulged outward from her face; her surprise was so great that Leah was suddenly afraid the woman might faint.

"You're dead!"

Leah, taken aback by the accusation, retreated a step, leaving Elder Keri to stand under her own power. The woman swayed but managed to keep her feet, and even stumbled forward a step, her hands reaching out.

"Are you real?" the Elder asked, her eyes hungrily devouring every contour and detail of Leah's face and body, which was still clothed in the light black and green armor worn by the Kindred Rogues.

"Yes," Leah said impatiently. "Yes, I'm real. I'm alive. I woke not five minutes ago among dead bodies."

"You were there because your heart stopped," Keri said, succeeding in coming forward and grabbing the younger woman's wrist. She searched for a pulse, felt it, and seemed too stunned to believe even that. She unceremoniously thrust a hand down the front of Leah's leather cuirass with the detached professionalism of a life-long physician, and felt Leah's heart beating against her palm.

"That's not possible," she said, staring wonderingly at Leah. "You were dead – I checked you myself."

"Well, I'm not," Leah responded. "I need Raven – where is he?"

"Gone," the Elder said immediately, her eyes clouding over as she thought back. "He struck me so I couldn't speak, couldn't move. And then he left."

"Why would he do that?" Leah asked, thrown off balance. Raven was never needlessly violent.

"I told him you were dead," Keri said, "and then he said he had to go, had to be with the soldiers for whom he was responsible. You have to find him. Bring him back here. Something is wrong with him – "

Leah stopped listening as Keri continued on, the words echoing in her head, bouncing around madly. She felt a rush of energy go through her like a wave, and all other thoughts left her but Raven. She began to move away, only vaguely aware that Elder Keri was still speaking, hobbling along behind her on unsteady legs. Leah sped up, breaking into a run down the hall.

I can't be too late. I won't believe it.

As she ran she searched among the Healers for one bearing the colored, striped sleeve of an orderly; she needed someone with information. There – a short woman with dark brown hair and clean hands.

"Where is Aemon's Blade?"

"Wha – what?"

"Aemon's Blade," she said, speaking as slowly as she dared. "The white valerium sword the Prince of the Veil carries. Where is it?"

"I – I don't – know –"

"*Then who does?*"

The orderly pointed immediately out the door of the hall, back toward the front entrance of the manor. "They-ey set up a command center – in-n the courtyard – whoever it is should be – "

Leah left, running flat-out now that she had a direction, knocking aside wounded and Healers alike. She shouted before her, calling for them to clear the way, but her voice was drowned out by the clamor of pained cries and urgent pleas for help, for mercy, for deliverance from the certain death the Wolf had brought down on them.

Dysuna's force must be on the Wall, or close to taking it. That's where Tomaz will be – and if I know anything about the damn princeling that's exactly where he is too, despite whatever wounds he has.

"Move!"

The chastised group sprang apart, leaving her way through the front door clear. She bounded down the steps of the walk, taking the barest fraction of a second to notice where she was and re-orient her internal map. The sun had indeed set, and the black haze above her was a combination of smoke and swirling storm clouds, ready to break at any moment. She was in the Inner City, with the mountainous ruin of the Cathedral of the Empress not a hundred yards away. The streets were made of beautiful paving stone, but nearly every space was covered with makeshift smithies, tents and quarters for the fletchers, runners and servants, and a hundred other trappings of a city under siege. A horse ran by, riderless, and no one seemed to care.

"You!" called a voice. Leah turned at the sound and saw a woman in white with red-blonde hair motioning to her. "Are you wounded? Healed? What?"

"Healed!" Leah called back. "I'm fine – who is in charge of the armory?"

The woman looked her over in a swift, critical fashion, and then shook her head. She glanced over Leah's shoulder back inside, looked dismayed, then angry, then shook her head again and her face became the neutral mask of a physician.

"If you can move, then we need your space," she said abruptly. "Go – your weapons are in the next house over if they were salvaged – "

"I'm a Spellblade," she said. "I know exactly where my weapons are, and I don't need your help finding them. *Who is in charge of the armory?*"

The woman paused, brought up short by Leah's direct manner and the ferocity with which she held her gaze. She did not look ready or able to speak, so Leah went to move past her, but the woman caught her by the arm. It shocked Leah a little – she wasn't used to people touching her.

"What?" she demanded, already contemplating ways to incapacitate the woman.

"The command tent," the woman said abruptly. "One of the Elders."

Leah nodded and pulled her arm from the woman's grasp, turning toward the large tent in the center of the huge Inner City square. She could just make out a number of men there, all hunched over what appeared to be a table of some sort.

I can't be too late. I can't be. What would happen if I were?

Blue lines spidered across her vision, shining with an azure brilliance like the tail of a comet. Images coalesced, of her shouting at someone, of a man with one red eye and one gold eye, and two Wolves fighting, one in white and one in gray.

The world came back to her in a rushing blaze of light that left her blinded. She staggered to one side, gasping and choking as if she had just sprinted a dozen miles. Her hand grasped a tent pole, and she held herself up by will and sheer, stupid determination.

And then she remembered the final part of what had happened in the Cathedral, the final part of what it meant to have Geofred's memories running through her mind.

He didn't just give me his memories – he gave me the Talisman of Prophecy.

Afterimages blinded her vision, but she waded her way through them, releasing the tent pole and stumbling a few steps forward before regaining her stride. She had no time to sort out what it meant to have what was now, through the purifying magic of Raven's Talisman and her own valerium Anchor, the Aspect of Sight.

Will it be like that every time?

Once again, vibrant blue lines, bright as flashes of lightning, spidered across her vision and engulfed her. She saw herself in the middle of an army, fighting foes on all sides; then she was in a command tent; then she was standing beside a teenage boy in the armor of a man –

"GO AWAY!"

Immediately, the visions given her by the Aspect of Sight disappeared. Her ironfisted will had clamped down, and she could feel her back teeth clenched so hard that they were ready to crack. Everyone in hearing range was staring at her, including the people at the huge wooden map table set up in the middle of the courtyard beneath the eaves of a side-less tent.

"Spader!" The Lawful Elder took a frightened, instinctive step back as she said his name. All of them were looking at her as if she were a Daemon.

"Where is it?"

"What?"

"Where is Aemon's Blade? You took it from him and stored it somewhere – *where is it?*"

"What – how did you know – ?"

She reached out her hands toward the ruins of the distant Cathedral, and *tugged* with her mind. The accustomed Spellblade muscle that connected her to her daggers was slow to move, but after an instant's pause it clicked into place. Spader, Ishmael, and the two Generals turned and looked at where she was gesturing, and in unison jumped back with cries of alarm. Two wicked, curved daggers, each over a foot long, broke out of the debris and rubble, pushing aside mounds of stone and mortar, and shot, whistling, through the air into Leah's waiting hand. The only one who did not move was Ishmael, the head of her order; he had seen that trick before a hundred times, and it was he who tried to intervene.

"Leah," he rasped, "calm yourself."

"*Where – is – the – Blade?*"

"The Blade is not yours," Spader said. "It is Raven's –"

"Yes, it is!" she shouted, rounding on him. "And when he woke, did he have it with him? No!"

"How do you know that – how does she know that?"

"Surely he is just as capable with another sword," Ishmael said, looking completely bewildered by her actions. "If he had wanted it, all he had to do was ask when he came to us, but he did not, he took a replacement – "

"Did you offer it to him?"

Spader shot a look at Ishmael before he could stop himself, and she had her answer. She moved forward and grabbed him by the front of his robes.

"Where is it?"

General Gates drew his sword, and Ishmael was suddenly at her side, a curved dagger of his own in his hand. "Leah, let him go," he rasped, his black eyes hard.

"I have no time for this," she said. *"You need to trust me.* Where is the Blade?"

"Why – ?"

"Because if he doesn't get it, we all die!"

The words rang true, even though she could not grasp the whole reasoning behind them. They were based on Geofred's memories, Geofred's thoughts, and those impressions had already mostly faded from her mind. All that had been left behind was the terrible, dreaded certainty that Raven needed that Blade. It wasn't just a sword, even though everyone treated it like it was.

Spader was gaping at her, putting her in mind of a fresh-caught fish. He and Ishmael exchanged a look, and then Ishmael tapped a finger to the back of his hand. Spader's eyes flicked to Leah, down to her hands, and widened. Leah looked down as well, and saw, peaking out just at the edge of her long sleeves, the swirling blue lines of the Eagle Talisman Geofred had forced on her. Spader's eyes flicked up and swept her hairline, then examined the rest of her, even though no other flesh was exposed, before his gaze zeroed in once more on her eyes. His mouth tightened into a hard line, and he nodded the barest amount. His hand lifted, pointed to the map table. Confused, she looked closer and saw nothing. She twisted his robes tighter and brought her face closer.

"Do not lie to me."

"He is not," came the rasping reply. Leah turned to see Ishmael dip to one knee and slash something on the underside of the table. A cable came loose, and with a ripping sound and a clatter of metal on stone, a shadowy bundle fell onto the paving stones.

"We had no idea what the Seekers or Bloodmages or Dysuna herself had planned," Ishmael rasped. "We could not let it out of our sight – we were going to give it to him when he woke, if he did, but when he came to us he did not even ask for it. And there was something wrong with him – something Spader and I both felt. You need to be careful if you are going after him – he is not himself. Are you hearing me, Leah?"

She wasn't; she already knew what she needed to know. She released Spader and went for the Blade, ignoring them all; as far as she was concerned, they had served their purpose, and for the time being had ceased to exist. The Aspect of Sight had infused a certainty in her that told her what she *had* to do, and none of it involved listening to their warnings, well meaning as they were. They could not see with the clarity she did; they barely saw anything at all.

The Blade was wrapped so that it could be safely handled – anyone but Raven would be sent flying a dozen feet through the air if they so much as ran their finger along the handle. It was too long to wear at her waist, and it would hinder her fighting there in any case. She swung it over her shoulder and pulled the edges of the wrapping sheet down in order to tie them across her chest, manipulating it so that the knot rested just between and below the slightly convex chest of her armor. She took a single glance at the top map on the table, saw that the Formaux Gate was the one that had been compromised, and left, sending Spader scampering out of her way.

"Let her go!" Ishmael rasped out as guards came forward. They looked back, confused, and she just walked between them.

In a matter of minutes she was halfway through Banelyn city proper, on her way to the east side of the city. The heavy clouds above her broke open, and she was doused in a downpour of warm spring rain that only lessened slightly by the time she turned a corner and saw scores of bodies littering the street before her. Long strips of paving stone were covered in mud made from the ash in the air and the blood on the ground. Leah saw it all in a series of distracted, oddly disjointed images – her mind was far overhead, piecing together a picture of the battle.

This street was invaded – the way the corpses fell – the pattern of fighting –

Several things came to her at once in the kind of sourceless, intuitive way her insights always did. She realized first that the battle had two fronts: the Kindred were fighting at the gate and had also been attacked from inside the Wall. The second attack had likely come over the secret passageway the Kindred themselves had used to infiltrate the city. And what was more, that second force had been made of both Imperials and Kindred.

Traitors.

She continued on, toward the Black Wall itself, following the tide of battle back to its source. She realized a reserve force had come to meet the invaders, and whoever led it had been brutally efficient, cutting straight through.

She pulled up short. Her breathing was suddenly ragged, her heart beating rapidly. A beautiful white stallion lay before her, resting beside a headless corpse in the trappings of an Exiled Kindred General.

I know that armor.

Knowing what she would find, she came forward and scanned the torn, gory patch of street that was the battlefield, until the lifeless, staring eyes of Henri Perci found her, his face pulled back in a final expression of all-encompassing hatred. Whoever had killed him... it had been personal.

Raven.

She left the grisly sight of Henri Perci's resting place and made her way to the Formaux Gate, her nerves on fire as the sounds of battle swelled. She braced herself for what she might find. If the Kindred were fighting inside the Wall, then this would be a very short siege. If they had managed to hold them so far... they had a chance.

She rounded the final corner and through a haze of falling rain saw a huge group of Kindred formed up before the gate – and another force, one in the tan and gray of Dysuna, attacking them from the flank. Her mind flashed back to Henri Perci's force, and realized she was missing something. Where was Raven? Where was the reserve force he had led?

Why would Raven kill Henri Perci and then just disappear? Where did he go, why didn't he continue the attack and join the others at the gate?

She scanned the battle, and then gave up trying to understand it. Men and women were fighting on the battlements – most were Kindred, but for every three of them, one Imperial was laying about with a broadsword. Somehow, they had managed to mount the Black Wall from the other side, and the siege of the city had begun in earnest.

A loud bellow rang out over the field, the bull cry of a giant man.

Tomaz.

She turned and scanned the upper battlements once more, this time looking for – there! A huge man, fighting in a sea of Imperial uniforms in front of what looked to be a hastily constructed siege engine of some kind. The giant was laying about with a sword taller than a full-grown man. An Imperial soldier attacked him from behind – and without hesitation, Leah flung a dagger that flew impossibly straight through the air, whirling end over end to sink into the soldier's throat. Tomaz saw the man go down, and even though he didn't turn back to see her face, the sudden smile that split his beard told her he knew she had arrived. She *pulled* the dagger with her mind, and it left the man and came flying back to her. She rushed for the closest stairway that led to the top of the ramparts, just as a number of fighting Imperials and Kindred swung in from the top. She rushed up to meet them, and her blades flashed and caught the light of the oil lamps and burning torches – she danced through them all, slipping in-between and sideways, like it had all been choreographed.

From the corner of her eye, she saw another man running to attack Tomaz's back, and she threw her dagger again. The man fell, and Tomaz's laughter roared out over the battle. But then two attackers, both of whom were very skilled, confronted her, and she was left with just her single dagger. She did not have time to *pull* the other. She bent and twisted, dodged and retreated, but she could not gain the necessary time or distance. A sword whistled over her head – she struck out and was repulsed. She switched directions – and was countered. Her only hope would be to –

A broadsword, thrown with all force and no finesse, flew out of nowhere and smacked the first man in the head, knocking him down. Leah and her second attacker both stared at the downed man for a long moment, completely surprised, before she spun and sunk a dagger through his throat. He fell atop the other man, and she took the moment to *pull* her second Spellblade dagger back to her, just as Tomaz began making his way toward her. As soon as he was within shouting range, she began to berate him.

"You could have got *me* you know!"

"I could say the same to you!"

They shared a small, grim smile. The battle around them had died down. The archers on the Wall were firing down into the Imperial troops, but many had thrown up shields to protect themselves while they hoisted new ladders, readying for a fresh assault. Leah looked over her shoulder into the city, and felt a sense of incongruity.

Why didn't they continue sending men over that hidden stair? They could have surrounded us and caught us in a vice...

And then all the pieces clicked into place, and she realized exactly what had happened. Raven hadn't followed the Kindred back to the gate – he had followed the Imperials back to the hidden stair. He must be there now, fighting to keep them from invading the city from that weak point.

Before she even realized she had made the decision, she was in mid-stride to retrace her steps and find her way back to the Seeker's Path. But before she could go, Tomaz held out an arm to stop her. There was shouting from over the side of the Wall, and with a series of *thuds* the second wave of siege ladders attached themselves to the battlements, and the Imperials began to climb.

"Leah – there are more coming! Where are you going?"

"I need to get to Raven!"

"Raven? I didn't even know he was awake!"

"He is! And this can't wait!"

"We must hold the Wall or all is lost!"

Leah growled and cursed under her breath, and realized she didn't know what to do. She had to make a decision, fast. What would happen if – ?

Blue lines – blurring vision – sword – red light – screams – silence.

Tomaz would die. She knew it with a sharp, cutting certainly that severed all thought of discussion. If she left now, he would not survive this assault.

I need to get to Raven – but Tomaz – I need to –

Men poured over the lip of the Wall – Imperial heavy infantry. Even as Kindred surrounded Tomaz in a tight group, the Imperial soldiers began throwing spears that killed them in droves. Once the spears were gone, they advanced, unsheathing thick, stabbing short swords and hefting long, curved shields that hid them almost perfectly from attack. They broke through the front line of the Kindred and stepped up to engage Tomaz.

"No! Stop – I'm coming!"

Even as she shouted, she threw her daggers. They spun through the ash-choked air, twinkling in the flickering light of oil lamps and torches lit throughout the city – only to glance ineffectively off of thick plate armor.

Fear coursed through her, shooting to the tips of her fingers, and she *pulled* the daggers back as two soldiers saw her. They turned to meet her, but their movement was half a beat too slow. She turned the first sword aside, slid a dagger through the armor-less area under the arm, and felt the first man go limp in her arms. She turned and kicked the second man off-balance; he swung his arms wildly, tripped over a fallen comrade, and disappeared back over the edge of the Wall.

She continued forward, slashing and cutting at every opening that presented itself, all the while moving toward Tomaz, who had been engulfed in a swirling tide of Imperials. She cleared the last men, fought her way to his side, and threw herself between her friend and the sword she had seen taking him in the back.

She was just in time. The blade, glowing a strange enchanted red as if touched by a Bloodmage's Soul Catcher, glanced off her daggers and away from Tomaz's unguarded back. She lunged forward and opened the man's neck.

"Good to see you," Tomaz grunted.

"You'd never survive without me," she gasped back, breathless.

Together they turned and looked over the edge of the Wall. More troops were climbing the siege ladders, shields over their heads, ready to mount the Wall.

"We just have to hold them a bit longer!" she called out over the fray.

"How much longer is a bit?" Tomaz roared back. "And how in the seven hells do you know how much longer we'll have to hold?"

Blue visions flashed across her eyes once more, and then disappeared.

"Something's about to happen."

"What?"

"Something is about to happen!"

"Shadows and light, what does that mean?"

Horns sounded – Kindred horns.

"Wha - reinforcements?"

Leah did not respond – she was busy trying to dispel more blue lines that had clouded her vision. "Not now!" she said harshly, and once more the lines disappeared just as they formed into the vision of her brother, Davydd, sitting astride a horse between his Ashandel partner Lorna and the Kindred Commander of the Light Infantry and Horse, Autmaran.

"Davydd?" she asked, stunned.

"Eshendai!" Tomaz called down to her, pointing over the side of the Wall.

Soldiers in the tan-and-gray surrounded the whole gate and accompanying sections of the Wall. There were thousands upon thousands of them, and the size of the army was breathtaking. The whole of the Outer City was gone as if it had never been, and all that remained in its place were the dying embers of the towering wooden shacks the Commons had once called home, now smoldering and letting off huge gouts of smoke and steam that billowed up into the weeping sky. A huge swath of the resulting muck had been cleared from the main road, giving the Imperials a perfect path up to the gate.

But beyond that, past the broken ring of wooden teeth that encircled the gapping maw that was now Banelyn, was amassed another force, one that was charging forward through the rubble, riding under the streaming banner of the Kindred.

As soon as Leah recognized the rose-and-sword banner, she turned and ran forward to the waiting siege ladders that were still spewing forth Imperial soldiers, Tomaz hot on her heels. They killed three soldiers apiece before those around them realized what was happening, and this spurred the others to action. Shouts went up all around them and the battle began anew, the Kindred heartened and the Imperials panicked.

There can't be more than a few thousand out there, Leah thought to herself. *It can't be reinforcements from Vale. What else could they be, though?*

The image of Davydd came to her again, and this time she saw him wounded, struck in the shoulder by an arrow and knocked from his horse. His face was different, though – it was half burned, with golden veins that pulsed and seemed to hum. Blue lines covered him, and suddenly she saw him facing off against a wolf, full grown and powerful. Davydd attacked; the wolf caught his arm in its teeth, pulled him to the ground, and crushed his throat between its jaws.

The images faded.

"By the Veil – *why does everyone need saving?!*"

She ran forward to the nearest ladder, dodging between confused Imperial soldiers, who followed her only to be cut down by Tomaz from behind.

"Where are you going?" he called out above the fray, sounding frantic.

"Davydd and Lorna and Autmaran are leading that force!" she cried back. "They need our help – we need to get them past the Wall!"

"What – *how the hell are we going to do that?*"

"Just keep them off my back while I clear the ladder!"

Without a further word, she turned to the siege ladder and looked down. Men were still climbing it, at least a dozen on the ladder itself and three times that number behind them at the bottom, waiting their turn.

Leah drew a deep breath and silenced her mind. She reached into her daggers, pulling her consciousness out of herself and sending it into the two curved blades. She could feel the steel – it was a part of her, like any of her arms or legs. With a shout, she leapt to the top of the battlements, so far out now that one wrong step would send her sprawling to her death, and hurled her daggers downward.

The first man raised his shield, thinking it would save him. The daggers sank into the wood and kept going. Leah grunted with the effort, and growled out a string of curses. The daggers sliced through the man behind the shield, and he fell sprawling backward, knocking loose two others with him. With a quick tug of motion, Leah *pulled* the daggers back to her with her mind, and they came spinning through the air to her hands. She repeated the process again twice more in quick succession, even as arrows flew up at her, one coming so close that it cut a line of red pain across her cheek.

But those at the base of the ladder had far more pressing things to worry about, and so quickly gave up the fight against the Spellblade girl. They ran from the Wall, trying to form up a double line of attack, even as Kindred bowmen brought down scores more behind them in the confusion. The Imperial horns were blowing, trying frantically to turn the host about to confront the charging cavalry, but it was too late.

The mounted Kindred struck the line where it was weakest – the bowmen had been pushed into the center over the weakened gate, where they could best bring down the defenders trying to attack the battering ram that had just moved into place. A pair of Earth Daemons flanked it, and they did not falter in their task, but instead began to pound away at the gate, throwing the huge cluster of tree trunks into the weakened gate over and over again. The Kindred tore through the archers and ripped apart their lines in a matter of seconds, and then were into the confused lines of the infantry behind them. Leah saw her opening.

"Let's go!" she called to Tomaz. She jumped over the Wall, grabbed the smooth sides of the ladder, and let her feet go out from under her.

She shot down the ladder, her hands burning even through her thick leather gloves, and with a *thud* that resonated up her legs and shook her entire body, came to a rest in the debris-and-mud covered stone of the Outer City. She looked up and saw the huge form of Tomaz jump off from the wall; she quickly dodged away as the giant came shooting down behind her.

She turned and ran for the fray, her daggers at the ready, knowing Tomaz would be only moments behind her. Out of the corner of her eye she saw others following them, men and women in the green, gold, and silver who were streaming down not just this ladder but others as well. Arrows continued to arch out from the Wall by the hundreds, taking down the Imperials in droves as they tried to form up to defend themselves from both sides.

She hit the first line of Imperials and passed right through, using the bulky armor of the soldiers to her advantage and simply sinking her daggers into the armor chinks that appeared when they turned their heads. Two others stepped up to engage her, but a shadow passed overhead, between whatever faint torchlight was left; Leah threw herself to the ground as Tomaz's greatsword Malachi parted the men from their heads.

And then other Kindred were there with her, a huge wave that continued to grow, and she was leading the charge through the Imperial force, looking frantically for her brother.

How are we going to get them back over the Wall?

Blue lines once more spidered across her vision, forming into an image of the Earth Daemons breaking through the gate with their enormous ram. She shook her head and the lines disappeared, just in time for her to duck a sword blow and slice the throat of the man behind it.

She shot a glance over her shoulder and saw the gate still closed. The metal was twisted, though, and even though the wood beneath held strong, it was only a matter of time. But if the Kindred could take the area around the gate at the same time the Daemons broke it open....

"TOMAZ!"

"WHAT?!"

"GO KILL THE DAEMONS!"

"What the – *WOMAN, HAVE YOU LOST YOUR MIND?!*"

"JUST DO IT!"

Tomaz ran off in the direction of the gate, fighting through Imperial soldiers as he did. Something caught her eye off to the side – among the mounted Kindred force were men and women fighting in Commoner brown, bringing their number from a couple thousand to twice that number.

Shadows and fire, where did they *come from?*

More Imperial horns began to sound – but not the call of retreat.

The men she was fighting heard the horns and immediately disengaged and fell back – not in retreat, but instead sideways, farther along the Wall. Leah jerked her head around to the other side of the battle and saw that there too the Kindred had been left chasing a force that was making its way farther down the Wall.

"FALL BACK TO THE GATE!" she cried to the gathered Kindred. "The enemy is regrouping – *fall back!*"

Those who saw her and knew her listened without question, and those who didn't were dragged along. The two Kindred forces met and mingled, having cracked the enemy down the middle and temporarily cleared a space. Leah turned and searched the crowd frantically. A figure on a rearing stallion caught her eye.

"Davydd!" she cried and ran for him, but before she even arrived she realized that the profile was wrong. The warrior turned to her, and she saw that it was Autmaran.

"Autmaran!" she called, rushing forward. "Where is my brother? Is he safe?"

"He's more than safe!" the commander called out in a fit of exhilaration. He flung his arm out and she saw Davydd and a group of men engaged with what remained of the Imperial force. Something about them tickled something in the back of her mind though, and suddenly she was afraid.

The colors... the colors are too dark. Why are the colors dark?

And then one of the men moved and the personal standard of Dysuna, in a deeper tan and gray than the common infantry, was revealed behind it.

"NO!"

She ran forward with all her speed, leaving Autmaran behind. As she approached, she saw Dysuna herself step forward and unsheathe a pair of curved daggers, almost identical to Leah's but longer and thicker, almost curved short swords.

Blue light flashed across the scene, throwing off her sight and disorienting her. It came from the sky – lightning. The rain had tapered off, but the clouds were still black and roiling. Lightning flashed again, crackling directly above them, no doubt drawn by the presence of the Daemons and the Bloodmagic that powered them. The thunder was so loud it shook the ground and threw a number of sword swings wide. The energy in the air was so intense it made the hairs on the back of her neck stand on end.

She turned her eyes earthbound once more. The fighters had shifted, and Dysuna was gone, but she could still see Davydd's group – could see his broad valerium sword cutting down soldiers with frenzied haste. Leah readied her daggers and went for him, cutting her way between two men who stepped across her path.

The crowd parted, and she saw Dysuna again; a spike of excitement that reeked of vengeance and hate flashed through her like the lightning above, and she saw her chance to end this all right then and there. She reached inside herself to quiet her mind, to touch her daggers and activate their Spellblade enchantments, but something stopped her at the last second. There was that other part of her now, that new bundle of energy hanging suspended inside her. It was a blue haze, nebulous and flowing. Even as she noticed it, she felt it reach deeper inside her, coiling around her insides until it was indistinguishable from who she was. What she did next was almost natural, like opening a door in her mind that had been locked since birth, a door that had given out occasional flashes and glimpses of brilliance throughout her life but never more. She reached out and touched that door, and it disappeared in a flash of sapphire light.

Blue shapes and figures exploded across her view of the battlefield, rushing, expanding, multiplying before her eyes, until they covered everything, all the men and women fighting on the field of Banelyn. The only thing that haze did not touch was the woman in gray – the Prince of Wolves. Dysuna stood alone, untouched by the Aspect, a gray fighter with a helm shaped like a weeping woman, with feet and hands bare and glowing with savage gray halos, grim as a reaper's blade.

I can't touch her – I can't break through.

She moved forward anyway, seeing in blue fore-images everything that would happen along her path. Men attacked her, only to find her dagger already in their throats. An arrow fell from the sky and would have taken her in the side, but she stepped away and it thudded harmlessly into the muddy ground. A horse reared and almost kicked her, but she danced around the flailing hooves.

Davydd dispatched the last Imperial soldier between him and Dysuna, and then stepped forward with a manic grin on his face. Dysuna fell into a ready stance, and Leah suddenly realized that Davydd wasn't wearing armor; he'd been relying totally on his newfound power, trusting in his luck.

But the Talismans didn't work on each other.

"Davydd! WAIT!"

She saw it happen twice, once in the blue haze of fore-vision and a half-second later in the harsh light of reality. An arrow, shot from the Wall, went wide and fell toward the pair of them. Davydd did not turn; he did not even see it coming. But in that moment, standing so close to Dysuna, his luck failed him, and the shaft pierced his side all the way to the feathered haft. He did not cry out, did not make a single move. The only thing that changed was his expression: shock and disbelief replaced contempt and condescension as he fell to his knees. Dysuna stepped forward and pulled off her helm, staring down at him with a snarling, feral animus ten times more woeful than the crying mask she had just removed.

"*THIS IS FOR MY BROTHER!*" she howled, the words echoing over the battlefield. She raised her arm –

Leah broke through the final crowd of soldiers, and both of her daggers sliced through the air toward Dysuna's face. Both struck true. Dysuna was impaled through the neck and the left side of her head; slowly, she swayed, and then she fell and did not rise. Leah ran to Davydd, and saw immediately that there was nothing she could do for him. The shaft was too deep – this was beyond battlefield healing; they needed a surgeon. Even moving him would be risking much – but he couldn't stay here.

She looked up and reached out to the nebulous blue light of her Talisman – and found it missing. Davydd's eyes suddenly shifted and focused, breaking through his shock and pain – focused on something *behind* her –

"Leah," he gasped, "*move!*"

She spun and rolled, and felt a tug on her hair as a pair of daggers cut through the space where her neck had been mere seconds before. Turning, her mouth dropped open and shock raced through her body. Dysuna stood behind her, the wounds in her neck and head glowing with gray light. As Leah watched, her daggers were pushed from the wounds and fell, harmless, to the ground.

Her Talisman works!

The Wolf Talisman, the Talisman of endurance and will, died down to the glow of banked embers seen through smoke, and Dysuna lunged at Leah. The Exile girl moved back, dodging and weaving with all her skill, but still the Prince of Wolves scored a dozen hits across her arms and legs in as many passes. There was no way out of this – no way to escape a truly skilled knife fighter. Leah knew it – she was one of them.

Dysuna's daggers flashed again, leaving more stinging lacerations.

Shadows and fire!

She rolled, reaching for her daggers with both her mind and her hands, but as they flew toward her, Dysuna struck them both out of the air and sent them flying.

It was over – there was no way Leah could win this without her weapons. She rushed Dysuna, and the Wolf simply moved aside and tripped her, giving her two new gashes along the side of her face as she went.

A white axe smashed into the Wolf's side and sent her crashing to the ground.

Lorna, Davydd's Ashandel partner, yanked the axe from the body of Dysuna and swung it high to bring it down in a killing blow. Blinding light pulsed from the Wolf's side, and she rolled away as Lorna came after her again. Lorna pursued, only stopping long enough to lock her stoic, implacable gaze on Leah.

"Get him out of here," she said simply.

Leah nodded once, and Lorna spun away, roaring a challenge at the fallen Child. Leah *pulled* her daggers with her mind, and they finally came spinning back into her hands. A rush of relief went through her, and the wounds she had sustained no longer seemed so dire. She turned to Davydd. He was too big for her to carry; she needed help.

A group of Kindred were fighting nearby, engaged with the last remaining Imperials in a small pocket of empty space. Leah threw her daggers, killing two enemy soldiers. The Kindred turned to her in surprise, and she immediately motioned them forward.

"Is that – ?"

"Yes! Grab him – hurry!"

Two of them picked Davydd up immediately, ignoring his shouts of pain, while the others spun, scanning the area for approaching soldiers. Leah took the time to look at the distant gate again – she saw the form of the Daemons fighting a man that was larger than life, a man that glowed with a bloody light. She glanced too at the two sides of the Imperial army and saw that they had finished regrouping. Horns sounded again, and the two halves of the enemy army charged toward the Kindred in the center.

"Go for the gate," Leah told them. "Sound the retreat – get everyone back!"

The rain began to fall again in earnest, and Leah felt the heavy weight of Aemon's Blade still slung across her back, weighing her down. Somewhere in the mess of battle was Raven. He needed that sword – why, she did not know. But somehow, in her heart of hearts, in that door that had opened deep inside her, she knew that without it, something unspeakable would happen. There was a darkness descending over the battlefield that was more than physical, more than a simple absence of light.

And Raven was at the center of it.

Chapter Five:

Loyalty

Lorna raised her gore-stained battle-axe and stove in the head of yet another Imperial Defender in the gray-and-tan. With a quick twist, she spun the double-bladed weapon free and turned back to face Dysuna, only to find the Wolf gone.

Surprised, she spun, crouching; she searched the battlefield, but saw no trace of the Imperial Prince, the Fourth Child of the Empress. She did, however, see thousands of other figures moving through the night, striving against each other in the bright flash of lightning that split the sky. It was so close now that crashing thunder followed directly on its heels. True night had fallen, and with it had come a thunderstorm the likes of which the Empire had not seen in years: rain fell in sheets, drenching them all and turning the already treacherous field of ash and blood into an unspeakable quagmire. The only man-made light came from braziers lit along the walls, the high Black Wall of Banelyn that had stood un-taken for four hundred years as a symbol of the Empress' glory and might. The Wall that now protected Her enemies from the army of Dysuna, Her Child. Lorna was one of the Kindred who had been born outside the Empire, born in a humble home to Eldorian miners south of the Kindred capital of Vale. Growing up she had never thought to see such sights... she had never thought of the Empire at all.

Not until that boy with red eyes came and convinced me to take on active duty.

The words of the Ashandel oath, taken during the ceremony before the Elders, rang through her head as they always did in times like these: *I swear to protect the Kindred, and to safeguard the Eshendai that is entrusted to my care. I swear that I will shadow him, I will shepherd him, and I will guide him through all that might do him harm. Through the night, I watch; through the day, I wait; and through the years, I stand fast. I am the sword that cuts the shadow, and the shield that gleams in darkness.*

Lorna made her way toward the distant gates where Leah and the others were headed, scanning the area around her.

Where is Dysuna?

The Wolf had sought out Davydd, had marked him on the battlefield as soon as she had seen the burnt half of his face that showed he had helped kill Tiffenal, and in doing so inherited the Fox Talisman. *She and Tiffenal are twins. That much I know is true.* The Wolf and the Fox were known throughout the realm as the only two Children who truly cared for one another. Never, in all their years of strife against the other Children, in all their time of shifting alliances, had they been on opposite sides of a conflict. To the contrary – it was rumored that they removed themselves from all plots that hurt the other. They had been born seconds apart, and ever since had been inseparable.

She will stop at nothing to avenge her brother. The Wolf Talisman is the Talisman of endurance and loyalty. It will compel her to take revenge.

The Imperial army was charging again, and Lorna saw them engage with the edges of the retreating Exiled Kindred. Time was short – whatever Leah had in mind better happen soon.

Another jagged spear of energy cracked across the sky, and in the brilliant flash that followed, Lorna saw a figure cloaked in gray plate armor, with a helm that bore the face of a weeping woman. She was at least fifty yards ahead, and had only turned back briefly in order to slay an attacker, before continuing on her path.

The Wolf was making for the Wall.

Lorna realized that Dysuna must have caught sight of the fleeing form of Leah; the Wolf was making her way through the clashing armies toward what remained of the Formaux Gate. More lightning came, and Lorna saw the Kindred trying to shift and regroup like. The force that had come from Formaux, the one that she, Davydd, and Autmaran commanded, had cut through the Imperials, killing three times their number, but it was hardly enough. The Empire's forces had overcome their shock, and they still outnumbered the Kindred. The Exiles were following Leah, and now Autmaran as well – Lorna could see his bald head and bright scarlet cape in the intermittent flashes of lightning. They were both shepherding Kindred toward the now-open gate as they protected Davydd. It looked as though the gate had been staved in by enormous force – and if Lorna wasn't mistaken, there was at least one Daemon still there, fighting with a huge bear of a man wielding a massive sword that rippled and shone in the night.

Tomaz killed one of them; with luck, he'll bring the other down as well.

The lay of the land assessed, all in less than a handful of seconds, Lorna hefted her axe and broke into a steady, loping run, her eyes on Dysuna. She circled to the left, using the angle with the Wall to close the distance; the Wolf was too fast for her to catch head-on, so her only hope was to come at her from the side.

Fear flashed through her as thunder rolled and shouted her onward; she wished for the thousandth time that she had never left Eldoras.

That boy needed protection. He still does. And there are worse ways to die.

Dysuna killed another man, this time one of her own soldiers who had fallen into her and slowed her down. She still bore her two long daggers that were almost short swords. The blades flashed and cut, never missing, always finding their target; the arms that bore them never tired, the legs that propelled the body never faltered, and with each man and woman that fell beneath the gleaming steel, the gray markings along the Wolf's neck and hands and bare feet grew brighter. She seemed to pull something vital from the cries of the Kindred, something that infused her with malevolent strength. And as she advanced, as men died before her, her gray hunter's eyes cast around continuously, locking again and again, unerring as a compass needle, on the distant form of Davydd.

Lorna fended off a blow from an Imperial soldier and carried on, not even bothering to strike back. Her path was set – already Dysuna was gaining on her quarry, and if Lorna was not in place soon, the Wolf would pass her by and the opening would be lost.

As she ran, a calm determination settled over her. It was the calm that came from knowing the outcome – the calm that came from knowing she would die if she faced Dysuna alone. But she had to. She had sworn to protect the boy, who looked so much like the one she'd lost.

I won't lose this one.

The distance began to close – their paths, Lorna along the edge of the fighting and Dysuna through the middle, were set to meet. The gap between them narrowed, Lorna careful to stay a single step behind until the last instant. Her precaution paid off: Dysuna did not look over, did not see the approaching Ashandel; the helm she wore narrowed her vision, and Lorna was perfectly hidden from sight.

Their paths crossed, and lightning flared. Lorna lowered her head and leapt straight into Dysuna's side. Her huge bulk crashed into the smaller woman, and the force of the blow carried the Wolf off her path, sending them both sprawling across the filthy ground. Lorna's momentum carried her over and off Dysuna, and as she rolled forward she grabbed the haft of her battle-axe and raised it, readying herself for an all-out attack. She was glad she did – no sooner had she fallen into a ready stance than Dysuna came to her feet as well and attacked with a shriek of anger. Lorna used her height and her axe to distance herself from the Wolf, who tried to close so that she could use her daggers. They both knew that as soon as Dysuna got inside the bigger woman's reach, the fight was over.

Lorna was good. As an axe fighter, she might even be considered great. But Dysuna had lived for hundreds of years and trained under the best fighters the Empire had to offer, and the disparity between them soon became glaringly obvious. Lorna swung her axe back and forth only trying to protect herself from the Wolf's attacks – she was able to gain no ground, only give it. She had to stay between Dysuna and the Formaux Gate, and to do that she could only move side to side and backwards. Her goal was not to defeat her opponent – that was impossible. Her goal was to survive long enough to ensure Davydd's escape.

Whole minutes passed with Dysuna unable to beat her way through. Her attacks became more vicious. She was so intent on getting beyond Lorna to the exclusion of everything else that the Ashandel even managed to score a hit – a huge upward swing that cleft her opponent's breastplate in twain, leaving the metal sliced open like a cooked lobster shell. The axe had even cut the skin below the armor, but Lorna felt no elation as she saw the wound. She knew the tales of the Wolf Talisman, and even before the wound began to shine with a gray light and heal on its own, she knew this was no victory, not even a temporary one.

The cut only enraged Dysuna further – and when she came at Lorna once more, this time the Ashandel found herself a constant step behind. It was as though the Wolf was speeding up, her blows coming faster than should have been possible. But Lorna had expected this too – the endurance was only half of what the Talisman drew from the men and women Dysuna killed. Speed was what made her truly deadly, and she was drawing on whatever stores she had gathered.

A rider-less horse screamed and went running past, buffeting Lorna in the process. She was forced to spin away and disengage, just for a split second, and in that time she saw that something was happening at the gate. The Kindred had made their retreat and drawn the Imperials in behind them. Davydd and Leah were nowhere to be seen – they had made the safety of the Wall.

Good.

The single thought spread warmth through her, a satisfaction that she had done all she could do to help. But Dysuna was on her again in the next instant, and that thought was the last she would ever have. She was alone now, surrounded by an Imperial Army while every friendly soldier had retreated. Arrows still flew from the distant Wall, but not nearly enough to keep her safe. As the Wolf's daggers finally succeeded in tearing her axe out of her hands and forcing her to the ground, she did not flinch, nor did she look away. Dysuna pulled off her helm and threw it to the side before approaching Lorna for the final time.

"I do not know why you chose to make this stand," she rasped, her voice a deep growl that seemed to come from the pit of her stomach only to force its way through a clenched, raw throat. She raised a dagger and stared into Lorna's eyes. "But no one defeats the Children."

The dagger gleamed in a flash of lightning, and Lorna's eyes slid peacefully shut.

But the stabbing pain and the numbing release never came. Instead, she was thrown violently to the side as something rushed past her. Her eyes shot open, and she found herself only an arm's length away from her fallen axe. She grabbed the weapon, fighting through confusion.

She spun to her feet, weapon once more in hand, only to stop short. A man had interposed himself between them with such violence that he had not only thrown Lorna to the ground, but Dysuna as well. The Wolf lay sprawled in the mud, a long gash ripped across her face. Lorna gritted her teeth and forced her eyes to focus, her breathing ragged and her thoughts disoriented. The man was tall, and he wore only the tattered, ripped remnants of a black cloak and some kind of black, ornamental armor. He towered over them both, standing nearly as tall as Tomaz – *was* it Tomaz?

But even as she thought the question, she knew the answer was no. This man radiated danger like a feral beast, and a black halo surrounded him that drank in what little light there was. That darkness seemed to feed off the carnage around them, pulsing like a fresh, bleeding sore, repulsing Lorna and making her sick to her stomach. Even the rain that still fell in sheets around them veered away from him at the last moment, as if the water did not wish to be polluted by his touch. Lorna made it to her feet and took an involuntary step back, trying not to retch. The man turned at her movement, his gaze impaling her like a spike through her gut, holding her in place. Her hands spasmed, and her axe fell to the ground.

It was Raven.

Fear struck her heart and made it falter and skip. He was not who he should have been – something had changed in him, something had broken or corroded away, leaving a hole behind that opened onto a pit of horrors. His eyes were terrible; they had turned his face into a mask of insanity. Lorna stared up at him – *up, how am I staring up? He must be eight feet tall! How is that possible?* – and found herself unable to move, unable even to think of fleeing.

But Dysuna was not caught in his gaze. She ran at him, snarling as she attacked. She might have been a child play-fighting with an adult for all the good it did her, though; without even looking, Raven dodged her blows and grabbed her by the throat. The Wolf's eyes bulged in surprise.

The hand began to squeeze.

Dysuna reached up and began to rip violently at his grip. She snarled and cursed at him, but all he did was watch her. She tore at his fingers, bloodying both him and her, reached for his eyes but came up short, kicked out to try and strike his knee, pulled her arms up in a saw-like motion that should have broken his elbow – but all the while the smiling mask plastered on the Prince's face never altered.

And as the moment lengthened, as Raven's hand continued to close about his sister's throat, she began to choke. The anger in her eyes disappeared and was replaced with fear that slowly turned to disbelief and raw terror. Her motions became more erratic, more desperate, and suddenly she was tearing at her own neck, trying to pull herself away, trying to *rip* herself away even if it meant leaving flesh behind, but it was all to no avail. Her face grew flushed and turned an ugly puce, and the Talisman markings on her bare feet and hands took on the pale, wan color of dying moonlight.

At the last second something caught his eye and he looked down; his eyes fixated on Lorna's axe lying beside him. A shiver passed over his face and he reached out a booted foot in its direction. Lorna tried to move forward to stop him — the axe was valerium, if he tried to handle it, it would burn him, maybe even knocked unconscious —

His foot slipped under the weapon easily, and with a quick flick of his toes, the weapon was up and in his free hand. His fingers closed and curled around the haft of the axe, and nothing happened. No, that wasn't true — the valerium did not throw him back, but it *did* react. It was as if the blade had been struck against a rock: a shower of sparks rained down, and the sudden, inexplicable sound of tortured metal filled the air. Lorna felt something deep inside her lurch, and the axe head broke off and fell to the ground, where it lay smoking.

Uncomprehending, Lorna looked back to the Prince and saw that he was holding a jagged splinter of wood that had made up part of the weapon's haft. The valerium in the axe head and metal reinforcing the wood had repulsed him — and fallen to the ground in a strange, smoking ruin. He grinned again, his teeth gleaming white in the darkness, and turned back to his sister.

With a simple twisting thrust he rammed the wooden stake into and through her right eye. Dysuna went limp, a look of shock and disbelief the last expression trapped on her face, but she did not die. Her arms and legs began to flail, the Talisman still holding her together, still keeping her alive. Raven chuckled, a sound like insects crawling inside a rotted wall, and he grabbed her head in both hands and simply ripped it off her neck.

Lorna watched in disbelief. A flash of light cracked across the battlefield, and the beautiful, flowing gray lines of the Wolf Talisman winked out. Raven stepped back and dropped the pieces of his sister, watching her body fall to the blood-soaked ground. Cries of disbelief and dismay sounded from around them, and only then did Lorna realize that a group of soldiers, likely all of those nearby, had gathered around to watch Dysuna. Some of them cried out now in horror, others in rage. The former fled, and the latter attacked, their weapons crying out in a chorus of shrieking metal that echoed the rage of their masters.

Raven met them, laughing.

Chapter Six:

Commander of the Gate

The Formaux Gate had been ripped from its proper place, and now lay shattered in pieces about them. Tomaz had done his best to defeat the Daemons, but this time had been unable to do so on his own. It was only when Autmaran and Leah arrived with a squad of Rangers bearing valerium weapons that the final creature was put down, but by that time it was too late. The battering ram had done its work on the gate, and what it hadn't destroyed the Daemons had succeeded in tearing down anyway.

"Into the city!" Autmaran shouted to his men, repeating the words over and over again. "Into the city! Go! *Into the city!* We fight them from behind the Wall!"

He saw Leah Goldwyn, the Eshendai Rogue partnered with the Ashandel Tomaz Banier, leading a group of Kindred with a wounded man at their center. As they shifted in their stride, a glint of unmistakable gold caught his eye and he knew immediately who it was. Autmaran gritted his teeth and hurried them past him.

Goldwyn always said luck only gets you so far.

"Archers!" he shouted to the men at the top of the Wall, but none of them could hear him. His voice was hoarse from all the shouting he had done already, and between the thunder, the rain, and the thrice-damned *war*, it seemed a miracle anyone could hear him at all.

"You!" he called out to a random soldier in the Kindred green-and-silver. "Get to the top of the Wall; tell them Commander Autmaran wants them to fire on anything that moves. We're all inside; shoot and *keep shooting* until there's nothing left!"

"Sir!" She saluted and ran.

"Sir?" another voice asked.

"What?" he snapped, focusing on the source of the question – a young man, dressed in the green, black, and gold of a Ranger.

"We have reports that the Prince of the Veil is still out there," he said. "The enemy attacked us over the secret stair we used to invade the city, and the men we sent to plug the hole – we had a runner from them not long ago that said the soldiers they relieved were in the company of the Prince until he ran ahead of them. They lost him, but they saw him go over the Wall."

The report made no sense to Autmaran, but there was no reason for the man to lie. There was a chance they had been seeing shadows – when men knew Children were part of a battle, a stray cat could become a Daemon through word of mouth. In either case, it was too late to do anything about it – if it was true, there was no way to track the Prince, and if it wasn't, then there was no need to worry about it in the first place.

"We have to get him," said a voice behind him.

He turned and saw Leah. She had made it through the gate with Davydd, and now that her brother was on his way through the relative safety of the Banelyn streets, she had returned in time to overhear the report. Autmaran scanned her quickly for injury, and saw the usual signs of battle, including a number of superficial but painful-looking knife cuts, but no debilitating wounds. The little armor that she wore seemed to have kept her mostly intact. He was about to dismiss her, but he noticed something strange: a long, wrapped bundle strapped to her back. It was in the shape of a sword, and, if the wrappings were any indication, it was made of valerium. He knew it wasn't hers: Leah hated swords. But he dismissed the thought as unimportant. It wouldn't be the first time someone had picked up a new weapon in the midst of battle.

"We don't know if the report is accurate," he said, turning and moving back along the way he'd come, scanning the crowd; he saw the way his men were moving, and knew the formations without having to ask the lower officers. He'd been a military man for a long time now – there were things he just understood. Everything was in order.

Until the Imperial army comes rushing through that gate.

"And even if the report *is* true," he continued, "there's nothing we can do about it. That's one man fighting in a field of soldiers – there are thousands of men out there, and the Imperials outnumber us five to one."

"*We must find him!*"

The vehemence in her voice gave him pause. This wasn't like her: she spoke her mind openly and freely, but she was even more pragmatic than he was. This wasn't some idealistic under-officer who wanted to bring back all his men; this was Leah Goldwyn, the daughter of one of the most brilliant military minds of a generation, and a budding figure of legend in her own right.

He caught a glimmer of something that distracted him, a flash of sapphire light that came from the base of her wrist before she twisted her sleeve to cover it. He looked up and caught her gaze, and knew she knew he had seen it. Those were Talisman markings; he'd bet his life on it.

The Wolf is outside and we killed the Fox… but this was the Eagle's plan all along. Shadows and fire, whatever happened to Davydd must have happened to her.

"What do you know?" he asked, dispensing with unneeded questions.

"That we need to find Raven."

"Why?"

"Because he needs his sword."

Autmaran paused and came to understand the bundle on her back.

"You have Aemon's Blade."

"Yes."

"You think he needs… why? It's just a sword."

"No – it's not. And he needs it."

"Why?"

"Because he does!"

A rumbling roar started, just at the edge of hearing, and Autmaran turned to see the Imperial force coalescing before the gate. The last of the Kindred were inside, formed up along the edges of the square and ready to receive the invaders, who would arrive in minutes. The Commander ran to his waiting horse, Alto, and mounted in one swift move. He gestured for Leah to follow and kicked his heels against Alto's sides, retreating behind the front lines of his army as they finished forming up in position.

Not my army, but my soldiers, at least.

He was the only senior officer on the front line – no one had heard from the Generals in hours, and from what the soldiers had said, they'd been giving confused orders for most of the night, responding too slowly to events that were already spiraling out of control. He reined in the horse upon reaching the back ranks where the reserves of light infantry had formed up along the city's central street. Leah had followed him. She looked ready to speak again, but he cut her off.

"Look," he said, "he's either dead, or he's coming through that gate. Either way, we need you here."

She snarled at him and spun away.

Damn it – if she tries to break through now, there's nothing I can do.

One of his jaw muscles spasmed as he tried to hold back his anger. He swung his gaze around the area inside the Wall and knew they would at least be able to put up a fight. The houses nearby had been torn and gutted – the walls of the lowest levels had been blown out by some huge force, and scraps of plaster and brick lay everywhere, covered in a thick layer of mud formed by blood, rain, and the ash of the burned Outer City. Furniture, doors, carts, and even dead horses had been pilled up at each of the entrances to the streets leading away from the gate, and the Kindred had formed up behind them, where Autmaran had told them to wait. Where he now stood was about to become a killing field, an unholy altar upon which the Imperials would sacrifice themselves in order to take back the city.

Horns sounded, and Dysuna's army attacked.

Autmaran pulled back as arrows shot through the open gate, heeling Alto behind the nearest building. He clamped down on his emotions and burned his fear within him, using it as fuel, so that when he turned back to the Exiled soldiers he was once more the Commander, in control.

"Hold the line!" he shouted. He couldn't let them break – if they lost this ground, that was the end. He looked up and saw the archers on the Wall, now joined by members of the Scouts, raining arrows down on anything that moved outside the Wall, but it clearly wasn't enough. Imperials rushed through the broken gate even as arrows felled them in droves.

"Hold!" Autmaran continued to shout, heeling Alto from barricade to barricade, passing between them via the torn-down walls of former homes. "Wait for them to engage! Stay behind the barricades and make them pay in blood for every inch they wish to take!"

The Imperial soldiers marched on, a moving tide of nightmare shadows. Autmaran reached the far end of the line and saw there the hulking form of Tomaz wedging half a broken cart further into the barricade. The giant spotted him as well, and gave a final heave before turning to go to Autmaran. His armor, what was left of it, was in tatters. Whole patches of his leather jerkin had been torn off, and bare skin showed in a number of places, glowing with a strange ruddy light that made him look bathed in blood.

"Where is Leah – did she make it back through the gate?"

"Yes," Autmaran said, his words clipped and terse, "but she won't stop looking for Raven. She's seen something – and I don't know what the Talisman has done to her."

Tomaz went pale beneath his black beard, and his beady black eyes, already hard as stone, turned cold as well, like chips of ice.

"Where is she?"

"The other end of the line."

"I have to go to her."

"We need you here."

"She is my Eshendai."

Autmaran hesitated only a fraction of a second before nodding. Tomaz would do what he could for her – and the two of them together were worth twenty men.

As the giant left, Autmaran leapt off Alto, knowing she would only get in the way now. He hoped he'd see her again. He moved back along the side of the nearest building and knelt behind the barricade, unsheathing his sword and taking his place on the line among a number of Rangers and Rogues. They nodded to him, their faces grim, and he looked over the top of the makeshift fortifications.

The Imperials were barely twenty yards away now. A good number of them had fallen to the hail of arrows shot from the Wall, but not nearly enough. Wave after wave of them marched through the broken Formaux gate.

"Stand fast!" he shouted to the men behind this stretch of barricade. "If we die today, we die as heroes! Every solider here who fights with me has earned the name of Exile, and we will make the Empire remember us long after we are gone!" Heat bloomed in the eyes of the Rangers and Rogues around him; arms shifted on weapons, jaws clenched, and faces hardened. "Follow me when I say the word," Autmaran continued. "We will be the first to engage when they reach the barricades."

They nodded, and waited.

The Commander turned and inched his head the barest fraction of an inch over the top of the cart in front of him, the wood scratching his bare left cheek. He caught sight of the approaching army, and it made his heart pound in his throat. It didn't matter, though; he had already made his peace with what he had to do. The Kindred forces had a minute left, tops, before the Imperial army was upon them. Autmaran shifted his gaze to the other barricades – five in all: two for the side streets along the wall, one for the main street, and two for the streets that led off the square at the corners. A large form caught his eye at the barricade where he had started – it was Tomaz, settling into position with the smaller form of Leah beside him.

A small flare of relief came to him, knowing that both of them had joined the fight. They were iconic figures – the Kindred would take heart just seeing them on the battlefield. He shifted took a final breath, soaking in the feel of air in his lungs, even though it was choked with ash and smog. He reveled in that last, frozen moment of time. If he died, he would do it admiring life, with a smile on his lips.

The way Goldwyn had.

I will see him when I wake.

"ATTAAAAAAAACK!"

Autmaran surged into motion, unsheathing his sword and mounting the barricade. The Rangers and Rogues around him rose up as well, shouting wordlessly; the Kindred at the other barricades took up the cry; the Imperials broke rank and came to meet them; the archers on the Wall continued to rain down a blanketing hail of death.

The battle was joined across the courtyard, and no one was spared.

It was the hottest fighting Autmaran had ever seen. Standing in the sludge of ash and blood, trying to see through the falling rain, cutting right and left with his sword, he barely knew where he was. It was almost cleansing, as if his identity had been pulled out of him. He felt alien in this sea of writhing humanity, inhuman amongst the snarling, bestial faces of his fellow men. His sword rose and fell over and over again with the regular beat of a metronome, lancing through the night to strike at any who stood before him. Bodies fell on all sides as lightning ripped the sky above, opening up the clouds and unleashing another downpour, this time so torrential it was as though nature, looking on, sought to drown them all for what they did. Autmaran's sword continued to rise and fall, and the blood of the slain polluted the falling water even as it tried to wash them clean.

The forces were matched, at first. The Imperials were bottlenecked, and their force had been thinned by the Kindred's surprise attack. But as more of the heavy infantrymen, clad in the colors of Tibour Province, pressed their way forward, the Kindred could not help but fall back under the weight. Soon they were fighting atop the barricades, and then at the foot of them. The Imperials marched forward relentlessly, and the battle was about to flow into the very streets of Banelyn.

But something changed.

The implacable tide of men, the steady, stoic movement of the Empire's army, faltered. It was no more than a slight ripple at first, and Autmaran thought the impression came from his own fatigue, his own exhaustion from being awake for almost two full days and nights and fighting through it all. His vision had begun to fade to a haze at the edges, and reality seemed more and more like a dream to him. But then the shift happened again. The formation of the Imperial army began to jerk and shift, somehow out of control. Voices rose in unison somewhere far in the distance, far from the Kindred barricades. Thunder rolled through the sky, wiping the noise away, but when the rumbling died the sound was louder. Suddenly there were no new Imperials to replace the ones that fell to Autmaran's sword. The Exiles surged forward and easily regained the barricades. They met the Imperials there, and two more men fell beneath Autmaran's blade, clearing his way. He reached the height of the barricade, now a ruined mass of rain-soaked splinters. Despite its sorry state, it gave him the height he needed to see through the rain, through the thick, black night; something was forming at the back of the Imperial ranks, something that made no sense.

The cries of panic mounted, rising one atop the other until a cacophonous insanity gripped the entire army. The men closest to the Wall were pushing away from it, running, *fleeing*, from something behind them. Autmaran imagined he could smell the terror in the air; the emotion was so palpable it should have had the strength to gain corporeal form.

"What's happening?" croaked one of the Rangers at his elbow, she too staring at the distant motion with wide eyes.

Autmaran opened his mouth to speak, but no words came out.

Leah... is this what she saw?

Lightning ripped through the sky, striking a metal flagpole atop the Black Wall, and the flash of light revealed a single figure in black, buried in a sea of gray and tan. The enemy ranks had turned around now, and the Imperials were facing the threat that had come at them from the Wall, through the open gate. Lightning flashed again, and Autmaran caught sight of the figure once more. His heart began to beat too quickly – what he had seen wasn't a man. It couldn't be. Had the Bloodmages created a new Daemon? A Daemon that had turned on the Imperial army?

Once more lightning, and this time the clap of thunder that came behind was echoed by a groaning, beastly roar. Autmaran didn't know what was happening, but he was a man of instinct and intuition: something was wrong. He didn't know what, and he didn't know how, but *something* had gone very, very wrong.

The Kindred on the barricades were forming up for an advance – they were readying to attack the confused Imperial force.

"No!" Autmaran called, motioning to them. His voice came out in a harsh creak, like an old, ill-used door hinge. He cleared his throat, and spoke again: "NO!"

The single word cracked out of his mouth like a whip, and the captains getting ready to lead the charge backed down as they saw him standing atop the central barricade with arms raised, his tattered red cloak flapping behind him. He turned to the Ranger at his elbow, a young woman he thought was named Yehana.

"Send word to the Kindred," he said quickly. "We hold our ground. No one moves past the barricades – we don't know what this is."

The woman nodded, shared the message with three others, and then all four were off and running. Autmaran turned his attention to the man on his right, an Eshendai Rogue, dark-skinned with a thin face.

"Find a way to get us more light," he said. "I don't care how you do it – build up the braziers on the Wall, light more torches, burn a building, whatever – we need to see what's happening. Go now."

The man nodded and left.

Autmaran turned back to the scene before him, trying to peer through the darkness that cloaked the swirling shapes. What was out there? What was happening? The shouts were louder, and there was a terrible sound coming from the center of the square, a sound of ripping and tearing that accompanied the clash of steel on steel. The closer Autmaran looked, the deeper the darkness at the center of the group seemed to be. Whatever was doing this was there in the middle. Autmaran peered closer, drawn in with a mixture of fascination and horror; he could just make out movement through the pouring rain: long limbs, black and glistening, swinging back and forth. Were there two things there? Surely no Daemon could –

"Autmaran!"

He turned and saw Leah coming toward him, flanked by Tomaz.

"You have to pull the Kindred back," she said quickly, her green eyes boring into him, even through the darkness. "They can't help – it needs to be us, and us alone."

"What are you talking about? We're in the middle of a battle – if we withdraw now, then there's no chance – "

"The battle is over," rumbled Tomaz. His eyes were bloodshot, and his beard crusted with blood. "We have won – unless we lose what happens next."

"What are you talking about?"

"You know who that is," Leah said, gesturing frantically to the distant fighting. "You know who is at the center of that."

"Who...?"

In a flash, it all came together. He spun and looked out again.

No... no, that can't be him. Please, don't let it be him.

"You!" he shouted, pointing to another soldier. "Send word – we gather here for a final attack; the Prince of the Veil is in the center of that force, we need to retrieve – "

Lightning struck the metal flagpole once again, and this time, through the thinning crowd of soldiers, Autmaran saw the figure clearly. Horror gripped him, and he faltered, taking a step back.

"S-sir? What do you – ?"

"Fall back," Autmaran said. "Ignore my last command – fall back! All Kindred, fall back to the Inner City, to the General's command post. GO – NOW! *FALL BACK!*"

The cry was repeated, and the Exiled men and women began to pull away from the barricades; but even as they did, the tide of battle changed again.

The Imperial army, which had turned inward to fight the intruder in its ranks, suddenly broke and turned. Men threw themselves at the Kindred without the slightest regard for their own lives and safety. Terror showed itself in the wide whites of their eyes, an image that put Autmaran in mind of spooked horses. It was an animal terror, the kind of fear that belies a predator that cannot be escaped. The Kindred stood on the barricades and cut them down in droves, but even when soldiers pushed through in large squads, they did not attack. They continued on, off into the city, followed by droves more. Imperial men died by the thousands, and hundreds more escaped to temporary safety in Banelyn City proper.

"Form up the Rangers," Autmaran said quickly to a captain nearby. "Any of them still with horses. Pull all the Scouts, get everyone off that Wall that you can and send them into the city. We find every last one of those men. Capture who you can, kill who you cannot – understood?"

The captain nodded, and Autmaran recognized her as Rahael, one of the women who had taken Formaux with him and Raven. He could see fear in her eyes, and more so, exhaustion. She was just as tired as he was, but she would do her duty. She left, calling together the Rangers and sending runners for the Scouts, and another thought crossed Autmaran's mind:

Raven's been in battle for almost three days straight.

The battle changed again, and the remnants of the Imperial army that had not managed to make it past the Kindred simply gave up. Many fell to their knees, praying to the Empress, while others threw down their swords and begged for mercy from the Kindred. The rain had doused all the battlefield torches, and the only light now came from the protected oil lamps farther back in Banelyn City. The darkness made everything more confusing, and Autmaran could barely trust what he was seeing, but he still imagined he was seeing... seeing objects go flying through the air... vague forms far too large to be arrows. They were pale and shapeless – no, not shapeless: one was round, another oblong; a third was –

Autmaran's blood drained from his face.

"He's not in control of himself," Leah said quickly. "We've only got one shot at this – if we don't clear the Kindred out, he'll come for them next. He's too far gone – he probably doesn't even know who he is anymore!"

"Yes," Autmaran said, tearing his eyes away from the sights that had already burned themselves into his mind. "You and Tomaz pass the word – whatever you have to do, get them back."

The giant and the girl ran to do just that.

Autmaran took a step to follow them, and realized his breath was coming in wheezing pants. The ash he had breathed on the first attack through the Outer City was taking its toll. As he spoke to the captains, the lieutenants, even the soldiers themselves, urging them to retreat, he felt as though he were moving through a fog. His body had begun to shut down, but he couldn't let it. Not yet. He had to keep going until the battle was through. He was in charge of these men – he wouldn't leave them without a leader.

"FALL BACK!"

His voice rolled out of him strong and steady, a crack of thunder in its own right. Men and women jerked around as the shout broke their trance. Roars and screams of terror continued to split the air, coming from base of the Wall, but they were fewer now. Slowly, the dam broke. At first it was only a trickle of soldiers, but then it became a river, and finally a flood. Thousands of Kindred fled the path of their Prince, not even knowing it was he they fled.

The Commander turned back to see the roiling mass of the Imperial army lying strewn and broken across the field like a rough child's playthings. The lights he'd ordered lit had never appeared – the rain was still coming down, though it had lessened. Autmaran wished briefly for another flash of lightning to let him know what was happening, but something deeper told him he didn't want it, something connected to his sense of self-preservation.

He felt Leah and Tomaz come up beside him, and they looked on in silence.

The sounds of battle stopped. All sounds, in fact, stopped in a single instant. The rain dropped off, the clash of steel ceased, and the only remnants of the battle were the distant, reverberating cries of fighting in the far reaches of the city that sounded eerily like echoes of the preceding slaughter. The silence truly was deafening – it was its own noise, so encompassing it seemed the world itself had taken time to pause after what it had just witnessed.

As one, the three companions peered closer at the center of the square, trying to push aside the curtain of darkness with their eyes. Shadows were layered one upon the other in such a thick, woven tapestry that no light seemed able to pierce it from any angle. All Kindred were gone from the spot, all except for a handful still manning the Wall, too wounded or exhausted to retreat.

And then, in the center of the square, something moved; something *breathed*.

"He's alive," whispered Autmaran. "How is that possible?"

"Something is wrong," rumbled Tomaz, speaking much closer to the truth of the matter. "Something is different."

Autmaran caught sight of an abandoned torch lying in a nearby building, wrapped to protect it from the damp. He crossed through what had been a ruined wall and caught it up in a single, smooth motion. With a quick strike of flint and steel from his belt, he had it lit. He came back into the street, holding the torch high above him, and as they advanced and the blaze grew, the darkness pulled back to either side like a theater curtain. A soft wind carrying the after-scent of lightning moved among them, whispering in their ears its own shock at the sight. Raven stood revealed, and they stared in horror at the thing he had become, at the monster that had been their friend.

He stood in the center of a bloody mountain of ruined bodies, covered from head to toe in the gory remains of a hundred men. He towered above them, far taller even than Tomaz, every tendon and vein in his body throbbing with unimaginable power. At some point during the battle his armor had been rent and torn so badly that it now hung off of him in tatters, blood-smeared and cracked. His back was nearly bare, and upon it was visible the outline of the Raven Talisman, the black lines of Bloodmagic power etched deep into his skin, skin that was now so dark it was almost part of the night. As they watched, those markings seemed to shift and writhe, like folded wings.

There was a noise to their left, and they turned just in time to see a lone Defender stand and run for his life. Almost before the thought could register in their minds, there was a terrible ripping sound, as if the fabric background onto which this scene had been stitched were being ripped in twain, and Raven crossed the distance to the man in a single bound that swirled with dark shadows of blackest pitch, shadows that looked like enormous wings and seemed to propel him faster than the eye could follow. He landed on the man's back and bore him to the ground, then reached down and removed the man's head with the same quick twist with which one might pick an apple from a tree.

He held the head aloft, still dripping blood, and turned to roar with an earth-shattering voice at the Black Wall. As he did, his eyes came to rest on his friends, and they saw that he did not know them. This creature's eyes were not Raven's; these eyes, black through and through with not a hint of white, were the eyes of the Lord of Death, the unleashed, true power of the Raven Talisman. Here stood the Prince of Imperial Prophecy, and Autmaran felt fear vibrate through him, fear that he had never felt before, not even when staring down a Daemon or the Prince of Oxen.

The Raven smiled at them, revealing sharp, wicked teeth, somehow far too large for its twisted mouth, and it came at them, dropping the head as it readied for this new challenge. Tomaz drew his sword, a huge swath of steel that looked no more than a play thing in the darkness that came from the creature before them.

"Run!" he shouted at the others, interposing himself between them and what had once been their Prince. But the Raven crossed the distance in the same time-defying leap as before, and Tomaz was on the ground, splayed out below him. The Raven pulled back its hand, a clawed thing that spoke of ripping talons, and bellowed in joy.

Leah came forward. "Raven!"

The cry seemed to startle the creature. It looked up, and as its black eyes met her green ones, the creature froze. "Come back to us," she said, her voice barely above a whisper, her tone pleading, something that Autmaran had never thought he'd hear from her. "Come back. I'm alive – I'm here. We're safe now – you saved us. All of them, the Imperials – they're gone. It's over. There's – there's nothing left to fear."

But the Raven didn't move. She took another step forward and a darkness that had nothing to do with the night sky enveloped him. The world warped sideways, and a snarl appeared on his face. He grew larger somehow, and the darkness spread from him, reaching out with searching tendrils.

"Raven!" Leah snapped, and this time, as she reached the edge of the shadow surrounding the creature, it looked at her, and its breathing began to slow. Its black eyes reflected her, and in their depths something human stirred once more.

"No! Wait – DON'T SHOOT!"

Autmaran spun and looked toward the voice of Elder Keri as it rang from behind them, slicing through the moment like a finely wrought blade. Arrows sprang from the Wall as the remaining Kindred fired at the creature. The shower of wooden shafts went wide, but two of the arrows pierced the creature's skin, at the shoulder and hip, and a third almost struck Leah in the thigh.

"STAND DOWN!" Autmaran roared, his voice cracking out in a tone of absolute command, and immediately the bowmen faltered, and the under officer – *Jallin, goddamn Jallin!* – looked down with a face suddenly ashen gray.

The creature threw back its head and roared into the sky, showing its wicked teeth, and then launched itself at the nearest form, slashing at it, mangling it, tearing it.

"*No – ELDER KERI!*"

A flash of white flew from beneath the Wall, from where the Formaux Gate had once stood tall and strong. It was the broken head of a battle-axe, and it hurtled end over end to bury itself in the creature's back. The Raven threw back its head and cried out; huge shapes emerged from its back – *shadows and fire, they are wings* – spreading wide as the creature howled in pain.

"Now!" cried a husky voice. Autmaran turned and saw it was Lorna, her blonde hair matted with blood, soot, and mud. "Whatever you're going to do, *do it now!*"

Autmaran spun. "Leah!" he cried.

She launched herself forward, running at the creature; Autmaran found himself standing over Elder Keri, who was no doubt here to seek out Raven herself.

Elder Keri... please, oh gods, don't let her be... no, he can't have...

Autmaran turned as the Raven managed to pull the axe from its back and fling it aside; the wound glowed a strange, burnished gray, and then began to move and pull itself together, the muscles knitting back into one, the spine bones repositioning themselves and receding back beneath the taut stretch of flesh. Leah unslung the bundle on her back and pulled off the wrappings. Fire blazed into the night as the sword burned white, and she threw the Blade forward, just as the creature turned to face her, a contemptuous snarl on its face.

The Blade twisted in midair, almost of its own accord, and struck the creature point first. The Raven threw back its head in agony, and the Blade once more lit up the world with a dazzling white light that blinded all those watching. The creature shrieked in pain and lunged forward, swinging its huge, disproportionate arms out to strike at anything it could catch.

Another huge form, this one wreathed in scarlet, came from nowhere and tackled the creature to the ground. The creature tried to throw the man off, but couldn't – Tomaz held it to the ground with superhuman strength, and Aemon's Blade continued to burn into its skin, trapped as it was between the beast and the ground. They all watched, entranced as the creature's form began to writhe and shift. The dark shadow that covered it began to lighten, to fade, and the light of Aemon's Blade shone through the Prince's entire body. The creature's form shrank, slowly folding in on itself, until it was only the body of an average-sized man. Tomaz pulled off of him, and stood staring down at the naked form of Raven, Prince of the Veil, lying in the middle of the battlefield.

"Is he... is he alive?"

No one answered him at first; they were all too stunned to speak, too focused on the transformed Prince and the pulsing black marks on his back and shoulders that were now matched by steely gray ones on his hands, feet, and neck. Leah strode forward, threw her cloak over him, and held her hand to his lips.

"He's breathing," she said, and though the announcement was what they had all been hoping for, the tension dissipated not one bit, and no one moved to help him. Autmaran turned back to Elder Keri. He bent down, unbuckling his own red cloak off his shoulders and wrapping it around her. He checked her pulse, felt for her breath.

He stood, and felt Leah and Tomaz approach him from behind.

"Get him inside," Autmaran said, finally finding his voice. "Bring Healers."

"What about Keri?"

"Get her... get her inside as well."

"And bring the Healers, yes?"

"She won't need them."

He caught their gaze.

"She's dead."

Chapter Seven:

Waking

Nightmares lined the path of Raven's dreams. He was moving on a road, going far and fast, and with each step new images broke through the barrier that separated his mind from the world around him, adding memories that were not his own. Shadowed forms chased him, and he was forced to break into a shambling run. He was running out of time, and his destination was far, far ahead of him.

His breathing came in gasping pants, and every muscle in his body ached. He looked down and realized every stone in the road was made of a human face, one for every man and woman he had killed. He continued on, unable to stop, forcing himself to continue as a voice from the deep memories of his childhood came at him from all sides.

"There will be a seventh child, a child not worthy of your line - Keep him! Do not cast him out, but around his arms bind your power; raise him as your own until his seventeenth name day, in which year he shall be both key and lock to your ambition. Upon that day, and not till then, take his life, for if he lives, so fall the other six Princes of Strife; should he live, he will bring about the rise of Light, but should he die, the fall of Night. That living Seventh Child shall seek to inherit the Kingdom of the Veil, and should he claim his right, all your strength shall fail. But if, before the year is out, the child is dead beyond a doubt, you shall reign forever on,

For all who might oppose you shall be gone."

Images of a chessboard and a tall, soaring tower with eagles nesting in the eaves came to him as the voice intoned the words. *That prophecy is old,* he thought to himself, not knowing where his certainty came from. *And incomplete.*

As if on cue, the second half of the Prophecy began to roll in his head, spoken in hushed tones, whispered at him from all sides. A voice spoke to him of secrets Geofred had kept hidden from the Empress... and of the hidden details of the Prophecy surrounding his birth.

If Mother kills me, she wins... what happens if I kill her?

Someone laughed behind him as he raced down the road, a road he now knew would end when he reached the city of Lucien and stood before his Mother. The laughter increased, and Raven knew it was his brother, and more than that, knew he was lost in his brother's memories.

Fine, you want to leave? cackled the voice of Geofred. *You can wake up – but the nightmare will continue.*

Raven woke.

The first impression he had of his surroundings was warm light and birdsong. He ran his hands along the bedding beneath him and felt cool linen against his skin. He blinked, and his eyesight cleared, revealing a hazy view of a distant door of polished mahogany, the frame carved at the corners into intricate spirals. The doorknob bore a Mage's Knot, one of the clever locking puzzles the Most High used in place of keys.

I suppose that tells me where I am.

He shifted on the bed, only to realize his hands were trapped between layers of sheet and comforter. Wriggling awkwardly, he managed to extricate an arm and reached for the coverlet, trying to free the rest of him, but found himself unable. A dull pain throbbed in his forearm, and he couldn't even grasp the edge of the comforter. He shifted his body further and managed to prop himself up and free his other arm. Sweat broke out along his brow, and the bird singing from the window behind him paused. Raven wondered if it was watching him.

From his new vantage point, he saw that the room was circular and bore an oaken vanity, a closet, and a heavily stocked bookshelf. There was also a second door, and this one was cracked, just enough to allow sound in, along with a thin sliver of vision.

"And what happens when he wakes?" asked a voice, drifting in from outside. It was hot and impetuous. "What will we find? The Raven? Or the Prince?"

"This has happened before and he came out of it then," responded another voice, one that brought memories of lavender and trail dust with it. "When we were on our way from Banelyn to Vale, he came to rescue me from a group of Defenders, and when he'd killed them all... he couldn't even remember who he was. He was like nothing I'd ever seen – and that was only twenty, maybe twenty-five. Who knows how many he killed this time? Thousands at the very least."

"Surely not that many," countered a deep, husky voice. The sound of it was oddly calming, and it brought with it images of gray eyes. "Between the Kindred and the general panic... "

"He killed so many that the entire army *ran away from him,*" rumbled a voice so deep and sonorous it vibrated the door on its hinges. "I've never seen anything like that. Shadows and fire, I've never even *heard* of anything like that."

"The point is," continued the second voice, one that came with the sound of steel daggers cutting through silk, "he recovered the last time this happened. It took him the better part of a week, but when he woke up he was himself again. He's been out for nearly that long this time – I can't help but think that same process may be happening now. His body must be... *purging* or something. He's still our Raven."

"I'm going to have trouble calling him that now," said the hot, impetuous voice. "I think I know now why he never liked it."

"But we all know he didn't do it," insisted the second voice, the one that came with visions of green eyes. "Whatever he became, it wasn't him. It was the Talisman – it was what the Tyrant tried to make him."

"Either way," rasped the third voice, "he did something unforgivable."

"But that's the important point – *he* didn't. Whatever it is that's him, whatever it is in him that is Raven, that *thing* out there was something else!"

"He's always said the Talisman is a curse... I never understood until now."

There was silence then, as they all thought it over.

Raven's mind finally started working again, and memories came back to him, fragments from both his life and... other lives. One life in particular, one of the most recent ones, one that he had told himself he had to remember, that he had to keep safe and... one that had begun to haunt his dreams.

Geofred. My brother, Geofred.

And then he knew who he was, and he knew at least some of his companions were standing outside this room in a house of the Most High, waiting for him to wake up.

His hands fluttered momentarily at the coverlet again, as if they knew he was supposed to rise, but they fell still again and lay lifeless. He felt the comfort of the pillows against his back, and the warmth of the sunlight streaming through the window behind his head. The bird had begun to sing again, masking the sound of his friends' silence, and he found himself lost in the warbling, nonsense notes.

His thoughts went back to Vale, to a cabin in the woods overlooking the white-stone city. He raised a hand to his chest and held it over his aching heart. There was nothing in the world he wanted more than to go back and leave this life behind, nothing more than to give the burden of his choices to another.

No, not yet. I have to go north first. I have to finish it.

The door creaked softly, and someone looked into the room.

"He's awake!"

The voice belonged to Davydd, Raven knew, but he couldn't bring himself to look up. He was just so tired... so very, very tired. Even the thought of lifting his head seemed a herculean feat, and holding a conversation seemed a goal as unattainable as touching the moon. He heard a rustle at the door; the hinge creaked as it opened wider. Davydd continued speaking to someone else, out of sight beyond the slice of hallway visible past the doorjamb. "You – go find Autmaran. The Prince is awake."

Leah was the first in; she pushed past Davydd and flowed forward with her dancer's grace to kneel beside the bed. She reached out a hand and touched his face, and then leaned forward and kissed him fiercely, taking him by surprise. Her lips were soft, but the kiss was hard and firm, almost as if she were using it to confirm to both herself and him that this was real, that both of them had survived.

She pulled back, and Raven stared at her in shock.

"You were dead," he managed to croak.

"I got better," she said with a smile.

"Shadows and fire," Davydd cursed. "He's already awake, stop that."

"Wouldn't have stopped me," Lorna said. "I tend to like men better when they're awake. More useful for kissing that way."

A huge form came up behind her, dwarfing even Lorna. "Let me see him!" rumbled the voice ferociously. "If you don't move I'll slice my way through with Malachi, don't think I won't!"

Lorna and Davydd moved out of the way as the bluff, bearded face of Tomaz reared into view. Pushing past them just as Leah had, he rounded the bed on the other side and, without pretense, bent down and grabbed Raven in a bone-crushing hug.

"Ah! Ack – Tomaz!"

"Shut up and let me hug you."

Davydd burst into laughter as Lorna gave out a huge guffaw that sounded like some poor animal being strangled. Even Leah smirked. Tomaz pulled back and examined him critically at arm's length, then nodded as if to pronounce Raven fit and himself satisfied. He rose back to his full height, almost brushing the ceiling with his head.

Raven cleared his throat, and they all fell silent. An apprehensive feeling crept into the room, as if all the fears and doubts they were trying to cover with their good humor had formed into a separate entity that stood with them and watched the proceedings, made of everything they wouldn't say.

"Where am I?"

"House of Werman, formerly of the Most High Blood," Davydd said. "You're a hero as far as the army is concerned, and Elder Spader made sure we put you here. Said it was a matter of decorum – the Kindred want to know their leader is living like a good little princeling should. At least until you recover, that is. When you're feeling better we're kicking you out, 'cause I want a turn too and feather beds are thin on the ground. Thin in the air for that matter. All around, not very plump. And besides, if you can kill a thousand men with your bare hands, you can sleep on the floor for a night."

His smile froze on his half-burned face and everyone tensed. The air in the room suddenly carried a charge, and all eyes were very consciously *not* looking at Raven.

Except for Leah. He felt a brief soaring feeling in his stomach knowing she was still alive, but it faded quickly. She was watching him with her stone face, that emotionless mask she wore when she was keeping her own council, and waiting to see how he would respond. He looked back at the others and opened his mouth to speak, trying to find a way to break through the silent litany of unspoken questions. Raven remembered only patches of the night, but those patches spoke volumes, and what he couldn't remember he was glad had been lost to him.

"Did I... ?"

His mouth was dry and he broke off, coughing. Leah shifted her hand, just enough to grasp his as he grabbed the coverlet, a move that surprised him almost more than the kiss. He swallowed and tried again.

"Did I kill any of the Kindred?" he finished.

Davydd glanced at Tomaz, but didn't speak. Lorna continued to stare, with dogged interest, at the carpet below her feet.

"You... did," Davydd said finally. "Do you remember any of it?"

Raven grimaced. "I remember rain... and killing Henri Perci." He squinted and winced at the memory, trying to focus on what came after it, but there were only flashes that made no sense. What came to him, though, he spoke out loud.

"A soldier in the mask of a weeping woman... running toward a broken gate... and then arrows, in my side, and confusion... and then ... dreams ... and now here."

They relaxed a fraction of an inch, but Raven knew something else was wrong.

"Do you remember what happened after you were hit with the arrows?" Leah asked. She swallowed and pinned him with her gaze. "Do you remember Elder Keri?"

As soon as she said the name, a flash of memory jabbed him like a hot poker. He gasped and clutched at his head. He remembered looking down at her, then Leah speaking and drawing him away, and then pain, and then he was ripping and tearing...

"I... killed her."

Saying the words out loud somehow made the act less real, not more so. To simplify what he had done to such a small collection of words did not seem right. It was a bigger thing than the words could hold.

"*You* didn't," Leah said, sudden intensity burning in her gaze. "The Raven Talisman did. The part of you that is still bound to the Tyrant – the part that you can hold at bay with Aemon's Blade."

Raven locked eyes with her and realized he had no reply. He was too numb to think about what she was saying. Instead, he swallowed again, his throat rough sandpaper, and asked the next logical question. "Were there any others? Any other Kindred?"

"Only a few that we know of," Tomaz rumbled softly, and the words sent a tremor around the room. The black chunks of rocky ice that were his eyes flicked to Lorna, but he said nothing else.

Slowly, Raven looked to her.

"I remember," he said slowly. "Standing over you." She nodded, her bowl-cut hair swaying gently. Her eyes were tight and her mouth and face neutral. "I almost killed you," he said faintly.

She nodded, just a simple jab of her head up and down, like a bird.

Raven reached inside himself, felt for what he was holding, and realized it was more than just the Raven Talisman. There was a well somewhere deep inside him, something he had never felt before. It was like a calm pool that spoke of endless depths, a pool that sparkled in a sourceless light and stood perfectly still, with not a single ripple disturbing its surface.

He reached down to his shirt and pulled it up over his head, fighting past the aches in his arms and back, chest and stomach. Tomaz came forward as if to stop him, but Leah grabbed his arm and stopped him before he made it more than half a step. They exchanged a look that Raven couldn't read, and in that look Leah convinced Tomaz to let Raven do what he would.

He looked down at himself as he laid the soft clothing over to one side, and saw gray markings at the curve of his hips, and lighter gray traces that moved down the front of his arms and curled up in the center of his palms. Pulling at the sheets, he managed to reveal the lower half of his body, and saw his bare feet peaking out from the ends of his pants also swirled with gray lines.

So he had two Talismans now.

He looked up quickly and caught Lorna's eye; this time she held the gaze.

It was supposed to go to her. I was supposed to use her axe to give it to her, to change it to an Aspect and break the Bloodmagic corrupting it.

But instead, it had gone to him.

"Raven," Davydd said, his half-burned face grimacing naturally, despite the damage to his skin, "there's one more thing."

"What?"

Davydd sighed and glanced at Tomaz. The big man nodded and moved to the vanity along the wall of the circular room. He grabbed something from the top drawer, and turned back to the bed; a small looking glass was grasped tightly in his enormous hands. The giant crossed the room and handed it to him. Raven took it, and slowly brought it up to his face.

Someone stared back at him from the depths of the mirror that he didn't know. It was a man with black hair and black eyes. He had high cheekbones, a narrow chin and a wide jaw. Lines creased the corners of his eyes and mouth, cutting furrows across his forehead and between his brows. His eyes rested deep in his head, and shadows had formed beneath them that were caused by age, not lack of sleep. This man was in his late thirties, possible more.

Raven had aged nearly twenty years.

He looked up and realized they were all waiting for him to say something.

"Well that's... surprising."

No one spoke, and a silence fell on the room that was deep and absorbing. Raven's mind had gone blank, and he just stared off into space for a long moment. Vaguely, he realized he was looking at Tomaz, Leah, and Davydd, all of whom had Aspects of their own now, and all of whom also looked to have aged. At eighteen,

Leah was only a year older than Raven, but now she looked like she was in her mid-twenties. Davydd was older than both of them, and now looked like he was approaching thirty, even barring the fact the whole left side of his body had been blackened and burned. Raven didn't really know how old Tomaz was, though the best guess would put him between forty and fifty. He was the one who looked to have changed the least, but now that Raven was looking for the changes, he saw that there were more wrinkles at the corners of his eyes, and while his thick hair and beard were still coal black, he too had deep furrows cut across his forehead.

It happened the first time I absorbed a new Talisman... the Elders said I had aged seven years exactly. I've taken four now... twenty-eight years in total. Some of that was probably smoothed over by the Ox and the Wolf. Call it at least twenty, though.

A flash of gold winked along the periphery of his vision; he looked over at Davydd once more, and saw again the Fox Talisman traced across his ruined cheek. It was more evidence of Raven's failure to take the burden of the Talismans on himself.

At least that isn't the case with the Wolf. Now I have two, and no one has to deal with either of them. No one has to –

A voice seemed to speak to him from inside his head, and though he knew it wasn't real, he still felt as though his brother Geofred was talking to him.

The Talismans each went to a separate Child for a reason, little brother. They were put into the Crown by Mother for the same reason. It isn't safe to carry them all around unaided. They pull at each other, tear each other apart if forced into one body and one mind. They are not safe – not for anyone.

He pushed the thoughts away. He would deal with them later. He would.

The Wolf wasn't meant for you. Just as your little companions were the Fox, the Eagle, and the Ox, so too is one the Wolf. The transfer was in motion, as it was supposed to happen, as I foresaw it happening. You cannot bear them all yourself –

He cut the voice off and refused to listen to it. The Lion and the Snake Talismans were both still in the hands of the Children. The path was far from clear, and until it was revealed more fully, there was nothing to do but protect the others as much as he could by keeping the Talismans himself. If he could, he would take the others that had already been transferred, but he doubted that was possible.

You will wait and your excuses will pile up, Geofred said, his memories speaking for him from beyond the grave. *You always do this little brother; you always make the same mistake. You cannot do this all yourself, you cannot hold them – not together, not like this. You do not embody all seven Aspects of Man – you embody one. One Aspect, one person. This Aspect is not your burden to bear; the others are not your burden to bear; you have your own, far greater, and if you are weighted down by others, all will fall.*

"You need to give the Wolf Talisman to Lorna."

Raven flinched. It was Leah who had spoken, and she was staring intently at him, unblinking. Their hands were still locked. The callouses on the pads of her fingers were rough against his skin, and she held him in place like a steel trap.

"No," Raven said. "I don't."

He reached over, holding her gaze, and pried his hand from hers. Her expression didn't waver – it was as if she had known he would refuse. He grasped the coverlet and comforter and pushed them back. His forearms still burned, and he realized now it must be the Wolf Talisman still settling into his muscles. He wondered suddenly how long he would have needed to recover if he hadn't taken the new Talisman. Could they even have brought him back?

The thought chilled him, and reaffirmed his decision.

He swung his legs around and rested them on the floor, only pushing himself up to a standing position after taking a deep breath and bracing himself. He managed to keep his back turned and hide his grimace as pins and needles swarmed over his lower body, blood racing to places that had been too long without adequate circulation.

When he faced them, his face was calm and his gaze was steady.

"With the Wolf Talisman, I have more control," he said. "I won't have to repeat what happened with Elder Keri – I won't ever have to risk becoming that *thing* again. Besides, we don't even know how to transfer it."

"So let's work on figuring out how," Davydd said, his eyes narrowing. He was a fearsome sight now, and even Raven, who was used to the physical appearance of Tiffenal, had to fight off intimidation.

"You can work at that all you want," Raven said, matching gazes with him. "But I'm not giving it to her."

"It's *hers*," Davydd said viciously, pointing to his Ashandel.

"Maybe," Raven admitted. "But I need it more than she does."

"Raven," Tomaz rumbled, "let's not do anything hasty."

"This isn't done in haste!"

His outburst was unexpected, even by him. The others all reacted immediately, taking a step back and grasping sword and dagger hilts. He looked around at them, slowly, trying to ignore the betrayal he felt at their reactions. He shouldn't be surprised – the last memory they had of him was as a senseless beast.

"You can't even be in the same room with me anymore without worrying," he said, voice remarkably steady. "By keeping the Wolf, that worry is lifted, at least in part. I can go further, stay awake longer, and even in the middle of a fight I won't have to kill more than I absolutely need to. I can keep the Wolf Talisman safe – and I can help keep all of you, all of the *Kindred*, safe too."

He looked them all in the eye, one by one, or at least tried. Tomaz looked wary, Leah looked resigned, and Lorna was once more staring intently at the carpet.

Davydd's lips had pulled back in disgust.

"I have to do this," Raven said slowly.

"I bet that's how it started with your Mother," Davydd snarled. "She only took the Talismans because she *had* to."

"Davydd!"

They all stared; it was Lorna who had rebuked him. Her head was up and she was frowning at Davydd like a disappointed mother or older sister. "I don't approve of this," she said. "But there is no need for that." Finally, she turned her gaze to Raven, and he saw that she was nothing but calm. Her face was neutral, her eyes simply observing. "You will give it to me when the time comes?"

"He needs to," Leah said softly. "He needs each of the Talismans to become Aspects – that doesn't happen unless he gives them away."

Raven swallowed hard past a lump in his throat.

No. I will not curse anyone with such a thing ever again.

And that was the heart of it. He knew what it was to bear a Talisman. He knew what it would be like for Tomaz and Leah and Davydd once the novelty wore away. For Davydd, it had no doubt already begun. He was burned for life – he would always be this way, affected by the luck he had earned, luck that would make him reckless and drunk with power. Leah would slowly start to lose her mind, finding herself unable to cope with the normal flow of life. Tomaz would gain arrogance with his strength, would begin to seek out ways to use it. He had seen it all happen before – he knew what this kind of power did to those who held it.

They are not us, said the voice of Geofred. *They are not the Children.*

"I will keep it as long as necessary," he said finally.

Lorna's eyes narrowed, but she made no sound of disagreement. Davydd continued to glare at Raven, his eyes, both red and gold, narrowed in the kind of fury usually reserved for men and women of the Empire.

Raven heard the scrape of a boot and the soft hiss of swirling clothing; he looked to the door. Autmaran was there, in a newly stitched red cape, bearing the four golden knots of a Commander on the upper left side of his green tunic. The dark skin of his bald head gleamed in the sunlight that streamed through the window.

"You're awake," he said, examining Raven and taking in the atmosphere of the room. "And I take it you've been reminded of everything that happened."

"You could say that," Tomaz rumbled, stroking his beard.

"Good then," the Commander continued. "The Elders and the Generals are meeting. You've all been requested." He looked at Raven. "All of you."

Chapter Eight:

Council Matters

Raven dressed quickly as the others filed out. He pulled his shirt back over his head, slid a belt through the loops of his pants, and donned his boots and the short coat that hung over them where they sat beside the vanity. He moved as naturally as he could, trying not to let the others see the tension he carried in his sore body. He turned to follow them, but was stopped at the door by Leah.

She watched him carefully, and as she did he realized again how beautiful she was. She had a new scar along the left side of her jaw, one that was healing well. Her black hair was pulled back behind her head today and her green eyes were bright and well-rested. Emotion gripped him with sudden force, and he had to mentally restrain himself from closing the distance and kissing her again. She glanced down at his mouth, the barest flick of her eyes, and he realized that maybe she wanted him to. But now was not the time, and here was not the place.

She's alive... shadows and light, she's alive.

But as the moment lengthened, he realized she was expecting something from him that was far distant from his current contemplation.

"What?" he asked warily.

She pointed to the far side of the room with her chin. He turned to look and saw, held on a small sword rack just out of sight, Aemon's Blade. "The one condition we all agreed on," she said. "You wear it every waking moment. We told the Elders and Generals that Keri was killed in battle, after you defeated the army almost single-handedly. There are rumors everywhere, but only those of us who were there know what happened, and the Kindred on the Wall were too far to see the details clearly."

She must have seen his face darken; she held his gaze, squared her shoulders, and faced him across the doorway.

"I didn't ask you to lie for me," he said.

"You were unconscious," she said, "and not in the frame of mind to ask me much of anything. Besides, this wasn't about you."

"I killed her – of course it was about me."

"Just do it," she snapped. "We need to know you're you."

She left with a last fiery glare. He turned and looked at Aemon's Blade: the white-metal gleam of the sword itself was hidden in a plain leather sheath, but the wrapped copper wire of the hilt glinted in the sunlight streaming through the window. He still remembered drawing it from the ruins of Aemon's tomb. Falling in battle to the Empress while saving the Kindred almost a thousand years before, the Kindred had buried and enshrined Aemon where he lay. The blade had been bound to the fallen hero through Bloodmagic, the same way Leah was bound to her daggers and Davydd to his sword. It meant that Raven, Aemon's only surviving ancestor, was the only one able to touch it, though controlling it the way Leah or Davydd could control their weapons was impossible due to the dozen of generations of blood dilution.

Raven crossed to the Blade and grabbed it, buckling it around his waist in one swift motion. As soon as his hand touch the hilt, a sense of calm descended over him, though it was short-lived. The Blade had always been as much a curse as a blessing, setting him apart from everyone else, marking him out as someone different.

But Leah was right; they needed to know he was himself.

He turned to follow the others, quickening his pace to catch them. The room he'd been given was in the downstairs corner of a mansion, and as they left they passed a grand stairwell and alcoves with various statuettes, carvings, and paintings. Whoever had owned this house had been quite the admirer of mythical creatures; everywhere you turned, there was another half-bird half-something fighting a beleaguered hero.

Which am I – the beast or the hero?

No one spoke as they walked, the only sound their boots clipping against the wooden floor. They passed an open door and Raven saw a man with bandages around his head resting in another bed like his while two others, also heavily wrapped, were doing their best to play cards on a gilded bedside table. Lorna and Davydd began to pull ahead, and as they did Leah and Tomaz specifically held themselves back, walking alongside Raven. The Ranger pair made it through the large marble foyer first, and out the tall double doors of the mansion.

"We'll be there shortly, so I'm going to make this fast," Leah said, breaking the silence only after the distance had widened between the two groups so that there wasn't a chance of the others overhearing. "We need to talk about Geofred's memories. And specifically about – "

"I know," Raven said as they crossed the threshold into daylight. He had to throw up a hand to block his eyes from the sun – it was noon, or close enough, and spring was in full bloom. The poplar trees that lined the streets here had not been damaged by the fighting, and they stood tall and strong. Birds sang from their branches, and a light breeze blew the smell of baking bread to him.

It seemed so wrong to Raven that he almost thought he was dreaming. It was so different from what he remembered happening that night.

Where are all the bodies? Have they all been burned? Nothing else to do with that many… no way to bury them all.

"If you know we need to talk about the memories," Leah said, annoyed at what she seemed to see as an unnecessary interruption, "then let's talk about the memories. What are we going to do? We have to let the others know. At least Davydd, Lorna, and Autmaran."

"Autmaran?" Tomaz rumbled.

"We need seven Aspects to challenge the seven Talismans," she said, launching into full analytical flight. They turned right and made their way down the street. Raven heard Leah speaking, but the words seemed to pass around him like wind over a raven's wing. He could not find it in himself to care very much about anything at the moment – perhaps the shock of what he had done was only just sinking in, or perhaps he still had not completely shook off whatever had happened to him when he'd been... that thing.

Can you ever shake off something like that? Are there things inside us that, once awakened, we cannot put back to sleep?

"Autmaran is the most honest man I know," she was saying. "He never lies, he never says anything but what he feels in his heart, and he is the best judge of character I have ever met. Of course, that's outside of you, Tomaz, but you've already got your Aspect, which means the others are meant for someone else."

"Glad you think so highly of me," he rumbled.

"So he's the Snake," Leah continued. "He is the one who will inherit the Aspect of Truth, or whatever it would be. That is obvious."

She looked to Raven for his input and he shrugged noncommittally. It could be. The Snake Talisman dealt with sensing honesty and truth, and if the corrupted version of it went to Symanta, a master of manipulation, then it would make sense that the pure version would go to an honest man, a man of the people. It could certainly be true.

But it won't come to that. And neither will the Wolf go to Lorna.

"That just leaves transferring the Wolf to Lorna," Leah said as if reading his mind. He stiffened, ready to have the fight again about giving up the Talisman, but it didn't come. He shot a glance at the Exile girl and was relieved to see she was too wrapped up in her own thoughts. He would have to be careful now that she had the Eagle Talisman. She could see the future, though just to what extent it wasn't clear, especially since she had only just inherited the Talisman from Geofred.

If I'm lucky, the Raven Talisman will partially cancel it out. Hopefully she will be prevented from seeing me. On top of that, it took Tomaz months to find a way to reach through his Aspect. Likely she can't even hold on to it longer than a few seconds.

"And what about the Lion?" Tomaz rumbled as they rounded a corner and made their way toward the main Inner City square, where the ruined remains of the Imperial Cathedral could still be seen. Leah grimaced.

"I'm still working on that one," she admitted. "If my father were still alive, or if Elder Crane were here… "

"He may be on his way," Tomaz reminded her. "They sent missives to Vale telling of our victory as soon as the battle was won." Raven heard what the giant hadn't said: "Missives telling of our victory… and Elder Keri's death."

Three Elders are needed to reactivate the sambolin *we retrieved from Tiffenal. With only Spader and Ishmael, all it remains is a fancy dagger.*

The whole reason they had gone to Formaux in the first place was to retrieve the *sambolin* the Prince of Foxes had stolen from the Kindred. The enchanted dagger held all the memories of the Elders who had worn it as Elder of State, and, even more importantly, was one of thirteen pieces that powered the illusions that had kept the Kindred homeland safe. Without the *sambolin,* the illusions had failed, leaving the Exiled Kindred wide open to attack. That was the reason they had invaded in the first place – the Kindred had been left with no other choice. It was either wait for the Empire to descend, or else steal the initiative and march north.

"But that's all beside the point," Leah continued. "What matters is the part of the prophecy Geofred held back from the Tyrant."

"What's this?" Tomaz rumbled. "It's been a week and you didn't tell me you knew something useful?"

"I wanted to wait for Raven," she said. "I've never seen another person's memories before – I wanted to confirm what I saw." She turned to him then, walking backward as she did so that she could more closely monitor his expression. "You saw it too," she said, telling him, not asking. "You saw it."

He just watched her, making no response.

"You know we have a deadline," she continued. "You know we have a chance."

"I know *I* have a chance," he replied.

For a few seconds, she did not respond, but then she swallowed hard and turned back around, her expression shutting down. She'd put her stone face back on. They were approaching the central command post, the one that had been set up during the siege. It now had its sides rolled down and the Kindred flag was flying above it, the rose and sword, flapping in the spring breeze.

"And what do you think you'll do?" Tomaz rumbled.

"I think what I'd like to do is sleep for another week," he responded, rubbing his eyes. "And I also think there are too many loose ends that need to be tied up."

As they circled toward the front, they saw Davydd and Lorna enter the tent before them. As they did, the Eshendai Ranger turned back and looked at them over his shoulder. His burns looked even more fearsome in the light.

Something finally stirred in Raven's chest, and he addressed the other two.

"He... how is he doing? Davydd. How is Davydd doing?"

Leah and Tomaz exchanged a glance, the kind that Raven had become quite used to – neither of them could so much as lift a finger without the other knowing what was meant by it.

"Well," said Tomaz, "he is the type of man that builds up walls of laughter, hoping they will protect him from invading armies."

"So you're saying he's vulnerable?" Raven asked.

"No," Tomaz rumbled. "I'm saying there's hope as long as he's laughing. He's going through hard times – but we all are. And he has his walls up – his laughter. It means he's fighting, and that's good."

"He doesn't seem so happy with me right now."

"He doesn't trust you to give Lorna the Talisman. You know how protective he can be. Give him time."

"But he's right," Raven said with a grimace. "Why should he trust me? I'm just as bad as the other Children. If I lose control again, I lose myself. It's why I kept the Wolf, and why I plan to keep it for as long as possible."

Tomaz stopped and threw out an arm to stop him too. Leah kept walking a few paces, her hands buried inside her coat, looking grim but also unsurprised.

"You having dumb ideas like that is exactly what I was afraid of," the big man rumbled. "And we need to talk about it before we move on."

"Here is neither the time nor the place," Raven said pointedly, and tried to continue walking. The giant stepped easily in front of him, stopping him once more.

"No," the man rumbled with a note of grim formality not unlike the final rock in a landslide settling over a blocked mountain pass. "You need to hear this."

"Hearing what you have to say won't change what I've done," Raven snarled.

Tomaz's eyes widened, and Leah was suddenly attentive; her hands shifted inside her coat, and Raven knew she was clutching the handles of her daggers.

"See?" Raven said. "I can't even get angry without the two of you thinking I'm going to try and kill you. What I did reminded everyone that I'm my Mother's son – it reminded *me*. You can try to forget about it all you want, you can try to pretend I'm just some High Blood runaway like Leah and Davydd, but what I am goes deep, into my *blood*. I am my Mother – not my father."

"Why do you have to be one or the other?" Tomaz rumbled; his black eyes had crinkled at the sides in lines of worry. "Sometimes the greatest strength of men and women comes from a combination of both their evil and their good. There is no pure evil, no pure good, or if there is it is quickly extinguished. Reality is both. There is good in everything, and evil in everything, and it is only given to us what to do with both."

"Then I have more of the evil," said Raven, pushing through the big man's arm on his way to the Council tent. "And that's the way it goes."

Tomaz resisted for a brief instant, but then let go and allowed. Leah fell into step just behind him, her eyes ahead and her face emotionless; she was once again limping slightly, her hands in the pockets of her coat. The heavy, steady tread of Tomaz's gait fell into step behind them, but Raven blocked it from his mind. They reached the tent, and, with a nod to the two guards flanking the entrance, went through.

"Do we know if anyone was able to apprehend Henri Perci?" General Dunhold was asking, not looking up from the maps he was buried in. "Some of these notes are in his personal shorthand and I cannot make them out – will we be able to question him? Perhaps we can find out how deep his treachery goes. There may be more turn cloaks, even Seekers, in our ranks, of which we knew nothing."

"Henri Perci is dead," Raven said. "I killed him."

His voice rang through the tent, even though he hadn't intentionally projected it; the words were flat and emotionless, but the weight of them was palpable and out of all proportion with their simplicity. Autmaran, Davydd, and Lorna had all dispersed to various parts of the tent, and they, along with the remaining Elders – Ishmael and Spader in their respective black and amber robes – and General Gates, in simple green and silver, rounded out the Council.

"And you've already asked that question," Leah said beside him, speaking to the General. "I'd like to remind you that no matter how many times you do, the man will still be dead."

She and Tomaz went to stand by the others, and Raven followed them. As he did, he noticed Spader and Ishmael watching him, scrutinizing every detail of his appearance. Dunhold paused and looked up, then exchanged an unreadable glance with General Gates, who stroked his mustache in agitation. But neither the Elders nor the Generals made a comment – the former simply went back to the maps and notes, while the latter continued to watch. He was suddenly conscious of the fact he looked far too old to be who he was. Certainly some of the way they were looking at him stemmed from that; he doubted they would even recognize him without Leah and Tomaz by his side, and the black-and-gold coat he wore.

What do they know about Elder Keri? What do they suspect?

He pushed the thoughts from his mind. The deed was done, and there was no going back; it mattered little if they knew or not, as long as they continued to follow him.

"Good," Davydd said, breaking the silence with an irreverent smirk. "He was an arrogant, traitorous ass that needed killing, and I'm glad someone did it."

Raven grimaced and hoped it would be taken for a smile, while the images of Henri Perci's life, of his father's dying words, echoed through him. Words he had told Leah so long ago seemed to ring beneath the images of his former rival's life: *I have no desire to know you, and therefore have no desire to kill you.*

He strode to the map table, rolled up the notes and maps covered in Henri Perci's bold, flowing script, and tucked them in to the leather holder full of scraps and useless parchment.

I am the Lord of Death, for my Mother cursed me as such on the day I was born. I know it as you never shall, and my life is tied to it as you should wish yours will never be.

"How do we stand?" Raven asked.

"Well," Dunhold responded. "We stand very well."

"How many did we lose?" he asked, steeling himself for the answer.

"Three thousand seven hundred and twenty-three," Gates said. "The majority from our invasion force, who manned the Wall. There are some still unaccounted for."

"Wounded?"

"Twice that number," Dunhold said, "but many are healing well."

"That doesn't sound 'very well' to me."

"Tell him the good news," Davydd said, leering at Raven.

"The Commons have flocked to us," Gates said, stroking his chin proudly. He even seemed to be grinning in his own odd way. "There are so many of them we've had to ask even the wounded to help train them."

"The Commons?" Raven asked, incredulous.

"Indeed," Dunhold said, handing Raven a sheet of parchment. "And with all the Imperial swords and armor lying about the field, we've even been able to arm them."

Raven glanced down at the sheet, though he knew before seeing the numbers that it didn't really matter either way. *Half-trained peasants don't stand a chance against Rikard, no matter how many of them there are.*

Leah came up beside him and held out her hand. He passed her the rough paper with the spiky, inked numbers, and turned away from her.

"You're certain this is correct?" she asked.

"I had the men count twice," Dunhold said. "I couldn't believe it either."

"That almost doubles our number of infantry."

"What?" Tomaz rumbled, coming forward as well. A single glance at the parchment and the giant let out a very uncharacteristic oath. "How did you convince them to join us? How can this be right?"

"We saved them," Autmaran said simply. "They saw us bring them inside the Wall, and then they saw Dysuna burn their homes. They saw us pull the High Blood from their houses and force them to stand trial as slavers, a penalty that requires death under Kindred law. They saw us seize what was left of the winter grain stores and give them an equal share. And all of that is just in Banelyn – we have hundreds of men and women from Formaux that stole horses and joined us as soon as we'd liberated the city. We also emptied Tiffenal's dungeons, and there were hundreds of Kindred down there – some were too injured to even walk, but half of them had the desire and the ability to burn the whole city down. We convinced them to come here instead."

Autmaran paused, and then looked at them each in turn.

"In the space of three days, we may just have equalized this war."

Raven was shocked. He'd had no idea they were so well off. If everything went perfectly, if they managed to maneuver themselves into an equitable fight with Rikard, then maybe, just maybe, they had a chance at victory.

They have a chance, he reminded himself. *I lose either way.*

"There is something else," Leah said, "something that I pulled from the Eagle's mind. A prophecy concerning Raven and his – "

"Yes," Raven broke in quickly, "I was about to mention that."

She looked at him, surprised and more than a little angered by the interruption, but as he continued she didn't stop him. Her eyes, however, narrowed, and he cursed himself: she knew what he was up to.

"The prophecy she is referring to," he said, "is one that... well, it is useless to repeat it verbatim, it is quite long. But the summary of it is... if we defeat the Empress before the month is out, we will overthrow the Empire."

Leah shot him a glance that was quickly covered over. Her eyes still flashed though, and he could see that she was on the verge of speaking. He caught her gaze and held it.

Do not speak, he thought at her. *For once, let someone else take the lead.*

Her jaw clenched and the fire in her eyes seemed to grow, but then just as quickly her face became stony again and all emotion was gone from it.

I'm going to pay for this later, I can already tell.

"We... we have barely enough time to make it north to Lucien with all our force intact," said Gates, stunned, and completely oblivious to the silent conversation that had just occurred.

"By the Imperial Road it should take us just under two weeks at a forced march," Raven said. "That gives us time to besiege the city."

"Days," Autmaran said, looking stunned. "It gives us *days* to besiege and take the greatest city ever built. Even an optimist would predict *months* before we saw battle."

"And you are also forgetting Lerne," Dunhold said, his staunch, unyielding face full of calculation. "Symanta will be there, and she – "

"Symanta will run for Tyne and the protection of Rikard," Raven said, cutting him off smoothly. "There may be a token force left, and that may cause us grief. They may even be anticipating that we will stop and take the city, allowing them to get between us and Lucien. They think that they are the only one with a deadline."

"They have a... deadline too?" Ishmael rasped from the shadows of the far side of the tent. "What does this mean?"

"It means that they need to kill me," he said simply. "The Empress needs me dead before I reach my nameday, which gives us exactly a month."

"Three weeks," Tomaz corrected. "Twenty-one days as of this morning, if I'm not mistaken."

Silence greeted this pronouncement, as everyone took a moment to absorb it. Raven waited, silently cursing himself for taking so long to recover. Another week could mean the difference between victory and defeat.

"So we win by invading Lucien," Spader said. "And forcing their hand."

"Exactly," Raven confirmed. "They are on their heels – we cannot let up."

"So we won't lay siege to Lerne," Gates said, before clearing his throat. "Will we simply march right by or will you… will you be taking care of it on your own?"

Everyone in the room fell silent and still. No movement was made, no cloth or clothing rustled. Even the wind outside that had been buffeting the tent with lazy, questing fingers, suddenly held back. All eyes turned to Raven, and he felt something rise up in the room that had never been directed at him by this group before: fear. Some had been apprehensive about his presence in Vale before his election, others had questioned his motives, and even Tomaz and Lead had been wary of him on their travel south to Vale so long ago. But now, their gazes held more. They were the companions of Raven, Prince of the Veil, not the creature he held inside of him, and the fear that creature inspired was breathtaking. It was an instinct, a feeling that went deeper than the mind into the bones and the gut, a danger made all the more frightening by its directionless nature, by the senseless way in which it emanated from its source.

It was the kind of fear his Mother inspired.

"No," Raven said quietly, unable to look any of them in the eye, especially Leah and Tomaz, lest he find them with the same look on their faces. "No – that was not what I intended to imply."

He moved to the map table, breaking the silent tension. The wind picked up again and buffeted the tent once more; the others stirred to life and exhaled long-held breaths. Gates and Dunhold exchanged a glance, and so did Ishmael and Spader. But Raven refused to look at Leah and Tomaz, Davydd and Lorna, or even Autmaran.

He finished his cross to the table as General Dunhold moved to allow him room. He quickly brushed aside the top maps that showed only Banelyn and the Elmist Mountains, and pulled out instead a larger map that showed the whole of the northern Empire.

"Here we are in Banelyn," he said. "And here is Lucien, where we need to get." He moved his finger slowly between the two marks he. "The distance is negligible compared to how far it was between Roarke and Banelyn, and if we skirt Lerne here, which is only a few days to the north, we have plenty of time via the main road."

"The main road?" Dunhold asked. "Are you sure?"

"Yes," Raven said, suppressing annoyance. "The main road. The Imperial Road."

"Won't it be easier for Rikard to find us that way?"

"Tyne is on the other side of the Elmists," Raven said, pointing to the map. "Likely he was waiting for word of a successful trap; he may not even know the details of what's happening."

"I think he might," Autmaran said. "We caught as many of the Seekers as we could, but I doubt we got them all when they fled the underground caverns. We cleaned them out – Leah and Davydd made sure we didn't miss anything."

"And there's the influx of new recruits," Leah said. "Some will be spies."

"There's no way to tell which are really members of the Commons," Raven agreed. "Fine – it doesn't matter. Either Rikard knows or he doesn't, but that only underlines the importance of leaving Banelyn now."

"Now?"

"Please don't continue making me repeat myself, Dunhold," Raven said quietly. To his surprise, the General paled and straightened up immediately.

"Yes, my prince."

Raven forced himself not to grimace – he had to be more careful with his reprimands. If he said something too harsh the man might pee himself. "Send the word out," he said, looking at everyone in the tent one by one. "Tell your troops, and all the Commons. We leave at dawn."

"Where shall we tell them we are going?" Gates asked.

"To Lucien," Raven said softly. "To kill a god."

His words sent a shiver around the room, and a silence descended on them all as they contemplated the road that lay ahead.

The final road. One way or another.

"Please leave me," Raven said. "I would like the room to myself."

Slowly, the others nodded. Davydd and Lorna were the first to leave; the fiery-eyed Eshendai did not salute or acknowledge Raven at all, though Lorna nodded as she passed. Autmaran was next, nodding as well, his face unreadable; Gates and Dunhold saluted and left together, already speaking to each other in clipped, rushed sentences before the tent flap had fallen back into place. Elders Ishmael and Spader followed, though they waited until after leaving to speak.

Tomaz was the last, and he left only reluctantly. For a long moment, Raven wasn't sure why he looked the way he did – as if he were worried for the Prince's safety. And then Leah rounded on Raven, and he understood.

"What was that about?" she hissed. "You know as well as I do that that wasn't all I wanted to say. Don't you dare try to dismiss this as unimportant – *they need to know!*"

"No, they don't!" Raven hissed back just as fiercely, shocking Leah and making her take a step back in surprise. He didn't blame her – his mood felt slippery, and he wasn't even sure himself if the next moment would find him angry, numb, or weeping.

"The only people who need to know are those whom it concerns – and only when it concerns them. For now, only you and I need to know, and that is fine."

"But what about the Elders?" Leah continued. "The *Generals?* How can they plan for something they don't know about? You know this means we will be attacked at every turn – you will be hunted by Death Watchmen, Seekers, *anything* the Empire can throw at you! Geofred had them convinced it was under control, but it wasn't, and now that the Empress *knows* you're still alive, she will come for you – she *has* to. This isn't about a battle or even a war for her – "

"*I know,*" he said intently, stepping forward so that their bodies were almost touching. Now that they were the only ones left, Raven realized that this was the first time they had been truly alone since she had kissed him goodbye before he'd left for Formaux. He saw the realization flash behind her eyes as well, and for a moment they both rocked forward on their heels, about to touch.

She reached out a hand and gently cupped the side of his face, tracing the line of his chin and cheekbone with her thumb and pinkie. He felt her skin rasping against the scruff of his unshaven face and hoped she didn't mind. He reached out to touch her face as well, to bring her closer, to remind both her and him that in spite of everything that had happened, they were still the same.

But at the last moment, Raven remembered what had happened to him, and knew things weren't the same. He looked old enough to be her *father* now – he had lived enough lives to be her *grand*father a hundred times over.

He stepped back, disgusted with himself, and saw the hurt and confusion in her eyes, but before she could voice her question, before she could speak and force him to air his insecurities, he spoke instead. "The Generals are less than useless," he said. "Both of them are in far over their heads, and with the death of Commander Wyck and what we learned about Oleander and Perci, I cannot trust them. Gates and Dunhold will stay behind when we attack – they'll hold in the Elmist Mountains should we need to retreat. They are defenders and ambushers – we will use them for that. As for the Elders... I don't know where their loyalties lie after Keri's death. I cannot confide in them. We need to march north, to attack and defeat Rikard and force a fight with Lucien – one way or another, we need to *end this,* or it will never be over. I may survive, but we both know the Kindred will not. They may not die today, they may not die for a hundred years more, but if we do not do this now, if we do not end it one way or another, the Empress will. We must… we must end it. Forever."

He swallowed past the lump in his throat. He looked up at her and saw she had masked her pain. "We need to tell them," she insisted again, this time gently. "Why do you always have to bear everything yourself, alone? They know the Empress needs to kill you before your nameday, why does it hurt to tell them you have to kill her?"

"Because it hurts *me* to even *think* about it!"

He felt tears of frustration well up in the corners of his eyes and he bit back his words, pulling his emotions back, keeping them hidden. "Because if I tell them the only way they survive is if I kill my Mother, then they'll make me do it," he said. "Because then it will become real."

"You have to know they already expect it of you," she said, coming closer again, nearly touching him. "They expect you to fight her. No one else can."

Raven's jaw began to cramp and he tried to loosen it. "No," he said. "They know we need to defeat her before I turn eighteen, and they know she needs to kill me. They may guess that will face her, maybe even hope for it, but that is different. They don't need to know the rest – not now. Maybe never."

He caught her gaze and held it. His hand twitched in an unconscious desire to grab her hand again, to hold her the way she had tried to hold him just now. He realized suddenly how much everything had affected him, and the sudden desire to run away and never stop invaded every corner of his mind. It did not help that he could see it from the outside, did not help that he knew he was acting out of fear and irrationality. She was right, but he could not admit it. His hands began to shake and his vision blurred, and suddenly he was back in that dark night. Images of spraying blood and flashing lightning rocked him, and the sensation of tearing and ripping bodies hit him with such force and vividness that he was half convinced it had happened only seconds before.

Leah touched his shoulder, and he flinched away.

"We leave at dawn," he said, and left.

Chapter Nine:

The Clock Ticks

Raven spent the rest of that day alone. He returned to the bedroom laid aside for him and told the Healers using the other rooms to use it for the wounded. They resisted at first, but he refused to listen. It was a large room, and before he left he saw that they had fitted two women with missing limbs into the bed, and two men, who were heavily bandaged but able to walk, on piles of blankets on the floor.

It wasn't hard for him to clear out of the room – he owned nothing besides what he wore, and the ceremonial armor of his office was stowed inside the closet. The pieces of his former kit were scattered over the battlefield, and not all of them had been found, so the armorers had simply made him a new one. It was identical to the last: hard steel, somehow dyed black, with golden scrollwork along the edges. He had the full suit – chainmail, breastplate, great helm, gauntlets, greaves, a leather jerkin to go beneath it all, and a full black cloak to be worn on top. It was much less ornate than most of the ceremonial armor he had seen worn throughout the Empire, but for the Kindred it was downright opulent. They asked him if he wanted to put it on, to wear it when he went out to see the Kindred. He declined, and told them to send it to the command tent. Before they left, though, he pulled out the long cloak and hid himself in its depths.

He walked the streets of Banelyn aimlessly for a time, keeping to himself. In the huge square outside the ruins of the Cathedral of the Empress, he saw rank after rank of Exiled Kindred training the stronger of the Commons in cobbled-together armor how to hold a sword. A number of the Eshendai had taken it upon themselves to teach short-sword and knife fighting to the more dexterous women who didn't have the musculature to hold a broadsword. Still others, those who did not rank high in dexterity or strength but seemed at least coordinated enough to keep the pointy end of a weapon faced toward the enemy, were being trained with spears and pikes.

Raven moved on, keeping to the shadows of the buildings. The hood of his long cloak was up, and without his bulky armor he was able to avoid most detection. Some who saw him pointed to him, questioning others nearby about his identity, but no one approached. The city was full of refugees, soldiers, and a general chaos that prevented anyone from wanting to get too involved with others. Everyone had their own urgent tasks to perform – worrying about the troubles of another who clearly didn't want company would only compound everyone's problems.

He wandered farther away from the Inner City, aimless. He soon found himself in Banelyn City proper, the area between the Inner City and what had once been the Outer City on the other side of the Black Wall. At random, he chose a path away from the center of the city's middle tier that went through a series of pleasant, well-kept houses with tall trees and green grass. He saw an entrance to an alleyway up ahead, between a row of houses of startling height. They towered above the surrounding structures, and while they weren't the gilded monstrosities of the Most High, they must certainly have belonged to the Elevated, those who had risen just high enough to leave the title of Commons behind. Raven moved toward the alleyway, only pausing in his stride when he heard noise further in. He almost turned around and walked away, but stopped when he heard voices.

"We can't leave him here."

"We have to – and we have to silence him. He knows too much."

"Killing would look more suspicious."

"He is fallen from the Path; convenience comes second to righteousness."

"Yes... and the Empress would be better served by us staying concealed. He knows enough to be dangerous."

"Indeed. They know there are Seekers; others who would defect have already been killed. One more death in a random alley will give them nothing."

"Very well. Make sure the gag is tight – finish it before someone comes."

"Hold," Raven said.

The two men, one short and one tall, jerked around at his voice. They were the epitome of average, which was to be expected. They both had nondescript brown hair, skin slightly blotchy from the sun, and simple clothing that was well mended but threadbare. Raven almost reached out through his Talisman to get a sense of their lives, but stopped himself. Instead, he drew on the Wolf Talisman, and felt warmth spread from the base of his spine down his legs and arms to pool in his feet and hands.

"Back away," the taller one said. He pulled out a punching dagger – the kind used most by Seekers, with a simple handle grip below a razor-sharp three-inch blade.

The fight that followed was over very quickly. Raven ducked the tall man's first blow, locked his elbows, and then rocked the man back with a vicious upward palm strike to the chin. Tallman staggered backward, unable to see straight, and Raven spun, smashing a booted heel against the man's temple, knocking him out cold. The man's companion, Shortman, swallowed hard, and tried to turn and run. Raven simply knelt, picked up Tallman's punching dagger, and threw it in a quick sideways shot. It sunk into the back of Shortman's knee, and he collapsed to the ground with a cry of pain.

Raven walked up to him as he tried to crawl away. With a sigh, Raven rounded the man as he tried to rise, and kicked him as well, smacking his head into the pavement at just the right angle, knocking him out cold.

He then retrieved Tallman's dagger from Shortman's knee, and went to the former subject of their attentions. He bent down and untied the gag from the mouth of the young man. He couldn't be more than fourteen. Raven gripped the punching blade and sliced the ropes that bound him.

"Find Leah Goldwyn," he said to the man, grabbing him by the collar. "Tell her what happened, and say that Raven, Prince of the Veil, sent you."

The youth, dumbfounded, could only swallow hard and nod. Raven stayed where he was, squatting on his heels, covered in his black cloak. It was quite clear the boy now knew to whom he was speaking.

"I just saved your life," Raven said. "Don't make me come find you."

The boy turned and ran, crashing into a building that jutted out slightly further than the others before escaping up the alley.

Odds he'll actually go to her?

He should have escorted the boy himself. Based on what he had overheard, he suspected that the boy had been something of an apprentice Seeker who had tried to back out. If it was true, he could be very valuable.

This war isn't going to be won based on how many Seekers we catch.

The sound of running footsteps disappeared, and Raven stayed where he was. He glanced at the two downed men, the two Seekers. If he had to guess, he'd say they would be out for hours. Still, he took the time to cut cloth from their robes and bind them. When he was finished, he looked up and noticed the roofs here were fairly low to the ground. If he wanted to, he could climb up to the top and even scale the height of the next building over, one of the towering Elevated houses.

He decided he wanted to, so he climbed.

He let go of the Wolf Talisman as he did, and the feeling of power and energy left him. Life dulled out, even though the sun was still in the sky; the bricks of the building were rough under his hand, coarse enough that his skin felt scraped raw by the time he ascended to the top of the first roof. He kept going, using a balcony to pull himself up onto the second building, then grabbing hold of an ornamental outcropping and swinging to a set of decorative buttresses that stuck out over the alley. With a final rush of breath, he rolled over the edge of an eave and found himself on a simple, slightly slanted roof made of flat shingles. He was breathing hard, and the honest strength it had taken to get him there made him feel good. His heart thumped fiercely in his chest, and he wished vaguely that he could just keep climbing. The exercise had driven the memories from him for a time; he could use more of that.

He looked around and was surprised to find that he could see all the way from the Inner City to the Black Wall. The ring of blacksmith hammers came to him on the light breeze that blew through the city, the sound mingled with strains of birdsong and underscored by shouts and clangs from the makeshift training ground. The smell of baking flatbread floated up as well, combined with the earthy smell of smoked meat – the camp cooks must be making as much food as they could before they left the city.

He walked up to the apex of the slanting roof and squatted down on his heels. He pulled back the hood of his cloak. The sun had begun to dip quite noticeably toward the distant horizon; he watched it sink, lower and lower, feeling the warmth of it, warmth only partly moderated by the last of winter's chill.

Time passed, and the sounds of the city changed. The orders to pack up and leave the following dawn had gone out, and he heard soldiers moving through the streets to form up outside the gates in tents so as to be ready for the march. He realized that he was muttering something under his breath and stopped. He swallowed nervously as he realized what he'd been saying, glancing around the rooftop, though he knew that there was no one there.

It was the prophecy Geofred had given him through his memories. He had waited as long as he could, put it off as long as possible; he had to confront it now. He began to recite the words under his breath, unable to keep them unspoken any longer.

There will be a seventh child, a child not worthy of your line - Keep him! Do not cast him out, but around his arms bind your power; raise him as your own until his seventeenth name day, in which year he shall be both key and lock to your ambition. Upon that day, and not till then, take his life, for if he lives, so fall the other six Princes of Strife; should he live, he will bring about the rise of Light, but should he die, the fall of Night. That living Seventh Child shall seek to inherit the Kingdom of the Veil, and should he claim his right, all your strength shall fail. But if, before the year is out, the child is dead beyond a doubt, you shall reign forever on,

For all who might oppose you shall be gone.

He stopped, feeling the pause, knowing that this was as much as his Mother had ever heard. But there was more, and the rest of it cast the whole into a new light. He continued on, going slowly, feeling the words roll out and tasting them as they did:

But with such chance comes perils too, for he, in equal measure, strives for you. If you go down this path so dark, you yourself shall bear a mark; for as you seek to seal your reign, so he will come to end his pain. A Mother's vow lives in her son, and if you find that bond undone, the sword you use cuts many ways, and seals you both to a term of days. If he dies before he comes of age, then you will return beyond the waves; but in that time he has the chance, to bring you death in a final dance. Until it is finished, up and down, you need always fear a return with sword and crown; for as he is your key and star, so too is he your bane and bar; and on that day he turns eighteen, either he, or you, shall reign supreme.

He stood up and moved along the rooftop.

There was a ripple of motion at the edge of his vision, and he froze, standing completely still. Hidden as he was by his cloak and the shadows, he thought maybe he would remain unseen, but it wasn't so. He'd been spotted – the form was approaching him. He turned to look, readying for another fight, and saw only a young boy. The boy looked to be maybe nine or ten, maybe older; Raven should know, but he couldn't remember. He had saved the boy's life during the winter he had spent among the Kindred, and when the boy's father had died, Tym had stolen away with the army as it had marched north. Ever since then, Tym had acted as a camp runner, fetching and delivering messages, particularly for Davydd Goldwyn, who had a soft spot for the boy.

"Prince Raven, sir," he began, his blue eyes shifting nervously back and forth under his cap of fine blonde hair as he panted hard, trying to regain his breath. Raven thought about the climb and was impressed the boy had made it all the way up here. "Ms. Leah said to thank you for the Seeker you sent her."

Raven nodded and smiled, a quick flick of his lips.

"And Mr. Davydd told me to say they're on their way."

Raven froze, feeling tension creep back into his shoulders. "What?"

"They – they're on their way here. Mr. Davydd said they wanted to talk."

"Who is 'they,' Tym?"

"Oh – Commander Autmaran, Mr. Davydd, Ms. Leah, Mr. Tomaz, and Ms. Lorna. They didn't tell me if they wanted me to stay. I can go if you like."

"All of them... you're sure, Tym?"

"Yes, sir," he said, looking confused. "I wouldn't say it if it wasn't true."

Raven nodded slowly, and tried to keep the sick, rising dread from overwhelming him. He wanted to run. "Thank you, Tym."

Tym nodded and turned to go, but stopped at the edge of the rooftop.

"Um, Prince Raven, sir, how do I get down?"

The boy looked back at him and Raven suddenly realized the boy's hands were shaking, and his eyes were so wide they showed white all the way around. He only wore a light tunic and brown pants and boots, and between the breeze and the height, the boy looked frozen half to death with fear and cold.

"Come with me," Raven said, taking off his cloak and wrapping it around the boy's shoulders. He strode to the edge of the roof and looked down, careful not to step on any loose shingles. There was no easy way down, not for the boy. Raven could do it, but not Tym. "How did you even get up here?" he asked.

Tym shrugged, and shivered violently in a particularly vicious gust of wind.

"Right," Raven said, reaching for the Wolf Talisman inside him. The energy came flowing through him once more; it was so different from the raw, jerking motion of the Raven Talisman. The Wolf built up slowly, like a finely wrought machine, humming along until it was at full speed and strength, ready to go for as long as necessary.

"Hold on tight," Raven said, as he picked Tym up. The boy let out a startled cry, and looked terribly distraught, but Raven ignored that. No doubt Tym thought he was dirtying Raven by touching him, or some such nonsense. The boy was far too polite, and twice as stuffy as the Most High.

Raven stepped off the roof, into empty air.

Tym screamed, and Raven held him tightly as he directed himself, making sure to aim his feet at the ground as best he could. They fell in seconds the distance it had taken Raven half an hour to climb, and when they struck the ground, small fissures cracked through the dirty pavement of the alleyway. The shock ran through Raven's legs, followed by intense, burning pain. He gasped as the sensations flooded him, but even as the pain broke across his body, shouting at him that he was injured, the feeling faded, and the wounds healed. Raven could feel the gray light rushing there, soothing the pain like a salve on burned skin.

"Impressive," drawled a voice.

Raven looked up and saw Davydd walking into the entrance of the alley, Lorna, Tomaz, Leah, and Autmaran all close behind him.

"M-Mr. Prince Raven, sir? C-can I g-get down?"

Raven knelt and set Tym on the ground. The boy walked a few paces away from him, looking unsteady and shaky, but on the whole just fine. He pulled off the over-large black cloak and handed it back to Raven.

"Th-thank you for the drop, Prince Raven. H-here's your cloak."

"You can keep it, Tym," Raven said, knowing the boy was still likely freezing. The sun had just dipped below the edge of the Black Wall and the air was rapidly cooling. The full heat of summer was still a few months away, and while sunlight warmed the days, spring chill still ruled the nights.

"I'm OK, thank you, Prince Raven," Tym said, handing the cloak back. Raven took it, standing up slowly as Tym took another few steps back, watching him carefully.

"We need to talk," Davydd drawled from the opposite end of the alleyway.

Raven didn't respond. He threw the cloak around his shoulders and tied it back in place before settling the hood on his head once more. The cold receded, and he felt warm and comfortable again.

"Did you hear me, princeling?"

"He heard you," Tomaz rumbled, pushing past the Eshendai Ranger, "all of Banelyn heard you." The giant strode down the alley, and Raven felt a small piece of trepidation settle in his stomach. The big man might be twenty years older than him, but Tomaz was still his best friend. Had things changed between them?

Tomaz finished crossing the distance and smiled through his dense beard, clapping Raven on the shoulder with a hand that could easily encompass the Prince's entire head. "I've missed our sparring sessions," he rumbled.

Raven felt a swell of relief and let out an unconsciously held breath. The Blade Master had his own history, Raven knew, but he was still under no obligation to side with him. He smiled weakly up at the big man, but said nothing.

"We can catch up later," Autmaran said, though not unkindly. His tone was businesslike, not antagonistic. "For now, we need to talk, where the Elders and the Generals cannot hear us."

Raven nodded slowly, looking at them all. The alley seemed much more narrow now that it was crowded.

"I see you took care of the Seekers," he said, ignoring Autmaran's invitation to speak about what had happened at the gate. Tallman and Shortman were both gone, the only remaining sign a small trail of blood from where Raven had thrown the knife into Shortman's knee.

"We did," Leah said promptly. "Thank you for that."

He caught her eye, but saw nothing there. She had her stone face on again.

"We need to talk about what's going to happen," Autmaran continued, stepping forward, separating himself from Davydd, Lorna, and Leah, and resting his back against the nearby brick wall. He shuffled his arms out of his red cape and crossed them over across his chest, the motion pulling at the tight-fitting black coat he wore.

"You mean the Prophecy," Raven said.

"He does indeed," Davydd drawled.

"What do you want to know?" Raven asked, suddenly too weary to care.

"We want to know what we can expect from the Empress," Autmaran said. "What will she send at us to get you?"

"Everything."

"And is there any way to prevent that?" the Commander continued. "What would she send after you if you ran?"

"Everything," he repeated. "And no, there's no way to prevent it."

"What do you mean?" Lorna asked from the shadows behind Davydd.

"I mean that if I run, I will likely only end up fulfilling the prophecy," Raven said, managing to keep his voice level. "I mean that if I run, the Empire will send everything they have straight for us. Death Watchmen, Seekers, the remaining Children, maybe even the Visigony. Every trap, every sentinel will be activated throughout the Empire, and in the end it will make no difference for them. If we run, they track me down, and kill me anyway. There's no place I can hide now – no illusions to get behind. We either fight together with a chance to win, or we fight separately and die."

"What is the prophecy?" Tym asked quietly, and they all looked at him in surprise, none of them having noticed he had stayed behind. The young boy became flustered by the attention; his cheeks grew red and he cast his bright blue eyes down at the floor. "Sometimes words are important... I just thought you ... I'm sorry I spoke."

"It's all right, Tym," Davydd said. "It's a good point."

"This is a conversation for adults," Raven said suddenly, not knowing why, "not children. Get him out of here."

They all stared at him, mouths comically agape. All except for Leah, who rolled her eyes in exasperation. "Shut up, princeling. You're starting to sound like Henri Perci."

Raven stiffened; he couldn't have been more surprised if she'd physically struck him. In fact, he probably would have been *less* surprised if she'd physically struck him.

"Everyone needs to calm down," Tomaz rumbled slowly, from behind Raven. "We've all been through several layers of hell, and we're still in the middle of a war. Everyone has a right to be tired, indignant, and scared. But we're people, not beasts. Control yourselves; be civil. We're all that's left now."

"There are still the Elders," Lorna interjected softly, though Raven noticed she said it more as if the point had to be brought up, not as if she believed it.

"There are," Tomaz acknowledged. "And they are important. But we hold the Aspects, and it is us who need to finish this war. It is us who will lead the charge."

"It is," Raven admitted. "But why does that mean we need to keep talking? There's only one thing we can do – go north, as fast and as hard as we can. I thought we'd already settled this."

"We still have things left to discuss," Leah said, her face a thunderhead of anger, but her voice steady and driving. "The first is the Return."

"The... what?" asked Autmaran. "Did you borrow something?"

"There is something happening," she said, "something that Geofred had in mind when he died, and something that is all throughout his memories. Something called the Return – and I don't understand it. But it's why the Empress is doing all of this – it's why she tried to kill Raven in the first place."

"We don't know that for sure," Raven said evenly.

"Shadows and fire, princeling!" she exclaimed, startling them all. "Yes, we do! Now stop being a *twit* and own up to what we *both know!*"

Raven realized his lips had curled up in anger. They didn't need to know all of this – all they needed to know was enough to get them to Lucien. If things needed to be explained afterwards, then so be it. But the more they knew now, the more danger they were in, and the more they would fear what was to come.

"*We. Don't. Know. That. For. Sure,*" he repeated, driving each word. "I have the same holes in the memory that you do. The Return – it's something that's been talked about for ages in only the broadest terms. It's a legend, nothing more."

"What is the legend?" rumbled Tomaz.

"That someday the Empress will return to the land She came from," Davydd said, surprising everyone. "That She will leave behind an Heir to rule this land, one of the Children, and She will Ascend back to the land from beyond the sea, where She will become the last and final Heir of Theron Isdiel."

He looked at Raven, the blackened half of his face and his new golden eye mocking the prince. "There are too many of us who have these memories now, princeling," he said frankly. "You can't keep things hidden anymore – we all have a piece of the puzzle. Like it or not, we're in this together."

"Fine!" Raven snapped. "That's the legend – don't interrupt me now, you want me to speak about it, I'll bloody speak about it!" Leah, Davydd, and Autmaran had all made noises as if they would speak, but at the Prince's outburst, they quieted again. "What Davydd says is true. It is a legend, a myth. I have never heard the Empress speak of it, and I have never heard any of the other Children speak of it expect in mockery of each other's ambitions, but the idea persists. It is not true – it is a creation myth, the idea that she came from another place and will someday return there. It's ridiculous."

"Finished?" Autmaran asked dryly. Raven almost lashed out again, but reined himself in at the last moment. "Yes," he replied, "for now at least."

"Good – then it's my turn," the Commander said. "It is easy enough for me to say that there is something more to this than myth."

Raven scoffed and turned his back on the man.

"Don't you *dare* turn your back on me!" Autmaran roared at the top of his voice, and the Prince froze in shock. The man was glaring at him now. "I stood for you and made you Prince. I stood for you when even you didn't think you could do this. I believed in you from the very beginning. And now I have lied to the Elders about what happened to Keri, because when I saw that monster you'd become, I knew, in my heart of hearts, that that beast could *never* be the man I have come to respect, the man I would gladly follow into battle. So you owe me an explanation. You owe it to all of us. We have every right to know what you are getting us into, and we have every right to know what the Empire is planning, so start talking, you sniveling, whining brat!"

For a moment, Raven could only stare in shock, but then anger flared up in him too, a black flame that burned. His hand fell to the hilt of Aemon's Blade.

Immediately, the others were all in motion. Tomaz put a hand on Malachi and interposed himself between Raven and Autmaran; Davydd, with his glowing eyes, was spinning a white dagger in his hand and eyeing Raven's neck; Autmaran had thrown his red cape over his arm to use as a defense, and drawn his short sword backhand; Lorna, still missing her axe, had simply settled into a grappling stance.

But it was Leah who reached him first, and it was she who stopped him in his motion. All she did was reach down and touch his hand, and as the pads of her calloused fingers grazed his skin, the anger left him. The human contact almost made him break down, and he had no idea why. He was losing control of himself.

"What happened when you turned?" she asked quietly.

The words and the tone calmed him, and the tension left his arm. His hand fell to his side, away from the hilt of Aemon's Blade. It was suddenly very hard to breathe. "I don't remember," he mumbled, very unconvincingly.

Leah stepped closer, and he turned his head away from her, looking toward the entrance to the alley, doing everything he could to keep himself from acknowledging her. It was too much – she was too close, she shouldn't be doing this where others were around. Her hand climbed from his hand, tracing the curve of his arm, until it rested on his shoulder. She was close enough that he could smell her, that lavender scent, and beneath it the clean warmth that was all her own.

"Tell us what happened," she said softly, though loud enough that the others could hear. "You don't need to worry; you don't need to be hard. The Generals are gone; the Elders are gone. It's *us*. Your... your family. Your true one."

His eyelids were so heavy they closed on their own, and when they reopened it was as if some huge rush of energy had gone out of him. His shoulders slumped, and his eyes felt like they'd sunk back in their sockets.

"It was... freeing." His voice was soft, and almost disappeared in the thin air of the alleyway. "I'm always so worried that I'll become my Mother, always so worried that what I'm doing might not be right. I hate that Kindred die because of me; I hate that Imperials die because of me. I hate death, and yet I'll never be rid of it. I worry every minute of every day if I'll be good enough to see this through, if I'm making the right decisions, if I'm dooming us all."

He swallowed hard, and blinked rapidly against stinging eyes. But the words continued to flow; the dam had burst, and it was impossible to stop it now.

"And when I finally let go, when I finally let it all just take me over, it was the first freedom I've known in my entire life. I just gave in, and everything was taken away. Everything felt *right*, and if I wanted to do it, then I did it. If I wanted to kill, I killed. I had no conscience, and I cut down everything that stood in my way. I felt *just*. I felt *righteous*. And I never wanted it to end."

He stopped and drew a deep breath, staring far beyond them now, into the few memories and sensations he could piece together.

"I felt like my Mother must feel every day," he finished, before lapsing into a long period of silence. "And then I killed the closest thing to a true mother I've ever had," he continued, looking at them finally. None of them could meet his eye now, not even Leah or Tomaz. "I killed her, and you're acting like it didn't happen. I killed one of the *Elders*, ruining our best chance of restoring the illusions around Vale that keep the Kindred safe. A woman loved by everyone, a symbol of Kindred goodness and strength, and everything that's good and kind in this world. I *killed* her. And you pretend it didn't happen. You tell me it doesn't matter – that I didn't do it. Then how do I remember it? How do I know what it felt like to sink my fingers into her and rip her apart? That's in my head – it's my head! That memory! I... it's... "

He trailed off as anger, guilt, and shame all came together and choked him. He looked around at them, his whole body quivering with the effort it took to hold back the full force of his emotions. But still none of them could meet his eye, and none of them could acknowledge what he was saying. They didn't want to believe it was true.

"SAY SOMETHING!"

His voice echoed up and down the alleyway, almost unnaturally loud. Each of them flinched as if he had struck them, and he realized his hands were balled into fists and his teeth were bared. His fingers and legs felt cold, but heat seemed to radiate from his chest and face, so hot his skin felt like it was burning.

"I did it. I lost control, and I *liked* it. That was me in that body, that creature is buried in me *right now* waiting for another chance to get out. So say something. Say *something*. Shout at me. *Strike* me. Please. Please!"

Still, they didn't speak, and still they looked away.

"LOOK AT ME!"

And they did, his words lashing them into action. Fury radiated from him still, fury that was as much directed at himself as at anything else. The silence lengthened, going on forever, and suddenly Raven felt a certainty come over him that none of them would speak, that none of them could forgive him now. He had finally done it – he had crossed the line, and whatever it was that they had had together was broken.

Davydd stepped forward. "Fine," he said, looking at the others, standing now in the no-man's-land that had formed between them and Raven. "Fine," he said again.

He took a deep breath, and they all watched him with apprehension.

"You're a dick."

The silence that followed this pronouncement was profound indeed.

"Seriously," he continued in earnest, his tone completely at odds with the mood of the gathered group. "You've done a lot of things since I've known you, and most of them have been at least half dickish. A few have been full-on assholic."

He took another step forward, standing tall, the burned half of his face making the gold of his left eye stand out brilliantly. "But you've also led us through some shadow-cursed awfulness. And for the most part, that dickishness has paid off. Don't misunderstand me, you're still a bastard for keeping the Wolf Talisman for yourself – it's Lorna's, and everyone knows that – and yes, what you just said makes me question your sanity. But I refuse to believe you would have done what you did if you were in your right mind. I have no doubts about you being a good person. Doubts about your decision making process, not to mention your haircut and wardrobe choices? Sure. Doubts about whether or not you're good enough for my sister? Definitely. But doubts about whether or not you're the right man to lead us through this and get most of us out the other side? No. Never."

He took another step forward, and thrust a finger toward Raven as if he were trying to pin him in place.

"So if you want a promise from me, then I'll make you one. I will never turn on you. *Never*. But if that *thing* comes out of you again – and yes, it is a *thing*, completely and distinctly separate from you – then I will do everything in my power to end its life and yours before it kills another person."

Raven felt a surge of anger mixed with pure, unadulterated relief course through him. That promise was what he'd wanted, and he hadn't even realized it until the man had said it. He swallowed hard once more, his throat dry and closed off. The silence lengthened between them as Davydd continued to stand where he was, letting his pronouncement hang heavy in the air between them.

"Thank you," Raven said softly. Davydd nodded.

"You're still a dick, though," he repeated.

"Yes, I understand that part," Raven said.

"Just want to be clear."

"Right."

He shifted awkwardly, and then spoke abruptly, his voice scratchy and hoarse, over the man's shoulder to the others. "Now you. All of you swear the same thing."

"Princeling," Tomaz began.

"Raven," Leah said, "the Blade – "

"*No*," he cut them off. "You swear, or we're done. I could lose the Blade, could lose one of you, could lose my mind. So you swear, or none of you comes near me again. I can't let it happen. *We* can't let it happen. You want me to trust you? Then fine – I'm trusting you. If you want me to be your Prince, then you need to swear you won't let that beast hurt another Kindred. Swear that you will kill me if I even come close."

For a long moment, no one spoke, moved, or even seemed to breathe. And then a small, lonely voice broke the silence.

"I don't know if I'd be able to," Tym said. "But Mr. Davydd told me what happened after Ms. Lorna told him, and... I see why it's important, Prince Raven, sir, so I promise. I – I promise to do it. I promise."

The boy was shaking slightly, and Raven knew he must still be cold, but even more so frightened. His fine blonde hair swayed back and forth as he earnestly tried to meet Raven's eyes, between sneaking glances at the others.

"Thank you, Tym," Raven said softly.

"I swear as well," Autmaran said, just as softly. The others shifted as he walked over to stand next to Davydd. "But only if you swear to set this behind you and continue leading the army. Continue leading *us*."

Raven swallowed again, thinking about what it would be like to live in a world where he dared say 'no.'

"You have my word," he said, instead.

"Then I swear, too," Lorna said.

"You already have my word," Davydd reminded him.

"Shadows and fire, princeling," Leah swore, suddenly turning and kicking the brick wall nearest her. She stood staring at it for a long moment, shaking her head, biting her lip. The open display of emotion was almost shocking on her.

"Very well," Tomaz rumbled, and as he said the words he caught Raven's gaze, and they shared an unspoken agreement, the kind that only exists between best friends: Tomaz would do it, and he would make it clean.

"Fine," Leah growled out, turning back, her hands on her hips as she paced back and forth. "Fine – I swear. But only, *only* if there's no other way. And I will be there, all the way until the end, making sure of it."

"Agreed," Raven said, and a huge weight lifted off his shoulders. "Thank you."

"Don't thank me yet," murmured Davydd. "I might just enjoy doing it."

"Now they need to know," Leah said, ignoring her brother and speaking to Raven. "They need to know everything – everything we know, everything we pulled from Geofred, and what you and Davydd pulled from Tiffenal."

Raven looked at her for a long moment, and then nodded.

"First," she said immediately, still pacing, "the first prophecy speaks of the Return. That's why the Tyrant wanted you killed, we both know it. She thinks it's real – how is she going to try to make it happen? What are her plans?"

"I don't know," Raven said. "I don't know. No one knows, like I said. But what I do know is that there are plans in motion to do… something. Geofred saw blood and death, huge waves of it, but I can't understand any more than that. But I do know that killing me is about the Return, and more than that, securing her rule for another thousand years through one of the Children."

"So one of the Children has to survive to inherit the throne?"

"Or somehow she Returns and yet stays," Raven said. "That's why I said no one knows – it's a prophecy, it's three-parts nonsense to one part logic."

"So how do we stop it?"

"I kill her," Raven said, simply. Leah stopped her pacing and looked up, locking eyes with him. She looked surprised, then approving, and, finally, sad. The rest of them were staring at him with redoubled intensity. "It has to be me, that's part of the prophecy. I can't understand it all, but that is one thing that Geofred knew for sure. It has to be me... and if I do it, I'm fairly certain that I'll die as well."

Raven watched this pronouncement sink in. Davydd's eyes went wide and he looked off to his right, thinking about something far distant; Tomaz watched Raven carefully, a look of grave concern pulling his brows in and down; Autmaran chewed the inside of his cheek; Tym kept looking between them all, as if unsure whether he was still supposed to be there; and Leah resumed her pacing.

"And if you don't?" Tomaz asked. "What did Geofred see happening then?"

"We all die," he said simply. "Everyone. Everyone dies."

Chapter Ten:

Good Use of a Tent

They left that alleyway after the sun had fully set and they could barely even see each other, talking over what Leah, Davydd, and Raven had pulled from their collective memories of Geofred and Tiffenal. There were numerous questions, from repeated 'was he sure?'s to 'how?'s and 'why?'s, most of which went unanswered. They questioned whether they could just let the Empress leave, but Raven knew the answer from Geofred's mind was 'no.' Raven's older brother had gone through every possible branch of this future, and he had found no way forward to thwart the Empress other than for Raven, her Seventh Child, to kill her, risking death himself.

And still Leah was not convinced.

"Words are tricky," she kept mumbling. "Every word can have myriad meanings in different contexts. Every word… "

She continued on like that even as she left for the tent she and Tomaz shared out beyond the Wall in what used to be the Outer City. Her eyes kept flashing back and forth from green to blue, and Raven knew she was trying to touch the Eagle Talisman.

No – not the Talisman. Since it went from me to her, it's now the Aspect of… Future? No, an aspect like strength and will… the Aspect of Sight. In either case, it would still let her see the future, though Raven wasn't sure how much of his she would be able to glimpse since his Talisman often negated the others. *Geofred was able to see me, but likely only because he had four hundred years of practice with the damn thing.*

They had agreed to break up for the night and reconvene on the road tomorrow. Davydd and Lorna were headed to check in with their troops, and Tomaz had gone to offer his services on guard duty. Tym and Autmaran were finding food; the Commander had started to show an interest in the boy.

Raven let them go without protest, preferring to keep his own council for the rest of the night anyway. He still felt somehow cut off from them, but it was better, at least. It was better for now.

As he made his way back toward the center of the city, he realized abruptly he had given up his bed before finding another. He sighed. *That teaches me to let altruism go unchecked.* Not knowing what else to do, he headed toward the command tent: there was a least one cot there, and it would be unoccupied 'til morning.

But he never got that far. As he was walking, he became aware of someone shadowing him. He couldn't see them, though: whoever they were, they knew how to keep out of direct sight, and he couldn't simply turn around to look without giving up that he had been alerted to their presence. Thoughts of the Seekers came back to him; the side street was deserted, a perfect place to attempt an assassination.

He reached out through the Raven Talisman, and felt the world snap into focus around him. Details started coming to him in a rush, the exact shade of purple the sky had turned, the smell of baking bread still thick in the air, and even more so, the sense of a bright golden knot of light walking just behind him.

Green and silver; honey and lavender; the sound of steel cutting silk –

"Leah," he breathed, just as she walked up beside him.

"It is still eerie when you do that," she said.

He eyed her sideways. "Says the woman stalking me?"

She arched an eyebrow at him. "I was on my way to find you. We've decided not to meet tomorrow morning."

"That's – no, we have to meet. We have a lot to plan, and – "

"It's done, princeling," she said, amused. "We're moving as fast as we can, and the Scouts won't have anything new to report until tomorrow night. An extra hour of sleep will do us all better than talk."

"But we aren't done formulating plans – "

"For now, the plan is go north until we find someone to fight," she said.

"You really are Davydd's sister," he said, dryly.

"Yes. Thanks for playing."

"I don't play."

"You should."

"I don't think that would be beneficial," Raven said.

"Sometimes it's good to have fun, princeling."

"You are acting strangely."

"Am I?"

"Yes. You are being strange. And, frankly, it's worrying."

"Hmm... well, I think you could use a frank worrying."

He opened his mouth to respond, and then realized what she was really saying, and closed it with a snap. The last few hours of inner torment evaporated as a terribly embarrassing flush spread across his cheeks.

"I don't know what – "

"You know *exactly* what I mean," she said, amused.

"We can't do that *now*," he insisted, scandalized. "That's – no, that's completely out of the question. We cannot do that."

"All right, if *we* cannot, then I'll find you someone else."

His head snapped back around immediately. Eyebrows raised and lips pursed, she looked the perfect embodiment of female indignation.

"I – you – *what?*"

"Well, I'm obviously not attractive enough to warrant attention, so let's find someone else for the mighty Prince of the Veil."

"No – no, that is not what I meant."

"What did you mean?"

"I meant that I do not want everyone to think we are... not that there is something wrong with people knowing – I am not saying I am worried people will know – and, it is not that I *want* people to know either – I mean, it's not like the thought never crossed my mind, it's just – "

"So you *have* thought about it?" she asked, taking a step closer.

"I – well – I – "

"It's a simple question."

"Well, I – "

"Just answer."

"Wait, that's not – "

"Stop stalling."

"Fine! Of course I've thought about it!"

"Whoa," she said, lowering her voice in mocking imitation of him. "No need to shout it so everyone can hear, I thought this was just between the two of us?"

Suddenly Raven realized that she was much too close, so close now, in fact, that he couldn't even look at her properly without his eyes going crossways. "All right," he said, stepping away. "I know what you are attempting to do."

"Do you? Go ahead: elucidate."

"You are trying to make me forget what happened. You are trying to make me forget about what we are about to do. But I cannot. I cannot just let it go, I need to be on constant guard, we all do."

She threw up her hands in exasperation and walked away. Before Raven even knew what he was doing, he was following her, speaking quickly as they headed back toward the main road. "All right, Leah, stop – no, I mean it, *stop!*"

He grabbed her by the shoulder and tried to stop her, but she spun around and threw him off. "What?" she demanded. "I was leaving you alone like you wanted!"

"That's not it – look, now just is not the time," he said, though the sentence came out much more sullen and sulky than he would have wished. "I can't. I can't just pretend none of it happened, I can't just – I can't."

"You should," she said, all teasing gone out of her now.

"Why?"

"Because in the end life goes back to normal."

"No. It won't. This is the end we're moving toward... there is no after."

"There is always an after."

She stepped up and raised a hand to his face. He tensed, just a flash of movement, but he realized there was no need. They had stopped in the deep shadows cast between two buildings, and there was no one nearby or even walking down the row of houses behind them. Her hand cupped his cheek, and she watched him silently, her face a quiet, stony mask, all except for her eyes. Those beautiful, green eyes that cut through him and made him want to reach out and –

No. No, I won't.

"I'm here," she said simply. "Be here with me. You are right; we cannot forget what's going on. But we also cannot control what is going to happen tomorrow, or when we reach Lucien. All we *can* control is what we do before that happens."

Her lips were inches away from his now, her breath mingling with his. She pulled him the rest of the way and kissed him. His head swam and blood rushed to parts of him that were suddenly very eager to meet her embrace. But he broke away before his mind submerged completely.

"No," he said, surprising even himself. The words came out in a strange half-croak that sounded like a frog's mating call. He cleared his throat violently, his cheeks once more hot. "I need... I need time. This is too fast."

She let go of him slowly, and backed away. She pursed her lips, took a deep breath, nodded once, and walked away. Before he knew it, he was after her once more – he couldn't leave it like that. He just couldn't.

"Leah, stop. That's not fair."

"What isn't? You said you needed time. I mean, we've known each other for a year, fought side by side in countless battles, even saved each other's lives. But you need time. So, fine. That's your decision – who am I to judge?"

They passed through the gate to the Inner City; guards saluted them as they went, and he stopped talking until they were through. He didn't know where they were going, but he'd be damned if he stopped before he told her what was on his mind. As soon as they were relatively alone again, he spoke once more:

"Leah, there are proper ways to do this. We cannot just – "

"Just be with each other?"

"No, that's not what I was saying."

"You don't seem to be saying much of anything."

"That's not fair, I'm trying."

"What's not fair?"

"You – twisting my – and then – and now we're – wait, where are we?"

Leah threw back the flap to the command tent and went inside without looking back. He followed her inside, where she was lighting a lamp. When the wick took and the oil began to burn, she turned to watch him, leaning casually against the central tent poll sunk into a soft patch of dirt where a paving stone had been unearthed, crossing her arms beneath her chest.

"I'm here to study the maps," she said. "What are you here to do?"

"I – well, I was planning to sleep here," he finally spluttered.

"Sure," she said, flicking her chin toward the cot in the back, placed there in case any of them needed to rest while studying maps late into the night. "Go for it."

"No," he said abruptly, suddenly feeling stronger, "not yet."

"Why not?" she asked wearily.

"Because I have looked through the memories of a thousand men, and none of the women they knew could ever hold a candle to you."

Something flashed in her eyes, and her demeanor changed completely. She... softened somehow, in a way he could not explain. She stared at him, unblinking, her mouth slightly open. Before he lost his nerve, he hurried on.

"But I... I do not know how to do this. I do not know how to be with someone. I do not even know if I *can* be with someone. I need to devote everything I have to the Kindred; I need to see them through this, see them to the end. They are counting on me in a way no one has *ever* counted on me before. I have come so close and there are only a few more steps left to go, and then... then – "

He broke off as his voice cracked, and he lowered his eyes, trying to keep the rest of it from her. He shook his head and cleared his throat, but said nothing more. She stepped forward, watching him from under veiled lids, and he realized she was choosing her words carefully.

"You did something wrong," she said slowly. "We both know it. You are trying to punish yourself for it – no, don't try to say you aren't – no, stop talking, *that's what you are doing*, there is no way around it. You are punishing yourself even though we both know you were not in control."

She stepped forward again, coming closer, holding his gaze.

"You need to learn the difference between what you can and cannot expect from yourself. You are not super-human. You are not above everyone else, either in good ways or bad. You have a gift, you have a destiny – but you are just a man. Like I am just a woman. And there is strength in that – there is strength in being nothing more than who you are. You cannot hold yourself responsible for something that you could not stop."

He just stood there, jaw set, staring at her.

"I do not want a gentleman," she said.

Raven's brow furrowed in an automatic reaction of confusion.

"I do not want someone to ask for my hand and woo me," she continued, watching him closely. "I do not want someone to show off at parties, and I do not want to tell the story of how we met. I do not want someone who will fix all my problems or devote his life to me. I do not want someone who will only touch me when it is the *right time* to do so. I want a partner. I do not want someone who will stand behind me; I want someone who will stand *beside* me. And I want that person to be you. I want *you*. Not because I love your eyes, but because I love the way you see. Not because I love your voice, but because I love the words you say. Not because you were born a prince, but because you deserve to be one. I want *you*, exactly as you are."

As she broke off, still watching him, he had no response. He was completely captivated; his mind was blank, and all he could do was focus on her voice.

"But I will not wait for you," she said, setting her jaw. Her brow furrowed, and Raven felt fiery panic begin to build in the tips of his fingers. "There is no time to sort through whatever it is you want to deal with. I do not want someone who says they want me back and then won't be with me. I do not play games, and I will not stand by while someone else plays them on me. So if you still want to go, then *go*. But if you walk out of this tent, then whatever we are, whatever we could have been, is over. I am not waiting for you. You are either with me, or you are not."

Slowly, his brain began to work again, and he found himself speaking. "Yes," he said. His hands began to sweat for no particular reason. "Yes. So I... I should go."

But he didn't move. He felt as though his feet had been nailed to the floor. Seconds passed, and then a full minute, as the light from the oil lamp flickered and played with the shadows across her face; shadows that never dimmed the brilliance of her eyes. A different kind of feeling came over him, a warmth that slipped beneath the panic and urged him to do something else.

He found himself focusing on a cut along her jaw, the one that had yet to fully heal. He had always assumed that scars detracted from beauty, that they took something away from the natural perfection that all of the other Children embodied and desired. But with Leah it was different. Each scar she had she had earned fighting the Empire; each was a mark of honor, tallied up against the world's harsh design. Her whole body was covered with scars... her whole body.

As if drawn by the thought, Leah took a step forward, and as she did he reached up and brushed against her arm with his fingers. When they touched, energy flowed between them that made his mouth go dry. Her breath caught in her chest.

"Are you all right?" he asked, the words brushing against the side of her cheek. She did not answer, and he did not blame her.

Heat seemed to radiate from them both, and they were so close now that they were almost embracing. His mind was consumed with a need for her, an endless yearning he had never felt for anyone else. He began to ache, his hands and body almost shaking. She swallowed and he realized there were bright spots of color in her cheeks. He opened his mouth to say something, and realized he didn't want to. He had a thousand and one excuses, and he no longer cared about any of them.

He could feel her breath rushing from her mouth, hot against his throat, the inside of which felt like it was coated with sandpaper. He was suddenly aware, with a strange unwavering certainty, that his hands and feet were completely, absurdly out of proportion to the rest of his body. He had never noticed that before, but in that instant it was abundantly clear to him that he had the body of a crazy sideshow act.

She moved an inch closer, a sudden, strange jerk that elicited an answering jerk from him, and then his fingers caught and gripped her hand. She continued to stare at him, not even blinking, and he stared at her too, seeing everything and nothing about her. His other hand moved on its own, up, up, until it came to rest against the nape of her neck, pushing back the thick curtain of her hair.

She arced her neck, pressing her skin into his palm, and the scent of her, the smell of leather and trail dust, lavender soap and femininity, encapsulated his mind, detaching his consciousness from the controls of his body.

Clothing began to fall to the ground. They both kicked off their boots at the same time. There was a ripping sound and he realized he had torn her shirt.

"I am sorry – "

"Shut up."

And then they were kissing, her lips full and fiery against his. She pulled him to the far corner of the tent, to the cot, blowing out the lamps as they went and plunging them into darkness just deep enough to cover them but not enough to leave them blind.

She removed her tight undershirt, and then her pants, revealing skin. He followed suit, and her warm hands slipped beneath his belt as he traced her scars. He grabbed a fistful of her hair, kissing her neck. He picked her up and held her against him before pushing her down onto the cot. She pulled him down to her, and cried out once before locking her legs around his hips.

Chapter Eleven:

Travelling North

When day broke, Raven woke alone. Momentarily confused about his location, and assuming by some strange quirk of his sleeping mind he was still in Vale, he looked around and realized dawn had filtered through the tiny holes in the canvas fabric of the tent. He reached over and felt the impression Leah had left on the blankets of the cot: still warm. He stood, the cold air turning his bare skin to goosebumps, and looked around. There was no sign of her.

Something fluttered on the map table, and he almost ignored it. But as he turned back to gather his clothing, he paused – there was a pen and ink there. Pulling his long cotton shirt from the floor and throwing it over his head, he strode to the table and saw a note, written in Leah's swirling cursive.

I've gone to find Tomaz; no doubt he's wondering where I was last night. I will see you on the march. I am glad you stayed.

Leah

He reached down and touched the ink: still wet. He turned back to his clothes and quickly pulled the rest of them on, smiling to himself like an idiot. Anyone who didn't know her might have been offended by the abrupt tone of the letter, but the fact she had written anything at all was a sign of how much the night had meant to her. He grabbed the scrap of parchment, blew on it to dry the ink, then folded it into a pocket, the whole while feeling as though at any moment he might lift up and start to fly.

He left the tent just in time, still shoving his right foot into his boot as Aemon's Blade bounced awkwardly against his left hip, the hilt tangled with his coat and cloak. The camp servants had come to take the tent down – *Not truly servants, are they? They're paid five times what an Imperial servant could hope to make* – and though they moved out of his way, they quickly set about their work as soon as he had passed.

His first thought was to find Leah again, to catch up to her and Tomaz and ride with them as the army moved out, but as he headed toward the Inner City gate he saw Commander Autmaran and the two Generals in heated conversation to his right, heading toward the rapidly deflating command tent.

Raven's thoughts darkened, and he realized the night before had been only a brief respite. He could not dwell on it – not now, at least. Something in his chest gave a strange, sideways lurch at the thought, but he ignored it. Leah knew it too – no doubt it was why she had left.

Maybe on the journey north....

He shook his head and moved toward Autmaran, trying to get the image of Leah's scars out of his head. Scars that highlighted the best things. Anyone who thought beauty was flawless skin had never been with a warrior woman.

After settling the dispute between Autmaran, Gates, and Dunhold – over whose part of the army got to march first, of all the fool-brained, asinine arguments – Raven found that he had been given the "gift" of a horse that had belonged to a member of the Most High. Autmaran informed him that the former owner had generously donated all of his wealth to the Kindred army after being found guilty of slavery, rape, and murder before choking his life away at the bottom of a tightly cinched rope in the ruins of the Imperial Cathedral. That wealth had included twenty-six horses.

"He's a handful," Autmaran said, handing Raven the reins of the sleek stallion, "but I know you like black."

Raven grabbed the bridle as the horse snapped its teeth at him. He pulled the reins to turn the stallion's head, but the horse twisted and snapped at him again. Raven stepped back and held up his hands, making soothing noises that seemed to calm the beast. Finally, he was able to come close enough to place a hand on the stallion's neck. He stroked carefully, watching the powerful rise and fall of the huge chest as the horse's lungs worked like a blacksmith's bellows.

"I would say thank you," he muttered to Autmaran, "but I have the feeling you find this amusing."

"Not at all. I just think it's nice when a horse and rider have similar personalities."

The Commander heeled his dun mare, Alto, down the road, and Raven found himself frowning at nothing but a retreating back. The horse snapped at him again – *shadows and light, maybe I should name it Biter* – but after a few more minutes of soothing noises and calm stroking, the stallion deigned to allow him to mount. Once seated and relatively certain he would not be thrown of, he grabbed the reins and carefully heeled the stallion toward the gate to Banelyn City proper.

His good mood was gone almost as soon as he crossed the city's threshold. For every man or woman who had joined them, there were two or three too sickly, too old, too young, or still too loyal to the Empress to do so. They would all remain in the city, under a skeleton guard to keep the peace, which, hopefully, would be easy with every pair of strong arms in the city either in Kindred colors, captured and placed in the city's prison, or else burned and buried after the battle.

As they left, Raven saw fear on some of the faces lining the streets; some directed at him and some directed at his departure. But there was nothing he could do for them, and so he turned his eyes away and tried to watch the street only, as a huge tide of Kindred, a river that swelled with each step as more soldiers came from side alleys and abandoned houses, swept out of the city by the Lerne Gate, heading north.

But for as many as they took with them, there were more they left behind.

How can there be so many to protect?

All told, their departure from Banelyn had little of the pomp and circumstance that saw them on their way from Vale. The army had a grim air to it now, and even the Commons who had joined them in huge numbers seemed battle-hardened. Many of them had seen their homes burned down, and many more had seen their neighbors, sons, husbands, wives, even children, murdered in those flames or by the attacking army. They shook the hands of those left behind and turned deaf ears to those who begged them to stay.

But despite the maudlin tenor of their departure, Raven saw in the eyes of the Commons a hunger that devoured grief and turned it into something new. The light was malnourished and sickly, and the hunger made their lean frames and pale cheeks look gaunt, even emaciated. When it shown brightest, it spoke of wildness, like a feral dog that had once been tame. They had seen both sides of the world, looking up at the Most High and the Children all their lives and down at the ditches dug for dying Commons. And now, even when death seemed ready to reap them all in droves, they had their chance to tear down those that had been set above them, and Raven knew, if the others didn't, that this was what drove many of them to join the Kindred. These were not men and women who fought for the Kindred – they were slaves who fought for freedom, and wronged souls that strove for vengeance.

And yet the only fanfare that saw them from the city was the crying of orphaned children and the hollow looks of those too far gone to care.

We will be back for them, Raven thought vehemently. *We will fix it. We must.*

As they left the city by the Lerne Gate, moving onto the wide, paved Imperial Road that ran the length of the Empire, Raven's thoughts turned to the resolve of his fellow Exiles. The Commons were with him for a simple reason: they knew who he was, they knew what he had done, and they wanted a chance at retribution.

But the Kindred were a different story. Part of him was glad the others had managed to conceal what had happened to him, at least in part, but another part of him wanted them to know. They had a right to know who they were following, didn't they? They had a right to know that he carried a monster inside of him.

Or did it even matter? Would they follow him anyway?

A monster that can kill an Elder.

In his mind now, when he thought of her, she was never "Elder" Keri. She was just "Keri," a woman who happened to have been an Elder. A woman whose life he had ended. It was strange, actually. Everything he felt now in connection to her death he had felt before when he had been forced to kill innocent men. He had even felt it when he had killed Henri Perci. But this death went deeper than before; this death *meant* more. He hated death, hated that he was bound to it, and hated bringing it about, even to those who had tried to bring it to him; but, before, that hate had always been nebulous, vague. The faces of all those he had killed had blended together, and the deed had become more dreadful than the doing of it. But now he had a name to latch on to, a form and figure – a face that belonged to a woman who hadn't deserved to die by any stretch of the imagination.

Why is it only now that I think of myself as a murderer?

He was glad he had the others' word that they would deal with him if it came to that. The creature was still in him somewhere, mindless and cruel, waiting to take over should he let his guard down. It was the part of him linked to the Raven Talisman, and it held him captive to his old life no matter how fast or far he ran.

The part of me that is my Mother.

He had stopped calling her that, or at least had tried to, when he was around the others; they were not comfortable with the constant reminder that he was one of the Children – now one of the *last* Children, a thought that brought both guilt and pride in equal waves. He shook his head to dispel the thoughts, and tried to focus elsewhere.

The next few days were a blur. The army moved as quickly as they dared, putting one foot in front of the other from the time the first glimmer of sunrise blossomed over the distant horizon to the time the last ray of sunset slivered into a mullion of light between land and sky. The Scouts brought no word of any approaching army, nor of any enemy scouts. Even the guard towers along the Imperial Road customarily manned by Defenders were empty, and stood silent watch as the Kindred passed.

And with every passing moment, the clock that had begun a slow but inexorable countdown in Raven's head continued to tick. Another minute gone... another hour... another day.

Everyone, from the soldiers to the Elders, was tired. Each march seemed longer, and each night of waiting more unbearable. The days did not so much wear on as stretch out, like an elastic band that, at some point, had to snap. Raven had learned that war was about long marches and short battles; even the siege of Banelyn, the longest such battle in recent history, had only taken two days compared to the weeks of marching and the months of preparation. But there was nothing to do but press on, nothing to do but move toward a battle that seemed as impossible as fighting thunder or punching air. Every eye slowly clouded with fatigue, every muscle began to cord with tension. Even the peaceful spring nights seemed full of dark and plotting shadows.

The sense of it permeated the Council meetings they had, where the Elders, Generals, and others all met with a rotating cast of under officers who came and went as needed. Their discussions were short, often terse, and made worse by the fact Raven refused to dally at Lerne. The others thought it necessary, even in light of the delay it would cause, but he had a gut feeling that warned him against it. Even if his sister had left her Principality, as he expected she had, they would be foolish to walk straight into her lair. Symanta bore the Snake Talisman, but would more aptly be called the Spider; this had all the makings of a trap, and Raven would exhaust every other option before being convinced to spring it.

The road they took was wide and unnaturally straight. Unlike the road north from Vale to Banelyn, this road was older, and did not conform to the contours of the earth. Instead, it went through hills and across plains that had once been forests, cutting through the landscape instead of following it, dictating its own path in defiance of any natural suggestion. The long, straight line, continuing on into the horizon, unaltered, was eerie, and completely alien compared to the curves of the natural world. And what made the feeling even worse was that every farmhouse and village they passed along the way was found to be abandoned; every watchtower and guard post was deserted. It was as if the people of the country they passed had all joined together in a mass exodus ahead of the approaching army and disappeared along the unnatural road, as completely and suddenly as dissipating mist.

The only sentinels along the road were the trees. They stood a lonely watch in a patchwork of large groves, poplar and pine, oak and cypress, but none grew next to the road itself. Raven found himself staring past them often, unable to pull his eyes away from the strange muted space between them. Nothing seemed to move when the Kindred passed; even the breeze fell silent and the trees stopped their wind-whipped whispers. The watching world took on the air of a hushed spectator, and it sucked in a deep breath, holding it until the outcome of their struggle was decided. Raven wished he could feel a sense of hope in that silence, but he did not, and could not, no matter how hard he tried.

Everything hung on a razor's edge, and the moment continued to cut them all in different ways. When each day's sun rose and burned away the morning mist, Raven felt as though another thin piece of his self-possession had been sliced away. He could see the same effect in many of the Kindred soldiers, in the other Aspect bearers, and even in the ever-composed Elders. It was not that they feared attack, nor even that they feared the battles yet to come. It was the knowledge that they were going up against an army that had never known defeat, led by an immortal ruler that had oppressed them for a thousand years. It took something from them, as if every step were part of the building crescendo of a death knell. Had the battle come on them suddenly, as it had at Banelyn, it would have been different. But now, the build up was almost as bad as the fight.

Yet there were those who fought the silence, and it was around these men and women that the rest of the camp congregated when night fell and shadows stopped their progress. Stannit, the former Roarkeman who had been an Imperial through and through until betrayed by his own leaders, would tell the tale of how Raven and Leah had saved the citizens of Roarke every night around the campfire, and Jaillin would continue it with how the Prince had cut down a thousand men inside the Wall of Banelyn. Leah was a figure of stories too, and Tomaz as well; both found themselves the subject of nightly ruminations as Raven's right and left hands, and they both, along with Raven, found these stories to be far grander in the telling than they had ever seemed in the living. Autmaran was praised as a military genius on par with his former tutor, the legendary Elder Goldwyn, and both Davydd and Lorna were spoken of as daredevil wonders, a pair that courted death with relish.

The stories gave the Kindred hope that while they faced forces beyond their ken, they were led by men and women who could give as well as they received. Their tones became reverent when talking to the Aspect bearers, and Raven found himself gritting his teeth every time he heard it. That anxiety shortened his temper and made him curt and terse, even when it was decidedly not the time.

"We need to – "

"No," Raven said, cutting off Gates yet again. "We do not."

"We *must* take the city," the General insisted again, his neck reddening as his mustache bristled. "To leave it open and behind us, that's insanity!"

"We will win or lose this war based on how quickly we get to Lucien," Raven said, trying to keep his voice even and his temper in check, though a headache had begun to build behind his temples. "Moving past Lerne is the right tactical move."

"But it *is* bad strategy," Leah said from the corner of the tent. Heat rushed to the tips of his fingers at the sound of her voice.

"You don't need to worry about leaving your own king unguarded if you see a clear path to check-mating theirs," Spader said, the only one who seemed to see Raven's plan, from beginning to end, and approve of it. The Elder, with his ever-present glass of amber liquid to match his flowing amber robes, winked at Raven in a way that showed support, but something less than affection. Their relationship had changed: whereas before he had treated Raven like a favored nephew, now he was more cautious, more wary. The friendly bond they'd shared had slowly begun to mend, however, and Raven found himself grateful for the support.

"A fair point," Tomaz rumbled.

"I just wish I could see it," sighed Autmaran. "I have trouble trusting what I cannot understand, and passing by a city we could, ostensibly, take in a matter of days seems like an unnecessary risk."

"Even a matter of hours is too long," Raven said, calm but insistent. "Time is the one thing that we do not have nearly enough of."

"How long now?" Tomaz rumbled, a question that elicited total silence from the others, even the ever-fidgeting Davydd. They all turned to look at Raven, though many of them no doubt already knew the date.

"One week, six days, and however many hours it is 'til dawn," Raven said.

One by one they nodded, doing internal calculations.

"By which time," Lorna summed up calmly, "either you are dead, or the Tyrant is?"

"That's the theory," Raven said.

"Something still worries me," Leah said. "And I won't stand here and stay silent; we need to have a contingency plan."

"We won't be attacked until we pass Lerne," Raven insisted. "There is no value in it for them. Surely you can see that."

"I see scales," she replied, her eyes flashing blue for a brief second, about as long as she had yet managed to hold the Aspect. "And I see shadows. That is all."

"Symanta?" Autmaran asked.

"There may yet be Seekers hidden in the camp," Spader added, with a wry twist to his mouth. "There are those who helped Henri Perci escape, and many of those who fled the Cathedral are still in our hair, even after Ishmael's thorough combing."

"We won't be attacked until we pass Lerne!" Raven exclaimed.

They all fell silent and watched him with wary eyes.

"We won't be attacked until we pass Lerne," he repeated at normal volume. He realized he was sweating; there was a fire in the tent with them, but not near enough to warm him. He passed a hand over his forehead and cleared his throat.

Shadows and light, why don't they just listen?

"Very well," Autmaran sighed, breaking the tension. "I will agree to drop the point on one condition: if we pass by the crossroads that lead to the city and see what we expect, then we pass on. If something is there, *anything*, that makes us think there is more to Symanta's plans than we assume, we revisit this."

Raven ground his back teeth together in frustration, but he nodded. "Fine. But unless that something is glaringly obvious and comes to us, then we move straight for Lucien. Agreed?"

One by one the others nodded, all except Davydd.

"What happens if you just run away?" the Eshendai Ranger asked abruptly. He stood up and began pacing wildly, throwing his hands into the air. "Huh? What happens if, magically, you and the Empress aren't in the same place? What happens if we just try to sidestep this thing altogether? I can't help but feeling like we're walking right into this one. Why don't *we* attack and *you* just stay out of the way for two weeks?"

"It wouldn't work," Raven said, rubbing his temples. "It's a neat loop-hole, but you can't avoid the future that way. Any step I take will eventually lead to that confrontation. Geofred was sure of it. All we can do is try to be ready when it comes."

"I agree," Leah said quietly but insistently. "I've seen this from the inside now, and the confrontation will happen one way or another. But this – us gathering and marching on Lucien – this is the only chance the Kindred will ever have to defeat her. Without him leading us, without him there to fight her, we lose."

"So, basically, you're bait," Davydd said, turning his red-gold eyes on Raven, sizing up his reaction, "and risking the fact you may die first and fulfill her side of the prophecy, all so you have the chance to kill her, in which case you might die anyway."

Raven swallowed hard and took a seat in one of the clever cloth folding chairs used about the camp. He dug his knuckles deeper into the knot in his temple.

"That about sums it up," he said.

Silence descended on the tent as they all consulted their own thoughts. Davydd had ceased his pacing and was now perched on a high stool, staring into his hands; Lorna was seated on the floor, back straight, watching them all; Tomaz stood in the shadows of a corner, expression unreadable; Leah's eyes kept flashing blue and then back to green as she tried to grab the Aspect of Sight, only to have it slip through her fingers; Autmaran was examining the maps, still shaking his bald head which glinted in the lantern light; Spader and Ishmael were standing side-by-side, saying nothing. The distant sound of a ringing bell that called for lights-out broke the tableau.

"We'll meet again tomorrow," Autmaran said, and they all nodded. They left in groups, until Raven was left watching the departing form of Leah, thinking how happy he had been alone with her only days before.

He saw Leah very little during the day. They had different responsibilities over the march: Leah, Tomaz, and the other Rogues were all being used as partial scouts, and also as guards along the borders of the army. In addition, when they weren't patrolling, they gave lessons in sword, spear, knife, and bow fighting to the new recruits. Raven had tried to join them one night as they practiced by the wane light of oil lanterns, but as soon as he'd entered the practice arena, everyone had gone silent, and the practice had stopped. Every eye had turned and trained on him, pulled like metal to a lodestone.

So much for that idea.

He nodded back, and turned to go. As he left, he caught sight of Leah and Tomaz, both of whom looked tired and worn. Leah took a step forward as if to follow him, her black hair shining with a glint of reflected gold in the lantern light, but he was gone before she did.

She should stay – we need all of them as trained as they can be.

But she came to him that night when the camp slept.

Raven was glad he'd had time alone with his thoughts after the first night they'd spent together. It had been... more than he thought possible. The act itself had been quite eye opening, but the time together afterwards, feeling her body pressed against his... it had made him long for something more, and that was the complication he had feared. If he wanted to win this war, if he wanted to get through the next few weeks, he could not spare thoughts for an after. That was what he had been trying to say to her the night they left Banelyn, and what she had stubbornly refused to hear.

But the way she pulled him was beyond what he could resist, and when she came to him in the dark of night, the whisper of moving tent cloth and the scent of lavender soap giving her away to his waiting senses, he didn't resist. He surprised himself, and her, with his own ferocity, something that he realized she found enticing, and something they both realized had been lurking beneath the surface of their relationship even as it began. To an outsider, their time wrapped in the shadows of the night might be mistaken for a fight; but as they lay gasping for breath after it was done, clinging to each other like lifelines, he knew that this one thing, in all his life, was good and right. They rarely spoke, and didn't need to; the silence encapsulated them like a warm cocoon, and their vulnerabilities, the things they had never shown another living soul, lay as open and on display as their bodies were.

But long after she had drifted off to sleep, he lay awake in the darkness. Thoughts ran around and through his mind in constant loops, building with each repetition, until it was as if voices were shouting at him from inside his own head. He'd find himself forced to his feet, his breath coming hard and fast, heart beating a harsh staccato against his ribcage. Leah rarely woke when he rose, and he was glad of it. At least one of them would get the sleep they needed.

And once he was up, he saw no reason to go back to bed, for the process would only repeat itself, over and over until he was up again. So he examined maps, and went over plans that had already been outlined in detail. He began to hold tight to the Raven Talisman, even when there was no need, constantly monitoring the camp around him, drawing on what reserves the Wolf Talisman could give him to wash away his fatigue. He would take walks, feeling the lives of the soldiers around him, the huge, nearly incomprehensible number of them, and a panic would begin to build in his chest, a pressure that made him feel as though something was about to burst inside him.

One night it became so unbearable that he left the camp entirely, and made his way up to the top of a hillside overlooking it. He avoided the guards easily – he knew exactly where they were without even needing to look, and so he slipped through their perimeter and made his way out into the night.

He sought solace in the stars, but they were no comfort. They held no answers for him, only more questions. He passed through a grove of trees, turned behind a hill; the sounds of the camp slowly faded out. He could hear his heart pumping in the silence. Silence – how long had it been since he'd stood in pure, natural silence? It spoke to a deep part of him that went beyond rationalization, a part that had been too long ignored, too long neglected. It made him yearn again for Vale, and the simple woodsman's cabin he had built there with Tomaz's aide.

I have been elected Prince, led armies across whole nations, and slayed men and women of unspeakable power. I have lived in the Fortress of Lucien, capital of the nation of Lucia, and stood beside my Mother, the Empress, as she ruled from the Diamond Throne. When people see me, they cower in fear or salute in honor. I hold the world in my hand; I am the stuff of legends; and all I want, in all the world, is to go back to a single-room cabin and watch the sun rise over white stone mountains.

He grimaced and turned back, leaving his thoughts and the glade behind. He wouldn't think of such things again; it only brought him pain. He had to focus on the next few weeks and nothing else. It was the same as with Leah – the same feeling of *after* and *more.* He couldn't think such things, not if he wanted to save the Kindred, to save Vale itself from destruction. Such nostalgia and longing would only weaken him, and blunt his mind. All he knew, all he had to deal with, was what stood in front of him. All that mattered was ending this, killing the last of the Children… and his Mother. What happened afterward – that was not his affair. What happened after the final battle would be up to the Kindred, the Elders, and any of his companions he managed to keep alive. That world was theirs, not his.

He would not live to see it.

Chapter Twelve:

Something to Lerne

Raven sat his new black stallion, freshly christened Melyngale, and felt the breeze blow in from the city of Lerne. They had reached a crossroads, the place where the Imperial Road met the Lerne Road, the former going from Lucien all the way to Roarke, and the latter branching off at a right angle toward the Elmist Mountains, in the shadow of which Lerne had been constructed.

A town had grown up around the intersection of the two roads like a swollen muscle around a heavily used joint. In fact, the town was nearly as old as Lerne itself. It was called Whitestone, though no one knew why. Any white stones that had been there had long since disappeared; the area was now a large collection of farms and a town center that did very well for itself with the passing traffic of the Empire. Indeed, the town buildings, of which there were several score, were all freshly painted or whitewashed, and a number of the main street buildings and inns were several stories tall and well made. The streets were wide and straight, and it was easy to see that while the town had not played host to any of the Most High, certainly a number of the Elevated would have made quite a comfortable home here.

All of which made the town's desertion more worrying.

"Word likely reached them a week ago that Banelyn had fallen," Autmaran said. He, Raven, and Tomaz were all in the center of town together, exactly where the two roads met and ran their respective courses. A three-story inn rose behind them, and two huge merchant outfits, one that looked like a general goods store, the other a combination smithy and farming equipment shop, pillared the road that led west, out of town toward Lerne. Raven's skin had begun to crawl the moment he'd crossed the first line of buildings. He knew the others felt it too – the whole town felt wrong. It looked as if everyone had simply left, taking nothing along behind, as if everyone, in one great mass, had simply decided to step out, but had never come back.

"And no one in their right minds would stand in front of an enemy army this size," Autmaran continued when Raven did not respond. The Commander's voice was more forceful than it needed to be, and a small muscle along the side of his cheek jumped uncontrollably.

"True enough," Raven said slowly. He saw the old arguments surfacing behind Autmaran's face, so he turned away and looked down the Imperial Road. The soldiers were swarming over the town, searching every building, taking what food they could to replenish their supplies.

But Symanta…

The cold, rational arguments he made each night about simply passing through the town still made sense to him. This was a trap, he could feel it in every bone of his body, and everything he knew about Symanta told him he'd be playing right into her hands if he let curiosity get the better of him. But there was a feeling that went deeper than that, something that even Raven couldn't ignore now that they were so close.

"Something's off," Tomaz rumbled, shaking his big head. "I can't say what, but it's something. It's like a bad smell, but it's not a smell."

Raven remained silent, but the words struck a chord in him. If Tomaz felt it too, it had something to do with the Aspects, and maybe, just maybe, it had something to do with the larger coming battle with the Empress. The big man heeled his huge destrier up beside him, and Raven found himself unable to look away from the big, bluff face.

"We all know time is of the essence," Tomaz rumbled slowly, his tone hedged with careful respect. "You convinced us all of that. But you know as well as I that there is something deeper at work here – the signs of it have been building and building with every new mile we've travelled. No guards along the road? Not a single sight of fleeing refugees? No trace of enemy scouts? And on top of that, this whole town looks as if it was inhabited as late as yesterday. The trees are well-kept, the fireplaces freshly cleaned; there's even a pile of weeds over there freshly pulled from the ground with roots that haven't even browned! How did the town know to empty in a matter of days if not *hours* if no one saw us coming? And are we supposed to believe the farmers left their homes weeks ago, in the middle of the planting season, without a single crop sown in those fields? Not even Lerne could support an influx of thousands, which all of the towns we've seen in this Principality would add up to be. Think about it, Raven. Think about the details. *It's all wrong.*"

And as they sat there in the middle of the town, with nothing but the wind whistling through the streets, Raven still didn't want to believe it. He knew too much about Symanta, knew her best among all his siblings as they were closest in age and had spent the most time in direct contact. His friend saw the stubborn look in his eyes.

"Check then," he rumbled, daring Raven, playing on his pride. "If you're so sure there's no reason, then use the Talisman and check."

Raven grimaced, but acquiesced. He reached out with the edge of his mind, sending just enough of it out through the Raven Talisman that he should be able to sense what was happening in their immediate area. The Kindred troop surrounded them, yes, so he pushed beyond that, until he came to a blank area he supposed must be the plain between the Imperial Road and the city of Lerne itself. He didn't sense anything there – just the background of plant and animal life, the kind of quiet murmur one might hear in an otherwise silent forest.

Nothing.

He felt Leah ride up beside him, but ignored the exchange of conversation she had with Tomaz. He had to push harder – he might be able to see the city if he concentrated, even from such a distance. Drawing on the Wolf Talisman, he tried to combine the two to add to his inner sight, but nothing happened. He pushed harder, pushing his mind out as far as it would go –

"Whoa!"

Raven opened his eyes just in time to see his horse bite at Leah, and with an uncharacteristically clumsy stumble, she twisted out of the way and fell against him, her eyes flashing blue.

Her hand touched the hilt of Aemon's Blade.

In a flash of blue light his mind *exploded* out of him. He saw for miles and miles, flying over the ground, completely unbound. He felt as though he'd been partially blind for his entire life and only now could see. If he tried hard enough, he might be able to see the end of the world itself –

But there was something closer than that, something only several miles distant, that drew his attention like a lodestone. There was something wrong in that place. It was like looking at a beautiful tapestry that had been ripped down the center and dragged through the dirt. The city itself was torn and bloodied, and even though he couldn't see the walls or the buildings, he knew that something terrible had happened, something monstrous.

There was no life in the city of Lerne – not one single person.

And then he felt himself being pulled back, pulled away by an inexorable force. Something had latched onto him and was forcing him back into his body, forcing his mind back into his skull –

He came back to himself with a strange *snapping* sensation, as if his mind had been tethered to his body by an elastic band that forced him to come back. His vision was strangely hazy, with a white light covering everything and bright stars winking at the corners. He was sprawled out on the ground, he realized that first;

his horse was prancing around in alarm off to the side. The next thing he realized was that Leah was beside him, staggering to her feet, looking for all the world like she'd just come from an alehouse drinking contest.

"Whoa, there!" Davydd said as he rode up to the group with Lorna at his side. Raven's horse, Melyngale, reared back and tried to strike out at him, shocked and frightened by the noise and action, but Davydd's horse, Aron, pranced out of the way. "I know you're falling for each other, but was a practical demonstration really necessary?"

"We need to go to Lerne," Raven croaked, before he started hacking and coughing. He felt as though his lungs had been wrung out, and any remaining air in them was not nearly enough. His fingers and toes were on fire, but not with lack of air – suddenly, he knew exactly where to go and what to do, and every second spent not getting there made him more and more anxious.

Leah was bent over, hands on her hips, coughing and hacking as well, breathing in huge rolling gasps as Tomaz tried to steady her.

"By the seven hells," Autmaran said, looking poleaxed, "what just happened?"

"This foolish slip of a girl touched the Blade," Tomaz said, his fear for Leah's safety manifesting as a bright flare of anger. "And she got thrown on her butt for her carelessness."

"That's – that's not all," Raven managed to get out. His vision was still hazy, but he was regaining it slowly. It was as if he'd used his sight all up at once and his body was only slowly restoring normal functions.

"Saw something – when I touched it," Leah gasped, holding to Tomaz for support. "Like – like Tomaz in Roarke!"

Autmaran looked at her with complete bemusement, an expression that matched the bewilderment on Lorna's face as well as Davydd's. But when Tomaz heard the words, he caught Raven's gaze.

"The Aspect of Sight went to you," he rumbled.

Raven nodded frantically, but spoke no more. A crowd of soldiers had gathered, and a number of under officers and platoon captains were approaching. "Is everything all right, sir?" asked the first to reach them – Jaillin, from the Wall at Banelyn. He still couldn't meet Raven's eyes – he spoke to Autmaran.

"Yes," Commander Autmaran said. "We move on as soon as we've cleared the town. Get your men to work, captain." Jaillin turned and started shouting to the others that there was nothing to be seen and that they should go about their business.

"We need to go," Raven rasped, his voice still weak but gaining strength.

"We can't leave yet," Davydd said, exasperated. "We know you want to go, but there's no reason to just move on. We need the supplies, and a few hours delay – "

"*To Lerne,*" Raven finished.

The others fell silent, and then Davydd threw up his hands. "Shadows and fire, princeling! I don't even have a clever thing to say – are you *intentionally* pissing us off?"

"What did you see?"

"It's empty," Raven rasped, trying to form his thoughts into coherent sentences but finding himself unable to do so. The shock of what he'd seen was still with him, and it was dulling his wits. He locked eyes with Leah, who was breathing deeply through her nose, and saw she was watching him right back. A shadow had fallen over her face, and he could see that she too wanted to be gone – *now*. Her green eyes were cold, like chips of ice dug up at midnight.

Had she seen the same thing? Was that how it worked?

"That's why we're refilling supplies," Autmaran said, "because the town – "

"It's not just the town," Raven said quickly, harshly. *"There's no one in the city!"*

The pronouncement didn't register with them at first. They all stared at him blankly, all expect for Leah, who was looking far away now, confirming for Raven that she too had seen the empty streets and the lifeless buildings.

"You mean no guard?" Autmaran asked. "You're saying we should take the city? I'll assemble the men – "

"No," Raven said, finally catching a full breath. "I mean *no one*. The city is empty – there is not a single life left there, be it guard, Commons, or High Blood."

He glanced quickly at Leah, and as soon as their eyes met he knew they wordlessly agreed on what to do next.

"How many?" she asked.

"Fifty at most," he said. "Only the fastest. Only Rogues. I don't understand the rest of it, but we're walking into a trap, and I have no idea how quickly we'll need to get back out again."

She nodded and left, mounting her horse in a dexterous leap, calling out names even as she did. Raven caught Tomaz's eye as well, and the big man nodded too, spinning to leave with her. Tomaz understood best what had just happened – when Tiffenal had infiltrated Banelyn and killed Elder Goldwyn, Raven had given Tomaz Aemon's Blade so that the Aspect of Strength would flow to Raven, allowing him the strength to follow his brother through the secret passage in the mountains. In theory, it was the same thing that would happen to any of them if they grabbed Aemon's Blade – it allowed them to transfer the abilities of their Aspect to Raven.

That feeling... like something had been torn....

"If we move quickly we can be there and back before sundown," Autmaran said, having caught on to what Leah and Tomaz had left to do. He stopped speaking when he saw the expression on Raven's face, and focused on him. "You saw something else, didn't you?"

"There is something there we have to find out," he said finally. "I cannot say any more than that, because I do not fully understand it myself. But we need to see it. If we don't... I don't know. I am not sure how it might affect us. All I know is that I was right when I said Symanta wouldn't stay behind."

"What do you mean?"

"I'm not sure," Raven mumbled. "Shadows and light, I am not sure of anything anymore. But we need to go – and we need to do it quickly, before night falls. We need to be back here, ready to move out, as soon as possible."

Autmaran watched him for a long moment, and then slowly nodded. "I assume Leah is out gathering a force and Tomaz is organizing the troops to stay here until we return?" he asked. Raven nodded. "When do we leave?"

"Now," said Leah, riding back into their midst, her horse breathing heavy. "Tomaz will meet up with us at the edge of town."

"I want to go too."

It was Tym, his blonde hair swaying as he looked back and forth between them, standing just inside their circle. The small boy was shaking slightly at his own audacity, as if amazed he'd had the courage to come forward and say what he'd just said. Davydd shifted uncomfortably, glancing quickly at Raven, and then at Lorna, who shook her head. He opened his mouth and then seemed to change his mind. His eyes flicked to Raven again. When he finally spoke, it was slowly, with none of his usual swagger.

"I don't know exactly what's happening, Tym," he said slowly, "but the feeling I get is that Lerne is no place for children."

"I'm not a child!" Tym protested hotly, his tone and gaze making him somehow hard to look at. "I'm your helper. All of you. That's my job – you said it was – and you don't ever let me help anymore. I'm here to help you win – I helped Tomaz beat Daemons in Banelyn, and I helped the Healers fix the hurt people, and then I promised I'd – we all did – that we'd make sure.... I'm a helper, and you might need help in the city, so I'm going."

His blue eyes were burning fiercely, and yet his chest and small hands were trembling with nerves.

"Tym," Raven said, as softly as he could, "it isn't safe. I'm sorry."

The boy's bravado and certainty disappeared like a puff of smoke, and suddenly he was looking down at the ground and his small, booted feet. "Y-yes, Prince Raven," he said, and Raven knew from the quiver in his voice that the boy was trying not to cry. Tym bobbed his head in a strange little bow, and then was gone.

Silence stretched between them all for a moment.

"He's right," Leah said abruptly. "He needs to be with us."

"Did you see something?" Davydd asked.

"I saw that he needs to be with us," she said simply.

"When we get back," Raven said. "Not now. I'm not putting him in harm's way."

Leah just stared at him, and Raven ignored her. He reached out and drew on the Wolf Talisman and Raven Talisman both, taking in as much of their power as he could. He would hold onto all he could gather; he might need it.

"Let's go."

They took fifty Rogues with them, leaving the Rangers and Scouts to circle the city and report back when they all returned to camp at nightfall. Raven supported Leah's choice: The Rogues knew city streets, and many of the ones she'd chosen had worked in Lerne before.

"Be ready for traps," Raven said quickly as they met on the edge of the city, on the road leading west. "The Seekers like to protect their secrets, and this is where they call home. Look before you leap – always."

He barely waited for the others to nod before spurring Melyngale to a full run, shooting down the road, pulling off to the side when possible to spare the horse's knees. His skin had begun to itch, and the anxious energy pooling in the tips of his fingers and toes did not abate. With every moment that passed his anxiety grew stronger. What had happened there? What was it they needed to understand?

An hour passed in silence, until they crested the final rise.

The city of Lerne was situated in a large bowl of land at the foot of the Elmist Mountains. The city itself, tall stone and mortar flying the green serpent crest of Symanta, shone in the morning sun. Mist curled around it like questing fingers, though the rising heat of day was already pushing the fog back into the Mountains. The sight was breathtaking, but it was not the beauty of the scene they focused on, nor the wonderful carvings that adorned the walls. It was the lack they saw, the emptiness that seemed to surround the city and engulf it, even more entirely than the retreating mist. No motion stirred, no noise rang out, but for the listless flapping of the banners flying from the unmanned walls.

The city was abandoned, and its gates yawned open, inviting them in.

"Do you sense anything?" Leah asked him.

"No," he said, trying to keep the growing apprehension from his voice, trying to ignore the way his heart was beating a beat too fast and his lungs were fighting against being squeezed.

"You're certain."

"Yes. I keep trying, but I can't. It's like... how I'd imagine it is being deaf. There's usually something – some kind of background noise almost, like a hum and a few clusters of light. But... there's nothing now. When I reach out, there's only darkness."

They looked at each other.

"Stay close to me," he told her, before he could stop himself.

"Likewise," she replied, holding his gaze.

They continued forward, now at a slower pace that gave them time to examine the outer rock wall of the city, and the way the light seemed to lose strength as it tried to force its way through the morning mist. Before they were ready, they were just outside the gate. There was no damage, either to the wood or the stone that held it; it had simply been left unlocked and open, like the door to an abandoned house. A group of Rogues, twelve in all, crossed through first, and after a brief, nerve-wracking time away, they returned and signaled the all-clear.

As the full mounted group rode through, the first thing Raven noticed was the smell of neglect. It was so strong that it was almost a feeling. The air was stale, as if it had been left unused for days, weeks even. There was a faint hint of rotting food in the distance, and human waste as well, maybe even coming from inside the houses. There was something below that too, something sharp and metallic, but it was thin and tenuous, as if coming to them from a great distance.

Raven absorbed the sight of it next, and with it the sound, the two coming together in strange harmony, for the only sights and sounds were those of objects, not of people. There were no guards on the walls, no men or women walking the streets. Doors hung open, swaying slightly in the kind of soft breeze that usually goes unnoticed, but in the strange emptiness seemed amplified.

None of them spoke; none of them dared. The silence felt both deadly and sacred, and they knew somehow that breaking it would be dangerous and wrong. The city was empty in every sense of the word, and carelessly so. The people here hadn't gotten up, packed for holiday, and left en masse. Doors were open up and down the street, and Raven could see through windows that tables had been laid and now sat abandoned with molding bread and meat still on the plate.

What has happened here?

With a small movement of his wrist, he signaled the others to follow him. They spread out: Leah and Tomaz moved to his right, Lorna and Davydd to his left, while Autmaran and the rest followed close behind.

The city was simply planned, with one long boulevard that bisected the homes into two groups and led straight for the distant Prince's Palace, a surprisingly modest affair on its surface compared to some of the other Imperial seats. The modesty, however, was only a façade. The Palace was set up against the steepest section of mountain, right before the cliff face took off, soaring hundreds of feet into the air, and Raven knew what was behind it.

"Strangely simple for an Imperial palace," Autmaran commented, echoing Raven's thoughts. His voice, normally strong and commanding, was muted here, and barely audible. He hadn't whispered, but it seemed like he had.

"There is always more to the Snake than meets the eye," Tomaz rumbled. His voice, unlike Autmaran's, could not or would not be muted – his deep bass echoed up and down the streets, and Raven had the sudden urge to shush the big man.

There could be shadows waiting in this silence.

"What do you mean?" Autmaran asked.

"He means what you see is an illusion," Leah said, speaking quietly. "It extends into the mountain behind it. The whole cliff side is hollowed out – its where the Seekers live."

"And where they pray to the lovely, lovely Empress for puppies and kitties to torture," Davydd added. "Don't forget that."

Autmaran looked about to speak again, but seemed to decide against it, looking around him at the rooftops still covered in morning mist. The others didn't press him – any noise at all seemed to be too much, even the ringing of their horses hooves on the hard paving stones of the boulevard. As they made their way further in, the city's divide became more and more clear. The Rogues came back and reported what they'd seen on either side of the boulevard, and their picture of the city became more complete. The houses on their left were cramped and narrow, with spider web streets that jutted out and around at odd angles to recombine in a strange patchwork farther in. The buildings themselves were painted wood, with the paint often chipped; cramped merchant shops seemed to occupy every corner, with the odd inn or two every few blocks, while every other building was a rickety panoply of living spaces.

The right side of the boulevard opened up onto wide parks, buildings with stone and plaster molding, and straight roads that met at right corners. The houses there grew more and more expansive until they butted up against where the wall met the mountainside; mansions lounged there, sprawling between walled gardens and once-flowing fountains that now lay silent and still.

But on both sides of the street, the shops were full of goods, the inns left vacant, and the homes, grand and poor alike, lay uniformly deserted.

"It's as if everyone just picked up and left," Lorna whispered, her hoarse voice barely audible.

"No," Tomaz rumbled. "It's not like that at all."

"Tomaz, speak softly," Leah hissed at him.

"Why?" he boomed. "If this is a trap, it wasn't for us, and it's already sprung."

"What do you mean?"

"These people didn't get up and leave, and we all know that. These people were taken from their homes – even the Most High."

Everyone in earshot, which, in the deadly quiet of the city, was most of the group, stiffened and exchanged looks. Many of the Rogues looked worried, and some even looked angry, but none raised a voice to disagree.

"There are no signs of struggle," Davydd said.

"No," Tomaz said, eyeing the shorter man. "But they are gone nonetheless."

"Where did they take them, then?" Autmaran asked.

"We're in the city of the Seekers and the Snake," Tomaz rumbled. "Where do you think they took them?"

With his heavily bearded chin, he motioned to the distant cliff side and the palace façade that footed it. He eyed them all and then heeled his huge black charger Gydion past them, taking the lead. They followed him, all at a loss for words.

The palace loomed over them as the sun climbed higher in the sky. The Rogues continued to scout to either side of the boulevard, combing through houses at random to see if a trace of anyone had been left behind. Some of them came back with torn clothing, and some reported dried blood – how long it had been there, they couldn't say. At least a week, was the universal guess.

A week. The city had been emptied only days after the Exiled Kindred had won Banelyn and killed Dysuna.

"When one of the Children dies," Raven said softly, "the rest of us can feel it. It's like being hit upside the head and kicked in the groin at the same time. You lose your breath, you can't see straight, and you start gasping for air. We're all connected through the Diamond Crown, and we can feel each other, though only to a very small extent."

He glanced at Tomaz and Leah, then Davydd and Lorna, before fixing his eyes straight again. "Symanta felt four of the other Children die, and three within days of each other. Whatever she did, my guess is that she did it then."

They absorbed this in silence and continued on. The last of the mist refused to evaporate, but instead continued to glide down from the heights of the Elmist Mountains and pool about the ground of the Prince's Square that lay at the end of the paved road. They reached the Square and entered, their horses' hooves echoing loudly in their ears; the earthy smells of waste and neglect grew stronger. Raven reached out again, and still felt nothing beyond their party. Not even rats.

This is a city – there should be something. Where is the background noise? What is so different here that even the rodents and insects have fled?

They crossed the courtyard, not knowing what else to do. There was nothing there, not even refuse. The city streets, aside from the broken homes, were spotless as if freshly cleaned, like someone had cared enough to wash up but not to lock the door. None of them motioned for a halt, nor did any of them feel it was necessary. The feeling that built up around them was not that they were being watched, but that they had entered a place that no one felt the need to ever watch again. It was the equivalent of walking through a hollowed out tree: towering, majestic even, but no longer growing, no longer organic. Something had been taken out of this city.

The life. All of the life was just... taken.

The gilded doors of the palace, shining with gold leaf and emerald-eyed bas-relief snakes, stood open wide. No guards stood at their posts, no locks or chains barred their way. A number of Rogues went first anyway, looking inside, spreading out, but came back once more empty handed. The rest of the party dismounted and ascended the long set of carved stone steps that would take them to the entrance.

As soon as Raven's boot connected with the first step, his vision winked out and the world spun around him. He crumpled, gasping in pain and clutching his head; it felt as though a needle had been shoved through his spine up into his brain.

He came back to reality to find Tomaz holding him in his huge arms, Leah looking into his eyes, checking his pulse along his neck. "He's fine," she said, pulling back. She had her stone face on, but he could see the worry in her eyes, could see the fine lines that showed she was concerned.

He pushed himself back up, and Tomaz let him go.

"What happened?" the giant rumbled.

"I don't know," he said. "But I saw… darkness. All around. And a haze, covering everything. I don't understand it. It was like looking at a scene through a transparent veil. It made no sense."

He looked over at Leah. "Can you look into the future?" he asked. "Can you try to reach out?"

"I've been trying to ever since we got here," she said, the edges of her mouth tightening in frustration. "I can't get it. There are flashes – " Her eyes turned blue, and then immediately back to green. "But nothing more. And it's like you just said: Everything I see is hazy; I can't make anything out. It's like trying to look through smoke. Like there's something… something… "

"Something covering the world," he said without thinking. "Like a piece of thin fabric, pulled tight. Only here it's been ripped."

As soon as the words had left his mouth, he knew they were true. They summed it up perfectly, and he saw the confirmation in Leah's eyes as well. She nodded slowly, and the others looked as if they agreed as well: Tomaz and Davydd were both nodding without realizing it. Lorna was solemnly watching Raven, expressionless, and Autmaran had his hand on his sword, scanning the area as he would a potential battlefield. The Commander moved past Raven and the others and strode through the doorway, his hand still grasping the hilt of his sword, his shoulders stooped, ready for an attack.

The others followed quickly; after whatever had happened the first time, Raven was fine walking through the door now, though he recoiled at the thought of reaching through the Raven Talisman again while he was here. Something told him that that was why he'd felt the shock and pain – something told him that this place wasn't just empty of life, but full of something else, something that had taken its place.

The antechamber was much the same as the outside of the palace: majestic, with beautiful tapestries, gorgeous carvings, and not the smallest hint of a living, breathing soul. There was one change, however: it was darker here.

They lit torches that had been readied when the palace was still occupied, and that gave light enough. The high windows let in only a paltry gray light that gave everything the half-seen quality of twilight even though it was only a few hours from midday. The flickering light of the flames cast strange shadows on the twisting, curved corridors they took through the palace; they passed large reception rooms that seemed alive with shadowy ghosts, and long halls lined with sitting rooms, studies, and lounges, each full of the lifelessness that coated the very walls.

Finally, they came to a long, straight stairway and began to ascend.

As they climbed the steps, they found themselves rising up through the center of an enormous audience chamber, with a throne carved into a sheer, unadorned rock wall at the far end. It was clear that this soaring cliff side, and the throne itself, were part of the living mountain, and looked to have been chiseled away from a gigantic sheet of granite half buried in earth. It was an astonishing feat of craftsmanship, and made even more impressive by the wan light of the torches and the shadows they cast. A row of double pillars lined the two far sides of the hall, running parallel to the group as they walked toward the rock wall, and the ceiling that started out low, rose exponentially into the sky until it towered above them, soaring hundreds of feet and thinning out until it touched and merged with the sheet of granite. Their footsteps echoed in the silence of the chamber, and the shadows flickered and moved with them, as if the darkness and the haze that Raven and Leah had seen were coalescing around them.

It was Davydd who reached the throne first, and as he did the left side of his body began to pulse with golden light. He didn't seem to notice – he continued forward, about to reach out and run a hand along the massive granite throne, when he stumbled, tripping over his own feet in a way Raven had never seen the lithe, graceful Eshendai do; his hands went awry, trying to catch himself as he fell, and he landed before the throne, arms spread wide as if prostrating himself.

Before any of them could react, golden light spread out from between his fingers, curling and weaving through the solid stone. It swirled and arched until it had outlined a space directly before the throne seven feet wide and seven feet long. Once the outline was complete, the light disappeared, there was a dull *click*, and then the ground began to move.

"Whoa!"

"Step back!"

Davydd managed to retreat just as the section of stone floor fell inward; it slid away in one solid piece on cleverly concealed hinges and settled with a loud clunk that resounded throughout the chamber, echoing around them before fading into that vast, unnatural silence. Raven was the first to act: he stepped forward and thrust a torch into the gaping black maw that yawned below them. The flickering light revealed stone steps that led down into the darkness, descending beneath the throne.

"I wouldn't trust that with all of us," said one of the Rogues. Raven glanced over and recognized Polim and Palum, Autmaran's right and left hands. They were twins, both older than typical for Rogues, with long silver hair, and both stalwart fighters. It was Polim, the Eshendai, who had spoken, and it was he who continued. "Let two of us go first to scout it – there may be traps."

"And you won't be able to disarm them," Raven said, not unkindly. "I'm not sending you down there to die – I go first." He turned to the others. "All of us – everyone who bears a Talisman. Most Bloodmagic cannot touch us; we go first."

Both Polim and Palum immediately looked ready to argue, as did some of the others, but Autmaran held up a hand and they all stayed silent. "Polim and Palum," he said, "you come with us. But you stay at the *back*." He glanced questioningly at

Raven, who nodded very slightly. "When we reach the bottom, or wherever this leads, one of you will come back and bring the rest, and the other will stay with us. But this is uncharted territory – no one dies here from stupidity. Understood?"

"Yes, sir," they said as one.

They turned back to the open hole in the floor, and Raven's mind suddenly clouded with all the tales he'd heard of Seeker's lairs, and what he had experienced when he'd been trapped in one.

Bloodmage enchantments... torture chambers... terror soaked into the very walls themselves.

He moved forward before he could lose his nerve.

The others followed quickly behind, though Tomaz had to go down leaning almost entirely backwards. The others all were forced to crouch, hunching their shoulders and ducking their heads; the passage had been designed to make them feel small, Raven was sure of it. It was part of the brain washing the Empire exerted on the Seekers and any others who passed this way – they were but worms beneath the feet of the Children, and their only desire should be to serve.

The stairway didn't twist, didn't turn. It just descended, down and down forever. The air was cold and stale, and as they went farther and farther down it began to take on a strange metallic taste – a taste that mirrored the smell above in the city.

Are we entering an armory?

They continued down, and they began to sweat. More time passed and thoughts began to race through Raven's mind: he began wishing he was elsewhere, anywhere but here. He heard Tomaz begin to breathe in increasingly short and erratic bursts, and Raven realized this was quite likely the first time the big man had been trapped somewhere his strength couldn't save him. After all, even Tomaz couldn't punch his way through solid rock. Davydd and Lorna were fairing the best, but even they were having difficulties – Raven glanced back and saw them both crouching down far further than was necessary.

A few dozen yards farther down and Raven felt the same feeling come over him. Suddenly there wasn't enough air in the staircase – the ceiling was too close, the floor rising to meet it. There was no room for them, no space – they had to get out of here – they were going to die, suffocated under the mountain –

He began to trip and stumble down the stairs, trying to move faster on cramping legs. His panic was contagious; the others began to stumble as well, and the one time he looked back he saw Leah's eyes had widened, showing white all the way around; Autmaran was behind her, sweating and even shaking as he looked from side to side, his hands outstretched as if to force the walls backward and away from him; Polim and Palum were clutching hands, alternating turns going first, as the shadows chased their footsteps to close in the group in a roving band of solitary light under the crushing weight of the mountain.

Raven stepped on a stair that shifted beneath him, and a violent gust of wind blew up at them from below; the torchers flickered, wavered, and went out.

Madness ensued. Someone shouted, two people screamed, and Raven felt himself pushed in the back, sending him sprawling down a dozen stairs. He shouted for the others to stop, but they didn't hear him; Tomaz roared for them to go faster; Leah shouted for the others to leave her alone, to stop touching her.

"SILENCE!"

The crack of command came from the lips of Autmaran, and his was the only voice that seemed able to penetrate, abate, and hold off the terror that had descended on them. "Everyone stay where you are, and listen to the sound of my voice."

They all stood still, though Raven felt as though the air around him had gelled and now clutched him tight.

"Raven – can you use your Talisman?"

He closed his eyes, reached out, and light blossomed inside his mind. Pure, unadulterated relief filled him, and he went weak in the knees as his lungs relaxed and he was able to take a full breath. They were all with him; he could see them in his mind.

But even as he held the Talisman, a dull ache began to build in the back of his head, at the base when his spine met his skull. He remembered the sharp pain he'd felt when he'd put his foot on the palace steps, and he knew that this was somehow related. It was a kind of primal sense that he couldn't understand or place, but that he knew was trying to drive him away.

If I was smarter, I'd listen.

"Yes, I've got it," was what he said out loud. "I can feel you all; everyone's here; we're all fine."

"Good – Tomaz, Davydd, reach through yours."

They did, and a low light of red and gold spread through the chamber, just enough to let them see. The walls hadn't encroached on them after all. They were all there still, Tomaz braced against both walls with his huge arms and legs, Lorna kneeling on the ground, Davydd and Leah both pushed up against the stone walls, their hands grasping at cracks.

"Good," Autmaran said, his own panic held at bay now that he had a task to do and something to organize. "Now move forward *slowly*. Raven leading."

They did as told, and began to descend once more.

"Where did that wind come from?" Lorna rasped.

"It was a trap," Raven said. "A hidden catch in one of the steps – not a Bloodmage enchantment, just something to induce terror in whomever passed this way. It wasn't meant for us – it was meant for the Seekers, to remind them that the only light comes from the Path. It's the same with this fear – it isn't natural. But it's low level enough that our Talismans – Aspects – can't fight it off entirely. If we weren't protected as much as we are, we'd be gibbering in terror right now.

"Leah," Autmaran said immediately, "can you reach ahead with the Eagle and see if there's anything else lying in wait?"

"I can't – something's blocking me. I can only see darkness – and a... what looks like a sea or something. I have no idea why."

"Very well – Raven, do your best to watch your step."

They all fell silent, and Raven regretted it; when they were talking, it was easier to forget where they were. Panic and terror were still waiting in the wings of his mind, hidden just out of sight and fighting to get in, but by holding the Raven Talisman he was better able to withstand it.

They descended for more time, and now with every step the sharp tang of salt filled the air, mixed with the same metallic smell from before. And what was more, something strange was building inside Raven's mind. It was like a ringing sound accompanied by a building sense of a headache behind his temples. It almost felt as if he should be seeing something, but something was preventing him.

"HOLD!"

Everyone froze, and Raven stood with his arms held wide, looking directly above him. A flowing, scrolling piece of script wrapped around an outcropping of rock that jutted down from the ceiling above them. It was in Bloodmage runes, he knew that immediately, but the inky blackness of them was indecipherable. He slowly crossed forward, knowing the Raven Talisman should protect him from any kind of interference, and reached out to touch the red blood-drop insignia, the sign of Bloodmage work.

As soon as the pads of his fingers touched the rough wall of stone, the script stopped, shivered, and faded away. Raven waited for a second, and then realized the trap had been deactivated.

"What was it meant to do?" Davydd asked from behind.

"Collapse the tunnel," Raven said grimly. "That rock must be a keystone for something – likely the enchantment would have moved it if someone not of the Seekers or High Blood had passed beneath."

The tension mounted, but they continued on, deeper and deeper into the all-encompassing dark, until they found their way blocked by a solid wall of stone. Raven had to fight the terror again, had to keep it at bay as best he could. There had to be a way through this – there *had* to be.

He examined the stone; on it was an image of the Diamond crown and the Imperial *triliope* – the single golden flower, the seven blades of grass, and the long black ribbon that bound it. The carving was wider than Raven's torso and nearly as long, and below it was writing etched in white fire:

Here lies the true sanctum of Our Goddess, the Diamond Empress of Lucia, Heir of Theron Isdiel, may She live and reign forever. Only those of purity and holy heart may enter here; all else must perish and hope for cleansing in the righteous fires of heaven.

Glory to the Empress! Glory to the Diamond Throne on which She sits! Glory to the legacy of Her Empire and Her Will!

"What does it mean?" rumbled Tomaz, from farther up. He looked calmer now too, holding his Talisman, but he was still forced to practically slide down the steps on his back. The fact he had made it so far spoke volumes about his mental fortitude.

"It means we need to speak the Path," Raven said. "Simple really... I don't understand why there weren't more traps. Why would Symanta leave all of this unguarded?"

"Why would she leave her entire *city* unguarded?" Leah asked.

"Good point. I don't understand it."

"My guess is the answer is on the other side of that door," Davydd said, impatiently. "So open it and let's get this over with."

Raven turned and spoke the words of the Seeker's Path: "I seek the one who seeks the light, and I mean to seek Her by following the path myself. I seek the Path so that my eyes may be opened to the Light."

There was a large cracking noise, and the outline of a door appeared along the outer edges of the wall. The words etched in white fire disappeared as a single line of pure white split the wall in twain, right down the center of the crown and *triliope*; the two sides began to slowly revolve outwards, leaving a space barely wide enough to fit between.

"Wait here until I call," Raven said. They all looked ready to argue, but none of them did, for which he was grateful. He turned and edged his way through the opening.

The immediate impression was of a huge space, but Raven could actually *see* none of it. The air was freezing, and the scrape of his boot against the stone floor echoed over and over, both above and to the sides. He laid a hand against the wall and traced it to the side, where he was out of the way of the stone door; his hand hit a metal bracket, and he realized there was a torch there, only half used. He felt around more and found below it a small pouch, with flint and steel inside. He quickly struck the two together, showering sparks on the still-oiled torch, which caught quickly. He turned, holding the flame high in the air, and looked around him.

Chambers and paths led off both left and right, to a number of openings honeycombing a cavernous space. The light from the torch didn't even reach high enough to touch the ceiling, but it did illuminate racks of candles, rows of seats, and prayer rugs worn by countless penitent knees and hands. He crossed quickly to the candles and lit them with the torch, adding their light. There were more racks further on, and he lit these too, watching carefully as the light began to build higher and higher. He saw more torches in wall sconces, and lit those as well.

"Okay!" he called out toward the door. "Come in!"

He turned back around, and felt his throat close up as the light suddenly bloomed bright enough to reveal his surroundings.

It was an underground Cathedral, one more splendid even than Banelyn's. Statues of angels and demons so lifelike Raven almost thought they were living creatures frozen in stone stared down at him from carved rock outcroppings. Water dripped somewhere far off in the distance, and he could see huge stalagmite pillars soaring hundreds of feet into the air, ringing a center area that was still masked in darkness. He stepped forward and raised his torch high overhead. The light fell on something else, something that he couldn't understand at first. He stepped forward once more.

As Raven raised the torch high, the light fell over the side of the empty space and shone down on the shores of an underground lake full with an ocean of blood. The torchlight guttered and spit as if the sight sickened even the unfeeling flame. Glints shone around the sides of the huge underground basin, and Raven's eyes raked over the image of metal holding hooks and channels that had been cut in the bedrock to funnel liquid – *blood, it's blood!* – down from higher levels. In the center of the lake, elevated high over the water and connected to its own platform by several long buttressed catwalks, was a stone platform carved with swirling red lines that pulsed dimly in the shadows of the chamber. At the center of the lines – the center of the Bloodmage rune – was a huge hole that looked terribly familiar. It was the hole into which a Soul Catcher might be placed.

Blood... that was the metallic smell, and the sea Leah kept seeing.

And in spite of the terrible sight, there seemed to be something worse at play, something that began to worm its way into Raven's mind. He felt... dirty. As if he'd been coated in slime. His very presence felt tainted, and he knew suddenly that a thousand years would never wash clean that feeling. No, all he could do, all he had to do, was step forward and let himself be taken by this too. There was no power in him to resist it – he was dirty, he was unclean, he had to offer himself up to the Goddess, the Empress, and know that through her – *only* through her – was there a path to salvation –

He reached out on instinct and caught at the Raven Talisman, and the thoughts cut off, leaving him in blank, shocked silence.

"STOP!"

Autmaran, who had just made it into the room, froze between the heavy stone doors. "Go back," Raven commanded. "No one without a Talisman comes through those doors – there's some kind of enchantment that's – "

Autmaran's eyes went blank, and he ran toward Raven. No, not toward Raven – toward the waiting lake. Raven stepped forward and rammed his fist into the man's stomach, then dealt him a blow to the back of the neck that made him go limp. He caught the Commander before he hit the ground and hauled him back toward the doors before anyone else could come through, his breathing coming in harsh, sharp pants as he tried to block the enchantment's thoughts from his mind by clinging to his Talisman.

He reached the entrance just as Leah was making her way through.

"No," he gasped, "go back!"

She caught sight of him and stared, then quickly pulled back to allow him to haul Autmaran through the doors. He fell to the floor inside, and Lorna immediately caught Autmaran and checked for a pulse, felt to make sure he was breathing. Polim caught Raven's torch, still grasped loosely in his hand, and lit the others that had been blown out, spreading light through the antechamber.

"What happened?"

"It looks like he's been hit... Raven – did you do this?"

"Don't go in," he said, breathless. "Lorna, take Autmaran – no, he's fine, he's just unconscious – take him back up the stairs. Polim and Palum – you guard this door. No one – *no one* – enters here until I say so. There's an enchantment that only those with Aspects can avoid."

He turned to Leah, Davydd, and Tomaz.

"Grab onto them and don't let them go," he said, trying to stress the importance of what he was saying. "No matter what happens, no matter what you see – "

– Oh shadows and light, what they're going to see –

" – don't let go of them. Hold them. Do it – now."

"What about Lorna?" Davydd asked.

"No one without a Talisman," he said.

"She'd have one if you'd done what's right," he snarled. "She's coming – she goes where I go."

"Then you're not coming," Raven said flatly, his voice cold and hard, without anger. Shock had driven any thoughts of anger too far from his mind; he was surprised he was still functioning.

How many people need to be drained to fill such a space?

Davydd caught Raven's gaze and went silent, no doubt sensing the shock written all over him. The Ranger's own anger disappeared and wariness took its place.

"Your hands are shaking," Leah said quietly, reaching out to grab hold of them, a rare moment of public contact that showed him just how frightened he must look. "What's going on? What happened?"

"What's beyond those doors?" Tomaz rumbled, the words shaking Raven's bones as much as the thought of what was behind him, of what had been done here.

Raven swallowed and held onto his Talisman with all his might, willing his mind to be still. "The answer to a lot of questions," he said quietly.

They didn't challenge him, but Davydd didn't back down either.

"Fine – then I stay here with Lorna. Polim and Palum can take Autmaran back – we're not leaving until you return."

Raven grimaced, but nodded, though Polim and Palum both raised their voices.

"Fine!" Raven shouted. "You can stay – but you sit on those steps and you go nowhere else. One of you at least go back up – tell the others not to come down. No one enters. Understood?"

They nodded as one, and then Palum took off running up the stairs, her silver hair glinting in the torch light. Polim grabbed Autmaran and positioned him on the stairs, trying to make him as comfortable as possible; the bald man's head lolled about on his shoulders, and Raven hoped he would be all right when he woke.

Please let the enchantment be weakening. Please let it be only confined to the chamber now.

"Hold on tight," Raven said to Leah and Tomaz, as they grabbed their Aspects, Leah's eyes flickering blue and holding, for once, while Tomaz's body glowed a deep scarlet beneath his armor. "Don't let go."

Raven turned back and led them in, forcing himself to walk even though his body was moving in barely controllable jerks and shakes. When they came close enough for the light of the torch to reach out and once more strike the surface of the underground lake, both Tomaz and Leah gasped. There was a thudding sound, and Raven realized Tomaz had fallen to his knees.

"What... what would have happened if we weren't holding the Talismans?" Leah asked. Her voice was hoarse and choked, but she forced it out anyway. Raven could see her eyes, but the blue in them was lost. They had turned purple in the light of the torch and the reflection of the blood.

"You'd have tried to throw yourself in," Raven said, talking in a monotone that didn't waver, afraid that if he stopped he'd be unable to start again. "It's an old trap. It was used often in the early days of the Empire, back before Bloodmagic was widely known. Bloodmages would go into an enemy town, inscribe the words on the most important stone of the city, and perform the ritual in the dead of night when no one was watching. By the next day... the whole population, men, women, and children, would have been drawn to the stone. They would kill themselves on it, and the Bloodmages would pull power from the deaths, storing life in their Soul Catchers."

"The whole population... you mean all of Lerne."

"I do. I think... I think that it might go even further. It might be Whitestone too, and maybe cities to the south and north." His stomach roiled, and he bent over, hands on knees, and vomited across the carefully laid stones of the Cathedral. He coughed and gagged, and through it all he could hear Leah doing the same not far away.

Hundreds of thousands of people... that's how much blood is down there. That's what it takes to make a sea of blood.

When he managed to stop, when there was nothing else to empty, he wiped his mouth, and turned back, forcing himself to look at it.

This is what we're fighting. This is the measure of their resolve.

He strode forward, toward the form of Tomaz, who still sat fallen to his knees, staring out at the sea. Silent tears were flowing down his face, and grief had etched itself into every line of his face. Raven walked past him, toward the walkway that joined the edge of the pool with the tall, elevated island in the center.

"Where are you going?" Leah asked behind him.

Raven didn't respond. Where Tomaz had gone from shock to grief, he had gone from shock to anger. It built up inside him, burning all other thoughts away.

He strode forward, straightening his back as he went, defying what they had done here, defying the emptiness he felt. The room shifted oddly about him, and he dismissed it as a trick of the light. The oblique *something* that had been wrong with Lerne was centered here, in this enormous room, and his anger, with nowhere to go, could only come out at what was left. "How could you do this?" he whispered to the Cathedral at large. He was halfway toward the middle island now, and he realized he was almost running.

This was like the Kindred Odeon – it was an amphitheater. That island was the pulpit, where the head Seeker would come to preach to the gathered masses below. This whole pool... it used to be filled with seats where Seekers sat to listen to the homily.

"How could you do this?" he repeated, louder; loud enough that the words echoed back to him from the corners of the huge, silent chamber. He reached the center and saw the gaping hole where the enormous Soul Catcher must have been, a crystal that would be half the size of Tomaz, and around it a ring of stones inscribed with the words of the Affirmations.

This is where the Seeker would stand to preach the glories of the Empress. This is where the Bloodmages inscribed their enchantment.

And even as he thought the words, black script blossomed and began to scroll along the edges of the stones, line after line of runes that he couldn't read.

"HOW COULD YOU DO THIS?!"

The room shouted the words back down at him, turning his scream into a screeching cry of despair, as if the stones themselves were shouting back at him, turning back his accusation with a protestation of their own innocence. He pulled Aemon's Blade from its sheath at his side and raised it high overhead, then brought it slicing down on the stone in front of him. The valerium sword bit deeply into the rock, throwing sparks off into the air and cutting the line of scrolling runes in half.

The enchantment froze, shivered, and then evaporated.

There was a long instant of silence, during which Raven could only hear himself breathing, the sound of it echoed over and over by the acoustics of the cavern. And then the world began to shift.

It was slight at first, only a distant rumble, but it began to build. One of the various honeycombed entrances in the huge underground cathedral exploded in a huge plume of dust. Two more followed on the opposite side, and then pieces of the ceiling cracked apart and fell, spiraling past Raven to land with a sickening splash in the blood below him. He pulled Aemon's Blade from the stone and ran. He saw Leah pulling Tomaz to his feet, forcing him to move, but the big man still seemed in a daze, unable to understand what was happening around him, unable to comprehend anything at all. Raven heard his own blood pounding in his ears, and he knew they didn't have much time.

He reached the shore just as Tomaz came back to his feet, and Leah shouted for him to follow them. More of the cavern collapsed, and as it did something strange happened in Raven's mind. The world began to shift in a way he couldn't understand. As he watched, the doors closed in and broke under the strain of the mountain, blocking their way and ensuring their death.

But through his anger and fear, Raven refused to believe it. He chose for the doors to be whole again – he chose for them to remain unbroken.

The world *shifted*, and became the way he wanted it.

Rocks fell from above him, crashing into where he'd been not a second before. Leah and Tomaz dove through the now-open doors, and Raven followed them himself, ducking beneath the sagging lintel. On the other side, the whole staircase was shifting and moving as well, and Polim, Davydd, and Lorna were staring with wide eyes.

"What in the name of the seven hells did you do in there?!"

"*Just run!*"

Lorna caught up Autmaran in her arms, and they all took the stairs as fast as they could manage them. The ascent took barely half the time it had taken to go down, but to Raven's mind it was much, much longer. Rocks fell all around them, and the torch he'd managed to light was knocked from hand and left behind. Only the light of the Talismans guided them now – Davydd out in front and Tomaz bringing up the rear.

"Faster, faster, go faster!" he shouted.

"Almost there!"

And then they were out. They burst from the staircase into the open air in a huge rush of dirt and flying stone. Cries sounded from all around them as the other Rogues shot to their feet, coming to their aid, but Raven pushed them all away.

"Don't stop," he said, his voice raspy, throat clogged with dirt and grime and a thousand conflicting emotions. "Not yet – it's not over!"

He pushed past them toward the stairs they'd taken into the audience chamber and throne room. He felt the other Rogues pause behind him, but Lorna, Davydd, Leah, and Tomaz followed him without question. And as soon as they were halfway across the room, the entire cliff wall behind them began to rumble and shake.

"Run, run, run, run, run!" Raven repeated over and over again, both to himself and to the others following. They couldn't stop – they had to get out of the palace. They had to get out of the city.

Far away – as far away as possible – away from all of it –

"RAVEN!"

He shot a glance over his shoulder but didn't slow. It was Leah – her eyes flashing blue, illuminating their future path; she was frantically motioning for him to move right. Without question, he did. An enormous chunk of rock fell from the ceiling the next second and crashed into the space where he would have been had he continued straight. With no time to thank her, though, he ran on, and as a group they descended the stairs and raced for the entrance hall.

The walls there began to shiver too, as if they had caught a cold and were in the throes of a violent fever that wouldn't break. And then the wood paneling that lined the corridor in front of them began to explode outward in huge sprays of splintered wood and ripped tapestries. The beautiful statues crumbled, split, and exploded. Raven felt his arm pierced by a sliver of wood bigger than an arrow, and a huge piece of marble crashed into his leg, leaving him limping. But still he ran, even as pain coursed up his leg and blood ran down his side, the wounds healing even as he watched. The others ran with him, no one slowing or pausing for any reason, Leah shouting out orders every other second, saving their lives multiple times over.

They exploded through the front doors just as the roof fell in behind them. Raven tripped and rolled down the steps that led to the door, only managing to catch himself once he'd already bruised every part of his body possible. The others came with him, some tripping themselves, and they were again racing, this time through the city itself.

At first it looked as though they had managed to escape the onslaught, that they had managed to get to safety. And then a *crack* sounded behind them so loud it was as though the skies themselves had been broken apart. Raven turned back to look and saw the entire cliff side under which Lerne was built now riddled with spider-web fissures from bottom to top.

The whole thing was about to come crashing down, wiping out the city.

"DON'T STOP, PRINCELING!"

At the sound of Leah's scream he realized he'd frozen, and the others were rushing past him. He turned and ran with them, now bringing up the rear. The ground buckled beneath them as the first of the stones rained down. Raven, unable to keep from watching, looked over his shoulder as the palace disappeared in a wave of mountainous rock that rolled forward like an avalanche. A huge cloud of dust preceded it, racing toward them, blowing out windows and staving in doors.

The boulevard bucked again, this time rising up beneath them and throwing them forward as the impact of the mountain into the ground behind them sent shockwaves racing forward. Buildings toppled left and right, even crashing in their path. Tomaz grabbed a handful of Rogues and hurled them bodily over one of the fallen structures, and then threw himself over as well.

Raven pounded along behind them, but soon began to fall back. His head was swimming, and he realized his entire side was sticky with the blood that had fallen from the wound in his arm. Something was wrong – the wound hadn't healed. Bright gray light was shining through the tear in his armor, but the wound wasn't healing. His legs didn't seem to be responding properly; he was losing control of his body.

"Tomaz!" he cried, but the big man was too far away to hear him.

He reached out to the Raven Talisman, unable to think of anything else that would help him, just as another building came crashing down from the sky not ten feet behind him. Rocks rained down like hail, breaking holes in the well-laid paving stones of the long boulevard, and Raven could do nothing but continue forward, praying, screaming, crying for his life to be spared.

He reached down deep, and felt again that strange *shifting* in the world that existed here, that pervaded the entire city, and he forced his will on reality.

A huge rock about to crash down onto his path changed direction in mid-air and flew the other way; the road suddenly bucked beneath him again, but in such a way that he was forced *forward,* not back or to the side. He stumbled again, and somehow paving stones rose to meet him. The Raven Talisman burned so hot along his shoulders and back that he felt as though he would soon burst into fire, and the hilt of Aemon's Blade shone like the sun.

And then he was through the crumbling gates, and sprawling along the side of the road where the others had gathered.

"Raven!"

"Grab him before he falls – "

"By the seven hells, that's blood – "

"I'm fine," he gasped. "I just need this shadow-cursed piece of wood out of my arm. Tomaz – pull it out."

The giant lumbered forward and did as requested. The pain was excruciating, but it was over quickly, and the wound began to close almost immediately as the Wolf Talisman set to work and healed his body. Crashing sounds came from behind them, and they turned as one to watch what was left of the cliff side detach itself from its precipitous perch and bury what was left of the city of Lerne.

"We need to be farther away," Raven said, getting to his feet. Someone had gathered the horses – whoever had had the presence of mind to do that was of stronger will than Raven could have thought possible – and it looked as though many of the Rogues had escaped unharmed, and all had escaped alive. Raven mounted Melyngale, watching the others follow his lead with strange, stilted movements that belied shock and pain. Lorna threw Autmaran over her lap and tied his horse's reins to her saddle horn. Two of the Rogues did the same with companions who'd been and couldn't sit, and when everyone was secure they left.

They didn't rein their horses in again until the town of Whitestone was in sight. None of them spoke during the whole journey back. Davydd and Lorna veered off when they reached the town, heading toward where the Healers had been setting up when they'd left; Raven looked over to see Lorna clutching a bloodied hand to her chest, face an ashen gray, Autmaran still sprawled across her saddle. The rest of the Rogues split off as well, going either for the Healers or their tents. Leah and Tomaz followed him to the command tent, erected in the center of the town square between the tall inns and shops, and as one they dismounted.

"I'll get the Generals," Tomaz rumbled, and then was gone.

"I'll find the Elders," Leah said, leaving too.

And so Raven entered the tent alone.

His mind was reeling and he searched frantically around the room for something to hold onto. He grasped the edge of the heavy map table, trying to crush the wood between his hands, and then let go. He picked up a chair and swung it into the air, ready to throw it or hit something, then dropped it instead. He threw an elbow into the center tent pole and only succeeded in bruising his skin. He cursed, and then took a deep breath, trying to calm himself.

He hadn't ever expected something like that. He knew his brothers and sisters were evil, knew too that his Mother had done terrible things all throughout the history of the Empire, but being presented with the evidence was something else entirely.

A lake of blood... all for what?

He remembered the empty space in the center of the pulpit, the space where a Soul Catcher would have been placed in a Bloodmage ceremony. The crystal itself would have to be enormous – to hold that much power, to harness that many souls, it would have to be nearly the size of a full grown man.

There was movement at the tent entrance, and Tym slipped in with a camp servant.

"My Prince," the servant said, "is there anything I can get you?"

"Fetch runners," Raven said. "Get the Rogues that just came in with me to the Healers, have every one of them checked, then tell them to rest. Wake Autmaran when you can and bring him here. I want everyone – the entire Council."

The man bowed and departed, leaving only little Tym behind. The young boy shuffled to the side, moving away from the center of the tent where Raven paced.

Shadows and light, thank the gods we didn't take him with us.

"Tym, you shouldn't be here, go – "

The tent flap moved again, and Leah entered with Ishmael, Spader close behind. As the flap fell closed again, Raven realized the sun was setting. A full day gone.

How long were we down there? How did I not notice that on the way back?

"What is this all about?" Spader asked. He had his amber robes on backwards, and was trying to turn them around without having to pull them off again. "Did you just get back from Lerne? You were longer than expected, but can't we debrief it all tonight after dinner?"

"Matters have become rather more pressing than originally thought," Raven said dryly. "But we need to wait for the others before we start."

"But what — ?"

"We need to wait," Raven repeated, emphasizing his words, "for the others."

Spader swallowed and snapped his mouth closed. His eyes glinted with anger at being treated in such a way, and Raven was reminded that this man, for all his pomp and dry swagger, was one of his true believers and not someone to alienate.

"I apologize, Elder," he said. "But we *must* wait. I thank you for your patience."

Somewhat mollified, Spader walked over to stand by Ishmael, whose eyes glinted darkly out from his scarred and pockmarked face in the waning light of day. A lamp sputtered into life across the tent, and Raven realized Tym was still with them.

"Tym, I told you —"

The tent flap moved again, and Tomaz entered with Generals Dunhold and Gates. Both were wearing their armor and riding boots, and it was clear that they, unlike Spader, had been expecting a summons at any moment.

"Generals," Raven said. Gates nodded and moved to the map table without another word; he knew by now that he would be called upon when needed and not before. Dunhold, however, stood near the entrance, looking confused.

"Where is Eshendai Goldwyn?" he asked. "And Ashandel Lamas? What about Commander Autmaran?"

Raven brushed past him and out of the tent once more. There were a number of soldiers gathered outside, all looking at the sudden flurry of motion with interest, but when Raven emerged they all found very pressing activities that needed their attention elsewhere.

"Sir?"

Raven turned just as a runner in green and silver broke through the closest group and saluted before him. "Good timing – I need you to find someone."

"Who, sir?"

"Three people," he said, speaking much more calmly than he felt. "Get me Rangers Goldwyn and Lamas, and Commander Autmaran if he's able to move."

"I just saw them, sir – "

"Where?"

"They're at the Healer's tent – "

"Bring them here on stretchers if you have to."

The runner saluted and moved off immediately, and while Raven turned away to head back inside, his mind clutched suddenly at the one part of the whole experience that made the least amount of sense.

We were trapped in that chamber, and then the doors were open... that boulder should have killed me, and then it missed... I changed the way the world worked. I... no, that's not possible. I must have imagined it.

The tent flap moved aside, and he was in once again, and found that everyone was talking at once.

"It was a trap," Leah was saying, "it was a trap the whole time. They knew we wouldn't just pass it by. Raven was right, we never should have gone."

"Eshendai," rumbled Tomaz, "you are speaking without thinking. Just because you can see that far in advance doesn't mean everyone can."

"What exactly happened?" Spader asked. "You say the entire city collapsed? Was that the roar we heard earlier today?"

"A plume of smoke rose up above the mountains," Ishmael said in his rasping voice, "was that a part of what happened?"

"The entire city was covered – "

"We only just managed to get out – "

"Everyone be still," Raven said, his voice low but intense, carrying with it the tone of command his brother Rikard had taught him to use. They all quieted, though they still looked ready to break into dialogue at the slightest provocation.

"We need to wait for – "

"Davydd and Lorna?" drawled a voice behind him. "Well, that's a pleasant change. I was starting to think we'd been kicked out of Raven's Happy Friends Group."

Davydd and Lorna entered the tent with Commander Autmaran not far behind, Lorna with her hand and shoulder wrapped in thick layers of bandage and Davydd limping slightly. Autmaran looked sore and shaken, but awake and mobile.

"Shadows and fire," Leah said, reaching for Davydd. "I thought the Fox Talisman was supposed to protect you from harm?"

"Aspect of Luck now, sis," Davydd grimaced. "And the Healers said an inch to the right and the splinter would've hit an artery, and an inch to the left and I'd've lost my balls. Splitting the difference, I'd call that luck."

"Young Goldwyn's balls aside," Spader said dryly, "we need to talk about what happened."

"Yes," Tomaz rumbled. "What *did* happen?"

"My question as well," Ishmael rasped. "Leah said – "

"Symanta arranged for the entire population of Lerne to take their own lives beneath the city in the Seeker's Cathedral," Raven said quietly. "The city was a grave even before it was buried by the mountain."

Leah and Tomaz exchanged a look, and Raven knew both were remembering the sight beneath the mountain, the pool of blood.

"What... what do you mean *all* of them? Surely there are refugees, this is not a thing that is so simple as rounding up all the citizens – "

"There was a hole left in the center of the space," Raven continued, as if no one else had spoken. "A space where a huge Soul Catcher, the biggest I've ever seen, could have been placed. Around that space was a pool of blood – a *lake* of it. I wouldn't even have thought such a thing possible, but it is. It's buried now, beneath the mountain, with whatever is left of the bodies, if they weren't moved or liquefied."

Spader, Ishmael, and the Generals were all staring at him in horror.

"That's... that can't be... " Dunhold looked around frantically, as if asking for someone to tell him this was a sick joke.

"The whole city," Ishmael said, watching Raven with blank eyes. It wasn't a question; he was simply speaking, trying to put into words a concept none of them seemed able to fully grasp. "The whole city."

"But then, what did they do with the crystal?" Gates asked, as if that were the one question that would stump them and prove the whole thing a fable. "If they made a Soul Catcher of such immense power, where did they take it?"

"I don't know," Raven admitted. "But my guess would be north, to Rikard or the Empress. If they gather enough power, no force we put in the field, no strategy we devise or clever tactic we stumble upon, will *ever* be enough to defeat them. The only thing we have on our side now is time. They will have to travel slowly with such a crystal, and once it is in place more rituals will need to be performed to link it to a user."

"How much time?"

"If we continue at our given pace," Raven said, "My guess is they could activate it hours after we arrive outside Lucien. And whoever links to it will have the kind of power that could level mountains."

Silence rang through the tent at this pronouncement.

"This changes our plan," Autmaran said, carefully eyeing Raven.

"This changes nothing," Raven responded calmly. "The plan is sound; it doesn't need to be changed. We continue on just as before."

"This changes *everything,*" Autmaran continued, his voice quiet, not raised the slightest bit, but full of intension and insistent pragmatism. "Our assumption was that we would bypass a city that was still intact. The implications in that are myriad – "

"We don't need to change the plan, the implications do not matter," Raven insisted, speaking just as quietly, with the same measured intensity. The conversation was becoming a battle of wills, and it made him feel oddly sick.

"First," Autmaran said, ignoring him, "we now know for sure that Symanta is gone, but we are by no means certain of where. Second, if she left straight for Rikard, she would have taken her armed force with her."

"She most likely did," Raven said. "She likely left the Bloodmages to do their work and ordered them to follow behind her. She might even have gone straight to Lucien."

"You're not listening to me," the man continued, with the same merciless, even tone of voice, driving his words into Raven's head. "I'm not concerned that she may have gone off to join Lucien and the Empress instead of Rikard. I'm concerned that she didn't do either of those things – I'm concerned that she did what she did in that city, sent her troops north, and then *stayed here.*"

Silence greeted this proposal, and Raven's mind started churning.

He does not know her like I do – Symanta is not a brave others-before-herself kind of fighter. She wouldn't do that. She wouldn't wait around to strike at me, or the Kindred, if it meant risking her own life. There is no benefit in it, no profit for her.

But fear began to gnaw at him.

"You do not understand her like I do," Raven said aloud, ignoring the emotions that roiled beneath the surface of his thoughts. "She does not do things that do not profit her. There's no reason for her to stay behind and strike at us now – even if she were to do damage, if she were to kill an Elder or – "

"It is not an Elder that I am worried about," Autmaran said, cutting to the heart of the matter with one swift statement. "You are a very rational person, and I think you are a better leader for it. But you have a weakness, a blind spot. You do not understand that sometimes people do things for emotional reasons. Your sister is a spider, not just a snake. She's the head of the Seekers of Truth, and she's just as slippery as any of her spies and informants; we all know that she prefers to spin her webs out of sight, where nothing can harm her, and to watch her prey get trapped by its own stupidity."

"Which is why," Raven broke in, just managing to keep the sharp edge of frustration out of his voice, "your fears are unfounded."

Autmaran once again ignored him. "But what if she has nothing left? What if Rikard gave her orders, or the Empress did, just like Geofred gave orders to Dysuna and Tiffenal. There are possibilities here you haven't considered."

"*You do not understand how the Children work!*" Raven snapped, the words coming out with more intensity than he'd intended. He tried to pull himself back; he was getting carried away. "The Children cannot order each other around. They can make deals, exchanges of loyalty, but not one of them is above the others."

"This isn't getting us anywhere – let's focus on what we do know, and what we can understand," Tomaz rumbled reasonably.

Who can understand any of this? What rational person can understand what has happened here? Thousands... they sacrificed thousands!

"What cities are left?" asked Lorna. "Did Dysuna do this before she left Tibour?"

"No," Leah said, "no, she couldn't have. She had no time – she marched north as soon as word came that we had."

"How do we know this hasn't been planned for years?" Raven asked quietly. "How do we *know* she didn't do it?"

"Would you follow the command of a woman who had massacred your entire city?" rumbled Tomaz. "Even if it was only the Commons, and the military and the High Blood were spared, would you feel safe, then? The High Blood weren't a part of the military force Dysuna led, either – that means that, likely, they were left behind. They aren't ones to get their hands dirty. They would have required slaves – "

"Unless the Most High were killed too," Raven interjected, his voice barely more than a whisper, "and the soldiers taken out of the city before it was done."

The group fell silent, and it was clear they were all thinking the same thing: if the Children and the Bloodmages could kill so many people so callously, why not twice as many? What number was too high to believe?

"We can only count the cities we've saved," Raven said, pushing forward with the conversation, trying to keep the discussion focused on the details, and on the pragmatic approach to dealing with them. "We know it was not done in Formaux, nor Banelyn. Roarke is gone, though we saved most of the population. The Kindred lands are safe – they won't have time to attack them while we are marching north."

He looked around, inviting the others to volunteer anything they had to add. When no one spoke, he started to count the other list, the one none of them wanted to think about. "We know Lerne is gone," he said, forcing his voice not to catch as he thought about what a euphemistic turn of phrase that was. "We have reason to at least suspect that the same happened in Tibour. The Eyrie was

Geofred's domain and I highly doubt he left behind plans to give the Empress more power after betraying her to save me. The only major city left is Tyne – and we have no intelligence about the situation there."

He turned to Ishmael.

"Do we?"

"None since the destruction of Roarke," he rasped in reply. "Some of our agents escaped the Lion and returned. Many have not been heard from since."

"So we're blind."

Ishmael nodded.

"Not for long." Davydd stepped forward, leaning on his crutch.

"I was hoping you'd volunteer," Raven said.

"No," Leah responded immediately.

"Yes," Davydd retorted.

"No," she said again. "Absolutely not. You are not going back there, into the heart of the Lion's den, just to make yourself look brave!"

"No," Raven said, his voice calm and hard as iron, "he's going back to get us the information we need to move forward."

Leah stared daggers at him, but before she could speak, Tomaz broke in. "He is the best choice, Eshendai. He has the Aspect of Luck now, and he – "

And then something strange happened – light seemed to burst inside Raven's head, and Davydd inexplicably dove to the floor. Leah's eyes went completely blue, like glowing sapphires, and both Ishmael and Spader pulled out their *sambolin,* holding them as if ready to do battle. Men in black cloaks came through the tent opening bearing crossbows, and arrows lanced across the room, striking both Tomaz and Leah in the chest.

"NO!"

Raven pulled out Aemon's Blade before he had time to think about what he was doing, and struck the hands off the man closest to him, sending the crossbow to the ground as the man cried out in pain and crumpled.

A golden eye on a golden chain fell from his black cloak.

Seekers.

Tomaz, his armor outlined in glowing red, roared out a challenge and cut down two of the men with his greatsword Malachi. Both the Generals and the Elders had been pushed to the ground, tackled by Autmaran and Lorna. Leah stood and broke off the shaft of the crossbow bolt where it had gotten stuck in her leather armor; she unsheathed her daggers and threw them in opposite directions, killing two Seekers simultaneously.

Shouts and cries came from outside the tent as well.

How many are there?

Raven reached out through the Raven Talisman and found himself blinded by a sickly green light that pounded behind his closed eyelids. He opened his eyes again just as his sister, Symanta, rushed into the tent. She wore no armor, and she was flanked by two men in black robes, wearing both the Eye of Truth and a Bloodmage crystal around their necks. They raised their hands and shouted words in a language Raven couldn't understand, and a crushing weight fell on them all, pushing them to the ground.

Leah flung her arms out wide, and brought them fast together in a loud clap.

Her daggers shot through the sides of the tent and struck both men in the side of the neck, downing them in an instant. The pressure disappeared, but she was too late; the men had served their purpose, and allowed Symanta to close distance with Raven. She strode forward, knelt over him, and stabbed downward with her dagger.

The razor sharp point pierced Raven's neck, and blood sprayed across the room. Pain shot through his body, and then a strange numbness covered it. He was so shocked all he could do was stare up at her, helpless, as his life rushed out of him.

"*YESSSS!*"

The cry was a hissing, boiling shout of triumph that filled the tent and set off a frenzy of movement even more frantic than what had been before. Leah dove for the two men in black as they tried to rise; Tomaz came for Raven, but it was too late.

"Die! Die you wretched *bastard!* You *traitor!*" Symanta spat the words at him, spittle flying from her lips as her hair cascaded in front of her wild eyes. "Die for everything you've done to us! DIE!"

She stabbed him again, once more in the neck, and then once in the chest and twice in the gut before Tomaz grabbed her by the scruff of the neck and flung her across the room to crash into the map table, sending papers flying and breaking the table itself into kindling. Raven gasped and bled where he lay on the floor, knowing he should be dead, but even as the thought crossed his mind, the Wolf Talisman drew on the energy stored within him, and his wounds closed and began to heal.

He heard a shout of incredulity, and realized Symanta was watching him.

"NO! No – that's impossible! You're the Raven, not the Wolf, you can't do that!"

She continued raving as she came back to her feet. Tomaz went to grab her once more, but she looked at him, the green lines glowing sickly along the sides of her neck, and dodged his arms and tripped him, sending him sprawling to the floor. Leah ran for her next, with Davydd right beside her, but Symanta evaded them both, sending Leah sprawling as she read the truth of her every move, and striking Davydd in his wounded leg, her own Talisman cancelling out his Luck when he got too close.

Raven pulled out Aemon's Blade and emptied his mind of all emotion, staggering back to his feet.

She'll read any emotion I have and use it to predict my movement. I'm an open book – there's no way I can regain enough composure to fight her fairly.

And then a thought occurred to him, and he reached down inside and pulled out an emotion he'd been holding down since Lerne: fear. He let it show on his face for a split second, and she caught it just as he knew she would. She came at him with her single dagger, already reading him, knowing what he would do next in his fear –

He stepped forward and rammed Aemon's Blade through her stomach.

The last emotion he ever saw on his sister's face was surprise. She slowly crumpled around the Blade, and as she died she looked him in the eye, opened her mouth to speak...

And spat in his face.

She went limp. Memories flowed into him. He pushed them away, tried to hold them down, and realized it was far easier than it had been with Geofred. She was nearly eighty years old, but that nothing compared to Geofred's four centuries of life, and though the memories were hard to bear, they were manageable. He saw the images flash before his eyes, but at the same time was able to stand up, wipe the spittle from his face, and look around at the others.

They were alive. The bolts that had hit Leah and Tomaz had been deflected just enough by their armor that they were wounded but not fatally so. Davydd was groaning but moving, and Lorna and Autmaran had forced the Elders and Generals to the ground, saving their lives. They were all there, all except for...

"Tym," he said, looking around everywhere. "Where is he?"

"Who?" asked Gates, confused.

"The boy – the *boy* – *where is he?*"

"Raven," Leah said. He turned and saw her bend over to pick up a small, unmoving form that had an arrow sprouting from his chest.

"No," Raven said immediately, "no no, no *no, no* NO NO *NO NO!!!*"

He ran to Tym and pulled him from Leah's grasp with a ferocity born of madness. He didn't know what was happening – the world was leaping by in flashes, and his mind wasn't able to catch up.

He's going to die, just like Goldwyn, just like Keri, just like everyone –

"No," he whispered. "No, not this one. Not this time."

He reached to his side, grabbed the hilt of Aemon's Blade, and pulled strength through it. He pushed it into Tym, taking his own life and giving it to the boy the way he'd done months ago in the city of Vale. He ripped the arrow from the boy's chest, using his new stolen strength, and blood welled up immediately. He pushed his hand down over the hole and reached deeper through the Talisman.

But the boy was too far gone. The mouth of the wound crawled and pulled together, but Raven had no reserves left to finish it. The blood continued to flow, and Raven knew that even if he closed the the wound, he couldn't heal what was inside. He didn't have the strength for it.

The Talisman.

"Raven, do it!" Leah said, reading his thoughts, spearing him with her eyes over the body of the boy. "Give him the Talisman – it's the only way!"

But there are two Talismans. Which one do I give?

The Wolf would save him, but even as the thought crossed his mind he knew it wasn't right. The Wolf belonged to Lorna, it always had.

But he had Symanta's now; he had the Snake.

The Snake Talisman... always sees the truth... always knows the truth... honesty... integrity? The Aspect of Truth? The Aspect of Caring? The Aspect of – ?

Innocence.

And just that quickly, Raven knew it was Tym, knew it had been him all along. The boy had been drawn to him, just like all the others. He grabbed Aemon's Blade and reached down inside himself like he had done with Tomaz at Aemon's Stand. He pulled the Talisman up and out and through him. His neck and mouth closed off and he felt as if he couldn't breathe, but the sensation passed and he gasped for air, pushing himself to keep going. The boy's body began to twist and contort, and though no sound came out, Tym began to scream. Most shocking of all, he began to grow before Raven's eyes, his body going through the gawky, lean phases of puberty and early adolescence in a matter of seconds. His legs stretched, grew; his arms shot out; his round, chubby face narrowed and hardened into a shelf of brow line and the beginnings of a strong jaw.

In horror, Raven tried to stop it, tried to pull the Talisman back through the bond he still shared with the boy, but it was no use. The Talisman was Tym's now, and there was nothing either of them could do.

The aging finally stopped, and Tym's mouth and nose cleared. He gasped a huge, rushing breath of air like a drowned man bursting through the barrier between sea and sky. Coughing and hacking, the boy looked around.

The boy... the young man.

He was searching for someone, and Raven grabbed hold of the boy's hand, so big now that it was nearly the size of his own. Tym felt the pressure of the touch, and his fingers sought and held Raven's pulse. The tips of his fingers glowed green, and so did the skin along his neck.

Tym turned and looked up at Raven with his bright, clear blue eyes. His throat glowed a pure, sparkling emerald, and he reached out a hand to touch Raven's face.

"Please," he said, "don't be sad."

Raven began to weep.

Chapter Thirteen:

Innocence

Raven fled the tent, dropping Tym unceremoniously to the ground before turning and rushing blindly out into the falling night. There were still shouts and cries sounding around him, but they were calls for Healers and guard patrols, not the sounds of battle. The attack itself was over.

It was meant for me alone. She wanted my head and nothing else. We stopped her.

But the cost was too high.

He heard vague movement behind him as someone else left the Council tent, but he kept moving, trying to get away. He passed into the first row of buildings, making his way through a confused ring of soldiers searching the area, dragging brown- and black-cloaked bodies across the courtyard into the light so as to count the number of their attackers. Barely any of them recognized their Prince; in the darkness, he could have been almost anyone.

A hand grabbed his shoulder to stop him.

His impotent rage boiled up inside him and blew the lid off his temper. He spun and struck the hand away, recognizing Tomaz only when he had turned to face the man. The big man was holding his Aspect.

Raven realized that he had let go of the Raven Talisman again.

I let go of it when we were fleeing Lerne, too. If I had kept hold of it like I said I would, I would have felt Symanta coming. Shadows and light, it's just like what happened with Tiffenal. I let them both in close when I could have given the Kindred warning far ahead of time.

The fight drained out of him. His shoulders slumped, and his stomach muscles relaxed. His knees wanted to buckle, and he thought longingly, for one glorious moment, of his warm bed back on the rocky hillside of Vale.

"Easy now," Tomaz rumbled, his voice soft and soothing. "Easy; hold on."

He caught Raven before he fell to his knees; he held him in a tight embrace, and kept him standing.

"I'm sorry," Raven said, his words slurring almost as if he were drunk. "I don't know why I – I don't know what I've been doing. I really thought I could do it all myself, I really thought that if I tried hard enough, I could… I thought I could…. For the past few weeks it's as if I've been sleepwalking. I've been living in a dream of some kind. I don't understand, I don't know why…. I'm so sorry, Tomaz."

Tomaz wrapped his thick arms around him and just held him there, knowing not to say a word. Raven heard someone approaching, and didn't need to look to know it was Leah. "Tomaz," she said quietly, "bring him in here."

They moved, but without any real sense of urgency. It was as if they were floating; Raven's feet barely even touched the floor. They entered through a door into a large room that smelled of sawdust and alcohol, and then up a set of wooden stairs to the top floor of an inn. They were in a hallway now with a long brown carpet running down the center of the floor, and a row of doors to either side. Leah opened one, and Tomaz led Raven toward it. Inside was a big four-poster bed with clean linen sheets. There was a vanity of good, polished wood, and a stone washbasin. The sounds of the army floated in through the window until Leah pulled it closed, wrapping them in their own private cocoon of space.

Tomaz gently pulled Raven away from him and sat him down on the bed.

"Raven," the big man rumbled, "how are you feeling?"

"I am feeling… old."

Leah and Tomaz exchanged a glance before the big man continued.

"Are you… are you whole?"

"What?"

"After what just happened, are you whole? Are you injured?"

"My body is fine."

"I was asking about your mind."

Raven swallowed and shrugged. He felt uncomfortable. He reached down and touched Aemon's Blade at his side; both Leah and Tomaz followed the gesture. They all relaxed when he touched the hilt and nothing happened.

"I should not have kept the Wolf," he said. "I kept it for all the wrong reasons. And it didn't even help."

"It helped to save you," Leah said softly.

"Something that could just as easily have been achieved by having Lorna pass me the Aspect through the Blade," he said. "It's hers, and always should have been. I was foolish to think I could keep it from her. I will give the Wolf to Lorna. I will. Now that Tym has the Snake Talisman, it doesn't matter. I can't keep collecting the rest of them. It didn't prevent any of this, and it won't prevent anything in the future."

He realized he had repeated himself a number of times, and that he was rambling. He began to stand.

"Raven, slow down," Leah said, grabbing his arm and preventing him from rising. "What are you saying? Please – let us in. You haven't been the same since... Banelyn."

The words "Elder Keri" hung in the air, and they all heard them.

"You argue with everyone about everything," she continued, "none of us ever know when your temper will snap, and you barely sleep. What's going on? *Let us in.*"

"Like you let me in after Goldwyn died?"

The words were out before he could stop them, and she withdrew from the venom in his voice as if he had slapped her. But her shock gave way to sadness, not to anger, and that was enough to make him pause. "I shouldn't have done that," she said, looking him straight in the eye, holding his gaze. "I shouldn't have taken my grief out on you."

Silence fell between them, and Raven was the first to break the moment.

"I've killed another of my sisters," he said simply, his eyes far away, seeing again Symanta's life. It was strange – she had lived for almost eighty years, a long span of time all things considered, but no more than a mortal man or woman. Where he had been crippled by the memories of the other Children, this time he could stand back and examine them as they came to him, flashing before his mind's eye.

"I didn't understand it before," he said.

"Didn't understand what?"

"The Snake Talisman. I didn't understand what it really was."

"It's the Aspect of Truth, right?"

"No," Raven said, shaking his head. "It sees truth, yes, and it sees emotion, but it also sees everything else. And that's just the effect, not the cause."

"Tym," Tomaz rumbled slowly, putting the pieces together. "You don't think it was a coincidence he was there. You gave it to him on purpose – you gave it to him because of how he is, the way his life feels."

"Yes."

"But what is he?" Leah asked, confused. "He's none of the things Symanta is. He's the opposite of her – he sees only the good. He doesn't have a deceiving bone in his body, he's – "

She cut off and looked at Raven.

"That's what you're talking about isn't it?" she asked, watching him carefully. "He's pure. He's innocent."

"And without pretension," Raven continued, still examining Symanta's memories. "The Aspect isn't about actual sight. I thought it was, but I was wrong.

Symanta guarded the real secret of it so closely that none of the other Children understood it – it doesn't *give,* it *takes.* It strips away the blinders we put over our own eyes, makes the bearer see the world unaltered, free from prejudice or subjectivity. It gives us the sight we were born with, and forces us to see the world as it is, not as we want it to be."

"And that's why it had to go to Tym," he sighed. "That's the way he sees the world already, at least in part. He's like you, Tomaz, but on the inside – he's got a strength that none of us could even imagine. He sees the world exactly as it is, and still believes it's good, still believes in good people. The Aspect heightens that, makes it much more potent. It was the same with Symanta, from what I can see in her memories, but in reverse – her strength was that she had no desire to hide from the world's evil. She saw everything – every flaw, every imperfection, and knew how to exploit it. But Tym – he sees the good. He sees every virtue and knows how to bring it out of you. He sees each of us... I don't know how he does it. How can you see the world that way all the time? How can someone be that brave?"

He shuddered, and slid off the edge of the bed onto his knees.

"Whoa there," Tomaz said, catching him. "Is it the memories?"

"Memories, yes, but not Symanta's. Mine."

"What does that mean? You have to let us in, princeling."

"I saw myself and what I've been doing," he said. "I saw who I'm becoming... I'm becoming like my... like the Empress."

He had to give them credit: both Tomaz and Leah took this comment in stride, without batting an eyelash. But maybe that was worse; did that mean they had seen it too?

"Part of why I wanted to avoid Lerne was to avoid killing her," he said abruptly, unable to look at them. "I didn't want to kill Symanta. It wasn't necessary, or so I thought. I don't want to kill anyone anymore... and with the Wolf and the Raven combined, and you with your Talismans and Davydd's, I thought it would be enough. I thought we'd find a way win anyway, despite all the odds. But what's the point? What's the point in fighting Her, if I can't control the outcome of anything I set my mind to? Everywhere we turn, there's another trap laid, another complication. Nothing is ever the same; nothing is *ever* easy. And now we have this impossible task before us, killing a *god*. How do we even go about that? How do you go about killing someone that has been here, like a fixture of the earth, for a thousand years?"

He broke off and realized his hands were shaking. He clasped them together to keep them still and started rocking back and forth, his whole body aching.

"I just... I'm so tired."

And with that final admission, he sagged into Tomaz's arms, and the big man slowly lowered both of them down to the floor; Leah kept her hand on his back, but made no move to come closer. She seemed to know he needed support, not affection.

"What do you mean when you say you feel tired?"

"I can't sleep, even when I try to," he said. "I sit up, every night, holding onto the Raven Talisman, feeling the lives of everyone in the camp, reaching out farther and farther, trying to sense an attack. And as I sit there, my mind just... it goes to dark."

"What do you mean by that?"

"I think of killing my Mother, like I've killed all the others." He swallowed past the lump in his throat. "And I realize I *want to*. I want to kill her. I think about killing her the way I've killed Tiffenal, Ramael, Dysuna, Geofred, and now Symanta. The way I killed Keri. The way I kill everyone. And I realize I'm becoming like them. With every one of them I kill, I go a little farther down the path they've all traveled themselves."

He fell silent, and for a long moment neither Raven nor the others spoke. He heard the sound of soldiers calling on the other side of the window, felt the warmth and heat radiating off of Tomaz along with the strong, overpowering masculine scent that was just *him*.

"The first time I went to Elder Goldwyn," Tomaz rumbled, the sound like a giant leopard's purr against Raven's ear as his head rested on the giant's chest, "I said something similar. I couldn't sleep, I couldn't think without reliving what I'd done. I drowned myself in any bottle I could find. But when he brought me out of my stupor long enough to speak, he told me that running away from it all wouldn't help. He said over and over again that those dark times happen to everyone, to one degree or another, and that the people who triumph, the people of true courage, are the ones who suffer through what they have to, and are strong enough to face their weakness. That's the phrase he used that's always stuck with me... 'strong enough to face their weakness.' I'd never thought about strength and weakness like that – not as a scale, but as relative terms."

He shifted Raven and pulled him up so they were looking each other in the eye.

"You're not one or the other," the giant rumbled. "Strength comes from accepting your humanity, not denying it. It comes from accepting what's been done, and knowing no life is perfect. You can only control so much, and your plans will only take you so far. Looking back, there's no way I could ever have guessed I'd be where I am now. I bet a year ago you never would have guessed you'd know me – or that you'd have met Leah, or joined the Kindred, or any of it. We can only see so far into the future."

Tomaz slowly stood, pulling Raven up with him.

"Strength is standing up after weakness pulls you to the ground," the big man continued. "It's knowing that glorious light casts terrible shadows. It's the way life is."

"How do you know that?" Raven asked softly. "How do you know it will get better, or that it will ever be anything other than this? We could all die in this war –in the next *week*. I could become my Mother, or could go back to being that thing, that *creature*. How can you hope for something better when everything is terrible?"

"Because I have to," Tomaz rumbled. "Because sometimes the only way to keep the glass half full is to fight gravity. There are some things you cannot change; there are some things you can; great men and women know the difference. You are your Mother's son – that you cannot change. You've taken many lives – that you cannot change. But what you choose to do next, what you choose to *do* – that you can change. And remember, always remember, that right here, right now, we're with each other, and until the end of my days I will remember you and what you've changed in *me*."

"What?"

"You gave me the chance to redeem myself. A chance I was convinced would never come. You gave all of us a chance to stand up and be counted for what we want our lives to be, what we want people to remember us for. You are not this image you have in your head of a Black Prince; you are not the cast-off heir of an all-knowing queen. You did not have to come to us; you did not have to take up the mantle of the Veil and lead the Kindred. But you did, and you became the stone that caused the mountain to split in half. You have changed forever who the Kindred are, and what we believe we can do. You have changed me, and what I think about redemption. And if for nothing else, I love you for that. I love you just for *being*, and for showing the world that someone who has lived through horror can keep going, keep living, keep caring."

The big man squeezed his shoulders in his huge hands, and Raven was shocked to find tears forming at the corners of the man's eyes.

"You are everything I ever hoped you'd be when I found you in the Elmist Mountains. Everything I hoped and more. You've changed my life. You've changed everyone's lives, and we'll follow you to the end for that."

He gave Raven's shoulders one more hard squeeze, so hard it hurt, and then he stood and moved to the door. Leah came forward, taking the spot Tomaz had left empty, and embraced Raven, holding him tightly.

"You matter to me more than I can say," she said softly in his ear. "Don't ever forget that. Don't ever forget what I feel for you; and if you ever need a reminder, ask me for it." She let go of him and smiled.

"Get some sleep tonight," she said. "We'll take care of what needs to happen."

Raven opened his mouth to protest, but no words came out. He was so numb, so tired, he couldn't even string a sentence together. He nodded, and she nodded back. Tomaz opened the door and stepped out, and Leah followed him.

When they were gone, he felt like a part of him had left with them.

Not knowing what to do, he went back to the bed and simply fell to his knees before it. He sat back on his heels, the tops of his boots digging into his calves and upper thighs. It hurt, but it was good. His eyes began to sting, and as he sat there, as the night rolled past him and the world did not stop, he found himself thinking about how easy it would be to simply let go. What would happen if he did? Would they miss him, and mourn him? Or would they consider him a coward for taking the easy way out, when they still had a war to fight?

You matter to me more than I can say. Don't ever forget that.

He scrubbed a hand across his face, trying to wipe away the thoughts plaguing his mind as easily as he could wipe away the tears clinging to his cheeks. And from deep within him, he realized that he wanted to be a part of it. He wanted to hold Leah, to laugh with Tomaz. He wanted to banter with Davydd and apologize over and over again to Lorna for keeping what should have been hers all along. He wanted to earn the trust Autmaran had put in him when he had nominated Raven as Prince of the Veil, and he wanted to give Tym back what he could of his childhood.

But there was a final barrier between him and them, something that still held him back. Every time he tried to push through and reach them, it was as if his fingers were wrapped in a film that left him unable to feel their touch.

You know what it is. You know. Symanta knew.

The black markings of the Raven Talisman on his back begin to heat as he thought about it. Those markings weren't the true Talisman, only a Bloodmage rune modified by the Visigony that gave him the Talisman's power. The physical form, the actual stone talisman itself, resided in the Diamond Crown of the Empress, along with each of the other six. Symanta had seen it, had known from the start: the Children were bound to their Mother not through blood or ambition, but through the Talismans themselves. And the reason Raven felt the way he did, the reason he felt as though the Empress was a part of him, that she was in his blood, was that she *was.*

Something fell into place with a strange *thunk* in his head, something he hadn't been able to understand before. But still the final conclusion lay just out of his grasp. Something about the Talismans, about Aemon's Blade... but it was gone, and he couldn't think of it. He moved to the bed, his head in his hands, pressing his palms against his temples.

There's an answer there... there's a way to win.

But the sudden flash of insight had left him as quickly as it had come. He sighed and fell back on the bed; immediately, the weariness of countless sleepless nights rushed over him. He managed to remove his boots and clothing before crawling into bed, but as soon as his head hit the pillow his mind blanked out, and he fell into the deepest sleep he'd had since leaving Vale.

Chapter Fourteen:

The Final Road

The next morning, Raven woke with a shock, jolted out of a dream he could not remember. His lips felt dry and strangely heavy, and his body was stiff in the way that only came from a full night's sleep. He blinked a few times, trying to order his thoughts, and idly noticed that bright, golden rays of sun were streaming in through the window in a beautiful cascade of light, playing with dancing motes of dust and lint.

Sunlight. Shadows and light!

He threw back the covers and started pulling his clothing on, wondering groggily how long he had been asleep and when he had taken his clothes off during the night. He hopped over to the window as he thrust a foot into a boot and looked outside. The tents were being taken down, and a number of soldiers were already walking toward the edge of town, lining up in formation. A bolt of panic shot through him – *why didn't someone wake me up?* – and he turned to run for the door.

It opened inward just as he reached it; he ran into it face-first.

"AHH!"

"ARGH!"

"P-prince Raven, I'm so sorry!"

Raven pulled back, holding his nose, which was throbbing terribly, and looked at the source of the voice. It was a young man, about seventeen, with fine blonde hair and blue eyes –

"Tym," Raven said, remembering in a rush what had happened the previous night. The boy was only a few inches shorter than he was now. Someone had found him new clothes – green and black soldier's gear over a thin leather cuirass, likely the only thing anyone had on hand that fit him. A sword had been strapped around his waist, though by the way he was standing it was clear he wasn't used to wearing it, nor did he have any experience using it.

"Prince Raven, sir," he said, his voice still a light tenor, though with the deeper roots that showed he had passed through most of his adolescence. "I – I was sent by Eshendai Leah and Ashandel Tomaz to tell you we're leaving. They've taken care of everything. Well, Commander Autmaran has taken care of everything, but either way, it's all done. All you need to do is dress and eat, and then meet them in the square."

Raven nodded silently, still examining the boy.

"Oh-okay," Tym said, turning to go.

"I'm sorry, Tym," Raven said abruptly. "I never meant for – "

Raven cut off as the markings along Tym's neck glowed a soft, soothing green, and the boy turned back to him, suddenly seeing *through* him.

"You saved my life, Prince Raven, sir," Tym said. "And now I have a way to help you. You gave me what I wanted: a way to be good." A lump started forming in Raven's throat, and the boy continued on, seeing and understanding the emotion immediately. "You don't need to regret anything, sir. You've saved my life twice now."

He smiled a brilliant smile, his full white teeth making Raven smile too, even though it was partially against his will. "I should be going," Tym said, bowing his head. Raven nodded back and watched him walk awkwardly away on his new longer legs.

Maybe something good came out of this after all.

Raven gave his nose a final rub, decided it was still intact enough to be getting along with, and turned back to examine the room to make sure he hadn't forgotten anything. He glanced through the window once more and saw Davydd and Lorna ride past. Surprised, he crossed the room and watched them go, a large group of soldiers riding with them in Rangers uniforms. They crossed to the edge of the town and disappeared into the morning mist.

They must have agreed to leave early for the distant city of Tyne with their handpicked men and women. The two of them, now with a pair of Aspects collectively, were likely a match for anything they might come across. Even a full group of thirteen Bloodmages would likely have trouble with them, and between Davydd's luck, Lorna's healing, and their valerium weapons, they were a force to be reckoned with. With a hundred Rangers added into the mix, the result was potent indeed.

Except... they were setting out to test themselves against Rikard, the oldest and most powerful of the Children. And not on an unnamed battlefield, but in his own city, in the middle of a war, when he had to be on guard and waiting. Raven knew Rikard better than any of his siblings save Geofred, because he feared him more than any of the others – all the Children did – and Rikard would be ready for this. There was no type of battle he had not fought or studied, no tactic he had not tried out or at least rehearsed. Geofred, the former Prince of Eagles, had been the one who could see events before they unfolded; Rikard was so battle-hardened he'd already seen the events unfold, and had come up with a response for each of them.

Something tickled the back of his mind, and Raven realized he still had the Wolf Talisman, not Lorna.

He shot back across the room, out the door, and down the stairs, oblivious to any of his surroundings. He looked around frantically outside, saw Melyngale tied to a hitching post nearby, undid the reins, and heeled the horse through the surrounding soldiers, who leapt out of his way.

He pulled up just outside the city, where Davydd and Lorna had stopped their group and were doing a final equipment check before heading out. When he arrived in a swirl of mist, they all looked at him as if he were crazy.

"What are you doing here, princeling?" Davydd asked. He was not sitting comfortably on his horse, and Raven realized there was one last thing he had to do before he gave up the Wolf. "I'm not kissing you goodbye, so don't ask."

Raven rode up to Davydd, ignoring the man's quip, and reached for him. Taken by surprise, the Ranger tried to pull his horse out of the way, but the angle was awkward, and there were others behind him blocking his path. Raven caught the man's head with his right hand, and touched Aemon's Blade with his left.

Gray light outlined his fingers, and energy moved through him, passing to Davydd. The Ranger's eyes widened in shock, and his mouth opened in a silent shout of alarm, looking almost as though he had been dunked in a freezing stream. The others closed in around them, some even going for their swords, but in the next second it was over.

Raven pulled back, and Melyngale was happy to go, eyeing Davydd's edgy horse with distrust. The other Rangers stopped moving and simply watched on, completely bewildered. Davydd was breathing heavily, and his eyes, both red and gold, were staring at Raven as if only seeing him for the first time.

"Shadows and bloody *fire*, princeling!" he said finally. "Warning would be nice!"

He shifted in his saddle, and it was clear the wound he had suffered the day before leaving Lerne had been healed. Still ignoring him, Raven dismounted and went to Lorna. When he reached her, she was watching him with cold reserve; if she had been surprised by what he had just done, she refused to show it. She and Leah should have a staring contest; rocks would weep before either one of them revealed a thing.

"I have something that belongs to you," he said. He reached out to grab her hand; she watched him carefully, her eyes narrowed, but she let him do it. Before she could object, he interlocked his fingers with hers, and their cold palms were touching.

Raven closed his eyes and placed a hand on Aemon's Blade, then reached inside himself and grabbed hold of both the Raven Talisman and the Wolf Talisman. He reached out and touched Lorna's life, a bright golden knot in his mind that radiated the smell of horses, the feel of iron bars, and the sound of a howl.

He pulled on the Wolf Talisman and added it to that golden knot.

Instantly, fatigue overcame him, and he realized just how much he had been relying on the Talisman to keep him going. He staggered back and disengaged from Lorna's life, leaving the Talisman with her and pulling his fingers free of her grip. He opened his eyes – *shadows and light, even my eyelids are tired* – and saw that her hands and feet were glowing so brightly that silvery-gray light was leaking out of her boots and gauntlets.

She was staring at him, shocked, and it was clear that a new vitality infused her. She wavered unsteadily and her eyes unfocused; Raven knew that she was mentally checking in with her body, feeling the new surge of energy that would power her past all normal human endurance. She swallowed, and looked at him once more, her former stoicism cracked.

"Thank you," she said, her voice the same raspy quality he had always known but with an edge of energy to it, like a crackle of thunder off in the distance.

Raven nodded and turned back to Davydd. The young man was watching the proceedings with a combination of surprise, annoyance, and gratitude. Reaching out, Raven stopped him from turning his horse away.

He won't listen, he never does. But I have to warn him anyway.

"Be careful," he said.

"I'm always careful," Davydd said.

"No," said Raven, "you're not. And this is no time for mischief. You're known in Tyne, and I know you have your own history there with your family – " Davydd's eyes narrowed as his jaw clenched and his nostrils flared; Raven continued before the man could break away in anger – *"But now is not the time to settle scores."*

Davydd stayed where he was, but still looked like he had half a mind to ride the Prince over as he left.

"Davydd, the Fox Talisman is intoxicating – you have to think of it like a drug. Remember me in Vale, when Henri Perci slipped me dopalin? It's very similar. That euphoria that you feel, like nothing can touch you, like you're all powerful? That's what will get you killed. You may be lucky, but you're not invulnerable. When you're up against Rikard, luck will only get you so far. And if you get too close... if you get too close, there's no telling what he might be able to make you do. He's mad, and powerful beyond what you can understand. Do not test him. If you come up against him, run and do not look back."

"Of course, my Prince," he quipped through a mocking smile that showed he had listened to all of the advice and heard none of it. He heeled his horse in the sides, and Aron leapt forward. The Rangers followed him – men and women in black, tight-fitting leather armor and green-and-gold tunics, all bearing a variety of personalized weaponry.

Raven cursed as he watched the Eshendai disappear northward through a haze of trail dust, and only realized Lorna had stayed behind when her husky voice broke through his brooding thoughts.

"The Talismans will offset, like they do when the Children come for you... correct?"

"No," Raven said quickly. "No – each of them reacts differently. I don't know why mine works the way it does – I doubt even the Empress knows. I've always had the most effect on the other Talismans, but some, like the Snake Talisman, are barely hindered at all by mine. I have always had the most effect on the Eagle and the Fox – and so does Rikard."

Lorna was watching him solemnly, and Raven, recognizing a receptive audience, continued on, desperate to make sure that if Davydd wouldn't watch out for himself, at least someone else would.

"When the Fox Talisman gets to him, and it *will*, you need to be ready to pull him back," he said, holding her gaze with all the intensity he could muster, trying to impress upon her mind as if with a physical stamp just how important his words would be to her in the coming confrontation. "Rikard will have little problem commanding him if Davydd loses his concentration. If Davydd lets go of the Aspect for the barest fraction of a second, just enough for Rikard to grab hold of him, then it's over. You, on the other hand, will have an easier time. The Lion has more difficultly holding the Ox and Wolf, or at least he did when Dysuna and Ramael bore them, and while he will still affect you, you will have a better chance, a *far* better chance, than Davydd."

Lorna nodded slowly, taking in every word.

"How long will you be gone?" he asked. "How long will it take to get there and meet us before Lucien?"

"Without needing to slow down for infantry," Lorna said, "we'll be there and out before the week is done. We'll meet you as you finish the journey north."

"The day before our time runs out," Raven said.

"Just so," she said. "Time enough for one final battle."

He nodded, and turned to mount Melyngale.

"Thank you." Raven turned back. She was looking at him with unspoken emotion in her eyes. "I have never felt this complete before," she said. "I feel... I feel like *me*."

He swallowed hard and nodded.

"Keep him safe," he said. "And yourself as well. We will need you both before the end. And I want to see you again before that end comes."

She smiled at him, a huge, beaming smile, the first he had ever received from her in all the time he had known her, and then she wheeled her horse about and took off. Raven watched until she was out of sight, and then made his way back to the Kindred.

*   *   *

After he found Leah and Tomaz, they wasted no time in leaving Whitestone themselves at the head of the Kindred Army. They were truly marching against the clock now, and everyone, even the Commons, knew it. The first day passed quickly, and so too did the next. Raven, Leah, Tomaz, Autmaran, and now Tym, met with the Elders and Generals every night to finalize plans, but everything truly hinged on whether or not Davydd and Lorna returned quickly enough to provide them with more information. If they had to deal with Rikard already in the city of Lucien, or if they had to deal with another Bloodmage crystal, foreknowledge of the fact might be the only thing to save them. Their supply chains were stretching far too long, and the small amount of food and forage they had been able to collect in Whitestone was not enough to help for long. They really would only have one shot at this – an all-out attack, and only that.

"We present ourselves on the Plains of al'Manthian," Autmaran said, "and we attack the city. There is no other way to do this. We will need to figure out a way *how* once we get there, but we have what the Empress needs: Raven. She cannot wait behind her walls any more than we can wait outside them. This will come to an all out battle with hundreds of thousands of men. We will need each captain to be in charge of their group independently, with general, flexible instructions about what to do. I will be in contact with each officer over the next few days to tell them what I expect on the day of battle, and to clarify our objectives."

He turned to Raven, Tym, Leah, and Tomaz.

"Our job is to stay in the center of the army until we know where we need to commit," he said. "They will have something readied for us – they know we have the Talismans now, and they know that you, Raven, are leading this army. We stay together in reserve, until the time comes when we are needed to bolster the most heavily hit parts of the army. Each of you is worth fifty soldiers on your own – and if the troops see you, they will rally."

The days passed and the plan solidified as the road continued leading them to Lucien. The trees began to thin out, and grass began to take their place. Spring took firm grip of the weather, and the days and nights both grew warmer. It rained at night, leaving behind fresh green leaves and the smell of mud and damp bark.

When they rode during the day, Raven thought of the map of Lucia he'd had to memorize as a child, and mentally charted Lorna and Davydd's progress. By his calculations, on the third day they should be at the city of Tyne, and on the third night they would infiltrate it and find out if what had happened at Lerne was happening there as well. The Kindred army itself was only days away from the Plains of al'Manthian – the wide, barren expanse of land that encircled the city of Lucien – and Raven knew that everything would be decided before the week was out. That thought made his palms sweat and the skin between his shoulders itch.

He watched the soldiers carefully as they marched, for signs of attrition or fatigue, and while he saw plenty of the latter, he saw barely any of the former, even though they woke as soon as it was light enough to see and marched until dusk. Raven expected protests, but there were none. Even when people had to be carried due to fatigue sickness and soldiers had to sleep with their feet elevated because they were so swollen and blistered, no one left or deserted. They just rose the next day when woken and put one foot in front of the other, with grim looks and set jaws.

"They have seen their Prince defeat an entire army, watched a capital city disappear beneath a mountain of rubble, and witnessed Dysuna, Ramael, Tiffenal, and Symanta cut down their friends, companions, and family," Autmaran told him when he brought it up. "Waking up early and walking a lot does not hold a candle to that."

"I... suppose that is a good point."

"Besides, they want to be here," Autmaran continued. "You may have been the one to start this rolling, but it has now become a movement far greater than you could have manufactured on your own."

"I suppose that's good," Raven said. "After all, I'm not the Commander."

Autmaran quirked an eyebrow at him; he seemed to become more broody and non-verbal with every day that passed, a quirk that Raven had noticed before the other major battles they had fought together.

"Well," he continued with a sigh, "there's only one Talisman left."

"The Lion," Autmaran said.

"The Lion," Raven confirmed.

Silence fell between them, and in it both saw the recognition in the other that the new bearer would have to be Autmaran. Raven wasn't sure why it had ever been a question, really. Autmaran was the Commander of the Kindred Army. If anyone should inherit the Lion Talisman, if anyone should be able to turn it from its black Bloodmagic purpose and make it a pure Aspect again, it was he. Now all they needed to do was engineer a situation in which Raven managed to kill Rikard, without Autmaran dying in the biggest battle fought in any single war since the founding of the Empire.

At least it wasn't a *hard* task they'd set for themselves.

"We are insane," Raven said out loud. "Really – we are."

"War is insane," Autmaran said. "And the right kind of insanity is what historians often call genius." He glanced at Raven, a small smile playing at the corners of his lips. "We're only insane if we lose."

"And if we win?"

"Then we'll tell everyone we knew what we were doing all along."

"So we lie to the historians?"

"Maybe bribe them."

"Or there's always blackmail – that doesn't cost money."

"Or extortion."

"Certainly an option."

"We could counterfeit an eye witness account."

"We could counterfeit *two* eyewitness accounts."

"Ah – corroboration, I like the way you think."

"Maybe we should try them all – that way at least one will work."

"Probably the safest way to go about it."

"Right."

"So it's a deal?"

"Sure. But if I die, you make me out to be a hero."

"Likewise."

They caught each other's eye and both broke into laughter at the same time, and the good clean happiness of camaraderie lifted the malaise that had fallen on them. There had been too little laughter lately – and there would be precious little more in the time to come. Melancholy rode with the army like a palpable force, it seemed, always just behind them, ready to overtake them should they falter.

But something held it at bay.

The change had begun after Lerne. Where before each step had seemed to take something from them, to drain away an essential part of what it meant to be human, now each stride felt like a conquered piece of land. The wind seemed to watch them with approval now as it blew past, racing south bearing news of their passage, and the sound of their feet on the ground was no longer the ringing of a death knell, but the beating of a strong and healthy heart.

And it was because of Tym.

Raven still, in his heart of hearts, wished that he had kept the Snake Talisman. For that matter, he wished that he had kept all of the Talismans, and found a way to turn them into Aspects without having to give them to the others. He still felt, and always had, that the burden was his to shoulder. He was one of the Children; he had a stain on his very being, turning the blood in his body black as night. It was his duty to repent for what his family had done to this land – it fell on his shoulders to bear the original task of Aemon and atone for the work of his Mother.

But when Tym walked through the camp now, not as a young boy but as a teenager on the cusp of manhood, he pulled away some of the stones Raven had used to barricade his heart from caring. When the boy picked up a sword for the first time and had the soldiers teach him how to use it around the evening fire, it soon seemed as if the whole camp was watching and laughing with him as he made an intentional fool of himself. On the march, when the men and women were the most tired, he appeared as if from nowhere with a smile and a welcoming hand, his eyes and neck glowing with the pure, innocent green of spring, echoed in the blooming world around them.

He was, in short, everything that Raven could not be. In a matter of days he became the heart of the Kindred, something Raven supposed the boy had always been, even though no one had realized it. They rallied around him in a way that was so natural it was eerie; it was not that they shied away from Autmaran or Raven, or even Leah, Tomaz, and the two Elders still with them. If anything, their relationship with the entire command unit was enhanced. But Tym gave the soldiers something that had been missing: hope and innocence. He reminded them what they were fighting for; reminded them that younger brothers, sons, nephews, even children not yet born, lived and breathed back home in the Kindred cities of Vale and Eldoras, Chaym and Marilen and Aemon's Stand.

And though Raven knew that the world did not work that way, that life did not care who was innocent and who was not, he felt the hope as well.

As soon as they were far enough distant from the city of Lerne, they found traces of the refugees that had been so severely lacking on their way from Banelyn: discarded clothing, bloody bandages, raided houses and burned ruins. The first group of people they saw was thought to be an aberration; when they were sighted, they were assumed to be nothing more than frightened Commons fleeing a war that was slowly and surely consuming the entire Empire. They came from what was left of the countryside to the north and east, from what Raven and the others came to realize was the implosion of Geofred's old province, the Eyrie, where the Most High had apparently found themselves unable to hold the territory together.

I knew he wouldn't kill them. I knew it.

More came hard on their heels, from every corner of the Empire, some even from the south on half-wild horses, bringing word that the countryside had been swept clean when Dysuna had marched north; she and her men had raped the land and taken what remained of the winter harvest and seed just as planting season had arrived, depriving thousands of life-giving crops. With nothing else to live for and no reason to stay on barren land, they had followed the rumors of a Kindred revolution, ready to extract a price from the Empire that had left them to starve.

And when they came, they did not ask for food, nor did they ask for shelter. They asked for swords and armor, men and women both. Children, if they could still be called that after what they had seen, volunteered for any work available. Soon, there was barely enough of anything to go around. Tomaz, Leah, and even

Autmaran himself, were soon found giving fighting lessons with any spare moment they had. Stannit became invaluable, and Jallin, the former Kindred captain, became his right-hand man. Together they formed what became known as the Free Commons, and they infused a fire into the rest of the army that burned hot and bright.

Raven offered his help, which was universally declined. In many cases it was out of fear: the men knew him on sight by the armor and clothing he wore, and the rumors of his deeds had spread far and wide. The men spoke of little else, and his legend grew still more around the campfires, stoked now by Kindred and Imperial legends both.

But while they rejected his direct help, they pulled something much more important from him: inspiration. At night, after the sun had set and they were bedding down for what little rest they could find, he would walk amongst the fires, and whispers would run behind him, swirling his cloak, snatching at his ear. When he passed the large swath of ground cleared for sword practice, the soldiers and Commons, many of whom had never held a blade outside of a plowshare, threw themselves into whatever they were doing with renewed vigor.

"You're more than a Prince now," Tomaz rumbled to him on the final night of their journey as they walked to their tents. The giant had run a short demonstration on how to defend yourself with a shield, something he considered much more important for a novice fighter than how to properly wield a sword, while Raven had watched on. "You're a symbol. You're the embodiment of their *why*, like Goldwyn talked about."

"I don't know if this is what he had in mind. I don't know how he would feel about me leading all these people to their death."

"Not death," Tomaz said, pulling up short and forcing Raven to stop and turn to him. "*Independence.* These people, they do not follow you, they follow what they see in you. They follow your cause. You – you are important, it is true, and your presence inspires them, something that will be invaluable on the battlefield. But they follow you because of what you *stand* for. They follow you because they have wanted to shout at the top of their lungs, to rail and scream and rant, against the Empress and the Children for generation upon generation with no release. Each rebellion stopped by Geofred, diffused before it could even start, each uprising brutally quelled by Ramael; every attempt by the Commons to fight back, to claim something for their own, to rule themselves in some small measure, to decide their lives – none of it has worked. But now there's you. Now there's *us*, the first in a thousand years to do what we've done, the first since Aemon himself to stand up and fight back against the Empress, trading blow for blow. They did not come here to die; they came here to *live*. They came so that they could know that they, for once in their lives, for once in the lives of every ancestor they have ever had, stood up to be counted. Some of them, like the ones from Banelyn and Roarke, have no home left to return to. One man at training lost his wife, his four sons, and his father in Lerne. He was gone – he had been sent by his Elevated master to attend a specialty market in the Eyrie. He didn't even know the city was gone until he found us on the road as he headed back.

"*That's* who you are fighting for. *That's* who these people are. You are the living manifestation of the tears they cry at night not knowing where their next meal will come from. You are their rage, their hatred, at a world they cannot predict, a world they cannot control."

He stepped up to Raven and laid a heavy hand on his shoulder.

"And you are my best friend," he said, "so listen to me carefully. Tomorrow will be the hardest day you have ever faced. Dig down deep, and fight for them the way they fight for you. You have a family now; you have a people. Do not forget it."

He ruffled Raven's hair, and moved on.

And so the final day faded into night, and no one slept as they contemplated what the next day held for them. The clock continued to tick in Raven's head, but there was nothing more he could do. All the pieces were set in place, all the corners of the board squared away. He went to Leah after darkness fell to spend one last night with her, and they both lay awake in each other's arms, watching the roof of the tent in silence. Raven's thoughts turned to the distant city of Tyne, where he knew his brother's forces were mobilizing and marching with equal haste toward them. Whatever had happened there, whatever Lorna and Davydd had done, it was over and they would meet them in the morning on the Plains. Thousands upon thousands of men and women from every part of the Empire would be there. All that needed to happen on all sides had to happen within the next two days; all events, the fate of the Empire, the Kindred, and hundreds of thousands of men and women, would be decided.

As the night closed in around them, the world took the time to pause. The flowers closed their petals, and the wind died away; the night fell and deepened, as it always did, and as it always would. The world turned on, watching.

And held its breath.

Chapter Fifteen:

Tyne

Davydd ran along the rooftop in the dark night, no more than a shadow among shadows under the slivered moon that shone fitfully through the dark clouds boiling overheard. A storm was on the way, one of the infamous spring storms of Tyne that made the land so fertile.

That will serve us well, he thought with a feral grin. *I do my best work in the night.*

He slowed when he reached the end of the roof and crouched on a merlon that jutted up at the corner of the building. He felt Lorna come up beside him, taking her customary position on his left-hand side; he fought right-handed and she left, and should they be surprised, they would need to react on instinct.

They were in the southernmost quarters of the High Blood, on the outskirts of Tyne itself. Tyne was unique among the cities of Lucia in that its Most High did not live in the center of the city; instead, they lived in elegant collections of manor houses on the far edges, with stables and acres of land that spread out from the urban center in rippling waves. There were well over two-dozen such compounds, and most were open to the rest of the High Blood, if not to the Commons. But the seven most powerful families, among them Davydd and Leah's birth parents, the Leoways, were protected by strong stone walls and connected to the inner most sanctum of the city by stone bridges, much like aqueducts. The bridgeways arched up and over the Commons quarters and allowed the Most High access to the city without the need to pass among the rabble, and led from the seven honored family homes directly to Rikard's personal compound, where stood the immense fortress castle and military training center of Tyne. Where Davydd and his merry band were intent on going.

Now we just need to wait for the watch.

Davydd and Lorna had done this a score of times now, and the key was always to wait for the guards, no matter how long it took. Once the pair of them had gone in too early and they'd had to fight their way free of the city only hours after they'd infiltrated it. Another time they'd gone in too late and been caught by a separate patrol on its way back. No, the best way – the *only* way – was to wait for the guards.

Speak of the devil. Luck is with us tonight.

He grinned at the thought.

A dozen men came slowly up the path that led from the adjacent manor palace toward the compound bridge. They were formed up in six pairs, each in the gold and white of Tyne with long spears that reached up above their heads, and shields that weighed down their left arms.

If they see us, I'll draw the attack and let Lorna deal with them. Right-handed spearmen never know how to deal with left-handed axes.

But, if all went according to plan, they wouldn't be seen in any case.

Davydd turned to look behind him, careful not to turn too quickly; his burned and blackened skin still twinged in response to sharp movements. The rest of the Rangers in the preliminary squad readied themselves behind him, easing their weapons in their sheathes, ready to go on his signal. He'd brought just over a hundred of them with him from the main Kindred force, but half were securing their retreat through foothills to the east, clearing the fields and manors of guards. It was exciting – this was the first time Davydd had been here in significant force.

We might even be able to force entrance to Rikard's personal castle itself if we take them napping.

Davydd could just imagine what it might feel like to twist the Lion's tail before running away with something of value. His toes practically curled at the thought.

"We take the guards silently," he said, barely more than a whisper. "We stow them in the stables below the steps, then we make the walkway. When you're up there, *stay low*. I don't want anyone to see our silhouettes as we pass over the city." He began to turn back, and then stopped. "And leave the front six for me." He flashed a manic smile. "It's been far too long since I've killed an Imperial."

They grinned back and passed the word, and he turned to watch the guards slowly move into position as they passed below. He gave the signal.

Arrows shot out of nowhere and pin-cushioned three men at the back of the line, killing them before they could utter a single word. Davydd ran forward, Lorna only a pace behind him, and jumped off the thirty-foot building.

He reached through the Fox Talisman, the Aspect of Luck now, and half of his vision became streaked with golden lines that seemed to pull and push at him with an inexorable force, like that of an ocean tide. As he fell he pulled two daggers from his wrist sheathes, and as his luck kicked in, the two front guards turned and saw him, just as he bowled into them from above, the force of his fall dissipated by their weight, his daggers sliding effortlessly into their un-armored throats.

He saw Lorna's axe flash out of the corner of his eye as she fell and rolled, the Wolf Talisman painting gray lines along her hands and feet, and another man lost his head. The remaining guardsmen were dispatched in a matter of seconds. Barely a minute later, the Ranger group was up and running again, ascending the staircase.

I love this, Davydd thought.

They crossed the bridge with no trouble, doubled over so that no one could see them above the high stone sides. The moon was out, and while it was unlikely for anyone to look too closely at the bridges at night, none of them were willing to risk it. When they reached the other side, Davydd dealt with the lock on the wooden door that led through the guardhouse by twisting it and hitting the pommel of his sword against the metal. It broke off with a snap, and he motioned two Ranger pairs to ready themselves to go through.

He opened the door, and they rushed past him. No sound came from inside, and, after a wait that couldn't have been more than thirty seconds, Terin came back and motioned for them to follow her. They passed through, and as they did Davydd noticed racks of weapons and large Black Powder barrels carefully packed in sawdust. The fact Tyne had never been successfully invaded had not dampened Rikard's vision of a perfectly defended city.

They were inside the Lion's compound now – a wide fortress made up of a large, double wall around a huge slew of military barracks and academies, along with Most High guesthouses, gardens, and shops run by the Elevated. The gate that led to the rest of the city was closed and barred for the night, with a number of guards waiting in front of it just down the street. Not many – ten at most, and with the Rangers' bows they were as good as dead already.

But Davydd held back. He didn't want to give away their position yet – they needed to find out what Rikard's plans were, and to do that they might need to infiltrate Rikard's castle itself, an enormous stone structure, all spires and towers with a dozen different flags flying from the keep. They already knew he hadn't done what had happened in Lerne or Tibour – the Commons were still here, and the city seemed to be thriving. Could he be planning something else?

Movement from behind Davydd – he glanced over his shoulder and saw a number of Rangers spreading out across the street, sticking to the shadows. But one of them, a tall male Ashandel, was moving toward Davydd.

No, not toward Davydd – *past* him.

Davydd held up a hand and stopped the grizzled older man from continuing on. The man barely held himself back from simply pushing through and moving forward, straight for the distant soldiers. He was one of those that had been found in the dungeons of Formaux – one of the few that had been there only a handful of months. In normal times he would have been taken back to Vale, possibly even to Elder Keri for an evaluation and medical care before being retested by Ishmael himself, but they had no time for such a thing. The man had working hands and feet, and appeared more or less unharmed, though Davydd knew from Tiffenal's memories the kinds of things that could be done that left no physical wound.

"Hold, Qoric," Davydd whispered. "We don't know what's happening here – we move slow and on my orders. Am I understood?"

The veteran looked down at him – *by the seven hells, this headache's tall* – and the thing behind those haunted, red-rimmed eyes could barely be called a man. But Davydd stared right back at him, knowing his own appearance was less than sweet these days.

Come on, big man. I dare you to even try it.

Without willing it, the golden lines danced across his vision, and Qoric glanced at Davydd's left eye with a sudden flash of alarm – the eye the Talisman had taken over, the one that glowed a burnished gold whenever his luck kicked in. Qoric swallowed hard and stepped back.

Davydd turned back to the task at hand, and saw Lorna watching him with a raised eyebrow. He smirked and she rolled her eyes.

A cry sounded from beyond the gate.

Surprised, Davydd looked at the wall, though that was, of course, no help. He looked up and saw no easy way to ascend it here, nor any lookouts up above. Strange, that. Come to think of it... there were far too few guards in general.

That group we just killed could easily have been twice that size, and why hasn't a patrol come down this street since we walked in?

He looked back at the guards manning the gate and realized they were at half-force. The last time he'd done this with Lorna there had been nearly twice as many, with men walking the streets as well. Tonight, aside from the men at the gate, the area seemed downright abandoned.

"Is it just me," he whispered to Lorna, "or does it seemed like a large portion of the guard is otherwise detained?"

"I noticed it too," she whispered back. "They may have been sent to join the army – they're massing just to the south, and we know they're leaving at dawn."

Another scream sounded, and then another right on its heels. Two men started shouting, and then there came the sound of what must have been a splintering door knocked from its hinges. Davydd caught Lorna's eye, and he knew they'd both realized simultaneously what was happening.

The ritual was taking place tonight.

Just our luck.

"Guess that gets rid of our need for more information," he said dryly.

"We can't leave them here," Lorna whispered. "We can't."

"How do we *stop* it? We have a hundred Rangers; they have an army just to the south of a *hundred thousand!* We can't even make them *angry.*"

"We can sabotage the dams," Lorna said immediately. "Like Tomaz did that one year. And not the ones at the grain fields – the Lionshead itself. If there's a skeleton crew of guards in the city, there must be barely anyone up there."

A chill went up Davydd's; now *that* would make for a great story.

"We send the retreat force to the dam," he said, "and the others stay with us to make a distraction?"

"Break the chain on that gate," Lorna said, "and with speed and luck, the odds are in our favor. It's the only way in or out of the compound outside of the bridges."

"Which we can break with the Powder," Davydd said, motioning back inside. The guardhouse was lined with Black Powder barrels, as all the guardhouses were. In the event of an invasion, Rikard had ordered the Black Power ready with fuses so that they could be rolled out and launched at attacking enemies from trebuchets anchored to the guard post towers. The last time Davydd and Lorna had been here together they'd even toyed with blowing them as a distraction, but Lorna had convinced him at the last moment not to, saying they shouldn't waste a trick that might work in the future.

"Have I ever told you how much I like working with you?"

"Always nice to hear it again," she said, her eyes bright.

"Qoric," Davydd said, motioning the man over. "I want you to pick ten Rangers and kill those guards – do it *quietly*, and when you're done, break the chain holding the gate in place. Wait for my signal."

The man's eyes blazed, and he moved off to pick his companions.

"Joli," Davydd said to another Eshendai nearby. "Take Paulia, Jamin, Kyr, and their Ashandel around the compound – there should be Black Powder stashed in each of the seven gatehouses, and if I'm right, the guards tonight will be at a minimum. Set the barrels at the base of the bridges and light the fuses. Make them long enough that we can get the hell out of here when you're done."

Joli nodded and moved off, just another shadow among shadows, whispering to the others to follow her.

Fifteen minutes, tops, to run the whole compound.

"This is going to draw *him* out," Lorna said. "We will need to be long gone by the time he tries to engage us."

"With any luck," Davydd said with a cheeky grin, "we will be."

Another scream came from the other side of the wall, then another as they began to multiply. It wasn't isolated now – Rikard's men must be pulling the Commons from their houses in droves.

"Topher," Davydd said to yet another Ranger, "get out of here and find the reserve force securing our retreat – send half of them to the west edge of the city with our mounts under Jasper, and tell the rest of them to break the Lionshead dam in... "

He glanced at the moon and marked its passage, factored in how long the rest of this would take, and how long it would take to get as many Commons out of the city as possible.

"An hour," he finished. "*Exactly* an hour."

The man grimaced and opened his mouth to speak, but Davydd cut him off.

"It has to be then," he said. "You're our fastest runner. Make it happen."

The man took a deep breath, then nodded, and sprinted back through the guardhouse, already moving at a fast, loping pace that ate distance easily.

"Qoric," Davydd said. "Go get your revenge."

The man took off with his chosen few, staying to the shadows, and ambushed the first group of guards, killing them all before they knew what had happened. Qoric himself took great pleasure in sawing his knife through his guardsman's neck. A few of the Ashandel disappeared into the gatehouse, and the sound of a snapping chain *clanked* out and rattled around the side streets by the gate.

Davydd caught one last sight of the castle, and suddenly regretted never having the chance to infiltrate it.

Well, maybe I'll get the chance to have a go at the Fortress of Lucien.

Qoric and the others came back after stashing the white-and-gold guardsmen in the gatehouse.

"Lorna," Davydd said, "can you – ?"

"Yes," she answered, and turned to lead the way back up the bridgeway as Davydd waited for Joli and the others.

Fifteen minutes... damn, what happened?

But just as he had the thought, she turned the corner with her squad, and began running toward him, gesturing frantically for him to run as well. Davydd turned and struck flint and steel to the Black Powder he'd been waiting to light, the one with the shortest fuse he could find, and as soon as it caught, he ran past it, following Lorna and the others, Joli and her squad right behind him.

They were halfway up the bridgeway when a series of explosions ripped through the air behind them. Gold lines spider-webbed across his vision, and he knew in the next instant exactly what they needed to do. The stone walkway on which they were running was one of the first to go, and as it titled drunkenly toward the city below, he shouted forward to Lorna, not needing to bother keeping quiet now.

"The house on the right!"

She heard him and veered right, just as the bridge, now unanchored, began to crash down into the houses below it. She jumped, and all the Rangers followed with her, just as the bridge fell past the roof of a seven-story house that looked ready to fall down at the slightest provocation. Luckily, it was sturdier than it appeared.

When Davydd reached the spot, he too dove forward, just managing to clear the ledge, with Joli and her fellow Rangers right on his tail. In a heap, they all crashed to the shingled roof of the building, which swayed dangerously beneath them.

Davydd spun around and looked across the city to see, in the harsh, chemical lights Rikard had had installed to light the streets at night and enforce the city-wide curfew, the six other bridgeways fall as well. Lights turned on across the city, as nearly the whole population woke in alarm, looking out their windows. Alarm bells rang inside Rikard's compound, but Davydd only smiled.

Let's see them sift through all that rubble in the time it takes the Commons to realize what's happening.

The soldiers already in the streets – it looked like a couple hundred of them, but in roving, ill-organized groups – suddenly started kicking in doors at random, all over the city, pulling men and women, screaming, from their houses.

"What do we do now?" Lorna asked.

"Wait for them to realize what's happening," he said.

He turned back around and checked the moon again. He hoped the others were in position – this was going to be tight no matter which way it ended.

And then again, flashes of golden light cracked his vision.

"Spread out," he said quickly. "We need to flank the main roadway out of the city and get them going this way. Kill who you can from concealment; *keep out of sight*. This needs to be timed perfectly, or else it'll all go wrong. Lorna, take that side, I'll stay here. When the guard finally gets through the gate, the Commons will come running right for us."

She nodded and took half the group across the street as he watched what was going on in the city below. The soldiers were emptying more and more people into the streets, but suddenly there was nowhere to go. They were trying to get into Rikard's compound, but with the gate locked and the bridgeways down, they were temporarily stymied. And with more and more Commons spilling from their houses, Davydd knew the situation would soon reach a critical peak.

As luck would have it, the two biggest bridgeways had collapsed at just such an angle that they separated the most densely populated half of the city away from where the Elevated lived. Two others bridgeways had broken into pieces small enough and far enough apart that they were quite easy to get around and through – except that their bases were still intact, and presented a huge obstacle to leaving the city via that route.

They've got to come this way, or no way.

Davydd shot a look across the street at Lorna on the roof opposite him where she had taken up her position. Shadows and fire, that Wolf made her bloody fast. Anyone else would have said her face bore no expression, but he knew her – she was just as excited as he was. She made a quick upward motion with her hand, two fingers out, then tapped her ears and just below her eyes and he nodded back. He turned and made the same motion to the Rangers behind him and then held up both hands, fingers spread, and jerked his head at the clock tower that stood visible over the city. *You have until the clock strikes ten.*

"Go," he whispered, turning back to the edge of the roof to look down once more as they left, swift shadows moving on the wind, making no sound at all, their hints of green and gold masked completely this night in black. He moved forward slowly, he and Lorna the only ones holding back as the others went forward, many jumping down and descending the sides of buildings to get to ground level where they could be even more deadly.

Davydd looked back at Joli and Qoric, the two he had kept back with him, and they knew, without him having to say anything, that the time had come. They both pulled out the battle horns they'd brought along, and blew them.

The sound rang out across the city, over the sound of the Commons screaming and fighting the soldiers as the men in the white-and-gold of Tyne pulled them toward a city gate still closed. Even from this distance, Davydd could see that they had started to grow frantic. There were already too many of the Commons – this wasn't the plan; they were severely outnumbered.

Kindred arrows suddenly shot out of nowhere, killing a number of the guards and freeing a number of the Commons, who ran unthinkingly back into the city, directed by the broken bridgeways toward the hidden Kindred.

Davydd stared hard at the fleeing crowd, urging the Aspect of Luck to tell him what to do next, waiting for the next move to come to him –

A Commons man running toward them seemed to glow with light, as if he'd been lit on fire by the sun itself, and Davydd launched himself off the side of the roof to the ledge below, then to a balcony nearby, then to another roof, and finally to the ground, heading for the man.

"You!" Davydd shouted.

The man turned, holding a young, crying girl in his arms. Davydd took in his face, saw immediately the black markings around his eyes and mouth, and almost killed him on the spot.

An apprentice Bloodmage.

"Exiled Kindred!" the man shouted, looking just as stunned as Davydd was.

"We're here to get you out of the city," Davydd said quickly, trusting in the Aspect despite his better judgment. "Rikard is trying to kill you – he's trying to create a massive–"

"Soul Catcher beneath the city," the man finished, speaking quickly. "I know – I left when I heard what they were doing, and I've been living as a refugee in the city. What's your plan?"

Davydd told him. The man just stared.

"Trust me," Davydd said, coming further into the light so that the man could see the burned half of his face and the golden eye in its bony socket. Davydd had to give the man credit – he didn't wince or cry out in alarm, but simply took a deep, albeit shaky, breath and nodded.

"So you're the one that got Tiffenal," he said. "Good. Man was a bastard."

I bloody well think I might like this Bloodmage.

Soldiers turned onto the street they were on, as more Commons fled their homes in a huge wave. The soldiers were laying about them with spears, trying to herd them all back toward the gate, but they were far too few.

"Will you follow me?" Davydd asked.

"Yes. And I'll spread the word – we'll see you at the edge of the city?"

"Spread the word?" Davydd asked incredulously.

"Yes," the Bloodmage said. "I'm not the only one who's changed his mind."

He disappeared, shouting names into the crowd, still holding the unconscious girl in his arms. A number of the fleeing men and women turned and caught sight of him as he shouted that the Kindred had come to save them, that the soldiers were trying to take them all the way they'd taken others in the weeks before.

"Follow that man!" the Bloodmage shouted, pointing at Davydd. "And you just might live!"

Davydd nodded, and turned to lead the way down the main road. In a huge wave, they followed him. More soldiers shouted and cursed at them, breaking in from side streets, trying to bar their way. Davydd pulled out his valerium sword, Titania, and cut them down where they stood. Men of the Commons who weren't carrying children or belongings bent and picked up the fallen spears, and started attacking the other soldiers themselves. When the tide was well and clearly headed in the right direction, Davydd ran for the nearest building and scaled it.

He emerged on top of the building just in time to see part of the great city catch fire. He glanced back at the huge clock tower and saw it was only fifteen minutes to ten now. He checked the moon and saw he had maybe fifteen minutes on top of that, a half hour total, until the other Rangers burst the dam. They needed to be out of the city and up the first hill before that happened.

"Damn," he cursed. It was going to be too bloody close.

But then a fresh wave of Commons rushed down the street past him, shepherded by the turncoat Bloodmage now waving a huge oaken staff and shouting vitriolic bile at the soldiers as he smacked them, knocking them off their feet with heavy swings and staving in heads, ribcages, and any other target presented.

As many as make it is as many as make it, Davydd told himself harshly. *I can only help so many; I just have to hope the rest can fend for themselves.*

He caught sight of Lorna and a number of other Rangers running down the street parallel to the main boulevard that led east out of the city, and went to go with her. But as he set his feet on the edge of the building and prepared to shimmy his way down a drainpipe, another huge explosion rocked the city, and Davydd saw the huge gate doors blast apart.

Of course – there was more Black Powder in the barracks.

Davydd watched as the dust settled, and a man dressed all in white – a white helm, a white cape, a white cloak, and riding a white warhorse in shining armor, emerged.

Ah, shit.

Davydd leaped off the side of the roof and slid down the pipe, crashing into an old crate that somewhat broke his fall – *ah, damn splinters!* – before he ran to catch up with Lorna. "Good to see you again!" he said. "Who're all your friends?"

She had collected a group of what looked to be nearly a hundred Commons men and women, all carrying commandeered swords and spears.

"I thought you'd abandoned me," she said. "I had to fill my dance card."

"Abandoned you? Now why would I do that? You're the prettiest girl here."

"And you take me to all the best places," she replied, face stony but smiling with her eyes.

They rounded the corner that brought the street they were on back to the main boulevard. The huge tide of people had swollen with fresh additions, and they were all running madly now, without restraint or abandon, away from the figure of Rikard.

Why doesn't he just command them to stay?

"His Talisman must be limited by distance," Lorna said, as if reading Davydd's mind. "He needs to be in earshot; it won't work if no one can hear him."

As one, they glanced at the clock and saw it was almost ten. Davydd's squad of Rangers had just returned, riding the wave of Commons down the street. But there were still more people coming. The clock ticked closer to the hour, and Davydd made a snap decision. "We need to buy them time."

"No," Lorna said quickly, "we need to get out of here, or we'll be trapped right along with them!"

"We need to buy them time to get up that first hill so they're out of the way of the dam," Davydd said. "We need to make sure he can't come after them."

"Fine! But not here – this is the center of the biggest street in the city! He's got guardsmen in spades all on top of being the shadow-cursed *Prince of Lions*. We cannot stand here!"

"And how far can we go before he can command them?" Davydd countered. "How far can we retreat before he can yell at us all to just stop in our tracks?"

Lorna growled deep in her throat, but dropped her argument and hefted her axe.

"You're going to be the death of me, boy."

"The rest of you," Davydd said to the Rangers and Commons around him, "go! Take everyone with you that you can, and make sure to secure the way!"

They left, which meant Lorna and Davydd were the only two standing amidst the flowing tide of refugees as Rikard rode out at the head of what looked to be hundreds of guardsmen; a rising tide of white and gold.

"This isn't a good idea," Lorna rasped. "Raven said –"

"Screw Raven," Davydd said. "I want my chance at the Lion." He felt a soaring feeling in the pit of his stomach as his luck took over even more completely, and any thoughts of warning or consequence were pushed out of his mind.

"This isn't about that," Lorna said immediately, her voice carrying a tinge of panic. "This is about letting the others escape. Right?"

"Two birds with one stone," he said with a manic grin. He saw her focus on his left eye, and he knew it was pulsing with golden light. Fear crossed her face, barely visible to anyone who didn't know her, but he didn't stay to listen to what she might have to say. The gold lines had returned, and they were telling him what to do.

He strode forward, his booted feet clicking against the paved street.

Rikard continued to move forward at the head of his guardsmen, his horse now at a trot as his men ran along beside him, and for the first time since they'd entered the city, Davydd found himself thinking back to the last thing Raven had said to them:

He's mad, and powerful beyond what you can understand. Do not test him. If you come up against him, run, and do not look back.

Davydd drew his sword, Titania, from the sheath slung across his back, and smiled. Lorna swung her battle-axe in a looping arc, making it whistle, as she kept pace beside him. He silenced his mind as he reached into his sword. He, like Leah, was a Spellblade, and he could send that sword anywhere he wanted if he focused hard enough. He swung the blade loosely in his hand, the valerium humming in anticipation.

He sped up, gathering speed, and then stopped and spun, swinging the sword in a huge looping arc, throwing it straight as an arrow at the distant form of Rikard. Pushing it with his mind, his eyes narrowed to slits, he watched as it flew straight and true, slicing through the air for the white figure. At the last instant, Rikard raised a sword, an ornate broadsword he wore at his side, and swatted the blade out of the air.

But Davydd was too fast for him, and at the last second he sped Titania up the last extra bit he could. Rikard's blow hit too high on the blade, and the sword sliced across his shield arm, the valerium metal cutting through his armor and biting into the flesh beneath.

The Prince of Lions threw back his head and shouted wordlessly into the night. Davydd felt his whole body rock with the force of the cry; he staggered back, and watched as whole rows of Rikard's guardsmen collapsed in mid-stride, screaming in pain as blood poured from their ears. A halo of white light suddenly burst from Rikard's great helm, and Davydd found himself nearly blinded.

With a mental *tug*, Davydd pulled Titania back to him, just as the clock in the large central tower began to strike the hour of ten.

"Time to go," he said to Lorna with a grin, and turned to run, just as Titania flew the rest of the way back into his hand.

A word that vibrated through their bones like thunder rang out from the center of the city, a word that seemed to roll around them and try to gel the air itself, holding them in place, but their Aspects saved them, and they ran for their lives. More words were shouted, words that made no sense but crackled with power, and they ran even faster, trying desperately to catch the flowing tide of Commons.

Next they heard the sound of hooves behind them, and Davydd shot a look over his shoulder to see Rikard charging forward, the guardsmen who hadn't been struck down by the Prince's roar riding and shouting along behind him. Davydd was running as fast as he could, but Lorna was already loping along in front of him, the Aspect of Endurance shining gray light out from her boots and gauntlets. His right foot had begun to pound terribly, and he suddenly remembered the crate he'd crashed into and the splinters...

"Lorna," Davydd gasped, "I think I might need a bit of help – "

She reached back and grabbed him, slung him across her shoulders, and began to run faster than should have been possible. Davydd looked down as he bounced about on her shoulders, and saw her boots break apart in shreds of leather, burned away by the brilliance of the light beneath them. Their speed increased even more, and they were running with such vigor that Lorna was leaving deep gouges in the earth.

"There!" Davydd said, pointing.

They had reached the edge of the city, where the last dam stood. The whole of Tyne was situated in a valley that had once been a deep lake. A series of dams that were heavily guarded in normal times held the water back now, water that was diverted to the huge grain fields to the south, what was called the bread basket of the Empire. But between the army gathering to the south and the men pulling out Baseborn for the Bloodmage ritual, it was very unlikely the damns were guarded well enough to fight off several squads of Rangers.

Let's hope my luck held.

Joli and Qoric emerged from the end of the rushing tide of Commons fifty yards in front of them, each mounted on their horse and leading two other horses with them. And not a moment too soon – the heavily reinforced metal of Lorna's breastplate was digging painfully into Davydd's chest and crotch with each long, loping stride.

Lorna swung him around and landed him on the ground beside her. His heel immediately began to burn again with an insistent fire, but he managed to take two limping strides and catch Aron's reins. He pulled himself into the saddle and watched Lorna jump onto the back of hers.

He spun Aron around and watched the retreating backs of the Commons; thousands had made it out and were now swarming up the hill, almost to the top. He glanced back at the clock tower and found it covered in shadows from their angle on the hillside. He looked up at the moon and saw it was nearly where it should be.

Five minutes, if that.

"You!" shouted a voice. "What's the plan now?!"

Davydd turned to see the Bloodmage from before, with the black markings around his eyes. There were nearly half a dozen others with him, all bearing the same long quarterstaffs that he was. All of them were young men, all just under six feet tall, and with the trademark dark, sunken eyes of their caste that made Davydd's lip curl up in contempt. Some still had freshly shaven heads, while others had weeks or even months worth of sparse growth that showed how long ago they'd left their black brethren behind.

This is what I would have become if my parents had had their way.

"Go!" Davydd shouted at them. "Go! Get as far away from the city as you can, take as many of the Commons as you can. Take the high road along the north side of the mountains for Lucien. Steal horses, oxen, mules and carts, anything you can. We will hold them until you are free of here."

"Make – make for *Lucien*?"

"There is a Kindred army marching on the city even as we speak," Davydd said breathlessly. "They are going to the Plains of al'Manthian."

"Impossible!"

"We have killed five of the seven Children and brought one to our side," Davydd said with a grin that split his burnt cheek. "I'm growing fond of doing the impossible."

He turned Aron and spurred him back down the hill toward where the other Rangers had gathered and were now shooting arrows down the hillside, using the height to increase the distance of their shots. Davydd spared one final glance behind him and saw the Commons, led by the group of six former mages, begin their flight down the Imperial Road; thousands were flowing over the city's final hilltop into the broad expanse of the Fields.

They needed just a bit more time, and he would buy it for them.

He hefted his sword once more, his beautiful Titania, and searched for Rikard. They were above the watermark – lines had been cut in the rocky hillside to either side of them, and he could see the layers where sediment had built up hundreds of years ago, still present as a marker of times long past – and he had to keep Rikard and his men from crossing that mark. Rikard and his men were making their way out toward them, past the wide, beautifully carved walls ringing the outer limits of Tyne, connecting each of the Most High compounds. The White City shone even in the darkness from the harsh chemical fluorescence of the streetlamps.

The Aspect of Luck grabbed him by the throat, and his confidence turned sour.

He felt it even as he embraced it, like a drug coursing through his body that he should have rejected, that in a sober state he would have realized as dangerous, but now couldn't resist. He rode the wave of it as it crashed inside him, and he heeled his horse forward.

"Davydd! Stop!"

He ignored the shout; he barely even recognized that it had come from Lorna, the one person who had been able to rein him in in times like this before. He rode forward, digging his heels recklessly into Aron's flanks. Arrows shot alongside him, knocking off the first wave of guardsmen as he engaged them, and suddenly his sword was flying, killing men left and right as they tried to get up the hill past him through the narrowed level pass that made the easiest ascent up the hill.

Lorna was with him in the next instant, laying about her with her axe, moving faster than should have been possible. Her gauntlets had split and burst now too, the metal going the same way as the leather in her boots and sloughing off in ragged strips that sizzled as they landed in the grass.

The Fox Talisman directed him, pushing him here, pulling him there, so that for every one man he would have killed before, he now managed to engage and dispatch five. Commons continued to stream by him in droves, and he realized more were still coming from the city, having rounded the far side. Many held children or belongings in their arms, and some even looked like guardsmen who had turned their coats. These latter ones stopped and fought with him, looking shocked by their own actions. They laid about them into whichever of their former companions happened to escape, and at the same time shouted behind them, urging on what Davydd realized were family members among the fleeing Commons.

But Davydd wasn't here to kill guardsmen. He looked around wildly, killing another man in a spray of blood as Titania feasted on the man's soul. Where was the Lion? Where was the one man here who could even attempt to stand up to him now, he, the Prince of Luck?

Arrows continued to rain down from the hill above them as the Rangers shot everything they had at the men charging from below, picking their targets carefully, killing or disabling with every arrow. Something tickled the back of Davydd's mind, something that was wrong.

The dam should have burst by now. They're late.

The thought almost brought him back down from the high the Aspect had sent him on, but at the same instant the crowd cleared as the battle shifted, and there was Rikard on his huge warhorse. He had pulled off his helm, and now shone in the night like a minor sun, the white light shooting from both his armor and the halo of his Talisman, which highlighted the statuesque arches of his cheeks and spread through his uncovered mane of long, golden-chestnut hair.

Davydd ran for him, cutting down anyone who stood in his path. Lorna called for him to wait for her; she wanted him to slow down, to approach with caution, as she always did.

Not this time. This time I do it my way.

Rikard laid about him left and right with a second sword, a long, two-handed claymore. He roared Commands left and right, felling men with only words, and knocking scores of others off their feet. The sound of the words even rocked Davydd, buffeting him but passing by, harmless.

Talisman cancels Talisman.

Golden lines pulled him right, and he went without complaint. A shower of arrows cascaded to the ground where he'd been a second before, and Davydd spun, throwing Titania as he did. It sliced through the air, flying end over end through the night. The white blade flashed and disappeared, and Davydd knew it had found its target. He *pulled* with his mind, and the weapon came flying back to him, the white valerium blade now steaming with gore.

Davydd turned again, cut down two more Imperial dogs that slashed at him uselessly with spears, and threw Titania, this time straight for Rikard's horse.

The white blade seemed to quiver in the air, but it didn't change direction; it flew true and took the white stallion in the chest as it reared back and flashed its hooves, intending to bring them crashing down on another solider. Triumphant neighing turned to a mortal scream of terror, and the steed fell; the Prince of Lions somehow managed to catch the motion, sensing it with his knees, and jumped from the horse's back. He landed, rolled easily, and came back to his feet, his voice ringing out with a single shout that dropped the dozen former guardsmen surrounding him to their knees, blood pouring from their ears.

Davydd snarled and *pulled* Titania with his mind, dislodging it from its place in the horse's ribs. He caught the blade with one hand, used its momentum to spin himself around, and then attacked Rikard with an overhand blow that could have cleaved a bull in two.

The blow was met by Rikard's shining, crystalline blade, and stopped dead.

"Die!"

The Command caught Davydd unprepared, and for a brief second the utter surety in Rikard's burning white eyes, the certain knowledge he would be obeyed, almost threw Davydd out of step; but he held to the Aspect and the instant passed, leaving him unscathed. He smiled, full and toothy, and Rikard snarled in his face.

Davydd spun and threw his weight behind a heavy sideways swipe; Rikard stepped back just far enough to avoid the blade, and then swung his own sword in a perfect backhand. Davydd slipped in the muddy grass of the torn hillside, and golden lines pulled him down. He went with his momentum, falling just beneath the edge of the blade as the claymore whistled past his chin. Davydd rolled and kicked out at Rikard, but the Lion anticipated the blow, dodged, and came forward.

Rikard caught him by the throat, and Davydd's mind went blank in complete shock; his mental grasp on the Fox Talisman, the Aspect of Luck, *slipped* somehow, and the golden lines that illuminated the world winked out like dying stars, fading in a blaze of glory like a shower of meteors crashing into the sea.

"*Do not touch the Talisman again; do not move; do not think; do not breathe.*"

The words vibrated through his skin, down to his bones, and latched themselves onto him, weaving the Command into his mind. Rikard saw the effect, and smiled.

Davydd felt fear course through him, the first real fear since entering the city.

A sound like a thousand trees splitting in half ripped through the air and Rikard jerked his head up in surprise. At just that moment, a figure with light streaming from gray hands and feet ran past him and grabbed Davydd in her arms, pulling him away from the distracted Prince of Lions.

Davydd found himself in Lorna's arms as she ran at break-neck speed up the hill. Water began to spill in huge tidal waves over the sides of the hilltop to their right, coming from the remains of the Lionshead Dam.

Lorna was shouting commands out ahead of her, while Davydd lay paralyzed in her arms. His lungs were burning with the need to breathe, but he was unable to break free of the Command, unable to even form a coherent thought. Titania had slipped from his grasp and now lay somewhere on the battlefield, while his hands, curled into unfeeling claws, were frozen in their final pose at odd angles.

Water rushed past them to their left, and Davydd heard Rikard shouting Commands behind them, shouting at his men to fall back, shouting at the water even to break to either side of them.

No... no, surely not, surely he can't control that.

But even as he had the thought, the water began to split, forming smaller rivulets, and Davydd cried out silently, trying to get Lorna to notice, trying to tell her she needed to do something.

I can think again – the Commands are wearing off with distance.

His mind went to his sword, lying somewhere on the battlefield, and he realized he could feel it, realized he could reach through his connection to it still. He *pulled* with his mind and felt it fly toward him. With every ounce of will power he had, he managed to shift in Lorna's arms, and she stumbled, dropping him to the ground.

"Davydd!" she rasped. "What are you –?"

Crouched on all fours, he saw Titania flying toward him. They were at the top of the hill, just above the waterline, but the water wasn't blocking the retreat now like it had been intended to: Rikard had Commanded it to flow around them, and it was doing just that. Davydd could see the man's eyes as he came toward them, eyes that were glowing white, the aura of absolute power flowing out around him like a lion's mane.

Davydd caught Titania, pulled the barest trickle of luck from his Aspect, and threw the sword toward the Prince. It flew true, and forced Rikard to swipe it away with his claymore. Davydd anticipated the blow, and pulled the sword back again, this time sideways.

Rikard was caught off balance, and the pommel of the sword struck him directly across the temple. He shouted, falling to the ground, and the white aura of the Lion Talisman winked out around him.

Immediately, all the Commands he had imprinted on Davydd's mind disappeared, and so too did the Command keeping the water at bay. In a rushing tidal wave, the water coalesced into one huge stream, and roared down the mountainside. Rikard pulled one of his own men off a horse, mounted it, and rode for the city, trying to escape the flood, and his men ran with him.

Davydd *pulled* Titania back to him with the last bit of will power left to him, and then sank back to him knees. Lorna caught him up and laid him over the saddle of her horse, and they galloped off into the night.

He'll be on us as soon as the water settles, Davydd thought as he pushed back against the encroaching darkness of unconsciousness. He saw again the hate in the man's eyes, and the lust for domination, those blank, terrible eyes that carried such unbearable, irresistible weight, and Davydd felt his chest shake as he tried to calm his wild breathing.

Well, that wasn't as much fun as I hoped.

Chapter Sixteen:

The Plains of al'Manthian

The Plains of al'Manthian were barren, and burned.

They had always been barren; only dirt, mud, and clay had been seen here for the thousand years the land had lain fallow. It stretched all the way south from the city of Lucien to the Elmist Mountains and all the way east and west from the Barrow Hills that led to Tyne in the west and to the Screaming Mountains of the Eyrie in the east. The Children had never directly fought over it, as it was a no-man's land; but the Empress had never claimed it as explicitly Hers, and so they had fought covert wars through economic and commercial means as She had intended all along. It had been planted with every seed, and trodden by every animal, but no crop had ever taken, and no herd had ever become self-sustaining. In the end, each Child who had tried to grab hold of it had been forced to abandon their claim.

And so still it stood, the whole plain a scourged ruin, a bald patch of ground that revealed hidden contours of tiny hills and concealed chasms that spelled a broken ankle for the unwary rider if not an immediate drop and eventual death. And the roiling clouds that covered the city of Lucien, the clouds that showed the Empress' power and dominance over the very sky itself, capped it all, like a solemn shroud that contained and held the grave and maudlin air of a burial ground.

Autmaran and Raven sat side by side on their horses on the high ridgeline of the final mountain before these Plains, as the Kindred marched past below them, expanding from their cramped, compressed trail columns into sprawling, full-blown battle formations. There were more archers than Raven was used to, and many more light cavalry, which he had never truly appreciated until he had met

Autmaran. All told, their force was massive, though looks were deceptive; nearly half was made up of untrained former peasants.

Tym shifted back where he was standing at the tree line, where he had chosen to wait for Raven and Autmaran's commands. He had become their most trusted runner, and, with his new body, one of their fastest as well. He had grown even more since Lerne, and was nearly the same height as Raven now, though he looked as though his bones had been stretched to make it happen, his skin gaunt and tight all over. The camp cooks said he ate prodigiously, and Raven had commanded them to give him all he needed. He refused to leave Raven's side now that battle was imminent, and Raven had stopped arguing with him. If the boy wanted to be near him, then fine.

It's better than having him out there, fighting. We need all the Aspects together.

Something about that thought caused him to remember what Geofred had implied before his death, what he had partially came out and said:

Only the Aspects can beat the Talismans.

But how could they all fight the Empress? They would be lucky if just one of them made it through to confront her face-to-face.

He felt a wave of unease pass over him, and again felt that nagging thought in the back of his head, the feeling that something had been left undone, that he had somewhere along the road missed a crucial turn.

Shadows and light... let Lorna and Davydd find their way to us in time.

They had still received no word from the Ranger pair, and none of their group had returned, though that was partly to be expected. With the distance to Tyne and the haste with which they had be forced to ride, it was hard to expect a messenger of any kind, even if they rode their horse to death.

The sound of approaching hooves broke him from his reverie, and he turned to see Leah and Tomaz coming up the ridge, their cloaks billowing out behind them under the force of the steady wind. "They're ready," Tomaz rumbled. "The captains are leading them into position now, and General Dunhold is keeping it all in order."

"He may be a little off when it comes to strategy," Leah said, "but he knows how to follow orders. They'll be in position before the sun has fully risen."

All of them had woken before dawn to get here, and the night's chill still hung close about them. As if in response to his thoughts, the wind picked up and blew fiercely past them, throwing Raven's hood up and over his head, partially blinding him. He reached up and pulled it down again.

"Damn wind," Raven muttered.

"Pray it dies down," Leah said as she dismounted and came to crouch on the ground beside them. Her tone of voice was grim. "It'll send our arrows flying every which way if it doesn't."

"I've always wondered about the story of a wind," Tym said suddenly from where he stood, his youthful tenor breaking easily through the whispering insistence of the rushing air. Raven, Autmaran, Leah, and Tomaz all turned to look at him with comically identical expressions of surprise.

"Think of all the things it's seen," Tym said, speaking almost to himself, his eyes far away, oblivious to their stares. "All the places it's been and all the places it has yet to go…. Imagine what that must be like – going on forever, just pushed from one end of the earth to the other, then back again. Sweeping over fields like this, playing in the leaves of trees, climbing mountains and racing back down again to who knows where."

Raven looked down over the edge of the ridgeline as the Kindred army continued to march below them, spreading out as instructed, and saw the wind passing between them all, playing with banners and cloaks and capes. It was like a small child, oblivious to what was coming, caring only for the moment.

"We stay in one place and the wind passes over us and then it's gone and we don't think about it again. Maybe that wind that just blew past us was the same wind that blew when we were born, or blew when we all met. Maybe that wind has seen us all our lives and likes seeing us again whenever it goes by. Or maybe it doesn't even recognize us 'cause it sees so many things. I could see it being either way. Maybe the whole world is like that – either everything is watched, everything is observed, every breaking of every branch and every twisting fall of every dying autumn leaf, or none of it is. I don't know which of the two I would prefer. I guess, though, if one is true or the other is, it doesn't really matter what I prefer, does it?"

As the easy, wistful tenor of the young man's voice faded away, none of the others felt the need or desire to break the silence. For the first time in weeks, Raven looked at the world around him, really *looked* at it, and saw the blooming spring. Flowers were budding nearby, a whole carpet of them interspersed with thick grass that led back to the side of the Elmist Mountains, and the trees that had shed their leaves only a few months prior were slowly growing them back.

Either none of it matters... or all of it does.

"Do you really think this is possible?" Raven asked quietly.

Tomaz shifted, sighed, and didn't answer; Leah grimaced and shrugged, shaking her head. Tym, it seemed, had expressed his thoughts as best he could, and so remained silent; Autmaran continued to stare off into the distance for a long time, so long in fact that Raven began to suspect he hadn't heard the question. He was staring into the horizon, looking over the plains as the sun rose in the east.

"I don't know," he said finally. The sun cast his face in a strange orange glow; his dark eyes were clouded, his brow furrowed. The responsibility of command had aged him, but where some crumbled under such weight, Autmaran had grown harder and stronger. As the weight of his responsibility had become more and more burdensome, he had become tougher in order to bear it, and now power seemed to sit on his shoulders like a mantle. A sense of calm directed purpose radiated from him, and Raven was reminded of the deep, assuring gaze of Elder Goldwyn.

"It *must* be," Autmaran amended, breathing in deeply; the dark skin of his face stretched tightly around his mouth as he set his jaw and pursed his lips. Tomaz grunted a rumbling agreement, approving the hard optimism. "Of all the things I have seen in the past few months – the death of Ramael, Tiffenal's infiltration of the Kindred, the siege of Banelyn, the very fact that you are here fighting next to me... nothing is impossible. One by one, things that I have *known* to be impossible have come to pass. It makes me question everything. Including the Tyrant's immortality."

Raven tensed but remained silent. Tomaz looked down at Autmaran, waiting for further explanation, while Leah nodded in agreement. Below them, the light cavalry was forming up along the sides of the Imperial Road as the heavy infantry lined up to act as the hard center that would bear the brunt of the attack. The untrained Commons were being formed up into roaming bands that would buttress weak points as they appeared, and the archers were staking out high ground.

This is really happening. It is finally here.

"Goldwyn started talking about it before his death," Autmaran said. "Not just with you, Raven, but with everyone. I spoke with some of the officers he chose as students, and they all said it was part of their conversations. He told them all that he felt sure of it. He always said that he didn't see the Empress as a God, but we took it as bravado. I should have known better. He's not the kind of man who says something without meaning it. I think maybe he was right. Maybe... maybe she's just like the Children. Maybe she's just a person."

"I'm sad for her Children," Tym said suddenly, his face incredibly despondent. Raven stared at him in shock and realized suddenly that the boy had never truly spoken ill of Raven's brothers and sisters. He had spoken of them as broken, as performing evil deeds, but never as evil.

"What do you mean?" Raven asked, watching the boy carefully. He realized that Tym didn't think of *him* as one of the Children. None of them did; at least not anymore.

Am I one of them? Was I ever really?

"I agree," Tomaz rumbled, taking over for Tym, who had wilted under Raven's gaze. "I *can't* believe it. I think they perform evil acts, but that does not make them evil. No more than a rabid dog is evil for biting and killing a child. A horrible tragedy it may be, but there is a madness in both cases."

"Madness... yes," said Autmaran, still staring out over the Kindred as they formed up below. The heavy infantry was now bordered by groups of spear and pikemen to fend off flanking attacks by enemy cavalry. The formation was almost complete – once the light infantry took up their place as reserves, the Rangers and Rogues would be spaced throughout as shock troops.

"The evil you read of in stories is not real," Autmaran said quietly. "Evil that wants to destroy for the sake of destruction, evil that does evil and knows it is evil, that is a fantasy. True evil, the evil that exists in the world, is the kind that does not know itself. It is the kind that does what it does for good reasons. Because it thinks the evil it does will bring about good, for itself and for others. Such are the Children, or so I have always thought."

"And the Empress?" asked Raven, his heart heavy and sad as it always was when he thought of his Mother, the woman who had tried to kill him, and the one who even now he couldn't help but love, whose approval he still yearned for. He felt sick inside, knowing that, but he knew it was true.

"I don't know," Autmaran sighed, shaking his head, the vision he had been seeing so clearly suddenly dispersed by the immensity of the thought presented to him. "A woman like that – an immortal – can she be human? Is there any humanity left after a thousand years?"

Raven opened his mouth to speak, but found that words stuck in his throat. He was unsure both of himself and Autmaran. He thought of what his Mother had done – tried to kill him, one of her Children.

Why me? Raven thought once more, the words jagged and ripping, like a fragment of broken glass. *Why wasn't I good enough for her?*

The wind howled around them like a tortured soul, grasping and pulling.

Raven said nothing, looking away from the others. He didn't even know if he believed the Empire could be saved anymore. He had dreamed that maybe there would be more like him, like Leah and Davydd – those who had grown up in the darkness of the Empress' shadow, but who, once given the chance, would be eager to change. He had hoped, before the death of Goldwyn, that there would be a way to keep from killing any more of his siblings, a way to avoid killing anymore of *anyone.*

But did he believe that now? Now, after all he'd seen? After what he knew of both the Kindred and the Empire?

A horn began to blow, far to the west, on the side of the plain that blended with the horizon and eventually led to the distant city of Tyne.

"Is that them?" Tym asked.

"If everything went to plan, then yes," Autmaran replied. "Everyone get ready –"

A speck of movement appeared on the horizon, and Raven immediately reached out through the Talisman, sending his mind questing over the land in front of them... only to stop short.

"Shadow-cursed piece of – Leah!"

She saw the request in his eyes and immediately came to him. He unsheathed Aemon's Blade and held the hilt out for her. She pulled off her gauntlet, grabbed the Aspect of Sight, and touched the valerium sword.

Raven's vision soared farther than before, crossing miles and miles of distance in a rolling wave, until it broke against a series of harsh lights that felt hard and panicked. There were... there were *thousands* of them.

Rikard? Had Davydd and Lorna failed and been beaten to the Plains by the Imperial Army?

But no... that didn't feel like an army.

"What in the world ...?"

"What is it?" Leah asked, her eyes glowing with blue fire, able to hold onto the Aspect for longer than a few seconds with Raven's help. Before he could answer, she stiffened, and her eyes rolled back in her head. Blue light streamed from the markings that swirled beneath her hair and down her spine, tracing her nerve-endings. She staggered, and Raven caught her.

"What happened?" rumbled Tomaz.

"I don't know," Raven said. "She must have seen something; she was holding the Aspect for longer than she's ever managed to before."

"Then what did she see?"

"I don't know," Raven replied curtly. "All I saw was that there are thousands of them out there; we need to form up and –"

He cut off as the lives came closer, crossing the edge of the field on the far distant side of the Plain, just visible now. He reached out again, going as far as he could without Leah's aid, pushing as hard as he could to get just one touch, one glimpse of that figure that was out in front of them.

He touched the figure with his mind, expecting Rikard and wanting to confirm it, just barely scraping the surface of his life... but what he felt was completely different.

That... that feels like Lorna.

"What is it?" Tomaz rumbled. "What do you feel?"

"It's not the Empire," Tym said before Raven could speak, looking out over the battlefield as the sides of his neck glowed a bright mossy green. "It can't be. That's not an Imperial formation; they're not marching, they're running!"

"He's right," Autmaran said, squinting through a scope he had brought along with him. "You've got fantastic eyes, boy."

"It's them," Leah said suddenly, breaking out of her trance and Raven's arms, coming to her feet. She shook her head as the blue light faded away, and focused on them. "It's Davydd and Lorna and half the shadow-cursed city of Tyne."

"*What?*"

"Davydd and –?"

"But those are Imperial horns," Autmaran said. "Who's blowing them?"

"Rikard is behind them," Leah said quickly. "They stalled the army and got in front – I don't know how, I didn't see it, but somehow they stalled the whole damn army, and brought half the city along with them."

"The plan was for them to bring us intelligence, not provoke Rikard!"

"He was always going to be here anyway," Raven said sharply; they had no time for should-have-beens. "That figure in front is Lorna – that means she's leading the charge and she's running from Rikard. We need to get those Commons behind our lines and meet Rikard in the field."

"We were anticipating the attack from Lucien –"

"We can't leave them to die!" Raven snapped.

"He's right," Autmaran said, taking over smoothly. " We always knew things would change once we got here – we'll adapt. Who is out in front – is it Lorna only?"

"Yes."

"But Davydd – " Leah began.

"He must be somewhere behind; I don't feel him at all."

"That can't be right."

"He can't be dead," Tomaz rumbled, though his inflection showed that the statement was half a question.

"He's not there," Raven said, straining once more and just barely touching that first life again. "All I can feel is Lorna – he should be standing out as bright as she, but all I can feel is the Wolf Talisman. The Fox –"

A glimmer of gold shot across his eyes, and the Raven Talisman grew hot across his back. Rocked, Raven took a step back as his vision swam.

"Whoa!"

"Catch him –"

"I'm fine," he said. "Davydd's there, but he's... he's so weak he's barely alive."

"What happened to him?"

"I have no way of knowing, but I'll bet Aemon's Blade against a hairpin he ignored my warning and sought out Rikard when they were in Tyne."

"You think the Lion defeated him?"

"If they fought," Raven said grimly, "I know he did."

"Tym, get the officers!" Autmaran called. Tym disappeared down the hill and reappeared within seconds, the under-officers running behind him from where they'd been waiting for further commands. Jaillin was there, as well as Stannit, Polim and Palum, and a number of others with bright patches of color sewn to their shoulders to show they were runners for particular captains.

"Two squads of Scouts to catch the stragglers," the Commander rattled off quickly, "with extra horses for any of the wounded. Yes, Jallin, I know we don't have enough as it is – *find them*. Three squads of heavy infantry to absorb the army on the west side of the field and hold off any attackers, one group of archers with them along the ridgeline; Polim and Palum, a full troop of Rangers to engage however is needed. The rest: turn to face the west side of the Plains, and hold formation. Go – now."

Raven only waited for them to be out of earshot before he spoke:

"We're already down enough Kindred without sparing more," he reminded Autmaran, doing his best to keep the bite of anger out of his tone. "What are we doing splitting our forces? We need to defend against two fronts as it is – we don't know what's waiting behind the walls of Lucien."

"We have the numbers," the Commander said, looking over the field quickly, his eyes flying back and forth so fast Raven thought for an instant he was having a mental breakdown. "It will be close. Very, very close. And we'll need to be on the Plains – there's no way to have them fully engaged without drawing them all to us."

"Autmaran," Raven started, but Leah cut him off.

"You mean to spread them?" she asked.

"In a fan there," he pointed, "and there."

"Where will you commit the archers?"

"There are ridges around the –"

"Perfect," she said, her eyes flaring blue for longer than normal – *has she finally gotten the hang of it?* – before returning to green, "they'll do damage."

"Will it truly pull them all the way in toward us?" Raven asked, suddenly catching on to what they were saying. The plan laid out before them looked... it looked *perfect.*

Nothing is perfect with Rikard thrown in the mix.

"Yes," Autmaran and Leah said together, before they both looked to him. Autmaran nodded to her. "You will need to detain your brother," Leah said softly.

Raven felt a thrill run down his spine, right between the wing-like markings of his Talisman.

"Sure we can't just fight them here?" Tomaz rumbled. He didn't look afraid – Raven wasn't sure any show of arms could ever scare the big man.

"They're not foolish enough to approach us here," Autmaran said. "With the ridgeline, we have the perfect defensible position. They will surround us if we don't come out to fight them on the field, and then crush us in a vice if they can."

"And we'd lose the people running toward us now," Leah said.

"Fine," Raven said, thinking of the clock ticking in his own head. "We meet them on the field – but we meet them on our terms."

"It's already in motion," Tomaz rumbled, mounting the huge horse Gydion. "My place is on the field. And so is yours, Raven, Leah."

The runners Autmaran had dispatched were already down the hill, and the Scouts they'd dispatched to catch the refugees were already speeding across the field.

"My place is here," said the Commander. "I'll send runners as the battle changes – but I need to be able to see it from here, at least for now."

"Stay alive," Raven told him emphatically. "I need to give you the Lion Talisman when this is done."

"Take care," he replied, and then turned to the others. "All of you."

Tomaz grunted his agreement and heeled Gydion's sides, throwing him down the hillside as he roared his battle cry. The Kindred soldiers took it up, the wordless ululation echoing back at them from the rocky lower passes of the Elmist Mountains. Leah grasped Raven's hand and caught his eye; everything they had gone through passed between them in that look, making him ache for her even on the cusp of battle. And then she left, jumping astride her pale gelding, Samsen, and following Tomaz with a cry of her own that was echoed by many of the women, particularly of the Commons. Tym crossed to him; his sapphire eyes scanned Raven.

"You *can* win," the boy said. "Just... believe it. As best you can."

Raven swallowed nervously. Fear rose up in him again as the clock in his head ticked down its final hours. The clouds above them blocked the sun, but some illumination broke through the cover along the horizon, the light finding a way to watch the unfolding struggle. The army below was moving, following Autmaran's instructions, and Raven could feel Lorna's life, strong and vibrant, coming closer now, and the fainter, weaker life of Davydd in her wake. They were halfway across the short side of the field; their horses must have been ready to fall out from under them, but still they pressed on as the force Autmaran had sent met them and passed beyond, surrounding the Commons and fending off the light cavalry division of Tyne that was harrying them.

And then the Imperial Army itself emerged on the far side of the Plains of al'Manthian, bathed in the white and gold of Tyne, with banners flying the Imperial sigil of the Diamond Crown encircling the *triliope,* and the roaring lion's head of Rikard himself. Drums beat and horns sounded as his brother's army spread out in rank upon rank, file upon file, covering the field with terrible radiance even as the clouds above blocked out the rising sun.

Raven turned away at last and mounted Melyngale, spurring the stallion down the side of the ridge to join Tomaz and Leah as they marched out onto the field. What dawn light had managed to make its way through the cloud cover forced him to squint.

They had twenty-four hours to finish this. The Empire needed him dead, and the Kindred needed him victorious. Twenty-four hours to kill the last of his brothers, to overthrow the capital seat of the thousand-year Empire of Ages, to fulfill prophecies so old the parchment they'd been written on had long since crumbled into dust.

One day to change the world.

Chapter Seventeen:

The Battle of the Plains

The armies met.

The first clash was so surreal that Raven felt as if he were living in a waking dream. He had been thinking of this moment for so long, dreading it in nightmares that repeated themselves over and over again, that as the reality unfolded before him, he found himself unable to distinguish it from his own anguished thoughts. The heavy infantry regulars of the Kindred army fought against the heavy infantry of Tyne, and spearmen and rows of pikes did what they could on both sides to contain the fighting and prevent a flank attack, while cavalry clashed and maneuvered for position.

Arrows flew from the Imperial archers, blacking out the sky and whistling catcalls as they lanced down and spited those too eager or too unwary on their terrible points.

Raven raised the shield Tomaz had forced on him at the last minute as they joined the army, and continued following the giant, knowing that in the tightest of spots, even his Talisman might not be enough to save him. His thoughts went briefly to Davydd, and he wished with a strange desperation born of panic that he had been gifted with the Fox Talisman instead of the Raven.

If only Aemon had made seven daggers that could transfer and share powers instead of just one sword.

Arrows *thunked* into the wood of his simple kite-shield, and he was suddenly grateful for the iron bars reinforcing it. As he watched, Kindred fell in droves as the clouds roiled overhead. More Kindred took the place of their fallen comrades, continuing the advance across the field. The Scouts and the ridgeline archers replied in kind, sending an answering flight of arrows arching through the sky, a deadly rain of broad-head shafts that would pierce armor and flesh with indiscriminate glee.

Tomaz came out from beneath his own shield, an enormous thing nearly as wide as he was, and roared out a guttural, animal challenge. His armor seemed to glow from beneath as if heated with burning embers; two or three Kindred stumbled away from him, stunned that he had grabbed them and saved them from the rain of death that had descended seconds before.

Leah, riding beside Raven, grabbed his shield and pulled it up; a late arrow stuck, quivering, in the wood instead of burying itself in his exposed throat.

"Stick close, princeling," she said as her eyes turned back from blue to green. The battle fever was on her; she was like Davydd: when she smelled killing, it brought something out in the her, something primal that was both beautiful and terrible.

The Kindred and Imperial armies both continued their advance, the first ranks now too mixed to distinguish friend from foe. Fallen men and women were already being pulled back from the front line by men and women in white robes – Healers, with Commons wearing white sashes running along beside them with out-stretched shields to protect as much as possible.

"Here we go," Leah said, looking forward. The front ranks were just before them; they were almost at the heart of the battle now, with Kindred behind them ready to step in when they tired or fell. Tomaz was to their right, still roaring, rallying the Kindred with his very presence, and standing out as a terrifying beacon to the Imperial army in front of them.

"Don't let me become that thing again," Raven said to her suddenly, almost viciously. "You do whatever you have to – but don't let me become that creature. You keep the promise you made – and you make sure the others do too."

Leah glanced at him, her long black hair flying across her face, her green eyes squinted against the wind and sound buffeting them.

"Hold onto the Blade," she shouted back, "and I won't need to!"

"That's not good enough!" he protested, grabbing her with his shield arm. "You promised – say it again! Say you'll do it if you have to!"

She looked back at him, and once again everything that had happened to them over the past year seemed to hang in the air between them.

"I promise," she mouthed, her words caught and taken by the wind.

And then they were in the thick of the battle that would define their Age. Raven unsheathed Aemon's Blade, the valerium metal standing out like a white-hot brand against the blackened, burned earth and the press of black-green-and-silver Kindred soldiers at his back. He slashed and cut. As soon as the first man was dead, his speed doubled, his strength doubled, and the world grew more vibrant. He killed a second, and then a third. He began to pull back – he cut hamstrings, parted hands from arms, and knocked men unconscious. Nothing could stand before him.

Tomaz worked beside him; Malachi swung through the air with screaming fury, ending men left and right and opening up a huge bubble of space around them into which no Imperial soldier wished to enter. He was an invincible force; with every life he saved he gained strength and power, and soon his skin was tough as leather so that not even the best-timed thrust could pierce him.

Leah's eyes continued to flash back and forth from blue to green, as she grabbed the Aspect of Sight for short intervals only to lose control again. But whatever glimpses she was seeing were enough – she dodged blows before they even appeared, and stabbed air where a man had yet to appear, only to have him fall on one of her wicked, enchanted daggers.

They pushed forward together, the three of them at the tip of the attack, cutting into the Imperial army and killing with impunity.

Raven had no idea how much time passed, or how many men he felled. The clouds above them blocked out any light or natural sign of passing time, and the sun had long since left the slim edge of space on the horizon where it was easily visible. Shadows fought alongside them now, dancing among them in the terrible faux-night. The Kindred soldiers behind him continued to rotate out in shifts, keeping the line of attack strong by moving the exhausted men and women to the back while fresh arms and legs moved to the fore.

"Raven!"

He killed the man before him, absorbing another life that gave strength back into his failing limbs, and turned, crouching low to prevent an attack from behind.

It was Leah – she was motioning to him frantically to return to her. Tomaz was by her side and the other Kindred were falling back as well. He turned back to the Imperials and found himself in a strange bubble of space where the two armies were breaking apart. Seams appeared in the line on either side of him, and he realized they were fighting now in the center of the Plains, and that the battle had somehow rotated. The Imperials were backing off, pivoting their formation.

And as soon as the soldiers were far enough away, the arrows began again, numerous as falling leaves in autumn. Raven ran, shield slung over his head, for the safety of the Kindred line, side-by-side with a number of other stranded Kindred soldiers; he was able to save two, but the others were too far away.

Leah caught him as he ran into and through the line in his haste to escape the onslaught, and wiped a gauntleted hand, thick with blood, across his face to pull his hair away from his eyes. She was holding out the reins of Melyngale, which he grabbed quickly. The stallion looked eager for battle, and Raven was sure that soon he would get his taste of it.

"What's happening?" he asked, his voice coming out rough and ragged; he had been screaming wordlessly for what must be hours now, shouting down the men who attacked him, screaming just to hear himself and prove he was still alive.

"Autmaran formed up the force to the west," she said, holding a message from a runner standing nearby. They were all crouched behind a wall of shields held by Tomaz and three Eldorians of similarly massive stature. "He's attacking — he needs us to pivot east and attack their rear and flank when they turn to meet him."

"Attack their flank?" Raven asked. "We're the smaller force — how?"

"Not anymore," Tomaz rumbled with a bloodstained grin.

"What?"

"We've decimated them," the giant rumbled. "Normal soldiers can't stand against the Aspects — especially not three together."

"Rikard must have known that," Raven said, bewildered. "What's he playing at?"

"Don't under-estimate Autmaran," Tomaz rumbled. "He's the only one who ever beat Goldwyn at a game of chess."

"I hardly think that applies to a real world battle —"

"Not the time, boys."

"Right you are," rumbled Tomaz. "LET'S MOVE!"

The roar carried even over the noise of the battlefield and their force began to circle the enemy. They crested a small rise, and as they did, Raven could see the Imperials, still an enormous force, reforming and milling in the center. The Kindred had split into three groups now — a central force, held down by Stannit, Jallin, and the ferocious core of the Commons and Kindred that had united together; a left flank led by Autmaran himself, with Lorna by his side and whatever force they had managed to rescue from Tyne; and the right flank, now led by Leah, Tomaz, and Raven, circling to close the Imperials in a vice.

"How did Rikard let himself get into this position?" Raven asked, shocked.

As if in answer, a single word in a black, incomprehensible language cracked and rolled across the battlefield. It passed over Raven, leaving him unscathed, but all the soldiers nearby, including both Leah and Tomaz, missed a step and stumbled. They turned as one and looked back toward the center of the battlefield, and saw the front row of the central force of Kindred fall as one, without a single sword, arrow, or fist anywhere close to touching them.

Rikard had simply told them to die.

"Shadows and light," Raven swore, panic surging through his blood like fire, "he's leading the attack himself – he's going to crush the central force and break us in half!"

Aemon's Blade was in his hand before he knew it, and he was astride Melyngale in a flash of forgotten memory. He was shouting wordlessly, calling for the Kindred to follow him, hoping frantically, *praying* with everything he had in him, that they weren't too late. He flew across the field, dangerously jumping concealed chasms and bursting up the side of the short, rolling mounds of burned land. The wind was blowing in his face again, and he realized he'd somehow lost his helm and his shield. Power from the men he'd killed surged through his veins, as the memories of their lives pounded behind his temples. He pushed the thought of them away; if he focused on the men he'd killed, if he put names to the faces, he might lose himself again.

He was halfway across the field, leading the charge, when a distant horn began to blow, the sound carrying the short, sharp quality that meant it belonged to the Kindred. Raven looked to his left, to the opening of the pass through the Elmist Mountains, the mouth of the Imperial Road, and saw Autmaran himself leading a charging horde of Kindred into the end of the faltering line that Rikard had attacked.

"*No – go back!*"

But it was no use: the roar of a hundred thousand voices and the clang of a hundred thousand swords thinned his shout and weaved it into the overarching tapestry of chaos and destruction. Raven dug his heels harder into Melyngale and the horse added as much speed as possible, racing across the field.

He reached the flank of the Imperial army just as Autmaran with his scarlet cloak of office disappeared into the middle of the fray, Rangers and Rogues fighting alongside him, trying to bolster the flagging Kindred.

"Thou shalt die!"

The words cracked out again in the tone of Command. All the Kindred around him stumbled and faltered, and the ones within twenty-five yards simply fell to the ground, never to rise again. Even Melyngale lost a step and stumbled. Raven vaulted over the horse's head, leaving him behind, knowing that if he brought the stallion any closer Rikard would only kill it.

"RIKARD!"

The shout ripped from Raven's mouth, but the man wouldn't be dissuaded. The Lion had spotted Autmaran, with his golden knots of rank, and he spurred himself forward, rushing for what was clearly a commanding officer. The Rogues and Rangers around Autmaran threw everything they could at the Lion, but his personally trained bodyguards were more than equal to the task of absorbing the blows, and soon it was just Rikard and Autmaran facing one another.

Autmaran unsheathed his sword, but Raven knew there was no chance.

"Be thou still as stone."

The words rolled out of Rikard's mouth, and froze Autmaran and twenty nearby Kindred in place. They were cut down in seconds, and Rikard spurred his horse forward, raised his claymore, and brought it down in a slicing diagonal cut.

Autmaran fell, a bright red line of blood traced across his armor.

No! NO!

Rikard began to laugh, and the sound made Raven laugh as well, even as inside him a small voice, drowned out by Rikard's Talisman, railed and beat against the inside of his chest. The laughter grew, and suddenly everyone was laughing,

laughing so hard that tears were rolling down their cheeks as Rikard's joy spread in ripples across the army. A woman nearby cut down an Imperial soldier, even as both of them smiled and laughed at each other, and two men in the green-and-gold of Rangers held their sides in mirth as they were spitted upon pikes.

Rikard turned, as if sensing that he was not alone, and locked eyes with Raven. He smiled, his handsome face creasing into the perfect expression of amused condescension. "That was the man you hoped to replace me with?" Rikard called out to Raven, his voice booming out, deeper and louder than Tomaz, more commanding than anyone besides the Empress herself. "How droll."

Raven threw himself from Melyngale's saddle and cut down three Imperials fighting beside his friend's body. He fell to his knees beside Autmaran and saw that the man was still alive.

There's still a chance. Shadows and fire, this is going to be way too damn close!

"I'll see you soon," he said, as Autmaran gasped for breath. Understanding blossomed in the man's dark eyes just before Raven sank Aemon's Blade into his side, killing him. He felt his friend's life pulled from his body, and saw Leah come up behind him, her eyes shining with blue light, already running for them, ready to keep the body safe, understanding and anticipating Raven's plan.

There's no going back now – if Leah can keep his body safe, then I can bring him back just like Tomaz. His memories are inside me, and if I can pull the Lion Talisman from Rikard, then I can use it to put them back.

"Leah! Tomaz!"

They turned to him, and he tossed them Aemon's Blade. Tomaz threw Malachi back at him in exchange, and Raven's hand caught the enormous hilt just as the giant's fist closed around the Blade and Leah dove to join him.

Light and heat exploded through him as both of their Aspects joined together and flew to him. Blue lines shot across his vision, and red light infused his body. He spun, the heavy six-foot-long steel ribbon of Malachi weighing no more than a broomstick, and launched himself at Rikard.

The Lion's eyes went wide in shock, and he threw himself off his mount just as Raven cut at where he'd been seconds before. The warhorse rose up on its hind legs and flailed its hooves at Raven before he cut it down with Malachi, sending it crashing to the barren ground. Raven turned to Rikard and advanced.

"*Stop!*" Rikard shouted at him, but Raven shrugged off the Command, relishing the terror in his brother's face.

"You hold no power over me," Raven said, feeling his voice roll out of him with a booming strength of its own as blue lines continued to splinter his vision, telling him where to go, and scarlet fire burned through his muscles, pushing him on. He launched himself again at Rikard, and this time the Lion had no chance but to parry and defend himself as best he could against the onslaught.

"*Die!*" Rikard hissed, and Raven stumbled as the word slammed into him. It didn't stop him though; he raised his sword again. "*Be thou dry as dust!*"

Something about that second phrase slipped past the defenses of the Aspects, and every pore on Raven's body suddenly gushed sweat. His head began to ache as he lost what felt like gallons of water and passed into the first stages dehydration.

"*Be thou cold as ice!*"

Shivers convulsed Raven's arms and legs, and his next swing went wide, missing Rikard once more. The Lion was smiling now, revealing beautiful white teeth in a gorgeous face made only slightly less so by spatters of mud and blood.

"*Be thou hot as fire!*"

A fever engulfed him, and he staggered, his head spinning. He was losing – he couldn't even focus his eyes. He had no idea where his brother was.

And then gray light infused him, coming through his bond to the Blade, and he saw Lorna standing beside Tomaz and Leah. The fever died, the shaking stopped, and his vision cleared. Blue lines formed into the figure of Rikard in his mind's eye, and Raven saw what he had to do next.

He fell to one knee, and heard his brother's sword whistle over his head. Raven dropped to his left, turned, and thrust Malachi upward with all the strength he could pull from the Aspects. The huge swath of steel sunk into Rikard's armored chest with barely any resistance, sparks flying as metal scraped against metal. In shock, Rikard locked eyes with Raven, and threw back his head and tried to speak a final word. All of those around him, including Raven, dropped to their knees and rammed fingers into their ears, but in the end no sound came out. His voice was broken.

We did it.

Raven felt the arm holding Malachi begin to shake and bend at the elbow, and memories began to seep through the bond between them, pulled from his brother's mind by the Raven Talisman. He pulled Malachi out of his brother's chest, and Rikard fell to the ground. Raven turned and raced back to Tomaz, Leah, and Lorna; the latter two had let go of the hilt and turned around to help fight back the tide of encroaching Imperial soldiers.

Raven's whole world narrowed in on Tomaz, who was holding out the hilt of Aemon's Blade for him, presenting it and beckoning for him to run faster, even as the giant himself stood and made his way forward, closing the distance.

Raven felt the markings on his back begin to shift and pull, and suddenly the link to his Mother's crown opened, and he could feel that black and evil creature, still a part of him, still lurking in the back of his mind, begin to stir and stretch its wings. The power of Rikard's life, the power of the new Talisman, had awakened it, awakened that dark part of him that was the Raven, and brought it forward.

Raven bore down, holding onto sanity with all his might. He reached out and caught the hilt of Aemon's Blade just before his mind was submerged completely, and a blinding white light blazed through him and threw the creature back and away.

Tomaz caught him as he gasped for breath, and then they both looked around. The Imperials that had seen Rikard die had thrown down their weapons and begun to flee. The panic caught on, and when Leah, Tomaz, and Lorna, all glowing with the light of their Aspects, began to chase them, the rout began in earnest.

Raven grasped the hilt of Aemon's Blade, holding it so tightly his hand began to cramp, but it worked. Whatever was special about the Blade was keeping him together, keeping him sane.

Rikard's memories rolled through him, buffeting him like a raging storm, but he stood firm in the center of it, holding onto the bright white light of Aemon's Blade. He saw a barely remembered childhood, saw the birth of each of the other Children, saw his visions for Tyne... and saw an enormous underground cavern, twice the size of what Raven and the others had found in Lerne.

Raven was able to detach himself from the flow of memories just long enough to realize this cavern must be in Tyne. No doubt it was the fate the Commons there had avoided when Davydd and Lorna had–

No... no, that's Tyne. That's Lucien.

And it was. He could see the streets, could see Rikard examining the underground cavern and ascending back to the industrial center of the city, leaving the Fortress and beginning his return to Tyne, already thinking of how to duplicate in his home Province the ritual he'd seen readied here. His Mother required it of him, for the Return.

The Return – *what was it?*

But Rikard had not known. Raven sifted through the memories as quickly as he could, discarding whole years of life, seeing Rikard grow up, seeing him embrace his Mother's ideals, fully embrace them, before setting off for Tyne to make a paradise that would be heaven on earth for the Empress and her Children. But Raven rushed past it all, pushing through hundreds of years of memories, trying to find the one crucial piece of information that would tell them what was going to happen next.

A memory came to him of a meeting of the Children, after Raven had been exiled. All of them were there, save Ramael, who had just been killed, and Raven, who had done the killing. He heard through Rikard's ears the sound of Geofred's voice as it recited the final lines of a prophecy:

The Sword shall be reclaimed,
The fruits of Empire sour,
But once the Lion shakes his mane,
So ends the Raven's power.

But... that made no sense. They'd won.

Hadn't they?

"Raven," said Leah in his ear, pulling him from the memories. He shook them away as best he could and looked at her. She'd come back for him, after chasing the group of routing Imperials, and she was looking toward the distant city of Lucien. He turned and followed her gaze.

A dozen enormous shapes had left the main gate of the city and were running toward them across the Plains. Behind them roared a second army, smaller than that of Rikard, but fresh and charging. The huge shapes each bore on their back a slim, gangly figure that seemed to shine with reflected light that came from nowhere. As Raven saw them, the image and sound of gears came to his mind.

The Visigony.

Each of the dreaded Twelve sat astride a Daemon, and the Trium, the three leaders, Vynap, Sylva, and Marthinack, rode Daemons Raven had never seen before: dark creatures that seemed to drink the light, with eyes a pale gray and slit like those of a snake. They were thinner than other Daemons, and their edges were strangely undefined. They were like nothing Raven had seen before – no Daemon looked like that. Daemons were drawn from the five natural essences – ice, fire, earth, wind, and lightning. Those three creatures – they were none of the above.

But... but there was a sixth element, one that none had ever managed to capture. The Children and the Visigony had both searched for it almost as long as the Empress had been in power, but in vain; it had always eluded them.

The essence of shadow; darkness itself. They found it. They captured it.

"We need to retreat," Raven said, but no one heard him. He looked around aimlessly, trying to find Autmaran, looking for the Commander in his red cloak. Only then did Raven remember the rest of what had happened. He spun away from Leah, rushing back to the spot he remembered seeing the man fall. He looked around frantically for the body – there were so many – which one was he? He couldn't find it – where had they left it? Had they taken him somewhere?

A scream like the screech of a thousand iron nails scrapped across granite rock filled the air, and Raven cried out in pain along with everyone around him. He turned to see the Visigony advancing, the three Shadow Daemons leading the charge, each of them with their huge, gapping maws open, revealing row after row of white teeth like lines of jagged, shattered glass.

Raven spun back around still trying to find Autmaran, and then Tomaz was by his side.

"Raven – we need to go!"

"Where's Autmaran?"

"What?"

"WHERE'S AUTMARAN?!"

He could feel the memories in the back of his head – they were still there. That meant he still had a chance to bring him back, and with the Lion Talisman, Autmaran could change the tide of battle, he could figure out someway, the only way to win –

"Raven!"

It was Leah's voice. He spun, combing the crowd of rushing soldiers, soldiers who were wavering themselves now as the giants beasts attacked. "Leah!" he called out as he saw her, waving her over. She ran to him, her whole left side covered in blood that he desperately hoped wasn't hers.

"Where's Autmaran?" he asked frantically.

"He's there," Leah said, pointing back toward the rear of the Kindred lines. "We took him back to the command post – Tym took him!"

"But we need him!" Raven cried frantically.

The Daemons screamed again, and then the Visigony on their Daemons were through the wavering line of the Exiled army, and the spine of the Kindred was broken. In the blink of an eye, hundreds died, and Raven watched with incomprehension, the way one watches a tidal wave rush forward or a meteor fall, knowing that no action taken could change the outcome.

"Raven," Leah called to him across a huge void of space. "Damnit, use the Talisman, princeling! *Use the Lion Talisman! COMMAND THEM!*"

Time caught up with him, the memories faded to a distant buzz, and power filled Raven's voice. "STAND!" he roared.

The Kindred who heard him, wounded, exhausted, terrified, all stood as one and hefted their weapons.

"FIGHT UNTIL YOU HAVE NO STRENGTH LEFT IN YOU ARMS! FIGHT FOR GOLDWYN! FIGHT FOR VALE! FIGHT FOR THE EXILED KINDRED!"

They shouted back at him as one, in one voice, crying his name, shouting "Raven!" over and over again as they moved onto the field again, even as more of them died, even as the Visigony continued to advance.

"KILL THEM – *BUT LEAVE THE DAEMONS TO ME!*"

The wavering line coalesced once more, and Raven ran forward holding Aemon's Blade high in the air, Leah running at his side. He went for the first of the Visigony, one of the ones riding the Shadow Daemon. It was Marthinack, one of the Trium.

He reached through the Lion Talisman and opened his mouth.

"*Die, Marthinack!*"

The Daemon reared back as if the Command had been meant for it as well, and the creature staggered, allowing the Kindred around it to retreat and shuffle the pikemen and spearmen forward to meet the attack. But the visor the machine-man wore covered his eyes, and, Raven realized, his ears. Commands were ineffective against him.

Pulling strength from the lives he'd taken, Raven ran forward and dove beneath the blow of the huge shadow-creature. It bore no weapon, but Raven realized it didn't need one. Its flesh moved and shifted, and when it swung its arms, the shadowy material altered itself and reached out, forming a razor-sharp edge that spread and cut through armor and flesh without distinguishment.

Raven swung Aemon's Blade, and the valerium metal sunk into the creature's skin, biting deep into the joint. The creature screamed, once more sending all the soldiers nearby to their knees, and Raven ran past it, just as the huge thing began to stomp its feet, trying to crush him.

Raven spared a single glance for the rest of the field, and though couldn't see the Visigony through their visors to distinguish them, he didn't need to. The Daemons they rode drove back the Kindred; two of them engaged Tomaz, who was on fire with light, blood-red strength pouring through the cracks in his armor; another engaged Lorna, who was moving so fast she was a blur of motion.

The Shadow Daemon spun with frightening speed and knocked Raven into a waiting group of Imperial soldiers, who attacked him as one.

"Thou shalt die!"

The words were out of his mouth before he realized he'd said them, and as soon as the soldiers heard them, their eyes rolled back in their heads and all eight of them fell to the ground, unbreathing. Strength and vitality flooded Raven in a huge wave, and as he found his way back to his feet, he set his sights on Marthinack. He ran forward, taking long loping strides that increased in speed as he went, and launched himself through the air, up and over the Daemon's shoulder, to crash into the Visigony's back.

Marthinack pitched forward, but managed to hold on to the saddle of black-gray flesh that had molded itself from the creature's body. The Daemon roared in confusion and reached up to swat at Raven, but before either the Visigony or the Daemon had time to react fully, Raven swung his sword down toward the neck of his former teacher, an action he'd wanted to take ever since that first lesson where Marthinack had had him beaten simply to show he could.

The man-machine's head parted from its body, and as Aemon's Blade passed through the flesh, it sparked and clanked against the Bloodmagic-powered gears inside the neck that had kept the man living long after his death.

The life that should have gone to Raven, the life that should have been culled from the man's dying body by the Raven Talisman, clanked and shook, like a gear forced into the socket of the wrong clock. The Daemon collapsed and exploded outward in a rush that threw Raven violently through the air, the shards of shadow slicing through him like broken glass.

He crashed into the ground, the breath squeezed out of him, and lost control of both Talismans.

The white halo around him winked out, and the power of his Commands disappeared with it. Terror returned to the Kindred: the size of the army before them, their own disarray, and the sight of the Daemons, all struck panic into their hearts, and they turned and fled. The remaining members of the Visigony went after them, the ones still standing, but two more went down, and Raven knew both Lorna and Tomaz had felled creatures of their own. The remnants of the Imperial army gave out a cry, proclaiming their victory as the broken, scattered pieces of the Kindred army fled.

The Daemons roared into the sky, but pulled up short, allowing the Kindred army to flee toward the Elmist Mountains in shambles as the Imperials reformed for a final charge. Raven didn't know how long it would take; they might have ten minutes or a few hours before they gathered what was left of their scattered strength and followed the Kindred into the mountains, but one thing was certain:

The Army of the Exiled Kindred was broken, defeated before they'd even reached the city of Lucien, before they'd even managed to confront the Empress.

They had failed.

Chapter Eighteen:

Why?

Raven didn't know how he managed to find and mount Melyngale, but somehow he did. He galloped back to the Elmist Mountains, chasing the scattered Kindred, calling out in the tone of Command for them to slow and regroup in the trees. It worked, to some degree, but there was no turning them around completely. Archers had formed up again on the ridgeline, shooting arrows that whistled over Raven's head into the enemy lines, providing a temporary deterrent to the Imperial army and securing a retreat as the Imperials tried to regroup their own half-fled forces for a final charge.

But Raven's first concern wasn't for the army: it was for Autmaran's fading memories stored in the back of his mind.

He'll know how to fix this. He's the Commander – he's the one who should be in charge, he's the one who'll know. He has to know.

He galloped through the Kindred infantry, shouting for them to move aside, combing the field with his mind for the telltale green-gold of Tym's life. Finally he found it – on the same ridgeline where they had started the battle, looking out over the Plains. Raven spurred Melyngale onward with a jab of his heels, and they soon crested the rise.

Autmaran was lying there on the grass, wrapped in his red cape, and Tym was by his side. Raven dove off of Melyngale and ran to the commander, pushing Tym aside. He touched Autmaran's ruined chest and dropped a hand to Aemon's Blade, then sent his mind through the Raven Talisman. The markings on his back warmed beneath his armor, and he frantically collected every memory of Autmaran he could find from among the hundreds of others he had gathered over the course of the battle. He bundled them in his mind, and *forced* them into his friend's dead body.

The memories rebounded, and snapped back into Raven's mind.

Raven made an unconscious sound of despair, somewhere between a moan and a grunt, and grabbed his friend's hand, pulling back the gauntlet so he could touch dark skin. Autmaran's face was bloodied, and his red cape, wrapped around him in a tangled web, was ripped and torn in a dozen places. He looked smaller than he had in life – as if the weight of his memories had somehow added inches to his height.

"Come on," Raven said, seizing hold of both the Lion and the Raven Talisman. He reached out again, throwing everything he could behind his friend's memories. Aemon's Blade warmed beneath his palm and his vision doubled as strength left him in a huge wave. Suddenly it was a feat of strength to even draw breath – his chest felt too heavy for his lungs to expand. Still the memories didn't want to go – it had been too long. The hour was almost up; the memories were fading and with them went Autmaran's life.

Raven snarled wordlessly and grabbed Autmaran's head with his right hand as his left cramped on the hilt of Aemon's Blade. Shadows and light, what would they do if this didn't work? By the seven hells, what would they – ?

Autmaran's eyes shot open and white light blazed out from them, blinding Raven. He recoiled with a yelp of surprise, and felt his sense of the Lion Talisman snap off and disappear. Autmaran's memories left him in a rush, pulled out of him with inexorable force, and returned to their proper place.

A hacking cough; a huge, wheezing breath; the former corpse tensed and rolled over on his side, retching as air hit his lungs again after almost a full hour of death.

"What," he asked, his voice rasping with disuse, "happened?"

"We had to retreat," Raven said, hurrying back to his side, nearly tripping over his own jerking legs. He reached down and tried to pull Autmaran up, helping him sit, but the transfer had left Raven so weak that he wouldn't have managed it if Tym, eyes wide and staring, hadn't come to help.

"We had to retreat," Raven repeated. "We defeated Rikard, we did it – Leah, Tomaz, Lorna, and I – but the Visigony attacked from Lucien leading a fresh army. They have new Daemons – Shadow Daemons, a new kind no one has ever seen."

As Autmaran listened, strength seemed to return to his limbs, and his breathing slowed. His eyes faded from white back to their accustomed brown, and he used Tym's waiting shoulders to lever himself back to his feet. He looked over the edge of the ridgeline. His eyes widened, and his mouth dropped open.

Raven followed his gaze and saw the Imperial army reforming, still with seven Daemons at its head, two of them the other Shadow Daemons, ridden by Vynap and Sylva. The remnants of Rikard's army along with the army that had been brought from Lucien looked to add up to at least three times the number the Kindred had left.

"What do we do?" Raven asked, trying and failing to keep the panic out of his voice. "What counterstrike can we make?"

"I ... I don't ..."

Autmaran continued to stare out over the field, and Raven saw now that his eyes had been drawn to the thousands of bodies scattered across the Plains.

"You have the Lion Talisman now," Raven said. "You can Command the Kindred – anything you tell them to do, they will do. Send word with me, or with Tym, and we'll tell everyone to gather where you need them. Somehow we can make this work, I know you can figure something out –"

"Is General Dunhold still alive?"

"General Dunhold?"

"Yes," Tym said. "He is, Commander Autmaran."

"Good – Tym," Autmaran said, turning away from Raven, "find General Dunhold and tell him to get all the troops we can into the Elmist Mountains – the site we talked about as a point of retreat. If there's anyone on the Imperial Road, get them off it and into the mountains."

"The mountains, but that –"

"Rangers and Rogues," Autmaran continued, ignoring Raven, "all that are left, spread out in full ambush. Keep the archers along that upper ridge as long as possible – until they're out of arrows, or we find a better place for them, whichever comes first. They're our first line of defense."

Tym nodded and left, running as fast as he could down the steep incline.

"Defense?" Raven asked, stepping in front of the man to draw his attention. "We need to attack – we need to get to Lucien!"

"We're not getting across that battlefield," Autmaran said, his voice taking on some of the tone that Raven had so often heard from Rikard. His eyes began to fade from deep brown to a sharp, cutting white. "If you want to help, get everyone into the trees and away from the road. We can't face them in the open field – we've lost that battle."

He strode past Raven, rushing to meet a number of runners frantically searching for him. One of them offered Autmaran his horse, and the Commander took it, shouting orders that sent the runners dashing off once more. He pulled off his split armor and handed it away; another man shrugged out of his own and lent it to the Commander.

"Autmaran!" Raven called, still unable to understand. "Are we regrouping for another attack? How are we going to get to Lucien? We must face Her!"

Autmaran spun his new horse around and raced up the hill, stopping just short of Raven before throwing himself off the gray mare and stepping right up into his friend's face. "We will be lucky to survive the rest of this day. We have done all we can; I don't know what happened when I was… but we have no way to win now. We can only survive – we can only do what the Kindred have done for a thousand years, and run, killing as many of them as we can before we flee again. We have the mountains – that will buy us time. But we cannot stand against that army. Not against soldiers, Daemons, and Bloodmages, with only a beaten and broken force and seven men and women with Aspects we can't fully control. If we survive this day – if we survive this *night* –"

"All we have is a *night*," Raven hissed back. "We have until dawn – and then you're right, there is no hope for us. If the Empress lives by morning, then we are all dead!"

Autmaran ran both hands over his bald head and paced away a step before turning back. "I will not send men and women out onto that field to die without a plan," he said flatly, all emotion gone. "I will not sacrifice them on the chance something *might* break in our favor. You can either help me save them and come up with a new plan, or you can try to cross that field yourself. It is up to you."

He left, mounting his horse again as Raven stared after him, open-mouthed. Autmaran looked back only once, and though Raven saw him grimace as if what he had done pained him, he did not take it back.

Raven found himself alone on the ridgeline, looking out over the Plains from the same spot where only hours ago it had seemed possible that they might win. Then, without really thinking about what he was doing, he found himself staggering away. As his grip on his mind slipped, some of the last remaining memories came back to him from the lives he had drawn into him through the Raven Talisman. Most were what he had seen countless times before – stories of wives and children, families, ordinary lives lived without distinction until the Empress had decreed an army was needed, and Rikard had come through, inspiring them with his voice alone. But there were other memories too; ones that were somehow sharper but strangely... twisted. He focused on them as best he could, trying to understand what they were, and realized some of them contained memories of *him,* struggling to learn his lessons as a child.

Marthinack.

That was why the memories were fractured and mechanical – they came from the mind of the Visigony. He was glad they were that way – Marthinack had been alive, if one could call it that, nearly as long as the Empress, and if Raven had absorbed all of that, he wouldn't be able to function. No, the memories were strange and disjointed, almost as if there were parts deliberately cut out, like a series of pictures with the middle, joining prints conspicuously absent.

But there was one, the last the machine-man had focused on in depth, which came across bright and clear.

The image was of another cavern, like the one in Lerne, painted with the enchantments from Bloodmage rituals, with three enormous crystals set in the center of an empty pool, pulsing with hungry light. It was the same memory he had pulled from Rikard, but much more recent. So recent it might even have been from earlier that day.

Three of them.

Two of the crystals glowed with a blood-red light that washed the faces of the waiting Bloodmages in terrible scarlet. But the third, the largest by far, sat ready and waiting... lying dormant. And in Marthinack's mind, amidst the sound of creaking leather and hissing, laughing steam, the words "Lerne," and "Tibour," came to him, clear as day.

All this time they only needed three. She knew we would stop some of them – but we couldn't stop them all.

One from Dysuna's city of Tibour, one from Symanta in Lerne... and the third, the largest, from Lucien itself.

"*What about the one from Tyne?*" asked Sylva.

– creaking, jumping, the vision split and then came together once more –

"It will help," Vynap gargled through his facemask, "but it is a security, nothing more. Three are needed – and with the arrival of the crystal from Lerne, we can forgo the others. After we perform the final ritual tonight and create the third, we have enough. Between the three Soul Catchers and the Talismans She already has, the Return is assured. We will all go home – provided the prophecy is fulfilled in its entirety."

"Well then," Marthinack said. "Let us begin."

Raven stumbled and turned toward the forest, grabbing Melyngale as he went and somehow managing to mount. He felt as though he were moving in a dream, and his actions seemed to make no sense. He heeled the horse's sides and shot through the trees, pushing forward deeper into the Elmist Mountains, galloping at breakneck speed for no reason, wanting to be as far away as possible. He started thinking about running again, something he hadn't contemplated since being elected Prince. Who cared now? They had no way to get to Lucien. They would hide out in these mountains until the Empress came from the city and crushed them all, searching for him.

Maybe if I run fast enough I can escape. Maybe if I go now –

The thoughts cut off as he emerged in a clearing that was strangely familiar. There was a tall tree, and a ravine off to one side. Why did this...?

And then they came to him, memories of his own rolling back across the inside of his eyes. He remembered seeing stars as he lay here, and feeling the rough fabric of a sack scrap against his cheek as he... lay dying.

This is the spot. This is where they brought me to die. I've come full circle.

There was movement and sound from behind him, and he turned to see Leah emerge from the trees. Her eyes were blue, but as she crossed to him they faded back to their vivid green, and it was clear to him that she had managed, somehow, to track him with her Aspect. She was becoming skilled with it indeed.

"Raven," she said, sounding half relieved and half confused, obviously wondering what he was doing here. "We need to go. Autmaran has formed us up to repel the attacking force. Davydd is well enough to fight now too; the Healers patched him up and his Spellblade talent sped his healing. With all of us together –"

"This is where I almost died."

His words sunk into the clearing like heavy rocks crashing into water. Ripples crossed her face, emotions swirling through confusion and astonishment and everything in-between. Slowly, she came forward, and in the silence of the glen he could hear her feet crushing the soft grass beneath her boots even as the distant shouts of the soldiers came to them through the clear, thin air.

"Raven," she said, "we need to go. We can still do this. We have a chance."

"No, we don't," he said with a small smile.

"Raven –"

"Autmaran said it himself." Raven shrugged. "It's over. I'll... I'll just wait for her here. It has a nice symmetry, doesn't it? Forcing her to come here and do herself what she was too afraid to do the first time. Hell, maybe I can even hold her off until the sun rises and then the whole prophecy will be for naught."

He tried to grin and realized it was more of a sneer.

"Raven," Leah insisted, her voice low and careful, "there is still a chance left –"

"No!" Raven snapped, stepping forward to snarl in her face. "There is *nothing* left. There is no chance! There is *NOTHING!*"

The word rang out unnaturally loud, far too harsh and guttural. It was the sound of a wounded, harrowed creature, backed into a corner and forced to watch its death approach, forced to watch the trap snap shut, knowing that all it had left was its anger and its hate, and some small ability to hurt those who could not save it.

"This war means nothing now," he continued, walking forward, forcing her back. The expression on her face was one of shock and worry, her beautiful eyes stretched wide, uncomprehending. He hated it. And he hated himself for causing it, for pulling such ugly things out of such a beautiful person, but he was past reasoning now, past all thoughts of remorse.

"We're living on borrowed time," he continued, savagely. "Do you want to know how the rest of this plays out? I can tell you – you don't need to even use the Eagle Talisman. We run, and we hide, as Mother comes down on us as I always said she would. The scattered remnants of our force fly like the torn pieces of a badly written play. We fight where we can, but we cannot stand against them. We are pinned down by the advancing the Bloodmages, cut off from retreat from soldiers flanking us."

"The Children are dead," Leah said, trying to burn her shock away with anger. "All of them! We beat them, we defeated what we once thought invincible!"

"And then the Visigony came," Raven said, "and broke our backs. They didn't even need the Empress! We wondered where Symanta's army went; now we know. They were in Lucien the whole time, just waiting for the right moment to strike. We've been out-thought every step of the way. Who cares what we've done? All that matters is that we have no way forward. Look, if you doubt me. Look through the Aspect of Sight, comb the future, and tell me what you see."

Her eyes flashed momentarily blue as she reached out, but they turned back to green almost immediately, and her face went slack.

"There, what did you see?"

"I... I couldn't see anything. It stopped; it just cut off and all I saw was black, and all there was around me was silence –"

"BECAUSE YOU DIE! BECAUSE WE *ALL DIE*!"

For a moment he thought he'd broken her, thought he'd made her see the darkness that awaited them, and immediately he wanted to take it back. But her eyes hardened, her brows furrowed, and she stepped forward and struck him.

He recoiled in shock, but before he could defend himself, she lashed out and struck him again. Shocked, he tried to escape, but she followed him as he stumbled away. She caught him and threw him down among the gnarled roots a huge tree. She crouched down and grabbed a handful of his torn and bloodied tabard and held him in place.

"Fine," she snarled. "If you want to die, let's get it over with. Right now."

She unsheathed one of her daggers and held it to his neck.

"If you want to die, then I'll help you. And I'll be glad to do it – glad to end the life of a coward, and the man who just called my father's death, and more importantly his *life*, worthless!" Her eyes were boring into his, drilling at him like green spears of light. "Just tell me to do it, and I will. Give me the word and I will open your veins and leave you here to water the ground, a much more fitting destiny for the craven imposter you turned out to be. I can't believe we named you *Prince!*"

He tried to push back against her and rise, but she choked back a sob and forced him back to the ground. Time stretched out between them, and Raven knew what he wanted from her.

"Do it with me," he said.

The words sank in, and she recoiled, almost as if touching him was somehow dirtying her. But he didn't take it back.

"Do it with me," he repeated.

"No," she said, his lips curled in contempt and disgust.

"Why not?"

"Because you're not all I have left!" she snapped. "I'm a warrior, not some dewy-eyed maiden. And if you decide to give up, if you decide to leave me here and take the easy road, then I won't follow you. Every day I live is a day the Empire hasn't won. Every day I live is a day I live free. And if that burden is too much for you, if you're too cowardly to step up and go on living, then you're not worth dying for, even if you are a Prince. If you would really do that, then you are much less than that title implies, much less than that man who stood before the Kindred and told them the story of a dream. You and he do not live in the same world, so I'd be glad to kill you, hoping maybe that by sending you out of it, I'd somehow be bringing him back. A Prince who would wear a Kindred crown, and fight until the last drop of blood fell from the smallest of his veins – that's the man I followed here. If you're not him anymore, then tell me so. Tell me!"

His whole body seized up as everything fell into place. He knew he was staring at her blankly now, knew that he should say something, but the shock of it was too much. Why had he thought of it only now? Why had he come up with the solution after they'd already lost?

A Kindred crown.

"SAY IT!" Leah shouted in his face. "GIVE THE WORD AND I'LL DO IT!"

And even then, even after he'd put the pieces together, he almost asked for death. It would be so easy to slip into the night that waited for him, so easy to leave everything here, to finally have a chance to rest, finally have a chance at peace. The darkness that waited in the wings of his mind, always waited, called to him, and it was only inches away from wrapping him up, warm and tight, in its eternal embrace.

"Well? What is it?" Leah demanded. She buried her second dagger in the ground, sinking it through the moist turf almost up to the hilt, and then grabbed him by the throat and started to choke the air out him. Her eyes blazed with pain and anger and deep, almost hidden, terror.

"No," he said with what breath he had remaining.

"Why?"

"Because I won't leave you."

"No!" she shouted, shifting the knife so that the edge of it was right up against the base of his chin. He could barely breathe without the razor-sharp metal nicking his skin. He knew he must be bleeding, though he was so numb he couldn't feel it.

"No," she repeated, softer, more intensely. Her chin was jutted forward; her cheekbones and brow stood out against the soft forest light in a gaunt silhouette. "Living for me isn't good enough. Living for Tomaz isn't good enough. Living for anyone but *yourself* isn't good enough!"

Raven watched her with a mind suddenly blank. That last primal part of him that loved his Mother – *No, stop the pretext. You do not love her, you fear her. That is what this has always been about, all your life* – could not let him do what she was asking.

"I can't do that," he said.

"*Why not?*" she hissed.

"How can you live in a world where you do not know the answers?"

"What? What does that have to do with anything?"

"If She is not all powerful, if She is not all-knowing, then how do we go on living? What is the point, if there is nothing to give us purpose? How do we know what is right and wrong when there is no one to tell us, no one who *knows*? How do we live when there are too many choices to pick from? When there is no absolute answer that *must* be right, when there are only shades of gray? I thought I could be the one to decide – I thought *we* could, the seven of us with the Aspects, but even that is impossible, and now I see it, and I know it, and I can't get it out of my mind!"

His voice, quiet and hoarse as he forced it around the blade at his throat, drifted off and faded away, like the insubstantial rush of air it was. What did words matter? He was insignificant; a tiny, single person in a world that held nothing but terrifying, huge possibilities. But as he felt himself spiraling down once more and drifting away, her gaze caught his and drew him out. She watched with understanding now, fierce and proud as she was, and the dagger slowly drew away. A shade of memory crossed her face, covering the brilliant light of her stare for the barest hint of time, something that had nothing to do with him, only with her.

"Every day I wake up and I fight it," he said. It all just spilled out of him, as if something had come unstuck and this wellspring of words was suddenly flowing up out of the stony ground. "Every day, I wake up and I try not to acknowledge the darkness I see, the darkness that calls me with every breath I take. I have the power to destroy the world, and all I want to do is destroy myself. I want to sleep. It... it's so hard to be awake, it's so hard to *feel*, and I can't... I just..."

Tears were rolling down his cheeks, and his words died off as his throat closed and choked him. He couldn't look at her anymore, couldn't acknowledge her or what he'd just said. He knew such thoughts were the thoughts of a coward, and they unmanned him even as he spoke them. There was no going back from it though; he could never be with her now, even if he wanted to. She knew his secret, knew he was weak, and even if she didn't tell the others, there could be nothing between them anymore.

She sank to her knees, and the knife dropped from her hand. It fell and lay abandoned at her side.

"Why ...?" She broke off and swallowed. "Why didn't you tell me before?"

"Wh... why would I?"

Her jaw clenched and a muscle twitched high up along her cheekbone.

"Because Goldwyn took me in after I... when Davydd told him I tried to... "

She stopped again, then ground her teeth together, pursed her lips, and continued, spitting out the sour, offending words. "I've fought that feeling for years. I've fought that feeling since the first night I spent in these mountains, having run away from my parents in Tyne. I fought that feeling when I realized I had no choice but to live life as an Exile. I fight that feeling every single day, even when life is wonderful – and I refuse to lose that fight. I *refuse*."

She continued to stare him down, her stony face a mask that held back more than he had ever expected.

"Why?" he asked, searching for hope.

"Because I'm not going down like that," she said. "Because screw the world and everyone in it. I'm going to live because I want to, and I will make of my life something of which I can be proud. That's how you fight it. That's how you *beat* it."

It seemed suddenly as if all sound had gone out of the world. When she stopped talking and stared down at him – fierce, proud, and invincible – the rest of life ceased to be. Nothing else mattered but her: she was everything. He wanted to be that man she saw; he wanted to drown in her, in everything she was and everything she stood for. She was more than just a woman; she was a symbol of everything that was right and beautiful about living. She was the unashamed, proud embodiment of hope. Not the hope in children's tales, the kind that came easy to heroes with simple tasks, but the hard kind of hope, and the hard kind of joy, that came from laughter forced through tears.

"I love you," he whispered.

The stony mask of her face cracked, the barest fraction, to reveal shock, and he felt the same emotion reverberate through him. The words had slipped out independent of thought; but they were true. They had been true since the first time he'd kissed her.

"I love you, too," she whispered back.

Thin, tendrilic warmth spread through his body, and the cold mountain air caught in his chest. The look of shock on her face was still there; her words had slipped out just as unexpectedly as his had. He reached up, folded his hands into her hair, and pulled her down to him. She came easily, letting go of the last resistance that had held her up, away from him. Her lips met his, and for a single, perfect moment, everything was fine. The darkness receded, the light took over, and silence cocooned them in the shadow of the grove. Her hands encircled him, pulling him close, and his did the same, wrapping around her waist.

They broke apart by inches, just far enough so that their lips could form words.

"I want this," he said to her. "I want it for the rest of my life."

"I want it too," she said. "Even if it lasts just for the rest of today."

He swallowed hard, feeling her breath warming his cheek, staring into her eyes, captivated as always. "I must face her," he said. "Even if it means death."

"Then I will get you there," she said. "Even if it means death."

They embraced again, feeling the blessed warmth of each other's bodies, and Raven found himself close to tears.

I want this. I want an after. Please, whatever gods may be, give me an after.

Noise very close: horses; shouts of men and women; the clash of steel.

They came apart and were on their feet in seconds. Leah had grabbed up her daggers, and Raven held Aemon's Blade before him in both hands, curved blade perpendicular to the ground. The noise came from the side of the small clearing opposite them, the side that looked out at the distant sight of Lucien and the Plains of al'Manthian. Raven reached through the Talisman and felt light blossom all throughout the forest before them: the rest of the army were arrayed downhill below them in loose ambush formation.

And closer, just beyond the nearest trees, was the life of Tomaz, burning in his mind like a fire, and the lesser flames of Autmaran, Davydd, Lorna, and even Tym.

"Who is it?" Leah asked.

"Tomaz, Lorna, Davydd, Tym, Autmaran," Raven rattled off. "But they don't seem to be fighting anyone. I don't understand what's going on –"

Small, sickly green pinpoints of light, half there and half not, burst into life before winking out, like stars through cloud cover on an overcast night.

"Death Watchmen," Raven hissed. "Dozens of them – get ready!"

Almost before he was done giving the warning, the Watchmen shot from the trees. There were dozens of them, all skeletal figures with flesh and muscle pulled tight across decaying limbs, kept alive only by the Empress's Commands. They raised onyx weapons – axes, swords, scythes – and shouted, their voices the rasping echoes of a death cry.

Raven dropped into a defensive stance and raised Aemon's Blade; Leah threw both daggers, striking two charging Watchmen straight through the eye, knocking them down and giving them pause, but not stopping them. The enchantment that powered them was inscribed into their spine – the only way to kill them was to sever it.

The first Watchman construct attacked him with a heavy axe, which Raven managed to sidestep. He then sliced a blow to the thing's knee, sending it tripping to the ground; he swung for the base of its head, cutting into its neck. The creature fell to the ground and began to decay immediately, producing the sickly-sweet smell of putrescence and then the horribly nauseating scent of weeks-old rot. Two more came for him, forcing him back, and he realized the true extent of the trouble they were in: these creatures didn't have life, not in the conventional sense. There was no power for him to absorb when they died; in this fight, he was just an ordinary man.

Leah came to his side, and together they fended off the attack of the Watchmen, retreating around the tree, only to see more coming from the other side in a huge wave.

"Where did they all come from?!" Leah cried.

"I don't know!" Raven called back.

An onyx dagger came whizzing through the air past them, just inches away from Raven's left ear. Two of the constructs rounded the far side of tree and came at them with matching half-moon axes bigger than Raven's head.

A roar sounded from behind them, and Raven felt the red-hot life of Tomaz burst through the pack of Watchmen, ripping them apart as he came. Lorna came after him, moving half a step faster than should have been possible, her movements jerky and somehow incompatible with normal eyesight. Her axe sliced the head of another Watchman clean off before it could understand what was happening.

But none of the Death Watchmen turned to defend; none of them even broke stride as they all came in a huge wave for Raven, even jostling each other aside in their haste to move forward.

Raven and Leah parried again and again, now standing back to back as they rotated, trying frantically to defend themselves on all sides. Raven was reaching as far through his Talisman as he could, his senses on fire with a thousand different impressions, all coming to him at the same time. He ducked a blade, only to roll away from another as it struck the ground where he'd just been, feeling every root and twig as it pressed against his back and shoulders. He swung around back to Leah's side, just in time to deflect a blow that would have caved in her head. She threw a dagger over his shoulder and knocked another Watchman off its feet.

The Death Watchmen's blades were getting closer, though, and Raven cried out as he felt the first of them score a slice along the back of his arm. Another blow glanced off his armored breastplate, but a third cut a line of fire across his cheek.

Leah's eyes were flashing with blue light, and she avoided nearly every blow that came her way, until there were just too many. The sheer weight of the Watchmen pinned them down, and Raven knew there was no way they were getting out of this on their own.

With a flash of steel, Tomaz cut his way through the Watchmen to Leah's side, just in time to save her from being run through by one of the razor-sharp onyx blades. Autmaran came next, mounted on Alto, cutting left and right, shouting Commands in the faces of the Watchmen, but to no effect: they were already under the Command of the Empress herself, and there was nothing he could do to break it. Davydd was mounted as well, and the left half of his face glowed with golden veins as he swung about him with Titania; Tym brought up the rear, a simple short sword in his shaking hands, killing Watchmen that had fallen but weren't yet dead.

They all surrounded Leah and Raven, and the battle turned. With each of them fighting side by side, using the Aspects, the Death Watchmen didn't stand a chance.

A sudden silence fell, and Raven realized the only sound left was their heavy breathing. He looked around and saw all the other Aspect bearers scanning the area as well, wide-eyed and staring.

"I'm glad you're all here," Raven gasped, "but how did you know to come?"

"Davydd," Autmaran said, trying to work moisture back into his mouth. "Davydd came shouting from the Healer's –"

"Went to take a leak and saw them running up the Mountain," Davydd panted, "dunno if I'd call that lucky, but I'll take it."

"There were more," Tomaz rumbled. "I have the feeling they came here for one reason – if I were the Empress, I'd do the same thing."

"Send them all running into the Mountains," Autmaran said, nodding and turning to Raven, "on a suicide mission straight for you."

"There were two groups," Davydd said looking around. "That was the first –"

"And here comes the second," Lorna said, raising her axe.

Trees rustled to their right, and more figures burst from concealment: another wave of Death Watchmen. Before they could more than shift in that direction, there were nearly fifty of them, and they split the group in two. Raven found himself forced back nearly all the way against the tree in the same spot Leah had thrown him earlier. He cut down two of the Watchmen, then tripped over a gnarled root.

He crashed to the ground, his cheek slamming into the rocky earth. He looked up and saw the closest Watchman raise his onyx sword, ready to bring it down. Raven rolled away as best he could, but the sword still caught in his cloak. He rose as far as he could, pulling himself free, raising Aemon's Blade, but he'd lost too much time. The Death Watchman was over him, swinging his sword with lightning speed. Raven managed to throw it back, calling out desperately to the nearest person to him:

"Tomaz!"

The big man swung around and sized up what was happening in an instant. He ran forward, abandoning the Watchmen he was fighting on his own, and brought Malachi around in a huge swing, parallel to the ground. The Watchman, too far away to swing its sword, pulled out a dagger instead, and hurled it at Raven even as Tomaz's sword cut into the construct's side.

The dagger flew straight and true, and there was no way Raven could deflect it.

Chapter Nineteen:

Elders

The dagger spun end over end in perfect form, even as Malachi cut through the Watchman's decaying flesh and severed its spine. Raven reversed his sword, swinging as fast as he could, but without the benefit of added strength and with the decided detriment of battle-weary limbs, it was like trying to swing an oar. He saw the dark, nearly black, onyx blade slice through the air toward him, almost as if time had slowed. He wasn't going to make it – the hilt of the Blade couldn't get there in time. The dagger was so close, its blade sliced through the swirling fabric of his cloak –

Something heavy hit him, and he was falling sideways. He slammed once more into the ground, the dagger flying harmlessly through where he'd been to imbed itself in a tree trunk twenty feet farther away.

The Death Watchman construct died and slid off the end of Tomaz's sword where it began to decompose on the forest floor. Beetles and worms dug themselves out of the fertile, black earth and began to gorge on it, making a meal of it then and there. Raven looked up to see his savior, expecting it to be Leah or Davydd, but instead the figure above him was dressed in simple gray robes of plain homespun. His hem was travel-worn, and the hood, shoulders, and back stained by the spring rains. A simple, well-cut gray beard, blue eyes –

"Elder Crane?"

The sounds of battle came from behind him, and before he could even force his tired body to react, Crane pushed past him, lifting a bow nearly as tall as he was. In the blink of an eye he'd drawn an arrow, notched it, and sent it flying through the gloomy mountains, striking a Death Watchmen engaged with Leah straight through the neck, felling the construct.

"Do it now!" the Elder cried.

Raven watched in shock as a number of other figures in the robes of the Elders of Vale, in red and blue, green, tan, and all the colors in between, suddenly appeared from between the trees. Lymaugh and Stanton led the charge with the others close behind, all shouting words of power that blistered the air. Spader and Ishmael were there as well - Spader with a long staff held tight in both hands, and Ishmael with a pair of daggers, one long and thin, the other thick and curved like a fang.

On Elder Crane's word, they all reached into their robes and pulled out the shining opal daggers slung about their throats on long silver chains. Unsheathing the daggers, they slashed the blades against their hands, and began chanting. Raven couldn't understand what was being said, but he didn't have to; the sound of it rolled over and around him, leaving him unaffected, only to drop dozens of Death Watchmen dead in their tracks, with flashes of green light leaving them just before they dropped.

In seconds it was over. The Elders had secured the clearing, and Raven saw that a number of Rogues had come with them; it looked like there were two for every Elder, acting as bodyguards. It was the last group of people Raven had ever expected to see here, everyone from Elder Dawn, the Dragon Lady herself, to Elder Ekman with his high forehead and bright blue robes.

"Spader, Ishmael," Crane said quickly, taking command even as the final body hit the ground, "I need you here. Everyone else, down the hill – the Visigony will attack shortly. Do whatever you can to slow their progress."

"We are weaker when we are not twelve," Elder Pan said, standing tall in his long brown robes, the color of a strong, healthy buck.

"The Visigony are no longer twelve either, but seven," Ishmael rasped, cleaning his daggers. "You will still outnumber them – show them the power of pure magic."

"We will," Elder Ceres said in her beautiful golden-tan robes, the color of blooming wheat fields. "I will lead."

"Good," said Crane. "I will speak with the Prince and his companions and be with you shortly. Buy us what time you can."

They nodded and were gone, leaving Crane, Ishmael, and Spader to wrap their cut hands while Raven and his companions all stared on, uncomprehending. As they left, Raven saw that Davydd was limping, having been pulled from his horse. He crossed to the Ranger and touched his neck, holding Aemon's Blade and the Talisman. Davydd let out a gasp as if he'd been plunged into freezing water, and then started sputtering and coughing, yanking himself away from Raven.

"Shadows and fire – *warning*, princeling, give me *warning!*"

He looked down at his boot, and Raven was pleased to see he had his weight evenly distributed. Whatever had caused the blood loss and limp was gone, the wound healed. Raven shook his head to clear the fatigue that had settled over him, and turned back to the others.

"So it does work," Elder Crane said quietly. His icy blue eyes were watching them both intently. Davydd, still shivering from the touch, looked like he couldn't decide whether to hit Raven or thank him.

"Elder," Tomaz rumbled, preempting any such conflict, a tone of wonder in his voice. "How are you here?"

"We received Elder Spader's message of Keri's death," Crane said quietly, his eyes flicking away from Raven to rest on the giant, "and we knew that our first plan had failed. You needed three Elders to rededicate the *sambolin* – and now you had two."

How much do they know? Raven thought frantically, keeping his face as calm and composed as possible. *What are they here to do?*

"But it was more than that," he continued. "We could easily have sent one or two of us with an armored guard racing along the Imperial Road to meet you along the way, but on the same night we met to plan the journey, we had something happen that has not occurred in my lifetime."

He turned to Spader and Ishmael.

"Elder Iliad came to Council."

Spader let out a snort of disbelief and turned around to the others as if to say 'look at this – even in the middle of a war he makes jokes,' before turning back to Crane and seeing he was serious.

Ishmael blinked. Once.

"That's impossible, though," Raven said, remembering his own encounter with the eldest of the Elders; a feeble man, shrunken in on himself, with so many memories locked away inside his head that he had been driven mad. He'd lost even the ability to feed himself; he simply sat staring out his sitting room window over Vale, day after day, answering what questions he could from those who came to ask him. As the Elder of History he held thousands upon thousands of memories in his *sambolin*, along with hundreds of prophecies, and to do so he had sacrificed what was left of his life.

"So we all thought," Crane said. "But apparently something was set into motion that Iliad felt all the way in Vale. He said it was something the Empress has done before, but not in nearly a thousand years, something he fears she plans to do again, something that may already have happened in a number of Imperial cities."

"The sacrifices," Leah said, stepping forward. "You know?"

"Spader and Ishmael filled us in with their reports," Crane said. "I think that was indeed what Iliad feared – and more than that."

"Me," Raven said simply. "He felt what I became when I slaughtered Dysuna's army at Banelyn."

"Just so," Crane confirmed, watching him carefully. "All those deaths... they cause ripples. They cause pain, and they tear at the world in ways many cannot understand."

"The Visigony will be on us any minute," Autmaran reminded them, his eyes flashing white as he reached unconsciously for his Aspect. "We cannot leave the men undefended – they need direction. They need us!"

"For now," Crane said, "they have the Elders and General Dunhold, who could hold a mountain pass if he were outnumbered five times over. We can wait. We need to talk about something that concerns you all, and the fact that, unless I miss my guess –"

Crane looked up into the sky, toward the setting sun. Raven realized the day was almost over, and panic kicked him in the gut, hard and fast.

" – a task that must be completed in the next twelve hours," he finished.

"Then we should go," Tomaz rumbled. "Storm the city ourselves – maybe one of us makes it through alive."

"Not until you know the story as I've come to understand it," he said. "Everyone knows that Aemon and the Empress came to this land together, somehow. The details are unclear, but that is unimportant. What matters is that they had a falling out, and Aemon chose to flee with our ancestors to the lands in the south. The Empress followed, eventually caught him, and tried to take the Aspect of Life by force."

"We know this, Elder," Autmaran said, "now is not the time for a history lesson!"

"Right," Raven said, "that's when she took the Aspect of Life and turned it into the Talisman I now have."

"But that is just what I'm trying to tell you: she *didn't* take it from him," Crane said slowly, watching them carefully with his cool blue eyes and wise, lined face.

"Of course she did," Davydd protested, "everyone knows she did."

"Not quite," Crane said, stepping forward and holding out a hand toward Raven. "May I see your sword, please?"

For a moment Raven didn't understand what he was asking, so foreign was the idea of lending anyone Aemon's Blade. It would be a strange enough request given the time and place, but it was stranger still since anyone who touched the Blade was likely to go flying through the nearest tree as soon as the metal touched their skin.

"I understand your hesitation," Crane said, seeing the confusion in his eyes, "but if I am correct, then I should not be hurt."

Raven nodded slowly and reached to his side. He untied the sword from his belt, still scabbarded, and handed it over, watching carefully in case he did end up needing to grab it back.

Crane grabbed it easily, with long, graceful fingers, touching only the sheath and staying away from the hilt. He closed his eyes and breathed deeply. The sheathed *sambolin* around his neck began to glow with opal light, and everyone else took a wary step back, until the light faded away and Crane opened his eyes again.

"Just as I thought," he said, an unmistakable tinge of excitement shot through his reedy tenor voice like a vein of gold. "I can't understand why none of the Elders ever tried that before."

"What did you do?" Raven asked as the Elder handed the Blade back to him.

"The reason this is no ordinary sword, not even an ordinary Spellblade sword, is that the final act of the man who carried it was an enchantment of its own. I have seen it happen before, but never suspected Aemon's Blade was the same."

"How is it possible for an action to enchant something unintentionally?"

"This gets to the root of what I came here to tell you. And why we came here as one when Elder Iliad told us what he'd felt. There are places in the world that are *thin*. The metaphor of the Veil is applicable here, but not in the strict mythological sense the Kindred use. Each myth has a root, and I think we've found the root of this one.

"The myth says that this world is separated from death by a Veil, so thin and sheer that you cannot see or touch it. However, if one knew just how to move, just how to turn, it is possible to lift that Veil and cross into the realm of death. The reality is that the Veil is a term used to describe the rules of the world. And certain events, to continue the metaphor, make the Veil thin, fraying it around the edges, bending the rules. One of these events is death: every murder changes the place in which it is performed. And that, I believe, is why the Empress brought you here."

Silence followed this pronouncement, and everyone turned slowly to look at Raven.

"Please tell me this is where you had a Mother-son picnic or something." Davydd said.

"This is where I found him," Tomaz said suddenly, looking around him with wide eyes. He turned back to Raven and saw that his young friend had already recognized the place. He nodded slowly. "This is where she took you to have you killed."

Raven swallowed and didn't respond.

"And why did she take you here?" Crane asked, watching him carefully. "Why on earth would she take you to this place, these mountains? Much more convenient to kill you in the Fortress, where she reigns supreme. Much easier to simply kill you with her own hand, and take the Raven Talisman in full force that way, don't you think?"

Raven opened his mouth to respond, but then slowly shut it, realizing for the first time how truly bizarre the assassination attempt seemed. Why *had* he been brought so far afield? Why on earth would she delegate the responsibility to others?

"Wait," Leah said, as always thinking much faster than the rest of them. "The Empress tried to take it from others, didn't she?"

"Indeed," Crane said. "In the early years, when we could still infiltrate Lucien, we learned that she tried over and over to give it to others and then take it from them the same way she took the other Talismans. Guardians, Seekers, even one of the illegitimate children she bore that failed the Visigony's inspection."

"And *none* of it worked?"

"That is what we suspect," Crane said with a nod, watching her closely with eyes that missed nothing. Leah looked up at the misted mountains and began to nod.

"This is where she did it," she said, almost too quietly to hear. "She killed the others here, the ones who had the other Talismans. The other Heirs of Theron Isdiel that Geofred couldn't find record of, the ones that always baffled him. She killed them and used their bodies to complete the ritual, binding the Talismans to her, changing them through Bloodmagic from Aspects to the corrupted forms she wanted, the ones that she could take and use even though she hadn't been given them."

Leah turned to face Crane.

"And you think Aemon broke that pattern – you think Aemon killed *himself*, meaning she never took the Aspect from him, he surrendered it. And she thought that by bringing Raven here, killing him at the spot she killed the others, she would be able to finish what she started a thousand years ago."

"I think so indeed," Crane said. "The pieces fall together that way. I've come upon no other solution that fits so precisely."

"But why should the place matter?" rumbled Tomaz. "Why would she want to do it here? If it didn't work elsewhere, what's special about this place besides simple correlation?"

"Crane is right," Raven said slowly before faltering. His throat was dry, though for what reason he couldn't be sure. "There are places where the world is... thin." His mind flashed to the Bloodmage rituals performed in secret caverns beneath the city of Lucien. "Where Bloodmagic has been done with great frequency, or with great power... something is lost. The deaths, the transfers... they *burn* something out of the world. It's like scraping off a layer of skin with a flaying knife. The first amount is small, barely noticeable really, but if it is done over and over in the same spot, the pain caused... it becomes unbearable for any but the Bloodmages."

He fell silent and he could feel the others watching him, though his eyes were fixed on the forest floor. The sounds of the remnants of their army gathering at the foot of the mountain came to them on a sudden breeze. There were the sounds of the Elders too, shouting out words that crackled with power, and the distant roar of what could only be Daemons.

It all seemed to be happening in another world.

"What makes these places special, Raven?" Leah asked quickly. She was close enough to touch him now, though she didn't, for which he was grateful. His mind was somewhere dark.

"Killing done in one of those spots is easier to do," he said simply. "It's like a void, where what you think you knew no longer matters. Rules are easier to change. Moral rules as well as physical."

"Physical?"

"Yes. It's where the Bloodmages gather power to put into their Soul Catchers, the ones they wear around their necks. Each one is made by the slaughter of an innocent, pulled from their heart after they are tortured and sacrificed. It's... the

Soul Catchers are *voids*, they're negative spaces. They're little pieces of that darkness that comes from killing, augmented by the power of the thin spots centuries of killing have created. Anything is possible in one of those spaces if you have the power for it. If you killed enough people there, harvested their energy in a crystal large enough, with an incantation powerful enough... you could remake everything. Change the world, rewrite the laws of nature any way you want to."

"That's what happened in Lerne," Tomaz rumbled softly. "And that's why the sky above Lucien is always black. The Empress has made the whole city into one of those thin spots, hasn't she?"

Raven nodded. "The city is ringed by Bloodmage circles that feed power to her crown. With the right enchantments, anyone who dies inside the walls gives her power. The crown... it's the first Soul Catcher. She made it from the bodies of her fallen enemies."

"Her fallen siblings," Crane said softly. "The other Heirs of Theron Isdiel. Which brings us back to this place... back to *this* thin spot. She brought you here hoping the ritual would work where it had worked before. She brought you here and removed herself from the equation in case it needed to be done by another's hand. What happens when the one wearing a Talisman dies of natural causes?"

"It has never happened before, at least to my knowledge. But I would assume it would return to the Diamond Crown, where the actual Talismans are kept."

"So she brought you here," rumbled Tomaz slowly, piecing everything together, "after drugging you and putting you through the ritual in the city. She poisoned you, and left you for dead, hoping that the Talisman will then return to her with full power, since she sacrificed a Child, in the same place she had sacrificed her brothers and sisters."

"But then how does that help her with the Return?" Tym chimed in from where he stood awkwardly to the side. Silent until now, he was there almost as an afterthought, even though Raven knew he was a part of this, tied up in it as tightly as the rest of them. His new height still looked wrong on him, but he was slowly growing into it, and he was assuming the stature of what would turn out to be quite a beautiful young man.

"I don't know," Crane said. "My only guess would be that with all of the Talismans together finally under her full control, she might then attempt whatever ritual would allow it."

"We may never know, but it doesn't matter," rumbled Tomaz, sounding uncharacteristically grave. "All of this is good to know, I suppose, but it doesn't help our current situation. We have an army approaching us, and we need to find a way to meet it, and drive it back."

"No," Raven said, breaking into the circle, standing at the center, and turning slowly to look at them all. They were all here, all seven, plus Crane, Spader, and Ishmael. "We're going to fight her. And we're going to do it with a weapon of our own."

"A weapon?" asked Tym, his neck and eyes glowing temporarily green as he unconsciously brushed the Talisman with his mind. "What does that mean? We have Aemon's Blade, is that what you mean?"

"Aemon's Blade is part of it, yes. But not the whole thing." He turned again, scanning the circle, before finally landing on Elder Crane, catching those bright eyes. "I need the other Elders, or as many as can be spared. And I need all of you," he motioned, arms wide, to the rest of the circle, "and your Anchors. We have the place, here, where the world is thin and malleable. Beyond that, we'll have to make it up as we go."

"Is that all?" Lorna asked, watching him in a strange confusion.

"Not all," he said. "We also need a *sambolin*."

"A – what? Why do we need a *sambolin*?" asked Davydd, thrown. "We can't ask Crane to give up his, we would need –"

He cut off and his eyes went suddenly big and round in a comical look of surprise as he put it all together. "The *sambolin* Spader has. The one he wanted to send south – the one Tiffenal stole from Goldwyn and we got back in Formaux."

Raven nodded.

"But – we were going to have the Elders rededicate it," Lorna said. "We were going to bind it to a new Elder of State so that the enchantment that makes the illusions around the Kindred lands would be reactivated."

"With at least three Elders present," Crane said, "we can do the rededication here. Though I am not sure I understand what your plan is – the memories themselves are valuable, and a little wisdom can take you a long way, but you will not be able to defeat the Empress with memories."

"I don't need them. If I'm right, then I only need the *sambolin*."

"What happens to the memories then?"

"If all goes well," Raven said, "the memories will go to you, Spader, and Ishmael when you activate the enchantments."

"But what are you going to do with the dagger itself?"

Raven took a deep breath and readied himself. "If I'm right, then the *sambolin* is very similar to a Soul Catcher, the crystal medallion into which Bloodmages pour the lives of the men and women they kill. It is the source of their power and bears a number of similarities to the *sambolin* – specifically that they catch the essence of a person and hold it inside the instrument, to be used at a later time for a specific effect. What is important to remember, however, about the Soul Catchers, is that they are based on a very important design – the Diamond Crown the Empress wears, the one that holds the power of all the seven Talismans.

"Now consider the *sambolin* – each new Elder is bound to it by blood, like a Soul Catcher, and when they die, their life is placed into the dagger. The only difference is that the *sambolin* is voluntary. All pure Bloodmagic is, in fact, voluntary, and it is the act of giving the Talismans that turns them pure again and makes them Aspects."

"So… you're planning on turning the *sambolin* into a Soul Catcher?"

"No! No, no, nothing like that – if we turn the pure Bloodmagic of the *sambolin* into the corrupted Bloodmagic of the Soul Catcher, then all of this is for nothing. No, what we have to do is something else entirely, something much more difficult."

He paused and watched them all with a careful, critical eye. He had to know what their honest response to this was – he couldn't have a single one of them unwilling to cooperate, or the whole ritual might be ruined.

"The Empress still holds us to her," Raven said, "because each of us, through the Aspects and Talismans we wear, still owes allegiance to the Diamond Crown, where the physical Talismans themselves are kept. We have already begun the process of breaking away from it, turning the Talismans back to Aspects – but we need to finish it.

"We need a Crown of our own – a Crown of Aspects."

Chapter Twenty:

A New Light

It took a moment for the words to sink in, but after they did, Leah and Tomaz seemed intrigued, Tym confused. Autmaran looked wary, as if they had just trespassed on some forbidden ground and what Raven was suggesting was a step too far, a move that broke some taboo; Davydd wore his excitement plain and open on his face, both the burned left side and the handsome right side creasing and breaking into a manic smile; Lorna's shoulders tightened, and she stood up straighter, but otherwise made no move, not even batting an eye.

"I know Prince of the Veil is a ceremonial title," he continued, "and if you are uncomfortable with me wearing the Crown, then we can give it to another, even Elder Crane since he is here – but what matters is that we make it. Right now, all of our Talismans, even though by technicality they are pure again, owe allegiance to a corrupted throne. As long as the Empress holds the stones themselves, the physical Talismans, we lose. But if we make something new – if we create a new crown, with Aspects instead of Talismans, and if we make that crown using Aemon's Blade, tying it to your Anchors, making it a *valerium* crown... then we truly owe no allegiance to the Empress. And what she has done to this world, the ways she has broken it – we can begin to repair the fractures. Just the act of breaking the Talismans in two, making two sets, one of Talismans and one of Aspects, halves her power. I know that – "

"Shut up princeling, you had me before the pep talk," Davydd said. "Not that the talk wasn't nice, a little pep is always appreciated. But we're doing this." His words shifted something in the clearing. The air around them began to crackle with excited energy. They weren't doomed; they had a chance. There was a way forward.

Raven looked then at Elder Crane, a quick and subtle shift of his gaze. Everything hinged on whether or not the Elder would go along with this. Without him, and without the other Elders, it was all pointless.

After a long moment wherein everyone seemed to hold their breath, Crane nodded.

"Thank you," Raven said quickly. "Elders, please go to collect Elder Goldwyn's *sambolin* and inform the others we will need more time. Dunhold will have to hold the passes for as long as he can." Raven strode out of the circle and began to make his way to the distant side of the clearing, moving toward the base of the first gentle slope. Without the slightest hesitation, they all fell into step behind him. "Tomaz and Lorna, go with Crane and get a description of the runes we'll need. Get ready to help the Elders craft them. And also... I need your Anchors. Everyone who bears an Aspect."

He turned to them.

"We don't have much time. Hurry."

Crane gave a curt nod and left in a swirl of gray robes, Spader and Ishmael following close behind. Raven breathed a sigh of relief that they were doing as he asked without rebuke. The others all reached hands into deep, secret pockets and pulled out their Anchors, Tomaz and Lorna dropping theirs – a red-edged sword and a small horse, both of beautiful design in valerium metal – into the cloak Raven was holding between his hands before running off after the Elders.

Raven realized distantly he was only several yards away from the side of the ravine that cut off one side of the clearing.

A man fell down there... I wonder what happened to his body.

Davydd, Leah, Autmaran, and Tym had all followed him while the others went about their tasks. He turned back to them, his black cloak whipping in the wind that came off the plains of Lucien and battered against the low mountain slope. He reached out with the Raven Talisman and felt the Imperial army massing below them, the huge lives of the Daemons out front, readying for an attack.

We need to do this quickly.

"This is it," he said, opening his eyes. "This is the spot where they left me, and, if Crane is right, it's the thin spot where the Empress thought she could kill me and fully claim the Raven Talisman. Spread out," he flung his arms wide and turned quickly, scanning the area, reaching through the Talisman and letting all the details of the outside world flow into him. "We need to clear this place of rocks and branches – we will need a smooth surface to carve the runes into the earth."

They nodded and set to work, and Raven's thoughts turned inward even as he helped Davydd and Tym unearth a large rock.

What runes do we need... what do I remember from the rituals I saw?

He remembered the black pit below Lucien, the way the runes glowed blood-red in the darkness of the underground caverns. Geofred had led him down there, to the place deep below the Fortress, the day he had turned five. As all of the Children were commanded to do at that age, he had killed his first man. It was the first time he had ever absorbed a life through the Raven Talisman, the first time he understood what it meant to be one of the Children, to be given power over the lives of others. And from the memories of the man he had killed, he had learned what evil was, what men could do to the world to make it a place of horrors.

Don't focus on the man. The rune beneath him... what was it...?

Finally it came to him, bubbling up from the back of his mind as all memories eventually did. There had been a labyrinthine rune there, one forming a perfect circle at least fifteen feet across. It had been sharp and angular in the center, and as it expanded out it had become more circular and begun to curve in long arching lines.

Tym and Davydd succeeded in unearthing the rock, and as they rolled it to the ravine to drop it over the edge, Raven knelt to the ground, where a patch of bare dirt now lay free in the middle of the grass. He began to draw what he could remember: angular lines in the center, the curving lines along the edge. Several times he scratched it out, and several times he redrew it, each time more confidently.

He heard voices from behind him raised in argument, and turned to see Crane emerging from the trees with Spader and Ishmael, both of whom looked disgruntled at being dragged through a forest, though for different reasons.

This might be the closest Spader has ever come to nature in his entire life.

Ishmael's discomfort, on the other hand, was soon made known by the man himself. "This will not work without the full circle," he said. The low octave of his voice did not prevent it from coming out with a sharp intensity, and it sawed the ear with its usual raspy quality, which today was even more pronounced. It was as if he were trying to force the words out to break something, pushing them forward to puncture the building excitement.

"We must try," said Crane.

"Hold on," Spader said with a hint of alarm, "let's not make any hasty decisions. This is untreaded territory. We don't even know if we can make our form of Bloodmagic touch him – he's been imbued with the Raven Talisman. Black Bloodmagic, the Imperial Bloodmagic... we can't work around that in most cases."

"We were able to swear him in as Prince of the Veil," Crane pointed out.

"That was with a full circle," Spader said, his voice calm but forceful.

"Not to mention the ancient runes of the First Elders," Ishmael continued, "runes of power that have been engraved in that stone for nearly a thousand years."

"It was *not* with a full circle," Crane said a note of impatience. "Iliad was missing, making us twelve. You both know as well as I do that while thirteen is nearly infallible, twelve is only marginally better than three. If we could touch him then, we can touch him now. Besides, I did not choose you for arbitrary reasons: the three of us are the strongest of the current circle. It is the same reason I sent you both north."

"That and the fact you know we'll go along with your damn schemes."

"That too," Crane admitted.

"Pan outstrips me," Ishmael rasped. "And Stanton does such things as I have never seen."

"On their own, they are very powerful," said Crane, his voice quick but measured, his eyes calm, a strong point of security in all the strange newness of the moment. "But in a circle, they are weak. They work well together, but not like the three of us do. We who have been together the longest, known each other, cared for each other since we were children. If there are any who can do this thing, it is the three of us. More will not make a difference; I doubt even the full thirteen, if such a thing were possible with Iliad in his condition, could outpace us when we are focused on a thing."

There was a long pause as the others watched him, and watched each other. Raven and the others could only look on in silence; they had all stopped what they were doing to focus on the Elders. There was something deep between these three, something even outside of what Crane had alluded to, that spoke of a long history.

It is no mistake Spader and Ishmael were sent with us when we went north. Crane made sure they were the ones, made sure that if he needed them here, they would be ready, and he wouldn't have to fight them like he would have had to fight the others in breaking a tradition of this magnitude.

"Fine," Spader snapped, "but this is breaking a hundred different laws about needing a full Council to decide things. Laws *you* made me write, I might add."

"I take full responsibility," Crane acknowledged. "But we are breaking the laws to save the nation, and for that I have no regrets."

"I never thought you were an 'ends justify the means' kind of man," Ishmael grimaced. "But I know I am. If this is what needs to be done, then my feelings are of little consequence. I may not like this course of action, but I can see no other way forward. It must be done."

"Good," Crane said.

There was more rustling behind them, and the two giant forms of Tomaz and Lorna appeared, each bearing what looked like hastily-constructed digging implements that had recently been pikes.

"Where do we start?" rumbled Tomaz.

"Here," Crane said, striding to the center of the space that had been cleared by the others. Raven moved forward to talk with him, but found his way blocked by the slight form of Ishmael. He looked down into the Elder's eyes – and was surprised by the realization he was taller than the man.

He could still kill me in my sleep ten times over before anyone realized I had stopped snoring. Thank goodness he's on our side.

"Show me what you've done," Ishmael rasped. "I will take to Crane what I think we can use." He bent over the lines drawn in the dirt and began to ask questions, which Raven struggled to answer. His loathing for Bloodmagic had led him to neglect it, indeed to shun it, and so he knew very little about the purpose of any of what he'd seen. Ishmael, however, seemed able to make something out of it.

"Besides the fact you drew it upside down," the Imperial Liaison muttered, "I think this was meant to be a dedication circle, very similar to what we use. If we improvise here and here to make connections, we may even be able to overlay the two runes to create an entirely new one. You say that this is used in the creation of a Soul Catcher?"

"Yes. A man is killed over the top of this rune, and his blood and body... dissolve. They melt, and... and *run*, as if every bond in his body holding him together had suddenly been snapped in two. The blood passes into the rune, the rune begins to glow, and in the very center – *here* – a Bloodmage stands, holding a ready crystal in his hand."

"The *sambolin* are not crystals," Ishmael warned him. "They are ornamental blades made of metal that, when enchanted, become... something more."

"Whatever they are, the spell is already a part of them. The only reason crystals are necessary is that they take the enchantment while other stones do not. If the Elders' Bloodmagic has already transformed the *sambolin* into a carrier, then there should be nothing to worry about. It should work the same."

"In theory."

"Theory is all we have at this point," Raven said, becoming exasperated. "No one has ever done anything like this before; we're going to have to make some things up as we go. Believe me, it makes me uneasy too. But it us necessary."

"Fine," Ishmael rasped. "Let us begin."

Within minutes the lines had been drawn in the earth, and the group formed up. Raven was standing at the center over a number of indecipherable runes carved deep into the black earth by Tomaz and Lorna, and the others were arrayed equidistant in a circle around him. There was little discussion for the most part, aside from the occasional disagreement between Ishmael and Spader as to the specifics of the runes beneath their feet. Crane stayed out of the whole affair, standing off far to the side, watching the whole proceeding with veiled eyes.

Does nothing shake that man?

Raven's gaze flicked to Tym, and he saw the boy looking at him sadly; Raven quickly looked away. The Snake Talisman had always been the one that made him the most uneasy – the fact that it had been transferred to Tym and purified hadn't changed that.

Huge bellowing roars sounded from down the mountain, and they all turned. Raven sent his mind out to check on what was happening and saw that the Imperials had stumbled into the first ambush the Kindred had set and been forced to retreat. They were reforming now, and the Daemons looked ready to lead the next charge.

They were very quickly running out of time.

"We must begin!" Crane called out. "Raven, do you have the Anchors?"

Raven nodded and pulled out the scrap of cloth in which he had collected the six Anchors, the little pieces of valerium that contained drops of his friends' blood and made them citizens of Vale. He was very careful not to touch them – particularly Davydd's, which was a miniature version of the valerium sword he wore slung across his back – it was just as sharp as the real thing. He took a deep breath, and carefully laid them beside the already waiting *sambolin*.

Elder Goldwyn's sambolin… *I wonder if his memories are inside it now. Shadows and light, if only he were here. He would know exactly what to do.*

He dropped a hand to his side and rested it on the hilt of Aemon's Blade. If this was going to work, it would all hinge on the very large assumption Crane had made that Aemon's Blade contained more than just a drop of Aemon's blood. If this whole thing worked at all, it would be because of something set in motion by one man over a thousand years ago.

Raven's hand moved with a mind of its own, unsheathing the sword and laying it in the middle of the pile before him. Head spinning, he nodded to Elder Crane, and just before the Elder began to speak, Raven's gaze slid sideways to Leah. She had her stone face on and was staring at him with a determination that was frightening in its intensity.

The word Crane spoke wasn't a sound so much as it was a vibration, like the first note of a primitive song, something low and deep, even deeper than Tomaz's voice. The Wise Elder held up his hand and pulled out his own *sambolin*, dangling on the chain clasped around his neck. He unsheathed the dagger, and its multi-hued blade caught the last rays of daylight and threw them across the glade in a hundred spangled flashes.

Ishmael and Spader mirrored him, and with all three of their voices joined together, the sound was suddenly unbearable. The notes didn't fit – they jarred, splintering into thousands of pieces. All three Elders slashed their hands in unison.

As soon as the blood began to flow, the sound changed. The cacophony melded seamlessly into something new, something easy and fluid like water running downhill. Crane's eyes widened in surprise, and Spader was suddenly smiling inexplicably, looking like he'd found an answer to a question he'd had for a very long time.

It was the others' turn now – all of those who bore an Aspect. Each of them drew out a dagger of their own, all of plain metal, and sliced their palms with it. With each cut, the air grew tighter around them, as if the violence done were pulling the air taunt.

Crane broke off his chant, and called out:

"On my count of three!"

Raven realized a background noise, completely independent of the Elders, had begun to build around them, so deep it vibrated him where he stood.

"ONE!" Crane shouted. Ishmael knelt and threw his hand to the ground. Raven flinched, but then realized this was part of the ritual: the section of the rune before the dark Elder turned a deep, unforgiving black, and the humming grew louder.

"TWO!" Crane cried.

Spader dropped to his knee and slammed his own palm into the ground. Another section snapped into a tan color flecked with lines of a deep tawny. The hum in the air and in the ground began to collect beneath the soles of Raven's boots, and the Anchors at his feet suddenly moved, snapping into a perfect circle around him, each leaping to a point directly between Raven and its owner.

"THREE!"

Crane, Autmaran, Tym, Lorna, Tomaz, Leah, and Davydd all knelt as one and slammed their hands into the section of runes in front of them. In immediate reaction, wind appeared from nowhere and tore at their clothing, sucked down in a sudden vortex that left Raven untouched but fiercely buffeted everyone else.

"HOLD STEADY!" roared Crane, straining to be heard over the rushing gale. "WHATEVER YOU DO – *DO NOT BREAK CONTACT WITH THE CIRCLE!*"

Crane, Ishmael, and Spader all began to chant again, their voices low and yet somehow loud enough to be heard over the whipping wind that had encircled Raven. The words cut through the air, and he watched in equal parts fear and amazement as the area of the rune in front of each person began to turn a separate color, each corresponding to the color of their Aspect.

Raven looked down and his heart leapt into his throat.

The Anchors at his feet were vibrating so hard and fast that they had begun to melt. The valerium metal was falling off of them in droplets and pooling on the ground beneath, burning the grass and blistering the soil. The center of each Anchor had begun to glow a deep, dark red.

Shadows and light, their blood is being distilled out of the Anchors.

He spun and looked at Aemon's Blade, and saw that while it continued to vibrate, no such thing was happening to it. It stayed just as it was, whole and unbroken, the lynchpin that held this all together.

Words continued to spill from the Elders' mouths, tumbling and tripping on each other, faster than any tongue should have been able to speak them. This was completely unlike anything he'd seen before. It was a violent fight with something deep and elemental, something that knew what they were doing and was trying to stop them.

Energy crackled in the air as the wind picked up speed, nearly blowing Tym off his feet before he dropped himself completely to the ground and grabbed a handful of turf to keep himself anchored to the circle. The smell and feel of lightning encompassed Raven's senses; the air had turned crisp and sharp, like before a storm. His anxiety spiked, morphing to fear inside his chest.

What happens if this changes me? What happens if this is the final step that sent Mother spiraling into the chaos that now consumes her mind?

The thought came out of nowhere, and he realized what this would mean when it was finished. He would be the master of all seven Aspects. The others would wear them, yes, but they would owe fealty, would be literally *bound* to him at the level of their souls, for as long as he wore that Crown.

Whatever gods may be, Raven prayed silently, *make my soul indomitable. Do not let me become her... do not let me fall the way she did.*

Crane broke off his chanting and began to shout at Raven.

"Grab the *sambolin!* It's your turn!"

In one swift motion, Raven knelt and grabbed for the dagger. He grasped the hilt, a single piece of smoothed ornamental stone that felt cool against his wrist, and sliced the opal blade across his hand. He fought back a sudden wave of pain and nausea at the self-mutilation, and slammed his hand into the ground.

A huge weight crashed down on top of him, trying to bury him in the ground. Air rushed out of his lungs; his vision doubled; and he nearly lost consciousness. He couldn't breathe, couldn't lift himself up off the ground, couldn't do anything but wait to be controlled by the huge forces now coursing through his body.

He reached out blindly, flailing with his free hand, and by pure luck grasped the burning hilt of Aemon's Blade. The rune around his splayed body burst into a thousand colors as the blood of each of the others on the outside of the circle finally reached it. The melted Anchors fell to the ground and six balls of light, the blood of his friends, shot into him, coursing through his body.

"AHHHH!"

The cry left his lips only to be echoed by each of the six Aspect bearers on the outside of the circle – the pain mounted, pulling at him, as thoughts and ideas and emotions flew through his head that didn't belong to him, impressions of life that could only belong to the others.

A new sound reached his ears – the sound of Crane shouting at the top of his lungs, only barely audible over the power of the circle.

"Use... the... sambolin!"

Raven looked down and realized in the middle of what had happened he had somehow released the dagger; it lay inches from his outstretched fingers, and yet seemed farther away than the moon. He reached for it, pulling his hand forward, even as the pain of whatever was inside him now ripped and tore at his mind. He was a bare fraction of an inch away – he was almost touching it –

He grabbed the hilt, and the light that had entered him left and flew into the *sambolin*. The dagger spun in his hand, moving of its own accord, and flew into the air. Flashes of white shot upward past him, and he looked down in alarm to see the pools of melted valerium ore rising into the air as if pulled by a magnet. In a quick rush of movement, the ore flew into the dagger, and turned it into something else – a roiling ball of molten metal that spun in the air above his head.

Crane was yelling again, but this time the sound didn't carry – it couldn't force its way through the gale-force winds that threatened to rip open the very ground they stood upon.

Why won't it come to me? What is still missing?

He felt the hilt of Aemon's Blade burning against the skin of his palm and realized what he had to do. He clutched the Blade convulsively in both hands, holding on to it so tightly that his knuckles cracked, and then thrust it up to pierce the fiery crown.

A blast went off akin to a whole storehouse of Black Powder going up in flame. He was thrown flat on his back, and the rune around him disintegrated as if it had never been. The Elders and the six Aspect bearers were all thrown backward, head over heels, and a sound like a thunderclap ripped the leaves off the trees for a hundred paces.

The silence that followed was the most deafening Raven had ever heard. It was a void, with him at the center, and no one and nothing sought to fill it. As leaves fell back to the ground and the dust of the blasted rune settled, one by one the others were revealed, all staring inward, all trying to pierce the haze to see what, if anything, was left of their friend. As one, they held their breath, eyes wide and staring.

A shape was revealed in the center, and they knew it was Raven, but none of them went to him. He was kneeling, left leg up and right knee down, and his hands were holding something that sparkled and shone with inner light.

As he knelt there, knowing the ritual was complete, Raven felt something bubble up beneath his thoughts, something old and barely cogent. It was a set of memories, so muted and distant that they were almost nothing more than whirling motes of dust on the flowing winds of time. But they were there – distant and vague, almost just impressions, but there.

Aemon. Crane was right. He was in there all along, and none of us had any idea.

And then a new shock ran through him. His palms hit the ground even before he realized he'd collapsed onto all fours, and tears came unbidden to the corners of his eyes. A single word rang through him and sang in his ears.

He remembered his name.

Chapter Twenty-one:

Crowned

He opened his mouth to speak it, to say the name out loud –

And couldn't. He tried again, but the word refused to come. The sounds wouldn't form. His teeth and lips and tongue were unable to say the name that now blazed in his mind, and even as he tried to force it out, his exhilaration faded. It was a dark name. It was a name meant for the bringer of death, and as the excitement of remembering faded, he felt uneasy, almost as if he'd encountered an old friend he wasn't sure was still a friend. He could *feel* the name; grasp it even, in an abstract way. It rested on the tip of his tongue, but the sounds wouldn't come and the letters wouldn't settle. He had broken his Mother's grip on him – but not completely. There was still something left to do, something that kept him bound to her.

She's my Mother. The very blood in my veins keeps me bound to her.

"How do you feel?"

He looked up. The question had come from Crane, the only one brave enough to approach him, though not by more than a step or two.

"Strong," he said.

It was true – the word described the state he'd entered in a way that none other could. Every ache he'd ever had, both mental and physical, had been washed away. Gold and blue haloes outlined the world, giving a strange, extra dimension to everything he saw. He heard the sounds of birds and insects, and somehow knew the truth of what they were saying to each other. He could see the veins in Spader's neck, the sweat beading on his pale forehead, and knew the exact shade of his fear and hope, and the way the two emotions battled inside him like marked warriors in a dueling ring. In a flash of blue he saw Ishmael leaving this grove and joining the other Elders to fight against a figure on a Daemon.

Bright colors caught his eye, and he looked around at the others. All seven of the Aspect Bearers, the new Heirs of Theron Isdiel, were lit with the glow of their respective Aspects. Autmaran's bald head was framed in a glowing mane of white light that traced around his head and down his neck; Leah's hands and neck were highlighted in blue as her Aspect traced her body's nerve ending; Davydd's veins pulsed with liquid gold, and the blackened, burnt skin on the left side of his face seemed darker by contrast; Lorna's face was clear, but her hands and feet burned so brightly with gray light that both her boots and gauntlets had split and fallen away; Tomaz towered over them all, his armor straining against his chest, legs, and arms as the straps sought to hold together despite the pulsing, blood-red light that had engorged his muscles.

And Raven could feel each of those same lights flow through him.

The light around his friends winked out, leaving them stunned and off-balance; but the light in the grove did not die. Instead, a new light blossomed, brighter than any of the Aspects individually. It seemed source-less to Raven, though each of his companions had thrown a hand up before their eyes to shield them from the brilliance. It took him a long moment to understand where it was coming from, and he only figured it out in the end because his head felt strangely... heavy. He reached up and his fingers touched something warm, and hard as diamond. Grabbing hold of it, he pulled it off.

Immediately, the light guttered out, and the sense of wonder he'd felt, the light that had infused the gathering, disappeared. He staggered sideways, catching himself at the last moment and managing to find his feet again before he fell to the ground – ground that now felt hard and unyielding, distant and colorless.

"Raven," Crane said. "How do you feel? Did it work?"

He looked up and nodded, dumb-founded by the sense of completeness he'd felt with the crown on his head. He held it up, so that all of them could see it.

It was fitted to his head, and neither thick nor thin but somewhere in-between. Unlike his Mother's crown, which was cruel and made of seven spires sharp as daggers, the Crown of Aspects was smooth, and all of one piece. It started thin in the back, and then gradually increased in width until it met again in the front, where a single, large gemstone was set: an opal, made from the blade of the *sambolin*. Light flowed from the large stone in varying shades and hues, pulsing and flickering with light that alternated between each of the Aspect colors.

"It worked," Raven said, answering Crane's question. "And now we attack."

His words seemed to break the spell that held all the others in place, and they all moved forward toward him. Leah and Tomaz came first to determine for themselves he had survived unscathed – the big man even went so far as to rest a hand on Raven's shoulder and look into his eyes. Davydd and Lorna hung back, moving closer to each other as they watched the proceedings warily. Spader and Ishmael joined Crane, flanking him directly to left and right. Autmaran and Tym came forward together, both staring in awe at the crown.

"Now we attack," Crane confirmed. "How will we go about it?"

"It would be a massacre if we attacked the Visigony in traditional lines," Autmaran said, shaking himself out of his trance. "Our best hope is to keep drawing them into the mountains, forcing them to come to us."

"We don't have time for that," protested Raven. "I saw something in Marthinack's memories – what he had of them."

"Marthinack?"

"The... Visigony I killed. He was one of the Trium – the three who have been here since the founding. He was one of the original Bloodmages to join the Empress."

"That tin-pot brain of his actually held something?" Davydd asked.

"More than something. A memory of a cavern beneath Lucien – a cavern like the one we saw in Lerne. A cavern that already holds two active Bloodmage crystals, from Tibour and Lerne, and has a third prepared. I'd give you three guesses when and how they hope to make it, but you'll only need one."

"You're saying if we don't invade the city by tonight," Lorna said slowly, "they'll sacrifice every Baseborn they can get their hands on. The same way they did at Lerne."

"Yes. And if the Empress gains that power tonight in conjunction with my death, then she'll be able to accomplish anything."

"She won't kill you," Leah said harshly.

"Not for want of trying," Davydd drawled.

"And if we stay in these mountains," Raven continued, "I can see her coming for us. And then there is nothing that will hold her back. We need to take this fight to her. *I* need to take this fight to her."

"To the top of the Fortress," Tomaz rumbled. "That's where she'll be waiting when she sees us coming. And she *will* see us coming."

Distant noise pulled their attention down the mountainside, away from the clearing. There were shouts and roars, and again the clash of swords.

"The other Elders have held them off as long as possible," Spader said quickly. "Whatever plan we come up with, we need to make it on the run."

Raven nodded, and as one they began to make their way from the clearing to the tree line, headed toward the sounds of battle. The sun had left the sky completely now, plunging them into quickly deepening twilight. Raven's palms began to sweat and his stomach roiled with apprehension.

By dawn it's over, one way or another.

"Tym," Autmaran said quickly, "we will need torches –"

"Yes, sir," the boy said, already disappearing into the trees.

"What about the Visigony?" Lorna asked, continuing their conversation. "They routed us, and they led that army across the plain – what makes you think that we can even get through them to begin with?"

"Leave them to us," Crane said simple.

"Then who will lead the charge?"

"I will," Raven said as he placed the Crown of Aspects on his head.

The light returned, illuminating their way, and driving away the lengthening shadows. Power swelled in him, and he breathed in deeply.

"You could have done that before I sent Tym running," Autmaran grumbled.

Raven smiled, but didn't reply. Wearing the crown, he felt no need to respond to the annoyance in his friend's voice – why was such a thing important? He could see the way the world worked, down to the smallest ripple and fold in the ground. He knew the truth of what he saw, knew how and where to move, and knew he would never tire, his limbs never falter. He was the perfect manifestation of humanity.

And as that thought crossed his mind, a sudden, sourceless sense of foreboding gripped him. He pushed it away. He felt powerful – why did he need to worry? For the first time in this whole war, their goal was accomplishable. He had the power to do what needed to be done now. The darkness he had spoken of to Leah was gone as if it had never been, and the hopelessness of only a short time ago was now nothing more than distant memory.

It was like a mountain had been lifted off of him.

The others continued speaking, and Raven realized absently that he should be listening. But his mind was far distant – he was thinking of grander things, about the turning of the world and what would happen after he deposed the Empress. The nation would be without guidance then. Someone would need to be installed, possibly even by force. The Kindred would never accept such a ruler, though.

But maybe... maybe *he* could be that ruler. He could be the Emperor his Mother never was, an Emperor that everyone could truly follow, Kindred and Imperials alike. Now, with his mind unburdened, with the clarity that all the Aspects brought him –

And you will end the same.

He convulsed, his body spasming, and he threw the crown from his head.

When the metal lost contact with his skin, his mind snapped back to who he really was. He stared at the white metal circlet where it lay in the grass like a deadly snake. His breath came hard and fast, and he realized he was shaking.

He became aware that the others were staring at him as if he'd lost his mind.

I think I might have.

"What happened?" Elder Crane asked.

"Nothing," he said. "Nothing – go ahead, gather the troops. I need some time."

They all paused. "Is it the crown?" Leah asked. "Are you seeing something that might happen?"

He caught her gaze and found he couldn't answer. He reached down and grabbed the Crown before he could think too much about it, and held it loosely, trying to keep his mind blank.

"Go," he said. "Organize the attack and call me when we're ready."

He turned and left them, trying to outdistance his thoughts. He hurried back to the clearing, where he stopped and looked at the empty space the ritual had left behind. He saw the matted grass where he had stood, and a glimmer of white stuck into the side of the oak tree.

Aemon's Blade.

He ran for it, grabbed the hilt, and pulled it from the trunk with all his might. The sword, though reluctant at first, slid out with a sharp jerk that left him stumbling. He grasped the hilt tightly in his right hand, and realized he still held the heavy weight of the crown in his left. He had never seen his Mother use a sword, and now knew why: she had never needed one. With the Diamond Crown on her head, her words Commanded the world around her, and the world obeyed. He could do the same now.

But this is more than just a sword.

He felt the overwhelming urge to put the crown back on his head, to feel that power again, that perfection, but something stopped him, something from the Blade that helped him resist. With a huge effort of will, he threw both Blade and Crown to the ground. He fell to his knees, holding his head in his hands.

This was supposed to fix everything. This was supposed to change it – the Aspects are pure, so why can't I use the crown? Is it me? Am I broken? Am I too much my Mother after all, so much so that I can't even touch the Aspects without corrupting them?

He became aware that he wasn't alone in the clearing. He turned: Elder Crane, in his gray robes, his lined face drawn and eyes narrowed, stepped out from the shade of a tree not a dozen yards away.

"How did I not sense you standing there?"

"It would appear you had other things on your mind," Crane replied evenly, taking a few steps forward before stopping well short of Raven's reach. He was wary; he knew what lived inside of Raven. "After all," he continued, "not even the Empress can have her mind on all things at one time. No one can."

The words, though speaking of the Empress, were pointed at him, and Raven knew it. How much did the Elder know? How much did he suspect? Those eyes were too knowing. They saw too much.

What would I be thinking if I still had the crown on? Would I see him as a threat?

The thought chilled him to the bone. He had already killed one Elder. Would he really think of killing another?

"What happened just now?" Crane asked.

Surprising even himself, Raven spoke the truth. "I started thinking about replacing my Mother. Not as a Prince, but as a King. As an Emperor. With the Aspects, I thought that I would be able to..."

He did not finish the sentence; he could not put that thought out in the open. To acknowledge it to another person was to acknowledge it to himself, and he could not t do that. He could not accept that he had thought such a thing – and if he kept it quiet, if he spoke of it in subtext, then he could deny it, even to himself.

Couldn't he?

"This wasn't supposed to happen," he said, looking at the crown, glowing softly in the dirt where he had cast it. "The Aspects are pure. They're not like the Talismans. They're meant to help people, they –"

"Are tools of power," Crane interrupted, "and made to be separate."

"But that shouldn't mean anything – they're *pure* now!"

"Unless they were never pure. Unless they were always tools of power."

The sounds of fighting swelled in the distance, and Raven heard the roar of Tomaz as the giant encouraged the Kindred. He needed to go to them – their time was up, every second he sat here was wasted.

But still he didn't move.

"What do you mean, tools of power?" he asked instead.

He tried to look at Crane, tried to pull his gaze away from the crown, but found himself unable. He wanted it. The feeling it gave him... the way it freed him from his fear and doubt...

"I mean," said Crane, stepping closer and breaking through the silence, "that the Aspects were never meant to be combined. These powers... they should not have been made. I think Aemon realized that in the end. He was never one of the others, that much has always been clear; he was an outsider in some way, and it gave him perspective. The Aspects have a purer outcome, and a purer purpose, but they do not make the bearer pure any more than the Talismans make the bearer corrupt. Why did you throw down the crown? What made you turn away from such power?"

Aemon. Whatever part of him was left tried to stop me from doing this.

"Raven! Elder Crane!"

The voice that called to them was distant, spread out and rounded, almost unintelligible. But it was deep, and Raven knew it was Tomaz coming back for them.

"Raven," Crane said, closing the distance and seizing the Prince's shoulders in a sudden forceful jerk. The motion finally broke Raven's forced concentration on the crown and brought him around to look at the Elder.

"This was never a story about good or evil. It was never a story about a bad Empress. It's a story about people. About everyday people, gifted with terrible power. And *people* are not good or bad. *People*, all of us, are *both*. We were never meant to hold the kind of power the Empress has; the kind of power you now possess."

"But I need to —"

"Raven! Crane!" The voice was closer.

"Yes," Crane continued, his reedy tenor voice becoming quick and clipped. "Yes, you do need to wear it. You're the only one who can — it's tied to you through your father's side. Your *father's* side, the side that *rejected* that power, knowing there was no way to keep it from corrupting the one who wielded it."

"But what if we did keep it? Think of what we could do!"

"No!" Crane exclaimed, bringing his face closer, so close that all Raven could see was the man's burning gaze. "You mustn't start down that path. You are equally the son of both your mother and your father — you have inherited the best and the worst of both paths, and if you start down one, you might lose the other forever."

"Raven! Where are you?" The voice was not a hundred yards away – Tomaz was on the other side of the tree line.

"You will have the choice," the Elder said fiercely, a frantic note creeping into his words. "Do not let this journey go to waste – *do not let it turn you into her!*"

"But I have to wear it, it's the only way to kill her – fire with fire."

"And when you're done, douse that flame before it consumes you."

Raven realized what he was saying, and felt his whole body revolt against it.

"We have little time," Crane said quickly, looking over his shoulder. "All of us are called on, at some point in our lives, to do something far beyond what we believe we can. But the value of an action is not in the succeeding, it is in the striving. You know what you must do. Time does not stop, even for Elders and Princes. The only choice we have, the only choice anyone *ever* has, is how we choose to greet what is already on its way to meet us. To walk forward or to be pulled.

"You have done everything you can to win with anger and hate and resentment," the Elder continued as Tomaz saw them and tried to hail them; neither responded. "Righteous fury, lent from the Kindred, has driven you here, but with it you have gone as far as you can go. It is time for you to move on; time to move on from doing this because of your father, because of Goldwyn's death, because of your love for Leah. This fight cannot be won if you fight on behalf of someone else."

"But I can only fight in one way – it doesn't matter *why* I fight."

"It *only* matters why you fight. The reason changes everything."

"I will not survive this battle," he replied, his voice low, telling the Elder what he had firmly come to believe. "If I kill her, I save the Kindred, but she kills me. We live or die together. I can feel it – I can't explain it, but I *know* it."

Crane grabbed Raven's head with clawed hands.

"The reason changes everything."

"Elder, Prince," Tomaz rumbled. He stood at the tree line bearing a torch that lit his bearded face with a ruddy glow. "We need to go. We are out of time for talking."

"Indeed," Crane said, nodding to Raven. "Indeed we are."

The Elder turned away in a swirl of gray robes as Tomaz beckoned them on, leaving Raven to sheath Aemon's Blade, grab the crown, and hurry along behind.

Chapter Twenty-two:

The Final Charge

They raced downhill toward the distant sounds of the army, all three of them moving as quickly as they could in what light was left to illuminate their way. They burst through the trees at the bottom of the mountain slope, and Raven saw that the remnants of the Kindred army had formed up to face the Plains. The Imperials had beaten through the ambush points and were forming up for another attack. Raven saw scores of wounded being pulled back by their comrades, and noticed that two shrouded, unmoving figures had been placed in a strange position of honor.

Elders. Two of them are dead.

He felt sick, but forced himself to move on. He reached for Aemon's Blade at his side; the weight of the hilt made him feel more in control.

"Raven!" Leah shouted, coming toward him with Melyngale. He mounted quickly and turned the stallion so that he could look down the mountainside. The Imperials had formed up and were advancing, the remaining Visigony spaced throughout the regular soldiers to make it harder for the Elders to engage them.

Leah gestured for him to follow and then spurred her horse toward the front of the army. Davydd, Lorna, and Tomaz followed close behind, mounted as well. Raven heeled Melyngale in their direction; they were heading for the distant form of Autmaran in his red cape. The gangly form of Tym was easily visible at his side.

He caught up with the others just as they reined in next to Autmaran, who was standing beside General Dunhold, giving him final instructions. They stood just outside a makeshift command post that was really nothing more than a sheet pulled over a branch behind a convenient rock outcropping.

"What's our plan?" Raven asked Leah, dismounting to catch up with her.

"We don't need to defeat the army," Autmaran said, disengaging from Dunhold and turning to face Raven, his eyes underlined with dark circles. "We've been looking at this wrong the whole time. We need to break through, that's the most important thing."

"The rest of the army will be slaughtered if we do that."

"Unless we force them to follow us," Leah said.

"We can't do that unless we take Lucien itself," Raven protested.

"My thoughts exactly," Autmaran said.

"And I'm willing to bet they forgot lock the doors," Davydd said.

"You think they left the gates undermanned?" Raven asked, incredulous.

"I think they mean to crush us," Tomaz rumbled from where he stood in the corner, keeping one eye on the progress of the approaching Imperial army. "I think they know they're out of time – they need to end this, just like we do. They need you."

And then it all fell together in one bright, clear line, blazing through Raven's mind.

"They'll follow me back to the city," he said in hushed tones.

"They'll follow all of us." Autmaran smiled. "They want you, but they want the rest of us just as badly. We're what they're looking for."

"Shadows and light, that's brilliant."

Leah flashed a dazzling smile at him.

"Then there are three things we need to do once we enter the city," Raven said quickly. He moved to Tomaz's vantage point and saw through a scrim of foliage that the Imperial army was moving up the mountain. He glanced at the maps on the table, mentally judging the logistics of the next leg of their journey: through the Imperial force, across the Plains, and straight for Lucien. "We need to stall the Visigony; we need to stop the Bloodmage ritual; and we need to draw out the Empress."

"You bloody well better be the one to volunteer for that last bit," Davydd said, eyeing him, "or else I'm going to tie you up and hand you over to the Visigony myself. Maybe there's a get-out-of-being-dead reward I could claim."

"Yes," Raven said. "Yes, I'll go against her, no one else. But I'll need help getting there – the city is not designed for easy access to the Fortress."

"So how do we help?" Tym asked.

"We split up. Between Leah and Tomaz, Davydd and Lorna, we can hit three sides of the city simultaneously. Autmaran and Tym – you stay with the main force while the others break off into two smaller groups and attack the city's east and west gates."

"That's three squads, but where are you?"

"I will head straight for the Fortress," he said, his voice grim. "We have until the sun rises; either I die, or she does."

A chill ran through the gathered group, but no one addressed it.

"Will we be able to use the Aspects while you wear the crown?" Lorna asked, barely audible over the army falling into place behind them; the Kindred were forming up to repel the Imperial attack.

"Yes," Raven said. "Distance should be no problem; it should work the same as the Talismans do with the Diamond Crown – we both have use of them."

"Good," Tym said, his thin voice rising above the din. "I think we're all really going to need whatever we can use."

"Just stick with the Commander, boy," said Davydd, not unkindly. "I want to see you grow up – *actually* grow up – after this is done."

Will there be an after? "Stop," he hissed to himself; the others didn't hear him over the noise of the marching men.

"We spear through the formation," Autmaran said, "with heavy horse in front, light infantry directly behind, and heavy infantry, archers, and the Scouts in the rear to keep whatever they can off our backs."

"How effective will they be while moving?" Leah asked.

"The Empire should be so surprised they won't focus on the rear anyway – my guess is that they'll break into two halves and run parallel to us while the Visigony try to deal with the Elders."

"We'll take the east side," Davydd said, motioning to himself and Lorna.

"Then we're the west," Tomaz rumbled.

"Excellent, we'll meet you in the middle. Where's the cavern?"

"It should be under the Fortress," Raven said immediately. "I think they simply expanded the existing Bloodmage caverns. They looked like what I remember."

"Great. Last one there buys the first drink back in Vale," Davydd quipped.

"Get ready to pay," Leah said with relish.

"I'm in front," Autmaran said, ignoring the banter, his voice harsh and no-nonsense, "and I want Raven beside me. This plan works best if you are out front with that crown of yours. The Kindred will see you and take heart, and the enemy will see you and run in the opposite direction. Once we're through, you pick the most promising side and go straight for the Fortress. Your job is the Empress – you leave the rest to us."

"Fine," Raven said, hating that he would have to abandon the others to fend for themselves, but knowing it was necessary. *How many people will die? How many will fall once we're inside the city and I'm not there to protect them?*

"When we hit the city," Autmaran continued, "we split like Raven said."

As he said the name, it jarred in his head – it wasn't the name that bound him to his Mother, the one that still held sway here so close to Her city. Shadows and light, he'd wanted to remember his true name for so long, and now that he could, he wanted nothing more than to forget it again.

Hold on to yourself – hold on to Raven.

"We're running low on time," Tomaz said. As if on cue, Dunhold bellowed a command and the archers released their first volley down the mountainside.

"To get to the caverns," Raven said quickly, "find a way into the Fortress and go *down.*"

"Down?"

"Yes, there are ways the Bloodmages use: they look like servants' pathways, but darker, and they're lined with traps. The traps shouldn't affect us – as long as you hold onto the Aspects and go first, the other Kindred should be fine. Touch any Bloodmagic runes you see; that should disarm whatever you come across."

They all nodded, and Raven realized that there was nothing left to talk about. The time had arrived. He balled his hands into fists to keep them from shaking.

Shadows and light. We're actually doing this.

"When we leave the trees," Autmaran said, bald head glinting in the torchlight, "we do not stop. No matter what happens, no matter who falls, we go straight for the city." He turned to Raven, and pointed a thick, gauntleted finger at him, spear-like. "And you don't stop for man, beast, or Daemon. You go straight for the Fortress, and you don't stop until you find the Empress. *Do – not – stop.* No matter what you see. No matter what trouble we get into along the way. Trust the rest of us to deal with it."

Raven nodded, his throat terribly dry.

Shadows and light... shadows and bloody, goddamn light!

Autmaran mounted his horse in a swirl of red cape, his head suddenly outlined with a glowing white halo. Moving to the front of the army, he spoke to the Kindred, his voice rolling out in rich, beautiful tones.

"We stand at the edge of a precipice," he said. "*I see that you are tired – and I am here to tell you that I am tired too.*"

The Kindred stood up straighter as his voice washed over them, even those leaning on one another just to keep from falling down. Raven felt it too – a soaring feeling that began to build in his gut.

"*I am tired of fighting to prolong the inevitable,*" Autmaran continued. "*I am tired of fighting not to lose. And so I tell you that I will do so no longer.*"

The intensity of the watching army increased, and many shuffled to see him better. Raven looked down and saw the Imperial army halfway up the mountainside. Two Shadow Daemons led the charge, the Visigony riding them clad in their visor helmets and gold-enameled armor. One of the creatures threw back its head and screeched a challenge that made Raven and half the Kindred army cringe.

"*Yes!*" Autmaran said, hearing the noise, seeing the reaction. "*Yes! That is what we face – Daemons! And the general in me tells me to run. The tactician in me says to retreat and fight another day. But I DO NOT CARE!*"

The shout truly sounded like a roar, and Raven felt the hairs on the back of his neck stand up. He grabbed a tighter hold of the crown he still held in his hand at his side.

"*I am tired of running,*" Autmaran continued, "*and I know you are too. I am tired of knowing that the Empire has invaded Vale countless times, but we have never seen the inside of Lucien. So I am riding for those gates; I am riding to put the fear of death into the would-be conquerors of all our people!*"

The Kindred listened, enraptured, and Raven saw many of them begin to swell with emotion. "*I am riding for the gates of Lucien,*" he continued, the white halo around his head glowing even brighter, "*and I will pass through them even if I have to break them down with my own two hands! I will attack the city, and I will take it; and if it is the last thing I do on this earth, I will show the Empire that I did*" not run, that I, Autmaran of Marilen and the Exiled Kindred, brought the fight for my freedom to her doorstep and spat defiance in her eye!"

Autmaran punched his fist in the air, holding aloft his simple, unadorned broadsword, and the Kindred roared back at him with a cheer so loud it left Raven's ears ringing. Autmaran smiled, a snarling grimace, turned to Raven, and nodded.

Raven heeled Melyngale forward and placed the Crown of Aspects on his head. Light broke out in the deepening night like the light from a minor sun, forcing Kindred to throw their arms in front of their faces even as they stared at him in awe. Raven kept a tight grip on the hilt of Aemon's Blade as he spoke, forcing back his anxiety.

"*As your Prince,*" Raven said, using the same voice as Autmaran, "*I ride at the Commander's side. I ride to depose the Empress – and I will not stop short. Not when my bones break, not when my blood falls. Not even when I can no longer raise my limbs to fight. All of us will fight –*" taking their cue, Tomaz, Leah, and the others rode forward, reaching through their own Aspects and adding further light to the bonfire that lit up the mountaintop – "*until no drop of blood is left in our bodies. We will fight, and even if we die, we will make the Empire remember us!*"

"*Who will join us?*" Autmaran cried. "*Who will blaze a trail through this waiting army at our side?*"

The army roared again, men and women shouting affirmations that they would follow even if it meant their death. Hands gripped swords, spears, and shields with renewed determination, and everyone from the lowliest Commoner to the best-trained Rogue had fire in their eyes.

Raven turned to face the Imperial army that was nearly upon them. He raised Aemon's Blade, and charged down the mountain.

Chapter Twenty-three:

Lucien

The Kindred fell over the mountain ridge in a crashing wave. Seven glowing figures, one wearing a crown that shone like the sun in the dark of night, were the first to ride out, and the rest followed on their heels. The Imperial army, heretofore undefeated and certain of victory, faltered in mid-stride. The wave crashed down on them, and in seconds the booming roar of a giant's voice and the thunderous howls of multiple thousand desperate Exiles split them down the center, rending the first dozen Imperial ranks asunder and leaving hundreds of dead or dying scattered across the ground.

The Kindred passed through line after line, sending ripples out before them. Raven and Autmaran were shouting Commands at the top of their voices, forcing men to throw themselves out of their way. The Visigony tried to engage them, but as soon as the first bulk of the Kindred army was past, the Elders rode forth and cried out ancient words that forced the clockwork men to fight those whose strength matched their own.

Raven rode with his mind open and soaring in a thousand different directions. He cut down one of the Visigony with nothing more than the words rolling from his mouth, simply Commanding the Daemon beneath it to dissipate. In an explosion of energy, the beast disintegrated, leveling Imperial soldiers for dozens of yards around it. He caught an arrow in his bare hand, his gauntlets having burst and split from the power of Lorna's Aspect. He grabbed a spear from a fallen Imperial and brandished it above his head before throwing it at another of the Visigony with such power and speed that it passed through the clockwork man's chest, spewing out flashing gears and twisted metal along with a gout of black blood.

The enemy in front of them began to run, turning and fleeing before them in confusion, as Raven, his companions, and the Kindred attacked with the vicious resolve born of a thousand years of hatred and oppression. Nothing could stand before the charge, and when the Imperials split and fled, running sideways off the trail into the mountain forest, the path across the Plains was clear and the race was on.

Raven and Melyngale hit the ground at the base of the Elmist Mountains and shot across the Plains. The Kindred raced behind them, steering around hidden chasms and unexpected dips, racing toward the dark city of Lucien as the clouds above them roiled and jostled one another for position. Horns sounded: Imperial horns that brayed out the call to reform and pursue, and Raven bent low over Melyngale's neck, praying for speed. Dark thoughts ran through his mind, coming from the crown, but he tightened his grip on the Blade and silenced them.

The city of Lucien rose before him as he led the Kindred through the night, and his breath caught in his chest.

He had come home at last.

He suddenly felt like two men squeezed into one body, the way he did when he absorbed a life. But this time it was his own memories, coming back to him across the divide of what felt like dozens of years. He remembered his first procession through the city streets, his coronation, and above all looking out from the Fortress over the Plains toward the mountains, wishing to see the world.

The city was a vision, something taken from the landscape of a dream. A single road connected it all, starting to the east, and curling inward one level at a time in a long, graceful loop. That road was bisected by two long, straight boulevards that ran east to west and north to south, two straight melody lines to give it form, marking the foundation of the city as both austere and indulgent, curved and straight.

The city built and surged as the spiral continued inward, a masterpiece symphony rushing toward its higher forms as the painted wood structures and simple black shingles of the Commons quarters gave way in fits and starts to sleek, plastered walls with tiled roofs and lavish balconies. Still further in, the structures began to rise still higher, soaring fifty, one hundred, even two and three hundred feet into the sky. Wide paths and archways spanned the distance between them, layering one upon the other, huge suspended walkways that linked the houses of the Most High so that their feet would never have to touch the sullied ground the Commons dared to tread.

And then the towering crescendo, the climax of the entire Empire's ingenuity and might, the Fortress of the Empress itself, piercing the sky and clouds like a tower built to reach the heavens. Made of seven inter-locking spires, the Fortress stood as the ultimate bastion of Imperial might, and anyone who had stood in its shadow knew what it was to be an insect beneath the boot of a giant. All who looked upon it trembled, and knew the Empress to be a god.

Raven tore his eyes away from the city and dared to glance behind him. The Kindred army was racing across the Plains in his wake, the cavalry flanking the infantry and lending help where possible. Already they had begun to split into their assigned groups, with captains shouting orders. When they hit the gates, they would be ready for the three-pronged assault.

Raven reached out farther, going past the Exiles, seeking out the twisted lives of the Visigony. He couldn't find them at first, but instead only succeeded in feeling the Imperial army, already regrouping with its eyes on the Kindred. Raven kept going, drawing on Leah's Aspect through the crown to give him farther sight.

There – three of them left, and coming hard toward them.

The Elders narrowed down their numbers at least.

He tried not to think about how many had died performing that task. Who? Crane? Ishmael? Ceres, Pan, Stanton? He shook the thought away and glanced at his companions as they rode beside him; they too were taking in the city, and he saw fear cross more than one face, followed by the realization that this might be the last time they were ever in each other's company.

They're looking at the greatest city ever built. Until now, I doubt any of them besides Tomaz really knew what they were up against, even when they fought the Children.

"GO!" shouted Autmaran.

He waved at Lorna and Davydd, Tomaz and Leah, and the two groups peeled off, followed by their separate forces, as the army split into three. Raven caught Leah's gaze one last time as she spurred her horse away, and he felt a sick sense of dread settle into the pit of his stomach. She disappeared from his sight and he turned back to face the city. The heavy cavalry rushed on like an avalanche toward the distant gates, the infantry running behind them as quickly as they could.

Autmaran and I will take the gate; it will be up to them to secure it.

As if on cue, whatever skeleton crew of guards had been left began to heave the wide doors closed, inch by inch, racing against the speed of the Kindred horses, taken completely unawares by the attack.

"We're not going to make it!" Raven shouted. "The gate is closing too fast!"

"We'll make it!" Autmaran shouted back. "Stay on my heel!"

He spurred his horse's sides once more, this time drawing blood, and Raven followed suit, the two of them riding neck and neck. They were within five hundred yards of the main gate, and had just merged back onto the long Imperial road that had led them here all the way from Banelyn.

"We won't make it!" Raven shouted as their horses' hooves rang out against the paving stones, adding to the already ear-shattering din.

"Yes, we will!" Autmaran shouted back.

Raven shot another glance to his left, then to his right. Both other parts of the army had disappeared around the edges of the city's outer wall.

"The gate!" shouted Tym.

Raven looked forward and saw the metal grill of the portcullis being lowered into place, just as the heavy wooden doors, so large they required twenty men to move, were being maneuvered into place.

"Five Rogue pairs – on me!" Autmaran called.

The soldiers behind them shifted, and Polim and Palum came forward with eight others as Tym fell back. They pulled ahead, galloping alone as they formed into a single column that could ride into the city through the narrowest of gaps.

"Shadows and light, shadows and light, *shadows and liiiiiight!*"

Autmaran, Raven, and ten Rogues shot through the opening just as the gate slammed shut and the portcullis crashed into place.

"Open the gate, and do not die!" Autmaran shouted at the Kindred. The Rogues set to work at once, and Raven watched in awe as they cut down the dozen guards in seconds, moving with perfect precision. Polim was the first to reach the gatehouse, and he and Palum cleared it. The gate reversed, and the other Rogues held their weapons to the throats of the gathered slaves – *slaves,* Raven thought, sickened by the collars and bare torsos that showed fresh whip lashings atop long-healed scars, *how long has it been since I've seen slaves?* – until they reversed the course of the enormous gates.

Alarm bells were ringing throughout the city, and already a panic had begun to spread. Raven reached out with his mind through the Talisman, the effect of it amplified by the crown, and felt the Visigony and the remaining Imperial Army coming for them from the Elmist Mountains, halfway across the Plains. He cast his mind the other way, into the city, and found the mental signature of thousands of Fortress Guardians spreading out in waves from the lower levels of the Fortress, taking to the streets with the bare few hundred common foot soldiers left in the barracks.

Shadows and light, the others need to take care of those Guardians or Autmaran will be caught in a vise.

The gate opened behind him, and the Kindred army poured in, the heavy cavalry pounding down the streets in carefully controlled squadrons, soon followed by light infantry and archer divisions gasping for breath and vomiting from sheer panic and exertion. Those who could, mounted and manned the wall – those who couldn't caught their breath in the bare handful of seconds they had to spare.

"Raven!" Autmaran shouted. "You have a job to do!"

Raven clenched his jaw and nodded. He pulled back on Melyngale's reins, and the Crown of Aspects glowed brightly atop his head as he drew on all seven Aspects. The Kindred watched him, and he reared Melyngale up and back.

"Buy me time," he said, his voice amplified by Command, *"and I will buy you freedom."*

Cheers and shouts from already ragged throats swept him onward as he spun and shot down the Imperial Road that led from the gate in a spiral toward the Fortress. He turned up a side street, taking the first in a series of shortcuts he'd learned as a boy that would take him directly to the Fortress. The Kindred continued cheering as he rode out of sight, but he did not share their enthusiasm.

This homecoming did not look to be a pleasant one.

Chapter Twenty-four:

Lucky Scoundrel

Davydd glanced over to his right just as the walls of Lucien blocked the charging column of Autmaran's force from view.

He looked back at the section of wall in front of his own force, just in time to see the portcullis slam down into place and the two enormous halves of the wooden entrance door swing shut. He reached out through the Aspect of Luck and golden lines flashed across his vision, pulling him, pushing him... upwards.

"UP AND OVER, FRIENDS!"

The soldiers behind him, a good number of them Rangers and Rogues, immediately shifted position, following his command. He and Lorna continued in the lead; Rogues pulled up alongside them to both their left and right, pulling corded ropes with attached collapsible grappling hooks from their packs.

Arrows started to rain down on them – but much less than Davydd had expected. He unconsciously spurred his horse to the left, and half a dozen arrows feathered the ground beneath his horse's hooves instead of the side of his body. He looked up and saw the gate was in a shallow alcove created by the wall, with two large watchtowers at either side, slightly sloped in ornamental fashion.

Davydd looked to his right back across the Plains and saw that none of the remaining Daemons had followed them. They must have headed straight for the main gate. It made sense – they had to know that they only needed to regain one gate in order to surround and crush the Kindred, and that gate was the closest.

He dove off his horse and threw the reins to an infantry soldier who had hitched a ride with one of the Rangers. The man caught them as he tried to catch his breath, the green and silver of his armor covered in dust and mud from their mad dash across the Plains. "Lorna!" Davydd called, looking for his Ashandel.

"What?" she snapped at him, her voice already coming from the direction of the wall. He spun toward the sound and saw that she had rushed forward with the other Exiled Rogues and was literally shielding them with her body, catching arrows with any part of her that could be interposed, be it flesh, armor, or bone.

"You're *crazy,* woman!" Davydd cried as he rushed forward, pulling a spare shield from the same infantryman who now held his horse's reins. The man gave a half-hearted shout of indignation and then let it go as he dove out of the way of more arrows. Davydd ran forward and interposed himself between Lorna and the wall, but she pushed him out of the way even as she ripped arrows out of her skin and threw them to the ground.

"We need to buy them time!" she rasped, the shouting only making the rough quality of her voice more pronounced.

"What, by making yourself the stupidest Ashandel to ever imitate a pincushion?! You can still die!"

"Says the idiot who rushed out to fight the Lion himself?!"

A brace of arrows *thunked* into both his shield and Lorna's breastplate.

"Dammit, you harebrained warrior diva! Cover yourself!"

"Watch who you're calling names you half-cocked ass!"

He roared out a laugh, and kept laughing even as a guard looked over the side of the wall and spotted them. In one smooth motion, Davydd unsheathed and threw Titania. The white blade caught the man in the chest and killed him instantly. Two of his fellow guardsmen caught him and pulled him back, twisting the blade inside his body.

The Aspect of Luck told him to *pull* the blade, so he did.

Stuck as it was, the sword remained trapped in the guardsman's body, and Davydd was ripped away from Lorna's side and pulled upward toward the lip of the wall with shocking speed while the guardsman's companions cried out in confusion as the body in their arms tried to pull away from them. They grabbed hold of their companion with all their might, stubbornly refusing to let his body go, which caused Davydd to shoot over the lip of the wall and collide with them like a bowling ball smacking a cluster of pins. As one, they slammed into the rocky battlements, the dead man's body still holding Titania captive.

Davydd managed to recover first, staggering back to standing. He smashed his booted foot into the face of the nearest guardsmen and felt his heel connect with bone. The man's head slammed into the walkway, and the man himself stopped moving. Davydd had lost his borrowed shield sometime during the startling ascent, so he switched to offense and unsheathed the dagger he wore at his belt. He dove for the final guardsman and opened the artery in the man's neck before he could free himself from the dead weight of his companion's body.

Well, that's one way to climb a wall.

With a grunt of effort, he pulled his sword from the body in which it was lodged and looked back over the lip of the wall. Lorna was staring up at where he'd disappeared with a look of horror on her face – as if she'd just seen the city eat him whole. He felt an insane urge to laugh.

"Lorna!" he shouted. "Catch!"

With a heavy swing, he threw Titania over the wall, straight for her. She jumped back out of the way, and it sank into the ground.

"Idiot woman, I said to catch it! Are you deaf as well as dumb?!"

She screamed something back at him that included the words "– you threw a goddamn *sword* at me you miserable son of a – ", but Davydd wasn't able to catch it all. His presence had been noticed, and five guardsmen were closing in on him in the uniform of Defenders, the common Imperial foot soldiers.

Seriously? They're being invaded by the whole damn Kindred nation and they put these idiots on the walls?

Golden lines splintered his vision, and he knew what he had to do.

I sure as hell hope she picked up the blade.

He hooked a toe under a fallen sword and kicked it up into his hand just in time to parry the first Defender's blade. He drove right into the center of the others, and when they shouted in surprise and cleared away, he ran through the watchtower door and forced it shut despite effort from the other side to keep it open. He crashed the bar down and into place, effectively barricading the door, and *pulled* on Titania.

Immediately, he found himself slammed against the door, and his lungs squeezed as though a giant the size of Tomaz was sitting on his chest.

Shadows and bloody fire, don't let me pass out before she gets here!

Shouts were ringing from outside, and he heard and felt pounding on the door. One of the bolts holding it in the frame popped up like a startled gopher. Stars began to wink at the edges of Davydd's vision as his heart beat in an awkward sideways manner that was exceedingly painful.

And then the pressure was gone, and Davydd heard, even through the thick oak of the door, a huge *crash* that sounded like metal smashing against stone. He stepped away from the door and grabbed the bar, still trying to clear his head and take a full breath, when the full length of Titania's blade sliced through the door right beside his head.

He fell backward, not even trying to dodge, simply shocked, and just barely managed to avoid being spitted on the end of his own blade. Shaking, he made it to his feet, threw back the bar, and opened the door. Lorna was hanging over the side of the wall where she'd ended up after Titania had shot over the edge.

Good thing she let go, she might have lost her bloody hands.

The five Defenders were still on the ground trying to figure out what the hell was happening when Davydd emerged. "Hello, boys," he said with a grin, feeling the gold veins pulse along the burnt half of his face. He reached up, grabbed

Titania's hilt, and pulled with both his arm and his mind. The sword came free just as Lorna pulled herself over the edge of the wall and unlimbered her axe.

Within seconds, the Defenders were down for good.

"Clever trick, right?" Davydd gasped, still trying to regain his breath.

"I'm not talking to you," Lorna growled back.

Davydd laughed and took off running as fast as he could toward the gate house itself. The Rogues on the ground had managed to make their way up the far side of the wall by the opposite watchtower, and they were attacking the Defenders on that side. A handful of archers along the top of the wall saw Davydd and Lorna approaching and shot at them. Two found their mark, piercing Lorna's arm and bare foot, but with a quick twist the arrows were out, and the wounds were healing. Davydd embraced the Luck Aspect as fully as he could, letting it direct his movements as arrows darted past him, hissing like snakes through the cool night air, and then he was among the archers, cutting left and right, the heavy weight of Titania swinging in deadly arcs.

Under the weight of two fighters bearing Aspects, the archers quickly folded and fled, retreating through the gatehouse, where Lorna and Davydd promptly followed them. There were Defenders inside, but in the tight quarters their numbers didn't matter, and Davydd and Lorna cut them down quickly.

"Go down!" Davydd called to Lorna as they dispatched the final man.

"We need to help the others!" she called back.

Gold lines danced across his vision, and Davydd shook his head viciously.

"*Go down!*"

She grimaced but complied and went for the nearest set of stairs, a winding staircase that was all in a steep, single column. They burst through the wooden door and found themselves on the ground at the mouth of the first road leading into the city. They were in a Commons area, and though many of the buildings seemed haphazard and shaky, the streets had obviously been kept clear and clean.

To their left was the gate itself, and a small alcove in which the winch that controlled the metal portcullis was situated. There were scores of thin chains lying nearby, and each was attached to the wrists or neck of a dead slave. There were nearly a dozen of them, and each had died in pain. They lay in the alcove, their sides and necks opened with hasty cuts that left red gashes smiling up at the clouded sky, their life drooling out around them.

Davydd bit back the wave of fury that threatened to overtake him and embraced his Luck, letting it control him completely, his only desire to wreak as much havoc as he could. He turned to the right-hand section of the wall, moving parallel to it from down below until he was directly in line with the Kindred and the Defenders fighting furiously up above. There was no smaller wall or balustrade protecting the Imperials from this side, and a cadre of bowmen could have picked them off like prize turkeys even from forty paces further back.

Titania.

"Open the gate," Davydd said quickly to Lorna, only pausing long enough to see her turn and go for the winch. He widened his stance, threw his weight forward, and launched Titania up toward the wall, where she sunk into the side of one of the Defenders, killing him instantly. As one, the two men flanking him looked down, saw Davydd, and started scrambling back for the gatehouse. Davydd *pulled* the sword back, and then threw it once again, killing a second man highlighted by the golden lines, this time at the front of the line. This man fell too, startling the others behind him so badly that they stopped in place and allowed the Kindred to surge forward. Davydd *pulled* again, just as he heard the sound of the portcullis winch winding up.

He glanced over and saw Lorna furiously attacking the winch, throwing her entire weight into it, the metal digging bloody gashes into her skin as she tried to perform alone a task that normally took a dozen slaves. She teetered just on the edge of raising the metal grating, but no matter how hard she tried, her strength wasn't enough. Davydd pulled Titania back to him, reversed the sword so he was holding the blade itself, and threw it backwards, pushing with his mind. The sword barely cleared Lorna's shoulder, but it did, and then a heavy *thunk* sounded as the pommel struck the arm of the handle and gave Lorna the last bit of force she needed to set the chains in motion.

Davydd pulled back on the sword, caught it in his right hand, and looked back up at the top of the wall. The Kindred there had finished what Davydd had started, and already they were chasing the remaining guardsmen through the gatehouse. Davydd went back inside to meet them, rushing up the stairs and killing the Defenders who weren't taken down from behind by the agile Rogues.

"Where are the others?" he managed to get out as he sucked down huge choking breaths. Only about half of the Kindred he'd seen on the top of the wall had come into the gatehouse.

"They dropped down the inside of the wall," said Tagel, a woman with brunette hair cut so short she was often mistaken for a man. "They went to help Lorna with the gate."

A ragged cheer came from outside, and the sound of heavy wood scraping against stone. Davydd and Tagel both grinned at the same time, and then dashed to the door. The gate was breeched – they were through.

"We've taken the gate," gasped Timon, one of the Rogues, as he ran up to Davydd holding the reins of his horse. "Should we bar it from the inside?"

"No," Davydd said as he watched his third of the Kindred army pour in, wave after wave flooding into the city. The infantry had all caught up by now, and it looked like the Scouts that had been charged with securing their flanks and rear had come as well. There was no sign of a following force.

The Imperials are all attacking that main gate… shadows and fire, Autmaran is going to have one hell of a time.

"No," he repeated, "pull all of the Kindred off the wall – the gate is nothing; the city is everything."

"Sir... you just want to leave it unguarded?"

"No," Davydd said.

"Then what should we do?"

"We destroy it."

He looked to Lorna, who was already standing tall again as her wounds healed. The final wave of Kindred passed through the wooden doors, and Davydd grinned at her. She nodded. Hefting her axe, she strode to the chain that held the metal grating of the portcullis, and with one huge swing, the valerium metal snapped through the metal links and sent the whole contraption crashing down.

"Bar the doors," Davydd said.

He turned, wheeling Aron around to face the city of Lucien.

Time to bring a little light to the city of shadow.

"Burn it, and follow me."

The Kindred lit torches and threw them against the doors with what was left of the oil from the gatehouse lamps. The slicked wood caught quickly, and soon the blaze was fierce, so hot that the iron bars of the portcullis and the wrappings that reinforced the doors began to warp, flow, and meld. No one was getting that gate open again now.

The clouds above them suddenly darkened, and they all looked upward. Strange... they looked to be coiling in around the Fortress, as if something were calling them. Davydd pushed the thought from his mind and spurred Aron forward.

Stop the ritual – that's our task.

He didn't know how to navigate the city, but he didn't really care. His objective was to get to the Fortress and find the cavern beneath it. He didn't know how he would manage to do it, but that didn't really matter either. With a third of the Kindred army at his back and Lorna by his side, there was nothing he couldn't do.

His luck surged within him, and he grinned.

Chapter Twenty-Five:

Innocence Lost

"Commander!" shouted a voice in his ear, bellowing over the cacophony. Autmaran turned and saw Jaillin standing beside him.

"Yes," he said, just managing to keep the irritation out of his voice. The man always seemed to yell with more force than was necessary.

"What are your orders, sir?"

"I'm trying to come up with them, man," Autmaran growled. "Go secure the gate however you can – and send me Polim and Palum!"

Jaillin saluted and ran as Autmaran turned to face the Plains. The Imperial army was coming straight for him. Most of his force was inside the city, either roaming the edges of the city and fighting what few guardsmen had been left behind, or else manning the walls in preparation for the coming onslaught; just under a third of them remained outside, still streaming through the gate.

Thousands of Kindred, and all dog-tired after that shadow-cursed run.

"FASTER!" he shouted, his voice cracking out across the blackened ground like thunder as he channeled as much of the Command Aspect as he could. But it wasn't enough: the remaining Kindred and Commons were already running as fast as they could without keeling over, their faces drawn and haggard. The Imperial Army was closing with deadly speed, the remaining three Visigony on their Daemons out ahead, flanked by rows of cavalry. As soon as they'd realized what the Kindred were planning, the three machine-men had spurred the army to action, forcing them across the field as quickly as possible and concentrating all of their force on the main gate.

Minutes ticked by as he watched, helpless. His heart hammered the inside of his chest so hard that he thought it might break one of his ribs.

We have to hold until Raven reaches the Empress.

They had to close to gates, it was that simple. There was nothing he could do unless they were safely behind the walls. If the Visigony regained the city, they'd be able to hold the gates and allow the rest of the army in. Once fighting began inside the walls, the Kindred were doomed. That gate had to close, and it had to close *now,* even if it meant sacrificing a few of the Kindred to do it.

And yet he was desperate to find another way. Each one of these men and women had come so far. Every one of them was willing to die for the cause, but... light, how could he throw them to the Imperials like that?

There was no choice, though. He gritted his teeth and turned to call Jaillin back, ready with the orders, but stopped at the last second.

A ripple parted the running wave of Kindred. Autmaran squinted through the dark night, cursing the wavering light of torches for throwing shadows and the harsher chemical lights of the city streets for ruining any hop of night vision. He caught sight of a group of Exiled infantry that had stopped and turned, standing their ground as their compatriots rushed past. The Scouts and the remnants of the main force split around this hard, compact core, diverting to either side like a stream around a boulder. Autmaran saw pikes and spears among them, as well as swords; he saw flashes of red and black, along with brown homespun and the cast-off colors of Tyne mixed with the green, silver, and black of the Exiled Kindred. Stannit, the huge bear of a man who'd been captain of the guard in the Imperial city of Roarke, strode forward and beat his armored chest, shouting wordlessly into the night.

"The idiots are going to get themselves killed!" Polim shouted as he ran up beside him with Palum, both staring over the wall.

The man isn't stupid... why would he make his stand like this?

Suddenly lessons he hadn't thought of in years were running through his head for no apparent reason, lessons drilled into him by his former mentor, General Goldwyn.

Everything is balanced. In life, as in war and battle, you need to work with opposites. Everything, no matter how powerful, has a weakness. The bigger the strength, the bigger the weakness, if you can find it.

Autmaran changed the angle he was looking at the battlefield, and realized that while the area fifty yards away from the wall was still cloaked in shadow, the whole area directly in front of the gates was lit brightly by the torches he'd ordered mounted on the walls for visibility. There was even a brazier over the wide gate itself nearly the height of three men in diameter that, if lit, would make it even brighter. Goldwyn's voice continued to roll through Autmaran's head.

Take, for example, Daemons, the deadliest of the enemy's weapons. They are immensely powerful, and in an area of their element, nearly invincible.

The remaining Visigony, Vynap at their head with Sylva close behind, barreled down toward the group, throwing the last of the straggling Kindred out of their way. What was happening? What was the last piece of the puzzle here that someone else had already put together? Were the idiots insanely brave, or did they have a plan after all?

Daemons cannot resist their opposite, Goldwyn continued. *Earth Daemons lose power when pushed into the air, Fire Daemons cannot cross water, and a torch thrown on an Ice Daemon will leave a mark worse than a burn on flesh.*

The last of the Daemons suddenly shot up into the sky and swooped down from overhead, landing on a number of Kindred along the walls. They shot arrows at the creature, driving it back, and as it pushed off again, Autmaran saw the ghostly figure and huge wings of an Air Daemon, its white skin so tight around its body that it looked like an enormous, skeletal bat.

"Sir!" shouted Palum. "Commander, what do you want us to do?"

The only way to defeat a Daemon was with weapons made of valerium, but there were precious few of those left, and he'd have to commit soldiers outside the gates. He could close the gates like he'd planned, but that would leave hundreds still outside to be slaughtered. He had managed to catch one Visigony off guard during the charge and Commanded the Daemon to dissipate, but there was little chance of repeating the same trick against them now.

"Sir, what do we do?"

Autmaran turned to Palum, but his mind had gone completely, utterly blank.

I'm not Goldwyn. His lessons can roll through my brain all they want, but I don't have his genius. If he were here, he'd know how to win. They deserve him, not me.

"SIR! *What are you orders?*"

Goldwyn wouldn't have needed valerium; he would have said Autmaran wasn't thinking about the problem the right way. Any problem with just one solution was a problem that hadn't been thought through thoroughly.

Great strength... great weakness.

Autmaran felt a shock go through him that he didn't fully understand, but without question he was up and running along the battlements, following the sudden understanding he had blazing through his head, the sudden certainly that whatever Stannit and Jallin were doing wasn't random, wasn't a desperate final call for death. He glanced back over the side of the wall again, out over the field, and watched the group of soldiers standing there shift as they prepared for the Daemons to crash into them, moving just enough to reveal a smaller figure standing beside Stannit. Autmaran pulled up short, halfway to the brazier.

He started screaming into the wind that blew over the wall. He felt cords and tendons tense throughout his throat as he shouted Commands with all his might, but the gale produced by the diving Air Daemon threw them back into his face. He continued shouting, his voice rolling out with earsplitting power, and still he wasn't heard. He rocked back on his heels, dazed, and realized the boy was on his own.

*   *   *

Tym pulled his sword from his sheath and stared wide-eyed at the Daemons rushing toward him. His body, now the long and lanky form of a seventeen-year-old, still jerked and shifted in odd ways when he tried to use it, and now he was shaking so badly that he was having trouble keeping his grip on his sword.

Prince Raven needs time – and I can't let the Visigony stop him.

He saw the truth now, everywhere he looked. On every face. Like he could read the heart of everyone around him as easily as he'd always been able to read a book. And what was more, he could see through the Bloodmage enchantments of the Daemons, could see right through their skin to the runes that held them together like enormous jigsaw puzzles or archways with intricately placed keystones.

And in that truth, he knew how to stop them.

Light – and then valerium.

His hand clutched the sword in both hands, though his sweat made the wire-wrapped handle slick. Tym had secreted it away when they'd gone north in case he needed it to protect Mr. Davydd. It was the only sword he'd known about, the only one that had been sharp and unspoken for – the sword Prince Raven had practiced with in Vale while Tym, hidden in secret alcoves, had watched.

He is Aemon's Heir for true. He can fix things. He needs time, though.

And so he had told Stannit what he had seen as they raced across the Plains of al'Manthian, and he had told Tym what they would have to do.

"Here we go!" shouted Stannit. "Those with valerium to the front!"

The ranks opened and the few men and women who possessed valerium weapons popped out of concealment. They were mostly Rangers and Rogues who had lost their Eshendai or Ashandel and had no desire to live past this battle. Tym could see the truth of their grief written on their faces, and felt sorry for them. Everything was so plain to him now, everything so clear, and there was so much sadness.

He hefted his own valerium sword, heavy and curved with a single sharp edge, and turned to Stannit. "Don't forget the fire!" he said, trying to speak over the shouting and screaming going on all around them. Someone was calling his name, but he blocked it from his mind, knowing if he listened he'd be trapped.

I'm sorry Autmaran, sir.

"FIRE!"

The archers they had recruited lit their arrows in burning torches and loosed them through the air. As the two remaining Shadow Daemons neared the gate, Sylva and Vynap sitting astride them, the last of the torches burst into light and the brazier on the gatehouse itself caught flame in a flash of glory, illuminating everyone with sudden light. As one, the two creatures faltered, stumbled, and threw black hands across their formless faces. Screams like a thousand tortured children rent the night as the Daemons shrieked in pain. The flaming arrows hit the apex of their flight, and fell, striking the exposed, inky flesh with hissing sounds as the light burned the creatures.

"CHARGE!"

Stannit and Jallin were the first to cross the distance, moving almost simultaneously, but Tym came on right behind them. The first Daemon swung its fist in rage and pain, and Tym felt the wind blow his hair straight back from his head. He pulled back his sword, praying to the seven angels that guarded the Veil path that his new awkward body wouldn't get in the way, and stuck the blade up in front of him as he ducked beneath the creature's reach and ran headlong into its abdomen.

The valerium flashed like fire, and the Daemon screeched in pain, spinning about and striking its fellow by accident. A chunk of the darkness above Tym fell off, and he found himself suddenly covered in black liquid that was choking him, closing off his mouth. He felt the ground rumble beneath him, and realized the Daemon had fallen to its knees. Moving as fast as his legs could carry him, lungs burning as if he'd inhaled salt water, the boy ran. He emerged from underneath the shadow, only to find himself facing an entire army of stunned Imperials.

For an instant, he just stood there, staring dumbfounded at the men lined up behind the Daemon, all of whom were watching in shock as the Visigony fell to the surprise attack. And then he was running, stumbling, falling backward, as the men shouted and broke rank, screaming murder at him.

The larger of the two Visigony rose in front of him, thrown from his seat on the back of the Daemon he rode, and Tym saw the truth of his name.

Vynap, the second of the Trium.

In his fall, the man-machine had lost the strange gold visor-helmet he had worn, and Tym felt horror and revulsion battle inside his chest and stomach as he looked upon the shell of what had once been a man. The Visigony's eyes were glass spheres through which light was collected, its mouth no more than a gash of empty space; open holes with rounded edges existed where its ears had been, and its nose was made of two slits in a metal mask. Gears clanked and whirled inside its chest, visible to Tym's eyes as he reached through the Aspect of Innocence, seeing the truth of the man before him, seeing him for the desecrated body he had become.

The two stood staring at each other for less than half a second that felt like an eternity: purity facing corruption, innocence gazing on depravity. They were seeing in each other polar opposites, and both were captivated.

And then time sped up beyond all recognition, and the Imperial army surged forward, making for the gates, ready to bash down the walls with their bare fists. Arrows shot from the sky, the Kindred on the walls trying to pick off the men on the periphery of the battle. The Air Daemon crashed down from above, folding its wings as it dove at the gate, smashing itself against the portcullis and wooden doors, which began to give way under the onslaught.

But Tym's focus blocked out all of this as the machine-man before him raised a scimitar and swung for his head. The boy evaded the blow, diving over the downed body of the Shadow Daemon even as the creature pushed against the ground, rising once more. But as Tym passed in front of it, he saw Stannit step up to the creature's head, gesturing frantically to Tym. With a mighty heave, Tym threw his valerium blade through the air to the former Roarkeman; Stannit caught it by the handle, spun it over his head, and sunk the whole length into the Daemon.

The creature folded in on itself, and then shot outwards.

Vynap disappeared as the shadows engulfed him, and Tym was thrown back a dozen feet. The first half dozen lines of Imperial and Kindred soldiers alike were flung off their feet and deposited on the ground as shadows knifed through them, rending armor and ripping flesh. Tym saw this and ran for dear life, tripping over a fallen soldier as he went. He looked around for Stannit, who had been with them since Roarke, and saw him, split in half, his eyes staring at the sky as smoking gears, all that remained of Vynap, rained down around him.

To kill a Shadows Daemon is to die yourself.

Arrows, lit from the brazier by the archers on the walls, launched into the sky, and Tym watched them as they soared like fireflies through the night.

It was only then that he realized his vision had begun to go fuzzy.

He looked down at his side and saw blood flowing from a hundred different cuts, each barely the width of a finger, and narrow as a piece of parchment. The

Daemon's essence had cut him as it had gone past; he might be able to make it back to the gate, maybe find a Healer –

But the thought died as the second Shadow Daemon, riddled with wounds and screaming in agony, rose up between him and the gate. Tym realized he had moved without thinking about it, and that he was now holding the valerium sword, his hands no longer shaking as they grasped the hilt.

Did I pick that up? When did I...?

He looked down and saw he was standing in the remains of Stannit, and had to fight back the need to retch. The sword was slick with blood, but it still shone like a white beacon in the dark night.

A swelling roar, like what the stories said an ocean sounded like, rose behind him. The Imperial army was still coming, trampling over their wounded and dead, and what was left of the small Kindred force outside the walls was scattered and broken. Captain Jaillin was still alive, but he was limping away, trying to rally what men still lived as the Air Daemon soared once more up into sky, ready to slam down one final time into the gate. One more blow would stave it in completely, and everything would have been for naught.

Tym caught a flash of motion from the top of the gatehouse battlements, and saw Commander Autmaran, his bald black head glowing with a white halo that shone so brightly it looked like a minor sun. Autmaran was beckoning to him, shouting what looked like words of encouragement, telling him he could make it back.

But Tym knew the truth.

He raised the sword and ran forward, using his new lanky body to cover the ground quickly, just as Sylva, the last of the Trium, turned his Daemon to lead the charge against the walls, forcing the creature through the harsh light coming from the brazier and torches. Tym ran forward, as if in a dream, and sank the valerium blade into the second Daemon's heel, all the way to the hilt.

The creature screamed into the night, and Tym felt his hearing go, shattered completely.

It is a good thing, he thought to himself, finding something positive like he always tried to do. *It means I don't have to regret losing the sound of music.*

The Daemon stumbled and fell to its knees, and Tym managed to pull the valerium blade back out of the creature's skin. It came out easily, in fact, as if repelled by the shadowy flesh. Tym climbed onto the creature's back, just as Sylva turned and hissed at him, slicing through the air was a sword of his own that cut a deep gash in Tym's unarmored chest.

Flaming arrows flew from the walls, no longer fireflies in the night but streaking comets that burned afterimage trails across his vision. They rained down, striking both the Visigony and the Daemon as the light from the torches, the braziers, and Autmaran himself, streamed over the battlefield and broke through their terrible strength.

There is light, Tym smiled*, and it shall always win.*

He raised up the sword, wrapped two hands around the hilt, and even as he saw Sylva come to take his head, he plunged the blade into the place where the Daemon's heart should be, parting the inky flesh as if it were true flesh, not the stuff of shadows. Even as the sword plunged home, arrows fell from the sky and pierced Tym in the shoulder, knee, and forearm. They burned, and made him hurt more than he'd ever hurt before, but the fire also touched the Daemon, and that was good.

The Daemon screamed again, writhing around the blade, and then pulled inward with a rush of shadows, knocking Sylva aside. The Air Daemon dove, brushing aside the arrows the Kindred shot at it, ready to crash into the gate one final time –

The Shadow Daemon exploded into a thousand razor-sharp shards of darkness that shot out over the field before the gate, dropping the enemy in droves, and piercing the side of the Air Daemon as it soared by overhead, leaving it to crash head-first into the wall. Jaillin and his remaining force attacked it, spitting it with valerium blades, pulling the final Visigony from its back.

The final image Tym saw as the blood drained out of the hundreds of cuts all over his body was of the Kindred cheering, and Autmaran staring, astonished, at what had been, barely fifteen minutes prior, a battle the Kindred had no hope of winning.

I'm the helper.

Tym smiled, and died happy, knowing it was true.

Chapter Twenty-six:

Exiled Guardian

"TOMAZ – ON YOUR LEFT!"

Tomaz turned and swung Malachi without hesitation; the huge swath of steel ripped into and through the body of a Death Watchman with a sickening crunch that severed the construct's spine and broke the enchantment holding it to life.

"Shadows and fire!" Tomaz roared. "How many of them are there?"

"Enough to keep us busy, that's for damn sure!" Leah shouted back.

The Exile girl's daggers flew through the air, deadly foot-and-a-half steel spikes, and sank into the neck of two separate Guardians held up in battle with a dozen Kindred. The giant men collapsed; the group of Exiles gave out a ragged cheer and moved on.

"Tomaz!" called Leah. "Anything look familiar?"

"I've been gone for twenty years!" he shouted back, saving a soldier from decapitation with a quick backhand slice that ended an Imperial life. "I think the best I can do is point us on in a general 'that way' direction!"

Leah's daggers whizzed past him, sinking into the eyes of two separate archers with bows trained on Tomaz's back.

"Wait – look!"

Tomaz turned and saw soldiers herding men and women out of their homes, pushing them through the streets with frantic haste as they eyed the approaching Exile force. Leah and Tomaz both launched into motion.

Arrows rained down, and he realized there were archers stationed on the rooftops.

"Leah – up!"

He pulled up short and held his hands out and down. They'd done this a dozen times before, and the moves were almost mechanical by now. She ran for him, landed both feet in the cradle of his hands, and pushed off just as he launched her with a huge, full-body throw. Powered by the Aspect of Strength, the Exile girl shot up to the height of the rooftop in a matter of seconds, caught the archer, and threw him down into the street as she switched places with him. She dashed off along the rooftops, already throwing her daggers out before her as she went, the steel blades winking in the harsh chemical lamppost lights.

Tomaz continued on below, leading the surging tide of Kindred as they crashed into the group of soldiers separating them from the Commons. Malachi cut through the air left and right, and the soldiers, barely two score, shouted and broke as soon as the full weight of the Kindred force crashed down on them.

"Run for the main gate!" Tomaz shouted to the gathered Commons, all of whom seemed ready to go anywhere but the way they were being forced. They began to stream past him, and were shepherded toward the front of the city by a number of mounted Scouts who appeared from the south side of the city and began to ride alongside them like sheep dogs protecting their flock.

By the Veil, I hope Autmaran's secured that gate.

Tomaz and a large bulk of the Kindred chased the fleeing soldiers down a side street, and then through a series of alleyways, trying to catch them before they managed to regroup. They caught up to them as they rounded a final bend, and though they turned to fight him with the determination of men who knew their time was up, the Kindred made short work of it.

The final man fell to the ground before him. He turned, trying to discern his location, and saw that he and his gathering force were now in the shadow of the Fortress itself. Old, old memories came back to him as he took in the faded stone and mortar of the street, saw the slightly crooked path it took. He knew this street, knew this view of the Fortress. The Blade Masters trained in the central tower, behind the one he now faced. This was the way they took through the sprawling city, the quickest way to get from the main gate through the towers.

I knew where I was going all along.

He turned, scanning the hundreds of faces along the road behind him.

Where's Leah?

The thought came to him out of the hazy shadows of confusion left when the heat of battle faded. He scanned the rooftops and saw her nowhere. That didn't make sense – she must have followed him. It was an incongruity that could not quite penetrate his thoughts to the level of understanding; when they fought, they were always near each other. How had they been separated?

"Where's Leah?" he asked the nearest man to him, a Rogue bearing the dagger sigil of an Eshendai. He was holding his shoulder, where he had tried to tie a scrap of his own uniform across the bleeding gash left by an enemy sword.

"I haven't seen her since she went up on the roofs," the man said.

The roaring call of a charging force ended their brief conversation, and both of them snapped their heads around to see a fresh wave of Imperials emerging around the corner of the long, circular boulevard to the right of the alleyway. Tomaz gritted his teeth and raised his sword. The Kindred followed suit, and as one they burst onto the main boulevard and hit the force of Guardians and soldiers in the flank. He broke through the line easily and dispatched a number of Guardians who were all taken completely off-guard by his Aspect-enhanced strength. He saved a dozen Kindred and gained more, and used it to redouble his efforts.

They emerged again onto the long circular boulevard that curled around the city, and suddenly Tomaz was having déjà vu. Memories of this patch of the city came back to him with a sudden shock, and he remembered running down this street as a child, remembered too the fist of Guardians who had come one morning to take him away.

He snapped out of the memories just in time to see a group of Guardians retreating down a side street, breaking off into smaller fragments that would be hard to follow.

"This way!" Tomaz called, gesturing toward the side street. The Kindred followed him without question, Tehanyu and Likal, the Eshendai-Ashandel pair of officers below Leah and himself, spread the word, and were the first to run to his side as he disappeared down the street.

He remembered this road. He had walked it over and over.

First as a Guardian… and one last time as a Blade Master.

That train of thought led him back to Leah, and he felt again her absence. She wasn't dead – she couldn't be. He would know, he was sure of it. Somehow, he would know.

They met a group of Defenders and cut through them with little trouble, then burst out of a side street back onto the circular boulevard. They were in a section of the industrial complexes with smokestacks that pushed against the sky and disappeared into the haze that hung just below the clouds.

The Fortress loomed before them, only a few streets away.

"Attack!"

The sound came from Tomaz's left, and he turned as one of the larger bands of guardsmen came rushing toward them. The Kindred force moved to meet them, but as they did, Tomaz heard the scrape of boots on stone and the rattle of unsheathing swords to his right. The Kindred were caught in a vise. He went for the second group as most of the Kindred went for the first. He cut down two men in a single swing and sent another half-dozen running wide. He brought up Malachi again and moved forward –

"Leave that one – he's mine!"

Tomaz froze as he heard the booming rumble of a voice, a sound that shook his bones even over the tumult of battle. He turned, and had to raise his eyes; the man standing across from him was his own height, not the shorter stature of even most of the Guardians. He wore plate armor with spikes at the elbows, shoulders, and heels, and shone bright white even in the dim light of the torches. The best of the Blade Masters took pride in wearing white armor to battle, armor that would show their skill in killing. Only those who were inelegant, only those base enough to be called *soldiers*, had to kill while spilling blood on themselves.

The man's eyes were as pure, blind white as his armor and long, flowing hair; shining red Bloodmage runes were carved into the skin of his temples, granting him sight even after he'd lost it. Rumor said that the new sight saw deeper than normal vision ever could.

Tomaz believed it.

"Valmok," the Ashandel growled, gripping the handle of Malachi more tightly. Memories began to trickle through the angry red haze of battle into the back of his mind, coming from some untapped reservoir he hadn't known was there. Valmok choosing him the day he'd been promoted to Blade Master; Valmok helping him forge his sword and teaching him the secret Forms; Valmok watching as the Blade Master tattoo, the brilliant blue-and-white star streaked with broken flecks of diamond, was etched into the skin of his back.

And underneath it all, like a hidden current in a rushing river, ran a torrent of fear. He pulled strength from his Aspect, trying to buffer himself, trying to drown out the thoughts, but it was no use. He might as well be a young boy again, standing before his old Master.

"I hear they call you Tomaz now," Valmok rumbled. "Did you choose the name immediately after you turned your cloak, or only after thorough consideration? I'm glad you couldn't keep the original, though I suppose you wouldn't want to. Just an annoying inconvenience, like your old loyalties, yes?"

Tomaz tried to steel himself, but he was shaken and couldn't quite grab hold of himself again. Shadows and fire, he should have expected this.

"It was my right to choose a name, as it was my right to choose my own fate," he heard himself reply, his voice matching Valmok's for intensity and strength.

Valmok smiled, revealing rows of large yellowed teeth.

I have the Aspect of Strength now – this will not even be a contest.

But the words rang hollow even in his own head. For all Valmok's size and strength, what made him so deadly was that he rarely had to use it. He moved with finesse and grace that would have made him a famous dancer in another age. Tomaz had fought skilled fighters before, Leah and Raven included, and more than held his own. His teachers had trained him in the Szobody Sword Forms and the Gunn Ax Forms since birth. He had faced Ramael the Ox Lord in single combat and held his own. But all the memories he had of sparring with his teacher were hard and angular, and each of them ended with him on the ground, sprawled out on his back, Valmok's blade at his throat. None of them ended in victory – not a single one.

He was a younger man then; his age will slow him now.

But as the Blade Master moved forward, his movements were not sluggish, nor were his reactions slow. Were it not for the white hair and eyes, he could have been a man half his age.

Even younger than me.

Valmok raised Jeremiah, the greatsword upon which Tomaz had modeled Malachi, and assumed the stance of Lion on the Hill. Tomaz flowed into Still Water Waiting, and began to breathe in controlled bursts, all senses tingling. They circled each other for a moment, watching each other for the slightest break in stride, the smallest weakness.

An arrow flew out of nowhere and passed inches in front of Valmok's face. He jerked his head back, a quick sure move that was hardly even there, but it was enough.

Tomaz rushed forward, Malachi flashing in the chemical streetlights.

Chapter Twenty-seven:

Raven Ascending

Raven struck the Guardian in the chest, pulling strength through the Raven Talisman and breaking bone even through the man's breastplate. A battleaxe fell from the giant's grip, and Raven picked it up faster than the eye could follow; he spun and buried it above the second Guardian's hip, slicing all the way to the man's spine.

Life drained from the Guardian and flowed into Raven, adding to the already raging torrent inside him that was, for the moment, contained and directed by Aemon's Blade. He dropped the axe to the floor where it rang against stone. The beautiful carpet beside it was smeared with blood and gore. Drawing on his gathered strength, he rushed on, his leather boots scraping against the floor, leaving echoes in his wake that reverberated in counterpoint to the flashes of his memories.

I ran down this hall the day Rikard gave me my first horse.

He turned left and pushed through a set of doors that had glowing red runes inscribed like enormous bas-relief carvings on either side; as soon as his hands touched the doors, the enchantment holding them shut broke, making a sound like shattering glass that echoed along the corridor. Raven pushed through, moving quickly.

The room he crossed was a cavernous hall, dripping in gold and silver gilding, watched over by life-sized marble statues of beautiful men and women in wall sconces. It was where he had first met Leah Monsunne, the young lady with whom he had been infatuated before leaving the Fortress.

What is it about girls named Lead?

He stamped down on the memories, trying to brush them under the edges of his mind, already a carpet of regrets and half-formed sorrows, but everywhere he turned another appeared, preventing such escape. He took the servants' stair, the one concealed in the corner, and ascended rapidly, drawing on the endurance of the men he had killed, using their strength to fuel his legs so as not to draw too much through the crown from Lorna or Tomaz. The memories of the men were mute and distant; after all this time, after all this killing, he had finally learned to numb the pain that came with it.

As he climbed the stairs, already halfway up the central tower of the Fortress, heading toward his waiting Mother, he felt the inevitability of what was to come.

Inevitable... how hard Goldwyn tried to help me escape that word.

He had become the thing he had always wanted to avoid. Even when he had still been in the clutches of the Empire, he had managed to elude it, managed to hold it at bay. But the darkness in his heart, no matter how deep he buried it, continued to build with every beat. His blood rushed through him like fire, throbbing behind his temples and burning in the pit of his stomach. His heart pumped hard with mingled anxiety and anticipation; anxiety that he would fail, and anticipation of the moment when everything, for good or ill, would be decided.

He left the circular way of the servants' stair and stepped out to find himself at the base of the final grand staircase that connected the tops of the other towers and went straight up to the throne room itself. Somewhere behind him, a clock struck the hour, beating out the stroke of midnight.

Time grows short.

He moved up the stairway, hoping everything was ready; hoping that the others had managed to find a way into the city; hoping that Autmaran had managed to secure the main gate and hold off the Visigony, somehow defeating the Daemons. And finally, above all, hoping that the Bloodmage ritual beneath the

Fortress had been disrupted, the enchantments left unfinished and the Commons saved from devastation.

Those thoughts took him the final distance, and he found himself standing before the entrance door to the Throne room, in front of doors carved in bas-relief with images of the Empress herself in haloed glory that took forty slaves to move.

Doors that now stood wide open, inviting.

Raven's hands began to shake, and something heavy fell with a *thud* into the pit of his stomach. His vision narrowed as his throat seized up and made it hard to breathe. He forced himself forward, every muscle telling him to run, to flee, every hair on his body trying to stand on end, quivering at every touch of air. His eyes darted left and right as he took in every last shadow, every last bit of information he could collect. He embraced the Raven Talisman fully – *not the Aspect, not truly, not after all she did to corrupt it* – and thousands of sensory details flooded through him: the sight of glinting gold and silver gilding; the empty sounds of unpeopled halls so often full of aristocratic Blood seeking favor; the smell of daffodils and lilies in floral arrangements that only just covered the smell of blood and death pervading the entire city.

He glanced sideways and saw the opening to the waiting chamber beside the door to the throne room, with the ornate mahogany door, behind which he had been attacked and abducted almost a year ago. His hands continued to shake, and he balled them into fists, trying to overwhelm the fear with anger, trying to drown it out in the bright flame of rage that had carried him so far, but he couldn't. That rage had burned out, and so too had his desire to save the Exiled Kindred; all of it seemed to mean nothing now that he stood here upon the doorstep of his childhood.

His feet moved woodenly, one in front of the other, and he passed the threshold of the doors into the throne room of the Diamond Empress.

The Prince of the Veil

The room was made of blackstone, the sooty black marble found only beneath the mountains that surrounded Lucien and bled into the Eyrie. The pillars that ringed the wide chamber were made of it as well, and inscribed with enchantments that caused the stone to shine with inner brilliance that negated the need for torches. The room itself was a heptagonal shape that seemed strangely modest compared to the rest of the Fortress, until one saw the Diamond Throne.

It lived up to its name. The Empress herself, using Bloodmagic that no one but the Visigony seemed to understand, had constructed it, and it shone and sparkled like the sun. It was a light that both illuminated and deluminated, making everything within sight brighter, but also harder to see.

She herself was there, of course, in her white gown and gleaming silver rings. She stared down at him from the throne, ringed with light and majesty, her flowing golden hair and perfect blue eyes watching him from a face that bore no lines, no scars, no hint of hardship; a face that was everything beautiful in the world, and somehow utterly mind-ruining in its perfection.

And there were the Talismans, embedded in the seven points of the Diamond Crown, each glowing faintly with its own light. They were no more than stones, indistinguishable from smooth pebbles one might find in any given stream or brook throughout the Empire; but for all their simplicity, they bore markings of power, letters of some long-forgotten language. Through them, the seven Talisman bearers were able to pull their power, using the markings etched into their skin by the Visigony, markings that were derived from the stone Talismans themselves.

She stood to greet him, abandoning the languid posture she had assumed, draped across the Diamond Throne, and the beautiful smile he still remembered etched itself across her face, like acid cutting through the perfect marble of a masterwork sculpture.

She spoke to him, saying only four words, but they hit him like a mallet upside the head. They rang in his ears like a bell, as a veil in his own mind was lifted, letting him remember what he had not been able to remember for almost a year, letting him remember what he could not quite remember on his own. He managed to remain standing, though the temptation to fall to his knees before her was overpowering, and he swayed with the desire. He grabbed hold of Aemon's Blade for strength, and hoped against hope that he was stronger than he knew.

"Hello, my little Azraeloph."

Chapter Twenty-eight:

The Wolf of Eldoras

Lorna rode beside Davydd as they led their third of the Kindred army away from the burning gate. The thick metal portcullis had already begun to twist and warp from the heat, making it an impossible snarl that would never open without days or weeks of labor. As they rode into the city, she knew that Davydd was leading them on instinct alone, headed for the distant Fortress that speared the sky.

Seven towers bound together by an impenetrable wall... how do we break into that?

As Lorna examined the structure, she knew instinctively that the central tower, the tallest and widest, belonged to the Empress. The area at the very top of that tower was expanded, and had balconies so large they were visible at this even distance, allowing a full-circle view of the city below.

When will she come out to fight?

The others had not addressed the issue, and Lorna had not brought it up, though now she wished she had. The question had begun to burn inside her ever since the clouds above the Fortress had begun to swirl and converge on the highest tower.

A huge shriek came from the distant edge of the city; a sound like a thousand nails dragged against steel, driving the thought from her mind.

Daemons. Gods, keep Autmaran strong and Tym safe.

Sudden lightning flashed across the rainless sky, and thunder rolled over them, seeming to constrict the air. The sudden smell of geraniums wafted past them, and as Lorna, Davydd, and their force of Kindred made their way closer to the center of the city, she became more and more on edge.

Tall buildings surrounded them now as they moved at speed along one of the side paths leading to the long circular boulevard that went from the gate to the Fortress. She and Davydd were mounted again, along with the Scouts, Rangers, and Rogues that still had horses, while the infantry soldiers were following as quickly as they could. They burst out onto the huge, circular boulevard, lined with towering structures and the houses of thousands. They passed a huge, ugly industrial complex of some kind with chimneys that looked eager, in normal times, to belch smoke into the dark skies of Lucien. The houses nearby were stained with soot, and the streetlights were an ugly fluorescence, alien and haunting, that left green afterimages on Lorna's vision even as she blinked and squinted to preserve whatever night vision she could.

Where are all the people?

The streets were too quiet – and there were signs of struggle everywhere: doors smashed in, clothing littering the streets, bodies left in the gutters.

Not like in Lerne – there they just set the trap and left, waiting for them all to die so that the Bloodmages could finish the ritual and bring the crystals after them. Not here – they had to do the dirty work themselves.

Lorna and Davydd shared a look as soon as they crossed the threshold of the first row of houses. They both knew what was happening. If Autmaran hadn't guessed it already, then he no doubt would soon, and hopefully he would send Scouts into the city if he could spare them.

Maybe that's why the Empress hasn't emerged yet... maybe she's waiting for the ritual to be completed.

Lorna couldn't imagine the woman being any more powerful than she already was, but she knew it was possible. If she gained the power of those crystals on top of the power from the Talismans, then there was no force that could stand before her if Raven fell. Even all of them together – Lorna, Davydd, Tomaz, Autmaran, Leah, and Tym – would be nothing more to her than a band of flies to swat away before she descended on Vale and wiped out the Kindred once and for all.

Figures moved out of an alley in front of them, and Lorna felt a chill go through her. She unlimbered her axe, reining in her horse, and heard swords free themselves from sheathes behind her as the Kindred followed suit.

Guardians. Hundreds of them. Each stood over seven feet tall, with blood-red plate armor and double-handed greatswords. They spread out, blocking the way to the Fortress. Davydd snarled low in his throat, raised his sword, and let it fall.

The Kindred charged, Davydd, Lorna, and those mounted in the lead. The Guardians ran to meet them, huge looming figures straight out of legend. The forces met, and in a matter of seconds, a dozen Kindred soldiers were dead. Lorna pushed herself to the front, drawing attention, and attacked with her axe, not even bothering to block or deflect blows that would only superficially wound her. Gray light flowed from her bare hands and feet, and she felt as though she would never need to sleep again, never need to rest at all. A sword bit into the exposed flesh of her neck, the break between her helmet and breastplate, and she retaliated by removing the Guardian's head from his shoulders. Her wound healed; his did not.

Davydd moved about beside her in bright flashes of brilliant gold that illuminated the night. Swords missed him, sure-footed Guardians aiming for his head stumbled over inexplicable obstacles, and through it all he danced with his valerium Titania.

The battle intensified, but with Lorna and Davydd at the center, drawing attention, the Kindred gave just as good as they got. But the Guardians died hard, and when finally Lorna realized they had made their way through the group, she also realized they had lost a full third of their Kindred force.

Somewhere, no doubt from a nearby square, a clock chimed midnight, and a second screech came from the gate; Lorna looked that way and saw an Air Daemon dive toward Autmaran's side of the city.

"Shadows and fire," she cursed to Davydd, "we don't have time for this – if we're not done by dawn – "

"On me!" Davydd cried, holding up Titania, the sheen of fresh blood that coated the sword shining sickly in the light of the chemical clockwork lights.

"For the Exiled Kindred!" cried one of the men, and the shout was echoed and shouted back. Davydd's side pulsed gold, the blackened skin seeming to grow darker, and he smiled, rearing back on his stallion, before he whirled and rode forward at full speed, Lorna once again at his side, ready to protect him should he fall.

He will not. Even if only one of us survives, it shall be him; this I swear by the blood of gods and men, and let them all be damned who try to keep me from it.

The next group they encountered was of common soldiers, rushing through the streets in the direction of the main gate, and unlucky enough to come upon this other group instead. Davydd and Lorna rode through them, cutting down a half dozen as they passed, and the rest of their force trampled them underfoot as they shouted and screamed down the road. More soldiers followed – they were closer to the Fortress now, halfway there. The streets widened, and battles began to take place in open courtyards, barren but for stone fountains that now ran red with blood and marble statues that stared on, indifferent.

They crossed through the mouth of yet another road, this one lined with carved statues of ancient warriors, and Lorna's eyes fell on a small rune, almost indiscernible in the darkness. It was etched into the base of a statue, and as they passed, she felt a thrill go through her, shocking her from head to toe and stealing her breath.

Bloodmage trap.

She opened her mouth to cry a warning, but before she could so much as utter a word, one of the Kindred soldiers stumbled into the plinth on which the statue stood, and a bloody red light lit him from below.

He looked down, gaping almost comically, until his head was removed from his shoulders. The entire street suddenly blossomed with light, bathing everything in waves of scarlet and ruby. Every single one of the marble statues, dozens in all, came to life and began to attack the Kindred.

Primal fear fueled Lorna to strike at the nearest statue with her axe, but the valerium blade glanced off, making a grinding noise that had her fearing the nearly indestructible metal would shatter like flawed glass. The statue swung its blade at her, nearly taking her head off, and she saw at least a dozen others do exactly the same to the Kindred surrounding them.

Lorna dove for cover, and, as she did, she saw Davydd still making his way across the road, dodging the statues. Imperial soldiers rounded the curve of the street and ran for them, shouting and brandishing swords. She stood and followed Davydd, dashing across the street and into the adjoining square, pulling deeply on her Aspect, gathering what endurance she could to help heal any injuries she might sustain. The Imperials clashed with the Kindred, rocking them back, and as Lorna turned to see what was happening, she collided head-on with one of the statues.

Red light blinded her, and threw her back. The statue exploded, taking down a wide patch of Imperial soldiers. Lorna picked herself up and, as mortal wounds in her side and neck mended themselves, she stared around, bemused. What Raven had said about the Aspects and the enchantments came back to her, and she knew what she needed to do. Turning, she ran to the next statue and *dove* for it. Both her bare hands grabbed hold of the smooth, flawless marble, and she bore the ancient warrior to the ground.

Again, upon touching her rough skin, the enchantment broke, and this time she was close enough to see the rune itself lose shape and disintegrate, cracking the statue into a thousand volatile pieces. She was blown up and into the air, soaring twenty feet only to crash down into a heap of Imperial soldiers, sending several flying like broken dolls.

She was up in a flash, and she could tell by the terrified eyes of the Imperial soldiers that her face and body were heavily wounded and healing rapidly. Raising her axe she struck out and cut them down where they stood, saving a number of Kindred lives in the process. More energy flooded into her – *I'm just like Tomaz; the more I save, the stronger I become* – and she turned and ran for where she had last seen Davydd.

She managed to break two more statues before she caught up with him, and saw him break one himself, having figured out the same trick. They had both lost their horses somewhere, though Lorna couldn't even begin to tell when or how. But they didn't stop: with the Kindred soldiers still behind them, many of them fighting so viciously they were nigh unstoppable, they rushed on, racing against time.

More evidence of destruction came with every twisting turn of the street now: more broken doors, shattered glass from windows, bodies, and even now screams from up ahead that had nothing to do with the fighting.

Have they started it yet? Has the killing begun? Are we too late?

They broke through to another square, this one bordered by even more impressive houses, though it contained no patrols. Looking up, Lorna found they were in the shadow of the Fortress itself.

Davydd stopped and turned back, grinning wildly, infecting the Kindred who had made it through with them; their looks of beleaguered terror turned to mimicked smiles of daredevil exhilaration. Davydd pulled his head back and howled like a wild beast, and the Exiles around him shouted and cried as well, and as one they crossed the square at a dead run, rushing for the looming Fortress, more of them following along behind, trying to catch up.

They'll follow the scoundrel to the ends of the earth.

The winding alley became a series of roads that intersected the circular boulevard and split into multiple levels. There were buildings with walkways between them towering hundreds of feet in the air; multi-layered mansions that twisted and warped and hurt the eye; industrial complexes big enough to hold a thousand Daemons with room to spare.

And as they went, more and more of their group found themselves drawn into battles with roaming Imperial squads. Lorna's axe was bloody from blade to hilt, and she herself was splattered with the blood of enemies, friends, and her own oft-healed veins. Guardians attacked them from shadowed alleyways with no warning, archers shot at them from the walkways spanning hundreds of feet above, and plain foot soldiers in roving bands attacked from every angle.

But they continued on, winning ground with every drop of blood they spilled, shouting defiance as one, each of them secure in the knowledge that if they fell, they helped the others go farther; they helped, in their own small way, to bring down the very city itself.

Death Watchmen, clad in the cast-off armor of their former selves, rose out of the shadows, no doubt summoned by the Empress herself to defend her tower. Guardians now roved the streets instead of soldiers, and Blade Masters, the most expert swordsmen in the entire Empire, commanded the forces arrayed against them. But Davydd and Lorna fought side-by-side, and, with the Aspects, won through every new challenge, following the road to the Fortress that only Davydd could see, the lucky path that would take them where they needed to go.

They burst out into a courtyard that surrounded a small mansion, into which thousands of Commons were being forced. Roving bands of Guardians patrolled the edges of the square, and there were archers on the rooftop, waiting for such a thing as the Kindred to appear.

Shadows and fire, we caught up to them.

She took a step forward, and pain ripped through her with shocking force, as if a thousand shards of glass had cut across her body. Her stomach clenched and her heart stopped. A terrible certainty came over her, so sharp and cutting it almost dropped her unconscious. She stumbled, and saw Davydd do the same beside her.

Tym was dead.

How can I know that? That's impossible.

But the feeling was undeniable. There was an emptiness in her as if something had been torn away, an emptiness that hollowed her out. The loss was so intense it was as if she'd lost a limb and was bleeding out.

"No," Davydd said beside her, stumbling forward. "No – not him!"

The Kindred force came up behind them and surged forward, only pausing when they realized both Lorna and Davydd had stopped. The Imperial force had noticed them; Guardians were loping forward, unlimbering their two-handed greatswords.

Lorna was so numb she couldn't think, could barely remember to breathe. But Davydd's face was a mask of fury, and he stood and shouted to the Kindred.

"KILL THEM!" Davydd roared. "FREE THE COMMONS!"

Lorna saw through clouded eyes Guardians pushing the people forward, cracking whips above their heads, forcing them through the large front door of the mansion, and her vision went red with the same fury that had overtaken Davydd. Sound seemed to disappear, and all she could see were the tears streaming down the face of a sobbing Baseborn woman whose child the Guardians were tearing from her hands.

Lorna remembered very little of what happened next, or how they won the battle, but when the clash of blades subsided, she found herself standing over a dozen hulking men that lay bleeding on the paving stones. Guardians, one and all. And there was something in her side... she reached down and grabbed a hilt, twisted, and pulled. The axe came out with a great gush of blood that immediately dried up. Gray light shone all around her, and she moved on.

She went straight for the open mansion doors, the doors through which the Guardians had taken the Baseborn. The surviving Kindred followed her like a green-and-silver tide. Inside was a clear path through the center of the expansive mansion, one lined with torn clothing, discarded shoes, and the blood of those with enough strength to resist. Lorna followed the trail, blood still pounding in her ears, righteous fury still filling her to the brim. She crashed through bolted doors, overturned beautifully crafted tables and chairs that stood in her way, and found, finally, at the far end of the mansion, a wall that had been torn away to reveal a hidden passage.

"Nice work," said Davydd, appearing suddenly at her side.

She grunted, and they moved down into the darkness, neither acknowledging what they had experienced nor questioning how they knew what they did. There would be time to know if it was real after the battle – time enough then to count the dead.

Not Tym... anyone but him.

They found themselves in a large stone cavern, lit by wan torchlight that revealed a single passage in the central room that led down into the earth. They crossed the room, getting as many of the Kindred in through the faux-wall as they could before descending. They left a dozen behind to bring what wounded they could inside the house and off the streets.

How many are left now? A few hundred?

The subterranean tunnel continued on and down, straight as an arrow, for miles; screams, echoed and magnified, bombarded them from down below. Lorna tried to quiet her mind but found herself unable. They were racing as quickly as possible, and she was already out as far ahead as she could be without leaving the rest of the group behind entirely, but it wasn't enough. They were still too late.

Halfway through the tunnel they encountered resistance, and Lorna felt like tearing her hair in fury. The tunnel was only wide enough for two to stand abreast, and because she was out front she killed almost all of the opposing force herself, staving in breastplates and helms with her axe. She didn't even try to block the swords that pierced her side and bent and scratched her already ruined armor.

She passed beyond, running, pounding the floor with steps that added to the tumult. She knew they were getting closer: the screams had doubled. She passed over a dip in the floor, ducked under an overhanging rock, and the tunnel widened, opening into a funnel that led them directly to the Bloodmage cavern.

The hollowed out space was bigger than Lorna could have imagined. The center of the gargantuan chamber was laid out in row after row of stone seats, carved out of the living rock. Everything seemed to glow with sourceless phosphorescence, perfectly highlighting the thousands of Commons that had been gathered by the Guardians of Lucien and led to a platform high above the rocky pews. One by one, they were being led to one of a dozen Bloodmages who were standing between two enormous crystals that glowed with a blood-red light. The Bloodmages forced the men and women to the ground, making them kneel before a third crystal, even larger than the other two.

And as soon as their knees hit the floor, the Bloodmages used black onyx knives to slit their throats.

Lorna watched, stunned into immobility, as a desperate man, eyes rolling in his head like a maddened horse or rabid dog, fought against the inexorable tide that led him up the walkway to the platform. He scratched and tore at those around him, attacking any and all living beings that he could see and touch, but it didn't help. The Bloodmages grabbed him, forced him to his knees, slit his throat to spill his blood across the crystal, and rolled his body off the platform. It fell, blood still spurting from his death wound, into a growing pile of bodies that rested in a pool of blood.

"Monsters," Davydd snarled from beside her.

He ran forward, eyes blazing hatred, and Lorna followed. A dozen Guardians turned to meet them, but between Lorna and Davydd they stood no chance. The rest of the guards, in the red-and-brown of Defenders, continued to whip and hack at the Commons, forcing them on faster. Lesser Bloodmages, those who weren't on the platform performing the ritual, shouted words of power at the huddled, screaming masses, words that burned anyone who dared move in any direction but forward.

Lorna moved toward them, ready to attack, but just as her bare feet fell on the cold, rough stone of the first step, the underground cavern seemed to *shift* around them, and a Bloodmage rune burned red and then disappeared beneath her.

The walls changed in a way that made no sense, and holes opened where there hadn't been any before. Guardians, each group headed by a Blade Master, surged into the cavern; Death Watchmen detached themselves from waiting shadows; shouts of surprise and terror sounded from the now-surrounded Kindred. The shadow armies of the Empress rushed forward, attacking the Kindred in waves, blocking the way to the Bloodmages who went about their grisly business.

"Break the crystals!" Davydd shouted at her as he ran back toward the other Exiles. "Do whatever you need to do! It's the only way to stop them – I'll buy you the time!"

He took off left, stepping into the center of the pathway down the side of the enormous rock cavern and planting himself at the head of the Kindred between two huge stalagmites that soared hundreds of feet into the air. The Imperials rolled forward, crashing into the exhausted Kindred, and Davydd was lost from view.

Lorna ran to the right, toward a long row of stalagmites along the right hand wall that gave a concealed way to the bridge that arched to the central platform.

She watched as another Commons was sacrificed, and then another. She caught a glimpse of Davydd as the tide of battle swept him away from her: he was fighting desperately to hold off both a Death Watchman and a group of Guardians. Lorna barely kept herself from running to his side.

She reached the end of the line of stalagmites, turned inward toward the Commons, and cut down the two Bloodmages nearest her. The others turned to her, grabbing hold of their Soul Catchers, and shouted words of power that had no effect, her Aspect pulsing as it shrugged off the magic. She strode through them and cut them down one after the other.

They turned and ran in fear, dropping their whips and shouting. She turned to the Commons men and women huddled before her. "Run," she rasped at them.

They ran. She turned and continued on up the line, shouting out a challenge for the other Bloodmages to come stop her. Her neck and foot suddenly sprouted arrows; she tore them from her skin and ignored the coursing pain. She engaged a Guardian who had come running for her, and though he fought with skill, her speed gave her the edge, and her axe cut him down.

More Commons were running now, but not nearly enough. Almost a hundred or so had made it to the edge of the amphitheater steps, racing to escape into the city, but thousands more were still being kept in check by Defenders and Guardians. She approached another Bloodmage and swung her axe into his chest, splitting him in two and ripping away his black cowl to reveal a bald and tattooed head. She moved forward again, and found herself at the edge of the bridge that led to the platform. Bodies were still falling to the distant ground as the Bloodmages spilt more and more blood, working with frantic strokes, like butchers trying to meet their quota.

Lorna shouted again for the Commons to run, and now the bulk of them were able to flee along the path she had cleared, giving her enough space to mount the bridge. As soon as she set foot upon it, every Bloodmage on the platform turned as one and began shouting enchantments at her, even as they continued to slaughter indiscriminately, throwing bodies into the pit where blood had begun to pool in astonishing quantity. Hissing, burning words flew at her as she approached, but they all passed over her like hot wind, momentarily ruffling her hair before passing on.

She raised her axe and cut down the first man, sending his body into the abyss where he had recently sent so many, and then turned to the others. Eight of them attacked, drawing cruel daggers, even as the final three continued sacrificing the dozen or so Commons yet to be freed. She cut the mages down easily, one by one, feeling a thrill of pleasure course through her as her blade ended each of them in turn. Soon enough, she was at the end of the platform.

One of the remaining Bloodmages – only four now – grabbed a Baseborn woman and raised his knife high in the air. Lorna dove forward, knocking him aside; the blade pierced her neck, and she felt it lodge in her spine.

The whole left side of her body went numb, and she fell to the ground. Her momentum knocked the Bloodmage off the platform, gaining her time and space, but a sense of foreboding swept over her. She dropped her axe and reached up with her right hand, grabbing the knife handle, but the blade wouldn't come free. She twisted, trying to pull it out, and pain shot through her, hot and blinding. She realized she had only succeeded in embedding the blade deeper.

There were only three Bloodmages left, the chief sacrificers, and none of them paused in their bloody work. Their onyx daggers continued to spill blood, and, as Lorna watched, the baby she had seen outside, no more than six months old, was pulled screaming from its mother's arms, and sacrificed. The tattooed face of the Bloodmage, half hidden by his black cowl, showed no remorse, no sign that he knew what he had done. Determination had set his square block of a jaw, and a light had infused his eyes that pulsed and throbbed in time with the blood-red crystal around his neck. He dropped the tiny body over the side, and grabbed the mother by her long, brown hair.

Lorna rose up, pushing herself to her feet with the working half of her body, rage forcing her past the bounds of human endurance. She grabbed the man by the throat and broke his neck with her bare hand, squeezing the life out of him, the coarse black fabric of his robe digging into his soft, pale flesh.

But the other two still continued. She realized now that they were chanting something as well, a string of words that seemed to electrify the air around them. They grabbed the mother, the final Commons on the platform, with frantic haste and held her over the crystal. She screamed once, but Lorna saw in her eyes that her heart had already stopped caring the moment they had slain her baby. The knives acted as one, and she died.

Lorna went for the mages, but they both retreated as she lunged forward, backing away as they watched something behind her with awe and reverence. Lorna spun, and saw the final crystal, coated in the blood of thousands, begin to pulse and throb like the others; slowly, all three crystals began to beat in time together, like a living heart.

That's what they were chanting. They were finishing the ritual.

Lorna crossed the last few feet to the crystal, knowing that somehow she had to try to break it, but collapsed to the ground. She couldn't even reach it – both the crystal and her axe lay just out of reach. She felt again the knife twisted in her neck, and recognized the debilitating rush of extreme blood loss weighing down her limbs, as the Aspect of Endurance was rendered useless. The dagger was stuck, and unless she found a way to extract it, her body couldn't heal itself.

She desperately arched her neck, feeling metal grind against bone, and searched for Davydd over the lip of the platform. She found him far away on the top row of the sunken amphitheater, besieged on all sides by Guardians with two-handed blades and Death Watchmen with sickly green eyes full of corruption. The

Kindred were retreating to cover the fleeing Commons, a number of Rangers pulling Davydd with them against his will, pulling him back to keep him from running for Lorna, where she lay fallen. His eyes met hers, and she was suddenly unimaginably sad.

Not even luck can do the impossible.

She faded away to the screams of her best friend and adopted son.

Chapter Twenty-nine:

Seeing

Leah realized that only the dead surrounded her.

Her breath rang hot and heavy in her ears, rasping through her raw throat like fire. Her heart beat a pained staccato against her ribs, and she turned and looked around the rooftop onto which she had ascended. Bodies were littered one atop the other, most of them with bows and quivers close at hand. There had been nearly fifty archers strung out across this section of the city; now there were none.

She didn't know when she had lost Tomaz, but it felt like years ago, lifetimes even. And then she'd felt the death of Tym – *Damn them! Damn them all!* – and what was left of her composure had disappeared. She had gone deeper into the city, all the time closer to the Fortress, seeking out vengeance.

She forced herself to release her hold on the Aspect of Sight and the blue, splintered visions of the future that had allowed her to bring down so many soldiers disappeared in a shower of brilliant sparks that left afterimage streaks across her vision. She breathed in, the air rushing through her burning lungs and clearing more of the bloodlust that had consumed her.

The Fortress towered above her. She stood on the highest roof of a series of buildings that were only a few hundred yards from the base of the towering Imperial seat.

Where is Tomaz?

Now that her bloodlust had cooled, she realized with mounting desperation that the one person she had always counted on, the one person who had always counted on her, could be anywhere by now. They had never lost each other in a battle before, never been separated for this long. Her skin itched with the need to fight beside him; it was part of the oath she had taken before the Elders that she would never leave his side when danger threatened. The longer they were apart the worse the itch would become, until she could barely think of anything else but returning to him.

She leaned over the side of the building and saw a way down to the ground through a series of balconies. She sheathed her daggers in one smooth motion and jumped down. Landing like a cat, she dashed forward again, launched herself into the air, and landed on the next balcony, and then so on story by story.

I'll find him at the Fortress. I can't spend time searching the city.

Her feet slammed into the ground on her final jump, sending shockwaves up her legs that should have crippled her, but were absorbed and dispelled by the Spellblade enchantment that bound her to her daggers and gave her some of their metal strength. Breath hissed in through her nose, and with it came the smell of soot, blood, and corruption. The city reminded her of nothing so much as a festering sore, a boil that had gone too long un-lanced.

She took off running, the leather of her boots thin enough to allow her to move naturally, but thick enough to cushion her against the hard stones beneath her feet. As she ran, she couldn't help but look up in wonder.

How can those buildings stand?

That was where the fighting now raged, she realized. It looked as though the original forces had split into roving bands of Kindred and Imperials, and the battle had become a citywide turf war. Soldiers fought for isolated blocks, hoping to join up with other members of their army, killing as many who wore the wrong colors as they could. It was what Leah had always feared would someday happen in Vale; except it was happening in Lucien, and the Kindred were the invaders.

If only Father had lived to see this, she thought.

A man fell off one of the arching bridgeways and crashed through a wooden gate in front of her, splintering it to pieces. She could not make out his colors, and whether or not he was Kindred of Imperial. It did not matter. She kept moving; her emotions were doused, the flames put out. There would be time to feel after the war, time to grieve. But until then, there was no place for sadness or regret. Feeling got you killed.

Two groups fought on the walkway high above her – she saw flashes of green and some of blood-red.

Guardians.

She threw her daggers and kept running; when she felt the blades bite down into flesh, heard the Kindred cry in excitement, she *pulled* the daggers back to her, and they came, heavy with blood, but still gleaming silver in the chemical lights of the street. She caught them just as she turned a final corner and came to a halt.

The Fortress blocked out the sky in front of her, soaring higher than she had ever thought possible. She craned her neck back to look at it, trying to take it all in, trying to grasp its size and dimension. It was made of ring upon ring of stone, with what looked like ribbons of steel laced all throughout, steel that shone bright, without a single hint of tarnish or decay even though the structure had stood for a thousand years.

And then she realized something more important: There were no doors.

She looked quickly to her right, and then back to the left, and a sense of panic began to batter against the tight-fisted control she had over her emotions. Raven was up there, and Tomaz was down below. She had to get inside.

Frantic, Leah dug deep inside her mind, pushing out thoughts and memories that floated across her vision. The blue light of the Aspect of Sight was nowhere. Panic quickened her breath, but she battered it down. Slowly, she took in the dank, soiled air of the city, trying not to care that it was rank with the smell of battle and spoiled humanity, trying not to care that the fate of everyone she knew and cared about might ride on her getting inside this Fortress.

She connected with the Aspect with a lurching, clunky motion that made her stagger and clutch at her head, but before she could do anything else visions were flashing before her eyes.

Tomaz was in a huge cavern, fighting a group of Bloodmages in black robes with glowing red hands, each falling before him one by one – *When is that happening? Now? Soon?* – before the scene shifted to the hulking barefoot form of Lorna and the burned and glowing shape of Davydd attacking the same underground chamber at the head of an army of Kindred – *They made it!* – before the world shook and turned sideways and everything blacked out.

Gasping, Leah shook her head, thinking the connection to the Aspect had been broken, but then the blue lines reformed out of nowhere and took her over again.

This time she saw what she hadn't been able to fully grasp before: the chilling black eyes and long, black hair of Raven. He ran, striking down opposing soldiers with Aemon's Blade, ascending the central Fortress tower. The vision shifted, and Leah felt as if she were being pulled along with it, as if the crown he wore, sparkling against his white skin, was trying to show her something.

Time disappeared and shifted, and Raven stood standing, silhouetted against the sky. Lucien lay in ruins beneath his feet, and the world shifted in ways that should have been impossible. Another form came from nowhere and met him, striking at him with eyes that burned, and the world unraveled into a thousand lines of brilliant blue light.

Leah came back to herself on the street, clutching her head in her hands, screaming as her entire body convulsed. When she became conscious of it, the scream cut off, and all she heard was the distant sound of battle.

And booted feet.

At the last second she turned to deflect the blow of the attacking Imperial soldier. His sword went wide as the girl he'd spotted turned out to be much more than he'd anticipated. She cut him down, snarling in his face.

She stood gasping over the body, pulled abruptly back to reality. She knew, with a sudden, sure knowledge that she wasn't meant to meet up with Tomaz, that she had been separated from him because she was being pulled somewhere else. Her gaze flew up, and she saw a low balcony jutting from the Fortress wall mere feet above the top of the aristocratic mansion to her left.

Somewhere a clock struck the hour of one, and the *gong* of the chime was a fist in her stomach, pushing her onward, forcing her to choose.

We have until dawn – that can't be much more than five hours away.

She thought of the height she'd have to climb in that time, how far she still had to go. She had no idea what she needed to do, no idea how to do it, and no sense of whether her life would be forfeit because of it. All she knew was that Tomaz would live, and Raven, the Raven she knew, would not.

I'm the only one that can bring him back.

Chapter Thirty:

Immovable

Tomaz dodged, only just avoiding Valmok's Jeremiah. He swung in the form of Morning Sun, but Valmok dodged as well, moving just as quickly as Tomaz, if not a step faster.

"Your swing is still strong," Valmok said with a straight face and gleaming white eyes, "but speed was always your weakness."

The Blade Master feinted left, and then reversed the blow, turning it into Leaves in the Wind, striking out with the blade in a series of lilting half-strikes. He reversed the blow again into a form Tomaz didn't know, and spun the blade around entirely to strike him in the temple with the pommel.

Stars exploded across his vision, and Tomaz stumbled backward, holding Malachi between them both, trying to slow Valmok even the slightest bit. But the Blade Master came on, striking Jeremiah against Malachi with such force it should have slipped from Tomaz's grip.

But red light flared and his grip tightened around the blade, keeping it in his hand. He used the momentum of the blow to turn the blade and bash his own pommel into Valmok's chin. The other giant's head snapped back, and he stumbled away. Tomaz felt a moment of elation.

"Well done," the Valmok said through a split lip. "Though it's too bad you only became a match for me once you inherited a Talisman. I had such hopes for you as a child – and now you can't even hold your own without help. Pathetic. If I die, it was not you that killed me – it was your stolen strength."

"You cannot taunt me into foolishness," Tomaz spat back, even though his former Master's words had affected him more deeply than he was willing to admit.

He hated it, hated to admit that he couldn't beat this man without the help of the Aspect. He had half a mind to let it go, to face him one on one...

He almost did it. He felt twenty years old again and invincible, and he wanted to prove both to himself and to Valmok that he could still perform the feats of his youth. He started to let go of it, to let the Aspect slide through his fingers...

And then he felt the life of a small, innocent boy, disappear.

It was as if a cord that had been tied to his heart was suddenly, inexplicably cut. He hadn't been physically wounded, but the feeling was the same. Somehow he could feel Tym's death, feel it as the boy fell, just outside the city. His vision momentarily faded and then returned, only to reveal Valmok rushing him, sensing the sudden weakness.

Malachi met Jeremiah in a flash of sparks. The clashing blow was so brutal that it would have snapped any lesser sword in half, if not broken the arm and wrist of the man holding it. But Malachi was not an ordinary sword, and Tomaz was not an ordinary man. The haze over his vision slowly cleared, and fury rose up inside him, directed both at himself and at his former Master. He saw Tym's broken body in his mind's eye.

This is why I left them. This is why I left the Empire.

He shouted wordlessly at Valmok and attacked with a sudden ferocity that pushed the Blade Master back. He pulled deeply on his Aspect, letting the red light wash over him, even as he felt tears of impotent rage build in his eyes and cloud his vision.

Tym – not Tym!

Valmok was struggling to keep up with him now. Each of Tomaz's blows carried with it the force of multitudes, and even the Blade Master's tree trunk arms could not hold off such an assault forever. Tomaz could see the muscles begin quiver and spasm with each new blow, and Malachi and Jeremiah were both notched despite their expert craftsmanship.

Tomaz reversed a blow, feinted left, and turned into Heron Cuts the Water a beat before Valmok could respond. Malachi sliced through Valmok's exposed throat. Blood cascaded down in a huge rush, and then began to spurt at irregular intervals as Valmok stumbled away, crashed into a thick stone wall, and fell to the ground. The Blade Master stared dumbly up at Tomaz, unable to comprehend what was happening.

"I may not be able to kill you without help," Tomaz growled as he knelt down and breathed into his former master's face, "but guess what? You're still dead."

He pulled back and swung Malachi, decapitating the man.

The body slid to the side and lay propped against the stone wall of a house. Tomaz realized the two of them had been fighting in an alleyway down the street from the main battle. The sounds of crashing metal and ringing shouts echoed over to him. But he stayed where he was, kneeling, trying to regain control over his emotions.

Dammit, why didn't the boy just stay where he was told?

He bit the inside of his lower lip, hard enough to draw blood. He couldn't believe it. He knew he shouldn't be surprised – this was war, and plenty would die. But he had never expected it to be...

I cannot save him. But there are others that I can.

He grabbed Malachi's hilt so hard his knuckles cracked, and then, after a pause, picked up Jeremiah as well. The blade was slightly longer and a little lighter, but in every other respect was Malachi's twin. He found himself moving before he'd even decided to do so, and his footsteps sounded far away. He had turned back toward the main street, and as soon as he emerged from the alleyway, he rejoined the battle with renewed savagery, using the strength from his Aspect to wield both swords as if they weighed no more than a feather. He fought his way deeper into the city, toward where he heard more shouting – the panicked shouting of the Commons.

The Bloodmage cavern. He had never been there, but he knew where to look.

"Tehanyu!" he shouted. She whipped around to see him. "Follow me!"

He took off, running toward the distant screams, already guessing they were using the Guardian entrance on the far side of the lowest tower. The Guardians trained in each of the seven towers – the bottom levels were designed for their exclusive use. He had been assigned to the seventh tower, the one Raven would one day grow up in, and during his time he had seen passages that went underground, passages that even Guardians were not allowed to enter without specific orders.

It must be there. It must be.

He rushed around a final turn and the Fortress rose up before him, towering into the sky. Before it was a final maze of multi-tiered mansion complexes, with walkways and arches going from one palatial building to the next. But beyond that, Tomaz could see a huge throng of Baseborn being forced into the seventh tower, the tower closest to the circular boulevard, just as he had suspected.

"Kindred – with me!"

His roar carried through the heavy air, and the Kindred force behind him, still nearly a thousand strong, ran for the distant group, all shouting their own battle cries. Tomaz ran out in front, his long legs carrying him in huge loping bounds, racing beneath the overhanging gardens and flowering vines that cultivated the Most High quarters; the last Guardians in the group heard them and turned, with just enough time to draw their weapons before Tomaz slammed into them. He swung Malachi into and through the chest plate of one, and then backhanded another with Jeremiah, sheering away half the man's head.

The Kindred caught up with him, and then more Guardians turned to join the fight as a dozen Spellblade daggers and swords flew through the air, whistling as they found chinks in armor.

But the Kindred weren't moving quickly enough. The rest of the Guardians had turned and were pushing the Commons through the doors, forcing them even as they cried and begged for mercy. Tomaz gutted another man in red armor, and pushed forward, trying to reach them in time. Kindred followed in his footsteps, filling the space behind him and killing any Guardians he missed, the big hulking brutes unable to find a weak spot in the cunning Rangers and Rogues that made up the foremost line of attack.

Soon they were across the space between the last of the mansions and the seventh tower, and they had bit far enough into the Guardian force that Commons were rushing by them, temporarily forgotten as the hulking men had to turn and engage the Kindred or risk being overrun completely. The red-armored giants gelled into a solid line, and suddenly it was the Kindred who were being forced back.

"No," Tomaz whispered.

He stepped forward, red light encompassing him, and kicked a man so hard in the chest he flew backwards a dozen feet. Another Guardian took the first one's place and sliced for Tomaz's head.

"No," Tomaz said again, louder.

He caught the blade between the hilts of his swords and broke it in half.

"No!" he repeated over again.

He swung Malachi and Jeremiah about him like a farmer wielding scythes in a wheat field. Guardians fell back, but their line did not break.

"NO!" he shouted.

He kicked another man to the side, then turned the other way and spit two men on his blades in a spray of blood. All the Guardians nearby turned to him, the Commons forgotten. The freed men and women streamed into the city, some shouting to head for the main gate, others simply running in whatever direction they could go. There were thousands of them. Some of the Guardians turned to follow, bellowing for them to stop, grabbing those they could and throwing them back along the appointed path.

"NO!!!"

He threw the Jeremiah end over end and saw it sink into the form of one of the pursuing men. Swords and axes cut in at him from all sides as the Guardians and even two Blade Masters attacked him as one, using Gunn Axe Forms and Szobody Sword Forms with the skill of true masters. But even when the blades found their way to flesh, they were repulsed. His skin had become as hard as steel, and no sword could cut it.

I just saved thousands. I could pick up the damn Fortress if I wanted to.

The fighting was hot, and it continued that way for long enough that Tomaz lost track of time. He slashed and cut and hacked, using every last trick and sword form he had learned as a Blade Master, until finally it was done.

The Kindred gave a ragged cheer. The section of tower the Guardians had covered was a wide opening with no door – it could easily have fit fifty men in a single line entering it, and inside they found training rooms and equipment. Tomaz led them quickly through it all toward the place he remembered, wrestling with old memories.

The place was the same, though it seemed smaller: a dark passageway in a distant corner, a simple circular stairway that led down to distant, unknown depths. Tomaz took a deep breath, and then plunged downward. The Kindred force still led by the Rogue pair Tehanyu and Likal followed hot on his heels.

The passage took them down, down, down, so deep that Tomaz began to feel the same claustrophobia he had suffered through in passage beneath Lerne. He balled his hands into fists and scraped them along the sides of the underground passage as he went, telling himself over and over again that he had air, that he could breathe, that he had space, that he would eventually be free.

Torches burned at every other turning, which helped, but not much. Three times he encountered bloody red runes that disappeared as soon as he touched them, giving way with a grudging but complete obedience. Once, the shadows moved about them and Death Watchmen sprang from concealment, hoping to take them unawares; but they were unlucky to come across Tomaz first, and then a knot of Rangers that dealt with the leftovers.

It was the changing quality of the air that Tomaz sensed first. It smelled ancient somehow, like dust and time – and it was full of crackling energy. Were they too late to save the captives? Had his fight with Valmok taken too long?

He rounded the final turning and emerged into a cavern even larger than the one beneath Lerne. Bodies covered the ground, and sounds of fighting came from the other side where Guardians were engaged with the last of a Kindred force that had been routed. They were fleeing up through another passage.

Davydd and Lorna.

He moved to go to them, but a glimmer of blood-red caught his eye and he glanced to his right. Three Bloodmages had appeared from a side passage on the far side of the platform in the center of the room, under which had formed a pool of blood. The Bloodmages were running for three crystals held on the platform – crystals that were all glowing with the light of activated Soul Catchers.

"Tehanyu!" he shouted. "Get the others!"

She nodded and called for the Kindred to follow her toward the embattled force, as Tomaz ran for the platform. The Bloodmages bent over the crystal and didn't even see him coming.

He ran the first one over, throwing him off the platform entirely. The other two scrambled away with shouts of alarm as the body of their fellow plummeted down to join the bodies of their victims. Tomaz saw they had drawn runes on the largest crystal in the fresh blood drying on its surface. One of the Bloodmages turned to him and unsheathed a black knife, while the second continued chanting.

Tomaz dispatched the first with a backhand that sent him flying over the crystals to the far side of the platform; he stepped forward and pulled the finally man up, grabbing him by the throat, just as the man's chanting ceased. He pulled his arm back and threw the man into the ground, where he stayed.

The Bloodmage's cowl fell back to reveal a head twisted and scarred. He was missing an ear and both lips, while other self-inflicted scars covered his skin like the cracks in a desert floor. The man began to wheeze, coughing in a rhythmic way...

Not coughing. Laughing.

"Something funny?" Tomaz asked, staring down at the man.

"We've finished it!" the mage said. He coughed, spitting blood that trailed down his lips and smeared across his cheeks in the shape of a fan. "The Soul Catchers are complete, and the Empress has all the power of a million souls! And your... your *Prince* stands no chance against Her!"

The blood drained slowly from Tomaz's face. He glanced at the crystals, each pulsing with bloody light. The Bloodmage took advantage of the moment and spat a word of power at him, one that cut away the stone at his feet. Tomaz dove forward, rolling toward the man, who had anticipated the move and pulled out a concealed blade etched with glowing runes. The blade came for Tomaz's chest –

A form came out of nowhere and dove between him and the attacking Bloodmage, wielding an axe made of white metal. The man died, and Lorna fell to the ground beside him.

Tomaz grabbed her up and knew immediately that something was wrong. Somehow, the Aspect that was supposed to heal her had stalled, as if something were holding it back. He examined her quickly and saw a blade stuck deep in her neck. It looked as if it had been twisted there, and blood flowed freely from the wound. Lorna locked eyes with him, and he realized his friend was dying. He reached for the knife and tried to pull it out, but she cried in pain and her whole neck bowed out. Shocked, he realized it had been twisted and caught in her spinal column itself. The only reason she wasn't completely paralyzed or dead was that her Aspect was spending every last scrap of energy it had gathered to keep her body working even when it shouldn't.

If I try to pull it out... she might lose her head.

The scrape of a boot on stone behind him – he turned and cut a vague figure in two, leaving a frayed robe and two flapping halves of a body that fell into the waiting lake below. Two more Bloodmages had arrived, and as Tomaz watched, the last of them stuck his hand to the crystal and shouted a single word. A hissing sound came from the center of the platform, and as the Bloodmage raised his hand, Tomaz saw that the skin was smoking but uncharred. The world seemed to tighten, and the crystals glowed with a renewed intensity.

The man was smiling, his bald, tattooed head covered in glowing runes that were slowly turning a shade of deep, midnight black.

"You're too late," he rasped. "The connection is complete."

"No," Lorna said, grabbing at Tomaz. "No – we're not!"

Tomaz didn't understand what she was saying, but she pointed frantically at the man and the crystals, coughing as she did, her eyes rolling back in her head as she fought for consciousness.

Tomaz looked down at the crystals, and then back at how the Bloodmages had been conducting the ritual.

Bloody hands...

He stepped forward, removed his gauntlet, let go of the Aspect of Strength, and drew Malachi across his palm; blood blossomed instantly, and he smeared it across the crystals, all three, one after the other.

The Bloodmage ran at him, shouting for him to stop. Lorna levered herself to her feet and sunk her axe deep into his belly as he passed; he died still gasping, trying to shout, screaming through a mouthful of blood. But Tomaz paid no mind to the man; he finished smearing the crystals, stepped back, and grabbed the Aspect of Strength again, knowing that he would need it. By the gods, he would need it.

He caught Lorna as she fell, and her blood mingled with his. She had other wounds that hadn't healed yet; wounds the Aspect hadn't been able to attend to as it kept her alive despite the dagger buried in her neck.

Both of us then, thought Tomaz brutally. *Both of us into the fire.*

The crystals began to pulse at a different rate; first one, then the others, like flames flickering out of synch, before they started to pulse to the same rhythm once more. Tomaz felt a *tug* on something somewhere behind his navel, and his mind went blank.

Pure light and power roared through him, flowing through the bond he now shared with Raven, splitting the power the Bloodmages had gathered to feed the Empress and funneling it in equal measure to the Prince. Light radiated out of him, blasting all thoughts aside, all hopes, all plans. The cavernous room shook with a light both red and white, blinding Tomaz and the few remaining Kindred and Imperial fighters still there to look at him. He pulled all the strength he could manage from his Aspect, and he knelt, resting the point of Malachi upon the ground, his hands and head upon the sword's pommel, as if praying to the gods of old.

Please, let it be enough. And please, whatever gods may be, grant me the strength to hold this bond until the battle is won.

He silenced his mind, and waited, kneeling like a mountain, immovable.

Chapter Thirty-one:

Prince of the Veil

Raven ran at his Mother. She raised a hand and flicked it at him, speaking a word of power that should have sent him flying across the room into the blackstone walls, but instead flew past him. He saw her eyes widen, and then she hissed, and her eyes burned red and she uttered the word again. This time it rolled out of her with such power that the air between them wrinkled like a piece of fabric, twisting and warping as the world bent to her Command.

This time Raven did indeed fly through the air twenty feet to crash into the blackstone wall. He spun back to his feet immediately, though, and paused. His heart had sunk somewhere between his knees and stomach, and suddenly Aemon's Blade felt like a dead weight in his hands. He saw again her eyes, glowing with a bloody light so brilliant he was forced to squint to look at her. She had thrown her head back and was laughing at nothing, her body racked with the ecstasy of overwhelming power, the sound of her voice crashing over him like waves.

The Bloodmages had finished the ritual. She had the power of three slaughtered cities at her command, and there was nothing he could do to equal it.

The others failed, he realized. *And I was too late.*

"That power is not yours," Raven said, still fighting with all his might to keep his nerve, locking his knees so they wouldn't shake. "Release it!"

"Too late," she whispered.

She threw back her head and thrust her arms out to either side. Light the color of blood flooded the chamber, shining from the cruel Diamond Crown, just as light so bright it paled the sun a thousand times over burst to life inside his head.

He drew as deeply as he could on the Crown of Aspects, throwing up his hands in front of his face, and suddenly power such as he had never imagined was flooding through him as well. His vision broadened, expanded, until he could see every crack and crevice in the stones around him, every swirling current of air, even the impossibly small flaws in the Diamond Throne itself. He saw how everything fit together, how the weight of the vaulting ceiling was dissipated by the blackstone pillars, how the beautiful gown the Empress wore had been sewn together, even the spells that had gone into making the Diamond Crown itself.

He saw the entire world and knew its workings.

How is this possible?

"No!" shouted the Empress. "No! It is mine – I need it all! Give it back!"

She spat a word of Command and a black sword that drank in the light from the Crowns materialized in her hand as she bent reality to her will, tearing the Veil. She flew across the chamber at him, moving so quickly it was as though she simply disappeared and then reappeared before him. He raised Aemon's Blade more by reaction than design, and caught the black sword, turning it aside. Her eyes widened as she truly saw the white blade for the first time; and, as her gaze touched it, the Blade glowed even brighter, its shining light eager and blinding.

"Aemon sends his regards," Raven snarled as he threw her away. She shouted a word of power as she fell to her knees, and flames encompassed him. The pain was so intense he almost blacked out, but in the split second it took him to understand what was happening, he had already opened his mouth and shouted another word back at her, a word that was more of a raw sound than anything else, full of intention but unformed. The power in him took the sound and twisted it, conforming reality to his will, and the fire winked out as a huge wind rushed away from him on all sides. The force of the gale was so intense that pillars around him cracked down their entire length, and pieces of blackstone fell around him as dust hazed the room.

He raised his eyes and met his Mother's gaze.

"*Die!*" she shouted at him.

The sound pierced him and his heart skipped a beat as his mind shorted out. For the time of a long, indrawn breath, he saw the yawning abyss that was set to swallow him whole. But in the space of that breath the Crown of Aspects flashed and threw the Command away, freeing him. Air rushed into his lungs, blood pumped through his veins, and the world exploded back into focus in beautiful, vibrant light. He staggered forward, regaining his balance, and raised Aemon's Blade. The Empress shouted a wordless cry of anger, and the sound of it shot a rippling wave of energy out from her in a huge, building swell that passed him by unscathed and instead broke against the walls with such force that it blew them out in a shower of stone and mortar that rained down on the other towers, breaking through the buttressed roofs and caving in beautifully constructed walls.

She raised her midnight blade, the darkness of it drinking in the light, and started forward. He raised Aemon's Blade and did the same, spinning the sword in his hands, feeling its comforting weight even as his heart and stomach clenched in fear.

They met with a ringing clash of metal, amidst a building, crackling energy that stood ready to consume them both.

*　　　*　　　*

The Imperial army was decimated, and as Autmaran watched, the remaining soldiers threw down their weapons and fled. A ragged cheer went up from the Kindred on the walls, a cheer that the rest of the soldiers on the ground behind him took up as well.

Shadows and fire... we just defeated the Imperial Army.

Their casualties were high, he knew that much for certain, but they had won.

"Polim - Palum!" he called down to the mounted Ranger pair. "Take all the mounted Kindred left and hound the Imperials all the way to the Elmist Mountains!"

They shouted back their affirmations and began calling for troops to follow the fleeing men. The portcullis was raised, the battered gates opened, and a sizeable chunk of the remaining Exiles departed, racing across the Plains of al'Manthian. After the Visigony had been dealt with, it had been the Kindred's fight to lose. Their position was superior, their force better deployed, and they were fighting for their very lives in hostile territory. The Imperials had attacked as if they were expecting at any time for the Kindred to be ambushed from behind, but no such attack had ever materialized.

And if it hadn't been for Tym....

Autmaran felt a lump forming in his throat and realized the corners of his mouth had pulled down. He coughed and shook his head.

Honor his sacrifice. There will be time for mourning later.

He paused, and turned.

Sounds were coming from further in the city, building slowly. The sounds themselves were distant and thin, but they were many, and as they began to crescendo, Autmaran realized the attack that had never materialized might just have come.

Dammit – I should have kept Polim and Palum here!

He shouted out commands, not using the Aspect, simply ordering the officers to form up their troops with their backs to the gates. He ordered the gates kept open – if the worst occurred, if Davydd, Leah, Tomaz, and Lorna had all fallen, then they would need a retreat. Shadows and fire, what did that mean for – ?

A huge vibration shook the ground, causing the entire city to ring like a gong struck by a mallet. The top of the highest tower of the Fortress exploded outward, walls simply blown out like glass under pressure, and from that came a ripple of sound that washed over them all, a sound like a distant roar. Autmaran's heart skipped a beat, and his knees went weak. He only just managed to keep himself from falling by grabbing the wall behind him. The rest of the Kindred and Commons had been similarly affected, and in droves of thousands, they clutched at each other and tried to stand, eyes wide with shock, confusion, and fear.

The battle has begun in earnest, Autmaran realized with a stir of dread.

But the moment passed, and the sound that had been building inside the city, the first sound, the slow crescendo, started up again and continued to build. Soon it was clear that a huge mass of people was moving toward them. Autmaran heard shouts and cries ring out as he descended from the top of the wall where he had been directing the flow of battle. The Kindred were forming up as he had commanded, this time with pikes and spears in front, infantry in the hard center, and what remained of the cavalry held in reserve. There was an urgency to their motion born of fear.

This city is not a place for mortal men.

The crescendo built like a wave, and just as it seemed ready to crash, Autmaran reached through his Aspect and shouted: *"Hold fast, Kindred! We have defeated the Visigony themselves, and sent the Imperial Army running across the Plains of al'Manthian! Whatever comes from this city, we shall meet it and turn it back!"*

Shoulders squared and chins raised; hands gripped tighter around weapon hafts and hilts. Autmaran felt a stirring in his heart as he watched – *his* men and women, *his* troops – and felt a pride greater than anything he had ever experienced. After all they had seen, after all they'd had to fight through, they still stood ready.

I am more proud of my people here today than I have been in my entire life.

He unsheathed his own sword, ready to join the fray should he be needed. The sound of the approaching force was enormous; they would spill out of all the streets simultaneously, it seemed, which meant the time for tactics and strategy was over. It was going to come down to a fight of total war, if it had not already.

"Here they come!" someone shouted.

A form on a horse emerged from the farthest alleyway, carrying a wounded boy across his lap and a child in his arms. Autmaran's mind couldn't grasp the image at first, bit then he heard bowstrings tighten and he leapt to action.

"HOLD!"

The Command bound everyone in place, except the man on the black stallion, who kept riding forward, untouched. More people emerged, all of them helping each other along, all calling out behind them for others to follow and hurry, that the gate was almost here. The man on the black horse rode forward; the burned half of his face looked gruesome in the combination of flickering torchlight and distant fluorescence as he reined in at the first line of spearmen and gave a mocking salute.

It was Davydd Goldwyn, and half the city of Lucien.

*   *   *

With every uttered Command, Raven felt the Veil tear further, like a ripping in his mind. He pushed away, running to another point in the throne room, and as he moved he saw that each footstep left a boot-print in the ground behind him. The world had become so strained that stone itself had ceased to be solid.

"Be thou consumed in flame!"

Fire sprang from nowhere and sought to envelop Raven.

"Be thy words as thin as air!"

The Command came rolling off his tongue before he'd even had a chance to examine it, but as soon as the words were said the world around him shifted, and the fire around him snapped out. His Mother's booming voice momentarily died, and she grabbed her throat in shock. She stared at him, her beautiful blue eyes showing white all the way around in pure astonishment, but then those eyes narrowed, and Raven barely stifled a shiver of fear. She took a step forward and broke through his Command by letting loose a shriek that shattered the pillars on either side of her, sending them crashing to the ground.

The air around her seemed to curve and bend before snapping back into place, and suddenly the ground beneath them began to shake. Without thinking, Raven looked down and shouted out another Command, pulling as deeply as he could one the energy flowing to him from the Crown:

"Reverse!"

He knew as soon as he'd spoken the word that he'd made a mistake. Rikard had always talked about specificity, and how, without it, Commands could go very, very wrong. Raven had meant to stop the stones from being pulled apart, meant to stop the Fortress from breaking beneath their very feet, but that wasn't what he'd said.

The gravity that held him to the earth abruptly disappeared, and was replaced with a force that pulled him upward, straight for the angular, vaulted ceiling with its sharp, blade-like carvings. Unable to understand what was happening or what he'd done, he threw his hands in front of his face and braced for impact; but before he could crash into the ceiling, the ceiling itself suddenly broke apart and flew upward into the sky, shooting into the encroaching clouds with shocking speed. Raven turned back, scrambling for ideas, mouthing words that made no sense, only to hear his Mother's voice ring out from somewhere close beside him:

"Let the laws of nature triumph!"

The force re-switched, and Raven found himself plummeting back toward the broken throne room. He drew on the Aspects of Strength and Endurance to fortify his body, and as he hit the stone floor he descended several inches into it, creating a crater where he'd landed, cracks running through the stone like streaks of silver.

"You foolish boy!"

Raven stood and spun, raising Aemon's Blade, but his Mother, who had landed easily on her feet, wasn't coming for him now. Her eyes were blazing with fury, but she remained where she was, clutching her long, curved black sword in her graceful hand, unmoving.

"You have no idea what power you hold, do you?"

"I know enough," Raven said, feeling his own rage burn within him. "I know it is power you created by killing *hundreds* of *thousands* of innocents!"

"But do you have any idea what you could do with it?" she asked, watching him with a flicker of curiosity. "Do you have any idea what I will do with it when it is mine and mine alone?"

Aemon's Blade flashed brightly, and Raven found himself speaking words he didn't understand, but words that felt *right*. "You will try to cross the sea," he said, his voice strangely flat and somehow deeper, "as you did once long ago."

His Mother's eyes widened and her mouth dropped open, revealing white teeth behind her perfect rosebud lips.

"And you will fail," Raven continued, speaking from the memories of Aemon, memories that flowed to him from the Blade, "as you failed then. You will fail as I always said you would – and I will be here to stop you, as I was then, as I am now, and as I shall ever be."

"*SILENCE!*"

The words snapped out of her with such power that Raven was blown back completely off his feet; he felt as though a huge hand had slapped him across the face. He flew back, twisting uncontrollably in midair, and landed on his stomach. His hands convulsed and closed around the hilt of Aemon's Blade, the wire hilt still cool against his slick palms.

"You are not him!"

"I am Aemon's Heir," Raven said in the tones of Command; he stood, this time ready for an attack, the Crown on his head flaring with light. *"And his blood flows in my veins, the same as yours. I swear it on my blood and body, and may the shadows take me if I lie."*

She was struck dumb by his words, and he could see that the fact he had spoken in the tone of Command told her it was real. The world didn't shift when he said the words; nothing changed, because nothing had to. He had spoken something that already *was*.

"Very well," she snapped, coming closer, her hand flicking the black blade like a lion twitching its tail as it stalks its prey. "So you are his heir. So your father deceived me. It matters little – I shall kill you as I killed him."

As she said the words "your father," Raven saw the barest flash of emotion cross her face, such a small twitch of it that he knew no one else would have seen a thing. But he knew it for what it was, and knew everything Goldwyn had said was true. She had loved his father, had loved Relkin, in spite of all that she was, in spite of everything she had done over countless years of tyrannical rule. She had loved him, even as she killed him.

She is only a person. A lost soul searching for meaning in immortality.

"Mother," he said suddenly. "Mother – abandon this. Stop it – you cannot do what you want to do!"

"You cannot convince me of such things, Aemon!" she roared at him, her eyes blind and full of madness spurred on by ancient pain that she had never let go, pain that had come to define her. "You tried once, but your words are still just wind! I killed you once, as I killed the others, and I will not stop until I have power over all! I will control the way the world works – I will make it work the way it should!"

The memory of that night flashed in Raven's mind, the night she had betrayed her brothers and sisters and Aemon himself; and then another night came to him, a night outside a white-stone valley, when Aemon chose to strike himself down as he fought her, using the Bloodmagic he hated to call down a bolt of lightning from the sky so that she would never have the power she craved. He lived the memories, felt the chill of the rain touching his skin on both those nights, felt the despair in his chest as he watched his best friend lose her mind.

Best friend....

"He mourned you," he said quietly, feeling sorrow for her for the first time. "He loved you like his own blood, and it tore him apart to see you fall."

"He *never* cared about me! He means nothing – I killed him; he was weak!"

"You never killed him," Raven said. "You never had that power over him."

"He fled before me, cowering like an *ant*," she hissed.

But as she spoke the words, more memories came to him, as if that first had been but the beginning trickles of a flood. He relived Aemon's flight on the night she had killed the other Heirs, and relived the despair Aemon had felt upon realizing his friend was gone, consumed by her grief.

And then another memory came to Raven, the memory of a single word that had been lost for as long as anyone could remember. It shocked him through and through, and in his surprise he couldn't help but speak it aloud:

"Alana."

At the sound of her name, the Empress froze, and something in her face seemed to crack and shift, like the façade of a statue falling away to reveal a hidden, scarred foundation. Here, where reality was so thin, the power of names was so potent that it could change a person altogether.

"Do not speak that name," she said, staring murder at him.

"It is who you are, Alana," he repeated. He realized his voice had mingled with Aemon's. He was speaking for them both somehow.

"It is who I *was!*" she screamed, and she came for him, her midnight blade swinging for his head. "You are not Aemon!" she cried out, railing against him with sword and Crown and sheer force of will. "You are my cast-off son! You are Azraeloph!"

"I am Raven!" he shouted back at her, his fear and doubt momentarily burnt away in the blazing light of Aemon's memories. "I choose to be someone new!"

The white and black swords clashed against each other with such power that both the Empress and Raven were thrown away from each other and sent rolling. They regained their footing and ran for each other again, channeling power and strength from their Crowns, breaking more of the throne room with each attack as the Fortress continued to shake and tremble.

"Fine," she snarled at him. "Then what will you choose to do?"

Black sword and white sword crashed together in a huge flare of sparks, both of them trying to control the world around them, both gaining an edge only to lose it again. The swords flashed out, back and forth, pushing, straining to break through.

"If you kill me and solidify your power," she hissed, "what will happen then? You trust the Kindred to treat the former Empire fairly? You trust that the corruption that is part of human nature will not seep into your new world?"

Raven shouted at her wordlessly and slashed at her head; she blinked, and was suddenly a foot farther away, sending his sword through empty air.

"And if you take the crown you wear now, this Crown of Aspects, and you keep it for yourself? What then? Then you live forever, don't you? Then you can take hold of this land and keep it pure, the way you want it, for as long as you live? How are you *any* different from *me?*"

"Is that it?" he spat back at her. "Is that what you think you are – some heroine who saved the world and kept it pure just like she'd always imagined it?"

She disappeared and reappeared on the dais of the Diamond Throne, out of range of his sword. Laughter rang from her open mouth; the sound and sense of it was beautiful bells ringing at a friend's funeral.

"This doesn't need to end like this," she said. "You can take this land – keep it. I need it not. All I want is to return home. You can have this land... *Azraeloph*."

The name burned in his mind, even holding Aemon's Blade, and he felt again that darkness inside him, the corrupted part of the Talisman he still wore, struggling to break free. The world closed in around him as he circled closer to her, trying with every ounce of effort not to show how weary he was, how weak he felt. He buttressed his mind with constant running thoughts of anything good he could bring to mind: Leah, Tomaz and the others; his cabin in Vale; his first taste of kaf at Goldwyn's manor; playing word games with Tym –

She killed Tym – she killed him!

He ran forward and struck at her, swinging the Blade so fast it was a blur of motion, but she met each strike, and even spun away, moving just as fast as he. He ran for her once more, but she slipped his blow and sent him sprawling. When he came back to his feet, she had moved to the center of the throne room and was watching him with wicked triumph.

"Let me show you true power, little Azraeloph!"

She threw back her head and flung out her arms. The world seemed to turn, and reality was forced to change again. As soon as the thinning stopped and the world settled, Raven knew something was different. She stood before him still, but she was somehow *more*.

She laughed, and rose off the floor.

Wings expanded behind her out of nowhere, beautiful white wings like those of an angel, unfolding in a huge spray of light. Raven dove to the side to escape the first rush of wind that came off of them, and then she was in the sky, soaring over the city. She cried out a word of power and lightning broke through the clouds, stabbing down at him where he lay. He rolled away, reacting by instinct, madly trying to find cover as thunder rolled around him, ruining his hearing as it cracked like an explosion of Black Powder.

"*Come to me, Azraeloph!*"

Raven turned back to the sky, fighting within himself to keep his identity, even though each time she said the name she'd given him he felt like he'd finally come home.

She is not my home – she is not my family!

But he knew he had to follow her. Geofred had known it too, somehow, and had told Raven what he had to do only seconds before his death.

When all hope is lost, when you are fighting her in Lucien, as you know you must, look to the heavens, and remember that where the world is thin, reality is what you make of it.

Raven drew power from his own crown, tapping into all seven Aspects, pulling together all seven strands and weaving them into a single, powerful Command that he let roll out of him in a wordless rumble of power. The sound of it alone, guttural and harsh, was enough to fry his throat.

But the world obeyed him, and warped. Sound changed, his vision blurred; he tasted ashes on his tongue. Everything snapped into place again an instant later, and he felt the Talisman on his back begin to writhe and shift. He grabbed a tighter hold on Aemon's Blade, knowing it was the rope that held him back from the waiting pit of insanity, just before black wings ripped out of the skin of his back, growing straight from his shoulder blades. The pain was terrible, but he refused to feel it.

He looked up into the sky, and followed Alana.

*   *   *

"What happened?" Autmaran shouted to Davydd as he rode forward, leading a huge rush of Commons. Kindred began to make their way out of the streets as well, and he realized the red-eyed Ranger had managed to bring out nearly a third of the force that had gone into the city. The Commons began to surge past him at the urging of the Kindred, and were soon rushing through the gates and out onto the Plains as the whole city began to shake beneath their feet.

"We were too late," Davydd said shortly, his face an expressionless mask.

"Where's Lorna?"

The Eshendai turned to him, and Autmaran saw the answer in his eyes.

Dammit. Dammit – not her too! Shadows and fire!

Another explosion rocked the Fortress, and Autmaran saw chunks of blackstone cascade down into the city, as what looked like whole columns of rock were blown apart. Davydd cursed and started shouting for the Kindred and Commons to move faster. Rangers and Rogues, the only ones who seemed able to keep their heads in the chaos, were standing guard in loose formations at every street into the city, on watch for any final Imperial soldiers.

"We need to leave," Davydd said. "Whatever is happening is only going to get worse – anyone inside this city while Raven and the Tyrant fight will die. We need to get everyone out and keep them out until this is over, however long it takes."

"It's barely an hour 'til sunrise," Autmaran said. "Two at most. The clock rang just before the shaking started."

Davydd cursed, and spurred his horse through the hard-won gate.

Another explosion rocked the Fortress, and this time the whole top of the highest tower, what must have been the throne room, split open like a popped boil, spewing blackstone debris that slammed into the adjacent towers, tipping them drunkenly as more stone crashed down into the city below. Shouts and cries could be heard, and claps of thunder that seemed to issue out in wave after wave with words on them that held all in hearing spellbound.

Autmaran watched the battle as the Commons streamed past him. Seconds passed, then minutes, and still he couldn't tear his eyes away. It was like watching a battle between elemental forces.

"Autmaran!" shouted Davydd from somewhere behind him, somewhere beyond the gate. "We have to go!"

But Autmaran couldn't move, couldn't break himself away from what he was seeing. His mind told him it wasn't possible, but his eyes told him it was happening. He felt a hand on his arm and knew Davydd had come back for him, was trying to pull him out of the city as the last of the Commons and Kindred fled. The Ranger was shouting in his ear, but Autmaran couldn't make sense of the words.

The two forms atop the tower had taken to the sky.

*   *   *

The walls and floor began to shake.

Leah was panting, breath coming in and out of her lungs so quickly that her throat and lips were raw and cracked. She knew no secret passageways, and the few glimpses of the future she could find through her Aspect did not include directions. Once she'd managed to pull herself onto the low-hanging balcony of the tallest tower, she'd been forced to take a huge central staircase that continued up and up and up, folding in on itself, circling around, doubling back, but always going higher. Doors and hallways branched off at every landing, leading to fantastically ornate apartments, audience chambers, and banquet halls.

She had met no one in these halls, and she was not surprised. The whole structure of the Fortress had begun to shake even before she had made it past the first staircase turning. Anyone of any sense had evacuated as soon as Raven had made his presence known. She had seen his handiwork as she passed, and knew that there were a score less Guardians to be dealt with.

She passed a large window that showed the city of Lucien spread out below her, and realized she must be nearing the top.

Please let me be nearing the top.

The shaking under her feet changed, and suddenly the whole tower lurched around her. She fell to the ground, clutching the stairs to keep from sliding backward, only to be lifted completely off the floor and thrown upward as the distant sound of a roared Command rang through the floors above her.

She shouted in alarm as she flew up and up and up, pulled by some relentless force, unable to make any sense of what was happening. She shot by a whole sections of stairs, and was only just able to maneuver herself around a stone landing before the force just as quickly reversed and pulled her back down again. Leah reached out and grabbed hold of a bannister as she flew past, slamming into the side as gravity tried to pull her back down the several flights of stairs she had just bypassed. She pulled herself onto level ground, and started up again, taking the stairs two at a time.

Whatever had happened, she was fairly certain it meant she was running out of time.

A huge explosion rocked the floors above her, and she dodged pieces of dislodged stone and debris as they fell toward her. She turned one final time and found herself facing a final length of stairs that led to a set of enormous carved doors, both bearing images of the Empress herself on either side, the Diamond Crown shining upon her head. Gold and silver gilding stood out everywhere she looked, and she was bombarded by the sickly-sweet smell of rotting flowers.

I'm here.

She heard a roar beyond the door, and a laugh that made her shiver uncontrollably. Rushing up the stairs, she heard what sounded like wings, and then the distant sound of crashing blades, but even as she came level with the throne room and the enormous doors, the sound began to fade.

She ran through the doors, still trying to catch her breath, and unsheathed both of her daggers, looking for the Prince and the Empress, but finding neither. The throne room was in tatters. The walls had been blown out by what looked like a huge concussive force, and only two blackstone pillars were left standing, the others lying strewn about the floor in collections of rough pieces that made the area look like a map room miniature of a mountain range.

Where are... ?

She heard again the sound of wings and shouted Commands that shook her to the bone, and she turned her eyes skyward. Her mouth fell open.

*   *   *

Raven was in a nightmare.

He was flying through the air of a black night illuminated only by massive flashes of lightning, borne on powerful wings he could not control, all while fighting for his life. She dove at him, hacking and slashing, shouting Commands and words of power that crashed into him, buffeting him like tempest winds. He attacked as well, flying at her, diving, trying to ride above her in the air, the whole of Lucien spread out below him like a hulking, black beast, but she turned aside every blow.

They fought in spiraling circles, racing back and forth over all seven towers. She caught and threw him into one, and his impact broke the roof and shook the top floors so badly that the whole structure looked ready to tilt over. He recovered just fast enough to disengage and take to the sky again, racing as fast as he could up into the clouds. She followed him.

He turned and struck out, the air shooting over him as he fell, but she rolled to the side, and he crashed into the roof of a second tower. He gasped in pain as he pushed off from the broken tiles, drawing on his reserves of strength and endurance to heal broken bones and torn ligaments. He rolled back into the sky once more, rushing for her, but she dove faster than he anticipated, and he was forced to roll awkwardly to the side, allowing her to swing back around over him, midnight blade held high.

She dove for him, sword extended and aimed at his heart. He tried to turn and meet her, but he was too slow. He saw it all happen and knew he couldn't stop it, knew her blade was moving too quickly, saw it racing down to claim his life –

Two daggers flew out of nowhere and pierced her through the chest, slashing the front of her beautiful white gown.

The Empress threw back her head, her golden hair spilling beautifully into the air, and shrieked in pain. She clutched herself and fell, spiraling toward the throne room at breakneck speed. Raven followed her, diving, shouting Commands downward, trying to *force* her into the blackstone floor, trying to bind her and stop her resistance.

"Be thou still as stone! Be thou full of pain! Fall with the force of mountains!"

But she rolled over, just before she hit the ground, and shouted back at him:

"Be thou tied to me!"

Raven felt a force attach to a point somewhere behind his navel and *pull* him forward as the Empress was *pulled* toward him. He rocketed downward and crashed into her, before they both shot down toward the throne room floor. In the back of his mind, he realized that the daggers must have come from Leah, that she must somehow have climbed the tower into which they were about to crash.

"Be she safe from harm!"

He crashed into the floor, the Empress following suit not five feet to his right, and the power of their combined Commands rocked the whole Fortress to its foundations. The tower shook beneath them, and with the sound of crumbling rock, the whole structure gave out. Suddenly they were plummeting through the air, the whole top section of the throne room floor crashing down into the level below it, and the level below that, not stopping. The walls bowed out around them and fell apart, smashing into the other towers and toppling them outward into the city. All Raven could do was hang on for dear life and hope that somehow his Command was keeping Leah safe.

They continued falling, breaking through barrier after barrier until they hit the ground itself, splitting it open to reveal an enormous cavern into which the stones and broken mortar of the Fortress fell. Raven heard the Empress shout another Command, and something rose up from beneath the ground, protected from the crushing weight of the stones, but he couldn't make it out. All other thought was driven from his mind as the throne room floor, somehow still intact, crashed to a stop.

He was thrown sideways by the final impact, through clouds of dust and powdered stone, and the whole world shook around him as he grasped desperately at Aemon's Blade. *I have to find her – I have to kill her now!* He knew he would have no other chance. She was more than a match for him, and only now, when the whole Fortress itself had come crashing down around them, would he be able to take her by surprise.

"Be my sight as clear as day!"

The dust before him parted like a thick curtain, and he saw her, pushing out from beneath a slab of blackstone rubble. He ran for her as the world settled around them. He caught a sight of something glowing red to his left, but he pushed the details from his mind. He raised Aemon's Blade and slashed at her.

She saw him at the last moment and tried to rise, but it was too late. The black blade was struck, spinning, from her hands. He spun and hammered her in the chest with the pommel of the blade, and she fell.

As the dust settled, he was revealed, standing over the Empress, white blade pressed against her throat.

He looked down at his Mother, at the Empress Alana, and saw that the fall had dislodged the Diamond Crown. It lay just out of her reach, flashing brilliantly, and she extended her hand out for it, desperate, but he gave her no chance. He hefted his blade, summoned strength through his own crown, and with one huge swing brought Aemon's Blade down upon it.

A huge wind rocked through the ruins of the broken tower, tearing at Raven's clothing, pulling him by the hair and slapping him in the face. Lightning shot through the clouds and thunder sounded, and a force rose up inside him, trying to overwhelm him, trying to force the Blade back and away; but it was too late, and he was now too powerful. The crown fell apart, and lay in smoking pieces upon the ground, each stone Talisman with its sparkling gemstone cracked in two, their powers broken.

He turned back to his Mother, and realized that without the crown she had been unable to survive the fall unharmed. Her breathing came in ragged gasps that whistled in and out through broken teeth. Blood ran down her face in a web like rain down a window. Her eyes held him still with her strength, but her crown was broken, her life was fading, and he had won.

"After all this time," she said with a broken smile that oozed and pulled, "after bearing seven hundred children, looking for the one to succeed me when I left this place... the perfect one I cast away."

"Shut up," he said, resting the gleaming white blade on his Mother's chest, over her heart. "Don't say another word."

"Why, Azraeloph?" She laughed, a hacking, wheezing cough of a sound that echoed without mirth, even in the huge empty space of the broken tower top; she still had power, even if it was waning. "Why, my son? Will you kill me?"

She smiled again, and Raven looked at her with horror and disgust.

"My name is Raven," he said softly, insistently.

"No," she said, her voice ringing with power, even separated as she was from her crown. Living so long with the power had changed her, had given her power of her own. "No – your name is *Azraeloph*. You are my son, my trueborn heir. I see it now. I should have known it was you all along – I never had the necessary ambition in the beginning either. I should have remembered. Yes... yes. It's you. This is it – it has to be!"

Triumph shone from her eyes like rays of tainted sunlight.

"You are him – you are the Prince of the Veil, just as in the prophecy! You are, you always were. Prophecies cannot be unsaid, they cannot be false – they must come true! You will kill me, you *must* kill me, and you will end my agony and become greater than I ever was! And in death – yes, in that death, I will finally go home. You will send me there. I must return. That was the answer all along. Yes! Azraeloph, my true son! *My true heir! KILL ME! FINISH IT! SET ME FREE!*"

"NO!"

He recoiled, his skin crawling, rejecting what she demanded. Aemon's Blade pulsed in his hands, and he felt something trying to worm its way into his mind, something on the edge of consciousness.

"You came here to kill me," she whispered, begging, pleading. "We want the same thing! Come, my love, my only Child, come and complete the prophecy. The power that I pulled from the Bloodmages is still in me – you cut me off from touching it, but it's still there. All of it – all of that power is yours to command if you kill me. Use it – use the Raven Talisman – live up to your name! Devour my soul, feed off of it, and all the other souls, and become my heir!"

She had pulled herself up now, the bone of her broken arm scraping against the stones as she maneuvered herself forward. She left blood behind her, flowing freely where she dragged herself.

"Do it," she said. "Please, my son. This was what you were meant for. Please... be my son again. Be my wonderful Azraeloph once more. I love you – I always have. This was all just a test – I see it now. We were both being tested – can you see it too?"

Raven, rooted to the spot, watched in horror as she caught at his boot and pulled herself up along him, her ruined, wasted body clutching at his.

"Do it," she hissed. "Be my son... love me the way I love you."

She grabbed his hand, pulling Aemon's Blade toward her.

"No," he whispered.

He tried to stop it, tried to stop from killing her, suddenly knowing, *knowing* with an absolute certainty, that she was right. If he killed her, he would become her. He would fulfill the Imperial prophecy. Somehow, killing her would change him. Here, in this place where the world was thin, where the Veil was torn almost beyond repair, Raven would become Azraeloph, the Lord of Death, once and for all.

"Stop it," he hissed, pulling back.

But there was still strength in her; too much strength. She fought him, pulling the sword forward, trying to bury it in her chest, trying to force him to kill her.

Kill her, said a voice deep inside him. *Kill her and damn the consequences. After all she's done, after all she's put me through, DAMN HER! DAMN HER!*

"No," he whimpered. "No – I won't do it. I'm not you. I'm not!"

"Yes," she whispered. "You are."

His strength failed as she said the words; the sword jerked forward, and sliced into her abdomen, spilling blood across them both. She smiled, her breath hissing out in a final sigh, and the Empress died.

And for a brief, perfect moment, he was happy. It was the way it should be – the evil die, and the good kill them. He had done it – he was finally a hero.

He, Azraeloph, was the conquering hero.

No... no, I'm not –

"That's not my name," he said out loud, stumbling backward. He shook his head violently, trying to clear it, and found he couldn't. His name... no, what was his name?

Azraeloph.

"No," he gasped. "No, that's not it – that's not it!"

He heard movement from behind him and he realized that it was Leah standing up. She had survived the fall after all, though her armor was half torn away and she was bleeding from a dozen places, including a heavy gash over her right eye. She stumbled toward him, reaching out a hand.

There was more movement, from the other side of him. He turned and saw what the Empress had tried to preserve, what she had Commanded saved from the falling ruin of the Fortress: the platform on which the Bloodmage crystals had been placed. They glowed with a bloody red light, and standing in their midst, only just coming to his feet, was the hulking form of Tomaz. His armor was blackened and burned, and whole sections of it had been completely obliterated. There was a body beside him, a body that Azraeloph recognized with a distant shock to be that of Lorna. But Tomaz was alive, and when he saw Azraeloph he began to move toward him.

"I can't remember my name," he gasped at them both, and also to himself. He couldn't – she had tried to take it from him, tried to turn him back to Azraeloph.

"Your name is Raven," Tomaz rumbled as he approached, his voice strained and exhausted. He continued repeating it, over and over again in a litany, seeing Raven still couldn't remember on his own. "Raven, Prince of the Veil. Raven, one of the Exiled Kindred. Your name is Raven –"

"Stay with us," Leah said from his other side. "Hold on. Don't give in."

He almost had a grip on himself – until the memories came. Memories, and with them the power the Empress had siphoned from the three Bloodmage crystals. Reality split into two as power broke from him and rolled across the city. He saw the world through his Mother's eyes, and through his own. The ground around him began to shake, and the city itself began to fall apart. Leah and Tomaz stumbled and braced themselves on widespread feet, still trying to remind him of his name, still trying to pull him back to them.

The memories started slowly, like the first spray of water from a cracking dam. They were short and painful, almost brutally short, as if they'd been truncated, the offending limbs shorn away. But they were enough: he saw her kill for the first time, saw her fight Aemon, saw her become the Empress.

"Tomaz! We need to get him out of here!"

"Where the hell do we go?! The whole city is collapsing!"

The huge mansions of the Most High cracked and broke apart, the beautiful arches and bridgeways crashing into streets hundreds of feet below. The destruction spread out, rippling away from them on all sides, shaking the earth beneath their feet. The memories intensified and Raven convulsed and vomited as his body tried to reject what was being forced onto him.

Her reign was steeped in blood. She reveled in it. The Visigony, her most faithful servants, were the same, and together they devised a means of pulling magic from the blood of her enemies. It brought her power, and it weakened them. She used it to extend her rule, conquering the disgusting savages of the land, all the while moving closer to the goal of finding Aemon in his southern refuge.

The clouds above them spun and crashed into one another, forming into a wild maelstrom that ripped more of the city apart. Azraeloph found himself thrown away from the others, toward the center of the throne room. There was red light there.

Azraeloph saw Aemon's death, saw the bolt of lightning shoot from the sky and strike him dead on the hilltop that would become known as Aemon's Stand.

Alana smelled the burned flesh, the crackling feel of the power and energy, and elation rolled through her. But her power was spent, and her army in retreat. It didn't matter; she would return another day to finish off the man's disciples.

The chemical lights of the city cracked and somewhere wood caught fire. The city went up in a blaze, and Leah and Tomaz both tried to make their way toward him again even as the ground bucked and rolled beneath them.

He saw the birth of Rikard, of Geofred, saw his Mother's determination to find a way to return to the land from which she'd come. The memories came faster, all the impressions of a thousand sensory details overwhelming him, submerging his mind. Memories of him, even, seen through her eyes. Azraeloph growing up, Azraeloph with black hair and eyes and features so similar to Aemon, who she had loved so long ago... so very, very long ago....

"Raven!" Leah shouted him. "You can't hold all of this in! You have to break the power! You have to break the crystals!"

Crystals... crystals... what was she talking about?

"Raven! You have to give it up!"

No. No, he couldn't give it up. There was something left undone. He couldn't do it. He couldn't – why couldn't he do it?

"I can't do it," he said, speaking the words aloud.

"Yes, you can!" said Leah, and he realized she was by his side again, shouting at him over the sounds of a storm. Lightning ripped the sky above them and the world shook and burned. "You must!"

"Don't give in!" roared Tomaz, his voice a huge boom of its own that broke through even the rolling thunder.

"Not yet," Azraeloph gasped. He began to smile.

The memories took him over and merged with reality, the two streams of thought melding back into one. He broke away from Leah and Tomaz as his limbs surged with power. He knew what he had to do. He knew what he *could* do, what he had the power to do. He stood tall and drew the power into him fully, taking all of the life stored in the crystals straight into his body through the crown.

"NO! Stop – wait – Raven, stop!"

Leah was rushing for him again, but, as he watched, the world slowed and stopped, leaving her several paces from him, hands outstretched, eyes wide and green and beautiful. An explosion of power roared through him, rocking back everything within a hundred yards. He filled himself with it, drinking deep until every inch of his skin felt electrified as he thrummed with supreme authority. He began to rise into the air without the need for wings, wind whipping him from all sides, and soon he was high enough to see all that was happening, all the city, and he knew what he had to do.

"Let light shine through the darkness!"

The Command rolled out of him and raced over the city, shooting into the sky, breaking apart the clouds, allowing the morning sun to send its first, tentative, questing rays out to them as it rose over the distant mountains.

"Let the ground be level!"

The huge sunken cavern began to shift and move in impossible ways, and the broken stones of the Fortress picked themselves up by the thousands and shot through the sky, crashing into the distant mountains. The ground shook, and the earth moved inward, filling the sunken pit beneath the Fortress so perfectly it looked as if there had never been a cavern there.

"Let life come to Lucien!"

Grass grew from the ground in spontaneous waves, coating the entire city. Trees, oak and pine, spruce and ash, sprouted and bloomed, reaching toward the sky, filling the space between broken hills of rubble.

"Let the dead live once more!"

And they did. All of them. All the Commons the Bloodmages had killed, all the Kindred that had been cut down. Lorna rose among them, pushing herself up from among the Bloodmage crystals, and Azraeloph felt Tym stand as well just outside the city, his wounds healing, his skin stitching back together.

He threw back his head and laughed, shouting his joy to the clear blue skies. He was a new god, a benevolent ruler that could mend the wounds of the world.

"I am the wind of change!" he shouted to the skies.

A huge wind sprang up, coming out of nowhere, in obedience to his will. He lowered himself back to earth and turned to Leah and Tomaz, who were barely able to stand. The wind buffeted the giant, throwing him back and rolling him away, until he flattened himself against the ground. Leah crouched low, her long black hair whipping in every direction.

"Don't you see?" he howled at her. *"I have even brought back our friends – I can fix it all!"*

But Leah's mouth was set in a grim line. *"That is not Lorna!"* she called to him. *"These people are not alive! You cannot make life like this – you are no more a god than she was!"*

Azraeloph laughed in derision, turning to the form of Lorna and moving toward her. He would show her. He would show her that –

He stopped short, as he realized that Lorna was staring at him with blank eyes... eyes that were slowly turning a sickly, corrupted green.

"No," he said. *"No – stop!"*

Lorna froze in midstride, but her eyes continued to glow. Azraeloph shouted at her again, yelled at her, but nothing changed. He reached out with his mind and grabbed hold of her life, feeling it, trying to find that sight and smell and feel that was completely hers – but it wasn't there. He reached down inside himself, into the crystals, and realized there was nothing there either, nothing that could make her who she had been in life. All details of the lives the Bloodmages had taken were gone, broken down into one single well of power. The memories were gone, and only blood-red light remained. He had the power to make her stand – but not the power to make her *live*.

I don't have her memories. I don't have them… they're gone forever.

He sent his mind racing across the city and found Tym, and realized that the boy too was becoming something corrupted, something unnatural. He had risen, his wounds had healed, but he was not the beautiful young man he had been before his death. All throughout the city, every single man, woman, and child who had risen…

Death Watchmen.

Azraeloph threw the thought from his mind, shouting in horror as he recoiled from the knowledge of what he'd done. The wind turned into a howling gale, and rain appeared from nowhere, clouds blanketing the city again in seconds as the weather mirrored his emotions.

"*Raven! Raven – stop this! You have to stop this!*"

He heard the shouting voice, and a small part of him remembered Leah. He turned and saw her, and felt something rise up inside him.

Stay away from her – she turned me back last time!

And as that thought crossed his mind, he realized what was happening to him. He looked down at himself and saw that the changes had already begun. His body was stretching and twisting as the power that ran through him changed him. Even the pure memories of Aemon weren't enough to save him now – there was too much in him, too many memories from Alana, too much power flowing through his veins, and all of it was jumbled in a terrible, incoherent madness. It was a sea, an ocean of souls that had been harvested and brought together through Bloodmagic, and it picked him up and bore him away like a twig on the tide.

The world around him stood out in bas-relief as the sharp light from the Crown of Aspects changed and morphed, becoming something harsh, something cutting. He felt himself fading away, becoming the embodiment of the Talisman he wore, a ruler that would replace his Mother and recreate a new and stronger Empire.

The Lord of Death, the Reaper of Souls, the Prince of Ravens.

He heard Leah's voice calling to him again, shouting over the maelstrom he'd created. *"Destroy it! Destroy the crown! Give the power up!"*

He shook his head, trying to dislodge the words.

"Think about your after, Raven! Think about what you really want!"

An image came to him, bidden by her words, an image that had nothing to do with Azraeloph, nothing to do with the Empire or the Children or any of it. It was his, just his, and it vibrated through his bones so powerfully that it jarred loose the raging power roaring through him.

A cabin among white stone mountains.

Not for her, not for the Kindred, but for him. The image took him over completely, and the knowledge of his name, Raven, the Exiled Prince, coursed through his body with such vehemence that the creature inside his chest was pushed aside. With a burst of lucidity, he raised Aemon's Blade even as the creature clawed for control, and pulled the crown from his head, flinging it to the ground. With a swing that nearly ripped his shoulders from their sockets, Raven crashed the sword down atop it, driving the razor-sharp edge of the Blade through the opal stone.

The tempest around him froze, and then the world exploded outward in a shockwave that warped reality. What little was left of the city disappeared, the reanimated bodies fell and moved no more, and the crown itself, now nothing more than a simple piece of valerium metal, split in half, broken. The Bloodmage crystals cracked and shattered, one after the other, and the thinness they had caused, the power they had pulled out of the world, flew back into it, healing what was torn.

He collapsed in a heap, his vision dark, and for a long time lay unmoving.

Silence held him, for how long he did not know. He seemed to float, weightless, somewhere in his own mind, for an eternity. He saw that the darkness that had lain so long on him was gone, rooted out and burned away, and a peaceful serenity had filled him in its place. He longed to stay here forever, floating in the comforting nothingness that somehow seemed full, but he knew he could not. Slowly, he was pushed back, by himself or by some other force, and he emerged once more in life.

The first sensation that came to him, the first indication that he still lived, was subtle warmth against his cheek. It was soft and golden, and gloriously simple. His eyes slowly opened, and he found himself staring at a lightening sky, going from black to violet to indigo, and farther to the east from blue to red to orange. He turned his head, following the warmth, and saw the rising sun shining on a land that had lain so long in darkness that it had forgotten the touch of light. But it rejoiced now at this reacquaintance, and reached up toward the sun, unfurling and embracing the warmth.

He noticed that his mind was quiet, and somehow empty. He reached slowly over his shoulder, feeling for the ridges of the black markings of the Raven Talisman.

He found only smooth, unblemished skin.

His hand fell back down to his side. He heard a rustling, and became conscious of someone coming up beside him only in the most distant way. The world had started to breathe again, and he could feel it. Nothing felt strained or torn – there was no thin spot here, not anymore. The Veil was whole again.

"Raven," Leah said, kneeling beside him. "Raven, can you hear me?"

"Yes," he said quietly.

"Are you all right?"

"Yes," he said. Tears began to leak from the corners of his eyes. The sound of that word, and the truth of that answer, was so good it hurt. He tried to breathe, and his body was wracked by a silent sob.

Leah levered a hand underneath him and pulled him up, helping him sit. He clung to her, feeling the warmth of her skin and the firm tension of her body. She held him and told him softly, over and over again, that it was finished, that it was done.

He grasped her hands; the blue lines of her Aspect were gone. He looked over to Tomaz, the giant still towering over them as he watched on, and there was no red light shining through what little remained of his armor. He swept a gaze around what had once been the Fortress, and, beyond that, what had once been mansion complexes and a dark, cesspit of a city. All of it was gone, leveled by the force of the falling Fortress, scattered to the winds by the sweeping power Raven had tried to wield.

And in its place was soft green grass, and sapling trees that whispered to him as wind played through their leaves. The warm, rising sunlight tossed shadows along the ground, and spring caressed the land like a forgotten lover.

The world was already moving on.

Chapter Thirty-two:

After

The cobalt sea lapped against the edges of the wide wooden dock. The tide had reached its height and was straining the huge ship against its moorings, thick ropes pulled tight. The sky was a clear, crisp blue, with dashes of white cumulus wafting lazily in the east.

Raven had never been to the Port of Valour before. The northern- and western-most city in the Empire, it had been built just north of where the Empress and her party had been stranded so long ago. Raven could still see it in his mind's eye. His mother's recollection of the place, while full of loathing, was more or less accurate. Little had changed in a thousand years. Buildings had gone up, and the natural harbor had been expanded and rounded, but the land itself was still the same. Trees still covered the hillsides, and wind still swept in from the ocean full of the tang of salt.

Raven had never seen the ocean before, either, and that had been the biggest surprise. That huge expanse of blue, going on forever... it really was possible to believe one could be lost in crossing it.

I wonder what that other world was like.

He caught a glimpse of his reflection in the windowpane, and was surprised again at the youthful face looking back at him. He had become so used to the years the Aspects had forced upon him that he still wasn't used to being eighteen again. It was strange knowing how he would age in the coming years. He wasn't particularly looking forward to the shape of the lines that would form across his forehead and around his mouth.

At least you have a full head of hair to look forward to.

"Hi," said a voice to his right. He turned. Leah was standing there, down the wood-paneled hallway, her eyes permanently returned to their natural, striking green. She had taken to pulling her hair back with a leather cord the way the women in the Port did, a style that revealed more of her smooth olive skin and sharp cheekbones.

"What are you watching?" she asked, coming up beside him. She looked out the window and saw what it looked out onto, and he felt her stiffen. She shook her head, spilling her black hair back over her shoulder, and turned away, leaning against the wooden frame.

"Has he come yet?" she asked.

"Not yet," he replied.

They lapsed into silence for a time, and Raven felt no need to break it. A new level of comfort existed between them that dead air couldn't threaten. It was something he had never shared with anyone else; something he didn't want with anyone else. She was the one who spoke first, as she often was these days.

"How are you feeling?"

The edge of his mouth quirked in the beginnings of a smile, but it stopped and faded away. There wasn't really anything funny about the question, only that she continued to ask it.

"The same as yesterday," he said, "and the day before that."

"Better," she said. "You're feeling better. Sorry – I know I ask too often."

"I appreciate it. It's nice to have someone care."

She nodded and turned back to the window. "I never thought I would love the sea this much," she said. The ocean sparkled in the summer sunlight, basking in her compliment. "Though I do miss the white stone mountains."

"Me too," he said with sudden yearning, thinking of Vale. The rooms they'd been lent here to recover were full and warm, but they weren't home. They lapsed into silence once more, now so close that their shoulders were almost touching. He was wearing his gray tunic today, one of the three he had bought himself. None of his clothing now was black.

"I thought of a question," she said slowly.

Raven nodded. "I promised I'd answer them," he said. "As fully as I can.

"You were convinced you'd die," Leah said. "Why didn't you?"

"Ah," Raven sighed. "I still think I was supposed to."

"But why didn't you?"

"Because I decided at the last moment not to kill her. She forced me to do it… she wanted it. I think maybe she wanted it all along. It's probably the only way she could return home. The closest way, at least."

She made a soft, pensive noise, looking over the harbor.

"Crane knew," Raven said with the ghost of a smile. "He told me, right after we'd made the crown: *the reason changes everything*."

She shook her head. "I don't understand – the action was the same, wasn't it?"

"That's what I said," grumbled Raven. "But he said it wasn't. And… I suppose he was right. When she died, it was because she made me do it. I did it because it was forced on me – all along I'd been trying to steel myself against the knowledge I would have to do it, and in the end it turned out I didn't."

"You really think you would have died if you'd been the one to do it?"

"Yes," Raven said after a moment. "I… you were there; you felt it, the way the world seemed so thin, like you could breathe on it wrong and everything would just drift apart like a broken spider web. We were connected – through blood, through Bloodmagic, and through the Crowns. The shock of her death… yes. I was so far gone into Azraeloph, I don't think I would have come back if I had killed her."

They fell silent and watched the waves roll in and out. The Port of Valour was peaceful, and almost abandoned. The ships that carried grain from Tyne to the docks in Lucien had gone south to collect their shipment, and the men and women of the city, one of the only cities unaffected by what was being called the Kindred War, were a private people that kept to themselves. They were very fair of skin, almost as alabaster as the Empress herself, and their city stressed peaceful non-involvement.

Leah moved closer to him, and he felt her lips touch the edges of his ear.

"I love you," she whispered; he smiled and grimaced simultaneously, feeling joy mix with sadness in his chest. He still felt the old pangs of unworthiness when she said it, but each time that feeling receded a little more.

"Even after everything?" he asked.

"Even after everything," she replied, holding his gaze with hers, steady and strong. He nodded, and smiled a real smile that she returned. A soaring feeling lifted in his chest, and he stood taller. He leaned forward and kissed her, reveling once more in the knowledge that he could do that anytime he wanted to. He ran his fingers through her hair, and she ran a hand down his cheek.

"There you are," rumbled a familiar voice.

They turned to see Tomaz walking down the long pillared hallway toward them, a red cape billowing behind him. After the deaths of Jaillin, Stannit, and dozens of other officers in the attack on Lucien, Autmaran had been unable to find competent replacements, and in turn begged Tomaz to fill in until one could be found. After talking with Leah, he'd acquiesced, and was now Captain Banier, in charge of the heavy infantry and reporting directly to Command Autmaran.

"Tomaz!" Leah cried out, just as surprised as Raven was. She moved forward to greet him, Raven only a few steps behind, and grabbed his arm in greeting, almost as if to confirm he was real. "Shadows and fire, what are you doing here?"

"Watch your language," Raven said with a small smile, "we're in the presence of a captain now."

"Stop that, princeling," Tomaz rumbled, smiling too, but as the old term of endearment rolled off his tongue, he froze and suddenly looked away, shifting awkwardly.

"It's all right," Raven said slowly. He swallowed past a lump in his throat. "Don't worry about it."

"So – why *are* you here?" Leah asked again, filling the space. "Not that it's not good to see you – it is, I've truly missed you – but this is the first time you've visited since escorting us here."

"Escorting *me* here," Raven said softly. "You're just a guest."

They both ignored him.

"I had some time on my hands," the big man rumbled. "There's a lot to do, but now that most of the city is in hand, the Kindred are being rotated out for a few days. We're trying to see how the city gets along without us."

"How are things in Lucien?" Raven asked, honestly curious. "Last we heard the Trials were being held."

"Yes," Tomaz sighed, crossing his arms and leaning against the wall that framed the wide window, looking out at the ship as they had. "All of the Most High, High Blood, and Elevated were rounded up. All that survived, at least. By unanimous decision of the Elders, Generals, and the new Lucien government, they were held to the standards of the Exiled Kindred. Every man or woman who owned or bought a slave was hanged. That was most of them. Though we went through them all, one by one. There were a few who we either had no evidence against, or who actually turned out to be good people – a few even asked to swear the vows and become Kindred. I've met one or two myself – they were in the early stages of organizing a way to smuggle slaves out of Lucien itself to the southern cities. Can you believe that? They're surprisingly decent."

"I'll believe it when I see it," Leah muttered, rubbing her temple. She did that now from time to time – she said her head ached when she thought too hard about the future.

The Aspects changed her. They changed all of us.

"Which families?" Raven asked, but changed his mind. "No – forget it, it doesn't matter. I don't want anything to do with it yet."

Tomaz shifted as if uncomfortable, but he remained silent.

"What about the Commons?" Leah asked. "How are they?"

"They're not Commons anymore," Tomaz rumbled with a smile. "The term is banned from all official documents. They were allowed to assume the name of whichever city they felt they belonged to, and many of them decided to be called Kindred and swore a modified version of the oaths. The Elders imposed the same laws that apply in Vale, most of which were greeted with cheers when they were read out, and were confirmed a few weeks ago by the new Lucien Kindred. The city is being cleared pretty quickly, and a new one is being built out of what was left behind. Elder Stanton is heading it; he's working wonders. Some of the others organized grain shipments from Tyne, since there are mounds of grain there for an army that no longer exists. They're not eating like princes, but they're full when they go to sleep. Autmaran sent missives to the other cities with the news of Lucien's fall, and Scouts to see what the reaction was. A large number of the Commons Davydd and Lorna freed in Tyne have gone back to the city – the growing season is here, and they can't miss it. We'll need all the grain we can get, and for the first time in a long time they'll get a fair price for it."

As soon as Tomaz mentioned Davydd, Raven found his gaze drawn back to the ship swaying easily against the dock as men in high-waisted white breeches and short blue coats began to load supplies aboard. His heart began to ache again as he thought of Lorna, which led to thoughts of Tym, and Keri before him, and

Goldwyn before that. Shadows and light... how could life still be going on without them in it?

"What are they saying about us?" Raven asked. "Me in the sky, and all of you leading the Kindred in the attack?"

"They're saying the prophecies were all fulfilled," Tomaz rumbled, smiling slightly. "There are people on street corners telling everyone who will listen that you battled death and conquered it, just as was foretold."

Raven sighed. A slight breeze picked up and provoked the sea to waves of agitation before calm descended once more. The sun was warm above them and the breeze blew through the open window, full of salt and promise.

A new day. The first of many.

"Do they know where we are?" he asked.

"No," the giant rumbled. "The Kindred and most of the Commons who fought with us – the ones we can be sure of – have all been consolidated under Autmaran's command. The Elders have stepped in to help organize the city."

"The Elders that are left, you mean," Leah grimaced.

"Indeed," Tomaz rumbled, "which is the other reason I've been gone so long. They finally have all twelve of the *sambolin* that came north, but it took far too long to gather them. They made another to replace the one we lost, and recovered the ones that Ishmael, Lymaugh, and Ceres died with. Add that to Elder Keri and Elder Goldwyn... there are five spots that need to be filled."

"Who do they want?" Leah asked, curious. "I can't imagine there are that many people lining up for the job just yet. I expect Demeter will take her Mother's place, and the others will be filled back in Vale."

Tomaz stopped leaning against the window frame and stood up, adjusting his cape about his shoulders, looking strangely nervous.

"Actually, they want us," he rumbled. "All three of us."

Raven felt surprise ring through him, then disbelief. He raised an eyebrow at the big man, wondering if he was trying to be funny. Tomaz was terrible at being funny.

"You're joking," Leah said, under the same suspicion.

"I most assuredly am not," the giant rumbled, looking slightly uncomfortable. He turned his gaze out the window so he wouldn't have to look at them anymore. "Elder Crane came to me himself. They asked me to fill Lymaugh's spot as the Elder of Mercy, and apparently Ishmael asked for Leah personally before he left for the battle against the Visigony."

Leah's mouth fell open in unfeigned shock.

"This is insane," she said, her eyes wide. "There hasn't been an Elder younger than fifty since the bloody founding of Vale! That's why they're *Elders*."

"I think collectively we've lived enough for a thousand lifetimes," Raven said quietly. They turned to him, and he met their gaze with a small smile – as much of one as he could manage.

Goldwyn would tell me to find the good. He would tell me to find the laughter.

Leah nodded slowly, her eyes far away, remembering, and Raven could swear he saw the faintest flash of blue in them, though he knew it was his imagination. The Aspects had left them, as had his Talisman, when he had destroyed the Crowns. Each of the seven bearers had been changed, though, and Raven knew it deeper than the others. Over time, the effects might become more apparent, clear enough for the others to see. He would be there to help them if they needed it.

"What about Raven?" Leah asked slowly. "What do they want him for?"

Tomaz swallowed, looking carefully between them both, and Raven knew in a sudden rush of understanding what the giant was going to say before he even opened his mouth. "Goldwyn," he sighed, feeling a strange sensation in his chest. "They want me to be Elder of State instead of Warryn."

"Yes," Tomaz rumbled. "They do."

Leah nodded slightly, as if he had only confirmed what she had suspected. She turned to Raven, and it was as if she were seeing him in a new light. "Yes," she murmured. "It's exactly what we need. Someone who knows both Kindred and Empire and can help us bring both together. Of course you're who they'd want."

"What about Autmaran?" Raven asked suddenly. "He was Goldwyn's protégé. Did they offer it to him?"

"He's Commander of the Kindred Army," Tomaz said. "And after discussing it with him, he and the Elders both decided the *sambolin* should go to you. I was there. His exact words were, 'I prefer to fight with swords against enemies I can see. Keep the politics to those who understand it.' I quite enjoyed that, actually."

Tomaz grinned through his beard at Raven.

"Besides," the giant continued softly, "he may have been Goldwyn's protégé, but he wasn't the one Goldwyn died for."

The words moved Raven, and he had to look away.

"Well," Leah said, looking between them, "what are we going to say?"

"Actually," Tomaz rumbled, roughly clearing his throat, "I've already said yes."

"*What?*" Leah asked, looking outraged. "Without talking to me first? If you say yes, then there's no going back to the life we had. We have to be Elders, and we have to give a damn about everything that's going on."

"There *is* no going back to the life we had," Tomaz rumbled, solemnly. He took care to stress his words as he said them. "This is a new world we've helped create. They will need us – all of us – likely for most of our lives."

"Of course," Raven said, nodding. "I will accept as well."

Leah glanced at him, searching his face for answers.

"I won't run *ever* again," he told her. "If there's anything I've learned after all of this, it's that. I can't turn my back on the world. Maybe the people who can are lucky, or maybe they're just heartless, but either way I've proved to myself that I can't do that. If I can help heal what is left of both nations, if I can stitch together even the smallest portion of the lives my family tore apart, then the request is but a formality. I may not be a prince anymore, but the title doesn't matter. It never did."

Leah nodded slowly. "Then I'll be there too," she said.

Tomaz let out a huge breath in a rush of air. He smiled and passed both hands through his thick black hair and immaculate beard, before turning to look back out the window. Something caught his eye, and he moved closer; Raven turned to look.

Davydd Goldwyn had emerged with two bulging tote bags slung over his shoulders. His face and body were once more whole and handsome, minus a few scars, and his golden eye had reverted back to its former glowing red. He walked with swagger down to the edge of the dock, and called greetings to various deckhands and Rangers who would be accompanying him. He seemed back to his cheerful self, but Raven knew it was an act. There was a tightness around his eyes, and his normally shaved chin bore several days' stubble.

"What are his plans?" Tomaz asked.

Below them, Davydd began to load his bags onto the ship. Other figures appeared, men and women that had decided to accompany him. Some were Rogues and Rangers; some were simple soldiers; one or two were dressed in the homespun clothing of the Commons and bore packs loaded down with navigation and map-making instruments.

"He won't say," Leah replied. "My guess is that he doesn't even know himself."

Raven nodded absently. His mind was still strangely sluggish at times, but he was coming back to himself bit by bit.

"I said goodbye to him this morning," Leah said softly, and Raven reached out to grab her hand, catching her warm palm before he realized what he was doing.

He worried for a moment that she would pull away, but after a moment's hesitation she interlocked her fingers with his.

"So he's going through with it," Tomaz said. "Does he have an idea where to go?"

"No one has an idea where to go," Raven said. "The Empress had that ship built to withstand anything, though. She was going to use it herself."

"Good," Leah said quietly. "Good. At least he'll be safe."

Raven felt her hand squeeze his, and saw tears forming at the corners of her eyes, tears that she refused to let fall. Her nostrils flared and her jaw clenched, and she forced the emotions back, keeping them in check.

"There's no chance of talking him out of it?" Tomaz rumbled.

"No," Raven sighed. "We've tried over and over again."

"Why not just tie him down?" the giant grumbled.

"He'd just get free and take a smaller boat. He's running from the memories of her death. He wants to forget. And besides, if anyone can make it, he can."

He squeezed Leah's hand tightly, trying to send her all the support he could, but his own heart was breaking as he saw the strong young man jump into the rope-sling that would pull him up on deck with all the belongings he cared to take.

"When do the Elder's expect us back?" Leah asked. "And will we perform the ceremony in Vale, or in Lucien?"

"Lucien," Tomaz said softly. "At least preliminarily. And the reason they sent me was because they needed someone to persuade you both to come as soon as possible. You've been gone for over two months. Everyone knows you needed time to recover, but we need you now. There's a new world to build."

"Then we'll go," Raven said, even as Leah tried to protest. "I've had long enough – and as long as you're both there with me, I'll keep getting better."

He fell silent, and they all watched as the rest of the crew climbed aboard the huge ship, trying to catch the tide.

"We won't see him again," Tomaz rumbled quietly, "will we?"

Raven swallowed hard, and tried to speak, but found no words. The sadness that continued to pool inside him was anchored to the man, in a strange way. Davydd had been ready right from the start to sacrifice everything to win, and despite his arrogance, he was one of the best men Raven had ever known. He deserved to have Lorna with him, deserved to have Tym trying to help him in everything he did, deserved to still have a father that would love him. Deserved so much more than what he'd been left with. But the war had torn him apart, and he couldn't find happiness here.

Raven tried again to speak, but Leah spoke before he could.

"No, we won't," she said quietly. "But he's going to have one hell of an adventure."

The ship pulled forward as the mooring ropes detached, and the three companions watched their friend sail out into the harbor, and then into the waiting sea. Raven held Leah's hand tightly, and felt Tomaz's presence by his side.

Time to make a better world. Time to make an 'after.'

Epilogue

The ship was big and sturdy. The crew took particular joy in handling her, which told Davydd all he needed to know about her craftsmanship. She was beautiful, quite honestly. He'd been eager to take her out to sea ever since he'd laid eyes on her, and now that he finally had the chance, he enjoyed it more than he'd ever thought possible. He loved the way it felt to have the deck rolling beneath his feet, loved the sturdy way his boots held the wood. It was a good ship. Part of him was surprised he'd never gone sailing before, though the larger part of him that knew he'd been fighting a war since he'd turned twelve really wasn't. The opportunity simply hadn't presented itself.

But it had now, and he'd seized the chance.

He remembered the look on Raven's face when he'd told him of his plans. That face with those dark eyes that reminded him so much of his father, Goldwyn, now, the way they saw more, much more, than they really should. He'd known what Davydd was asking, and he'd still agreed anyway.

I'll miss him, and Leah. But I have to go.

They'd sailed for weeks now, straight into where the sun set, using the stars to guide them. There'd been a storm, their first, not too long ago, and Davydd had found it the most exhilarating experience of his life.

Guilt wormed through him, but he ignored it.

She'd want me to enjoy life. She'd want me to take a risk.

He didn't know if that was true, but he didn't care. After all the death, after everything he'd given... no, he didn't care. He'd stayed for her funeral, for *both* funerals, and he'd wept in solitude, refusing for days to leave his room. But after the initial grief had passed, he'd known what he wanted.

He was born for adventure; he ached for it.

He was a Ranger, first and foremost, and what Rangers did was explore. No one knew what was out beyond the western sea – no one had ever tried to cross it. With their provisions and their new ship, they had the chance to explore, and to see if the stories Raven had gleaned from his mother's mind were true.

Davydd, in the deepest, darkest part of his heart, wished they were.

The storm he'd been waiting for hit that night, and he lost himself in it. Some of the crew were frightened, but many more were hopeful. They wanted this the same way he did, and together they fought the storm with all they had in them. Hours passed as they were tossed about like a scrap of bark in a sadistic child's bathtub.

They lost the foremost mast first. It broke in half with a sound like cannon fire and plummeted overboard, crashing into the sea, pulled down to unknown depths almost immediately. Davydd and a gang of crew with hand axes ran forward and cut the rigging, lest it drag them down as well. Seawater sprayed in his face and rain cascaded down in veritable sheets. Men and women were thrown overboard, including the pilot, and more pieces of the ship were torn off, but still the crew fought on. Their hands were bleeding from handling ropes and lifelines, their bodies racked with pain and the disorienting, stomach-wrenching drops and climbs of towering waves.

But Davydd grabbed hold of the ship's wheel and laughed and jeered at the shouting wind, mocking it as it sought to drown him. He shouted at the storm, taunting it, telling it that he still stood, that no mere squall would turn him back now. The crew joined in, shouting and laughing through their fear, roaring into the wind.

The Lucky Scoundrel grinned and steered them on, his eyes like glowing coals.

Glossary

Ashandel (AH-shan-DEL): Meaning "Sword" or "Blade" in the old tongue of Kindred, an Ashandel is part of a Rogue or Ranger pair. He or she is meant to compliment the Eshendai to which he or she is paired. Ashandel are typically the physically stronger of the two, though this is not always the case. Ashandel can be Spellblades, but it is rare.

Bloodmage: A Bloodmage is a member of the Empire who, through ritual sacrifice, has given up his life in exchange for the ability to manipulate the lives of others. They are exclusively male, and ritualistically shave their heads. They do not eat, but instead subsist on the strength of the lives they harvest. The basis of their magic is the Raven Talisman, as well as the other Talismans to varying degrees, and as such their magic and enchantments cannot bind the Children. Their nominal head is The Seventh Child, the Prince of Ravens, but until he comes of age they are under the command of Rikard, the Prince of Lions.

Children, The: The seven living children of the Immortal Empress. Each of them bears one of the Seven Talismans and rules a province of the Empire of Ages.

Daemon (DE-mon): An elemental creature created by Bloodmagic. The formation of a Daemon requires raw material – i.e. the essence of a storm, the heart of fire, or the strength of earth – in addition to human sacrifices, and all Daemons require a full circle of thirteen Bloodmages to summon. Once Daemons are summoned, control is in the hands of the leader of the circle, and the Daemon is connected to that Bloodmage's Soul Catcher.

Elders, The: The governing body of the Exiled Kindred, made of thirteen men and women who are responsible for distinct areas of Kindred society:

Elder of Wisdom – Crane

Elder of Truth - Ekman

Elder of Justice – Dawn

Elder of Mercy – Lymaugh

Elder of Agriculture – Ceres

Elder of Arts – Rose

Elder of Health – Keri

Elder of State – Warryn/Goldwyn

Elder of Innovation – Stanton

Elder of Animals – Pan

Elder of Law – Spader

Elder of Imperial Liaison – Ishmael

Elder History – Iliad

Eshendai (EH-shen-DIE): Meaning "Dagger" or "Knife" in the old tongue of the Kindred, an Eshendai is part of a Rogue or Ranger pair. He or she is meant to compliment the Ashandel to which he or she is paired. Eshendai are typically the smaller of the two, and are extensively trained in healing, strategy and tactics, and map-making as a basis for their work. The majority of Spellblades are Eshendai.

Exiled Kindred: A people made up of the original inhabitants of the land of Lucia, of which there were few remaining survivors following the war between Aemon and the Empress, and those who have been Exiled from the Empire itself. No one knows how large the nation is, though the population has varied throughout the reign of the Empress. All who escape the law of the Empress are known as Exiled, and are hunted throughout the Empire. They are traditionally known as a refuge for thieves, criminals, and murderers.

Lucia (Loo-see-uh): Refers to both the continent and the Empire upon it.

Lucien (Loo-see-en): The capital city of Lucia, and the seat of the God Empress.

Ranger Pair: A pair of Exiled Kindred made up of one Ashandel and one Eshendai, who are charged with protecting the borders of the Kindred lands, as well as searching the Empire for any Imperial men or women who have been Exiled and wish to join the Kindred.

Rogue Pair: A pair of Exiled Kindred made up of one Ashandel and one Eshendai, who are charged with various infiltration and sabotage missions executed throughout the Empire.

Spellblade: A man or woman among the Exiled Kindred who has undergone a process of binding that has linked them to a specific weapon. The binding is not possible for most people, but those who have the ability can link themselves to their weapon of choice, enabling them to exercise a limited amount of mental control over that weapon. The binding also lends them strength and endurance, and speeds their recovery time. Most Spellblades are Eshendai.

About the Author

Hal Emerson was born in California and currently lives near San Francisco, where he works as an author. He graduated from UCLA with a BA in Musical Theatre, and has an undying obsession with raspberries.

Made in the USA
Middletown, DE
14 March 2021